AGNES'S BROKEN DREAMS

JUDY KING

Matador
Unit E2 Airfield Business Park,
Harrison Road, Market Harborough,
Leicestershire. LE16 7UL
Tel: 0116 279 2299
Email: books@troubador.co.uk
Web: www.troubador.co.uk/matador
Twitter: @matadorbooks

ISBN 978 1803135 199

British Library Cataloguing in Publication Data.
A catalogue record for this book is available from the British Library.

Printed and bound in the UK by TJ Books Limited, Padstow, Cornwall
Typeset in 11pt Minion Pro by Troubador Publishing Ltd, Leicester, UK

Matador is an imprint of Troubador Publishing Ltd

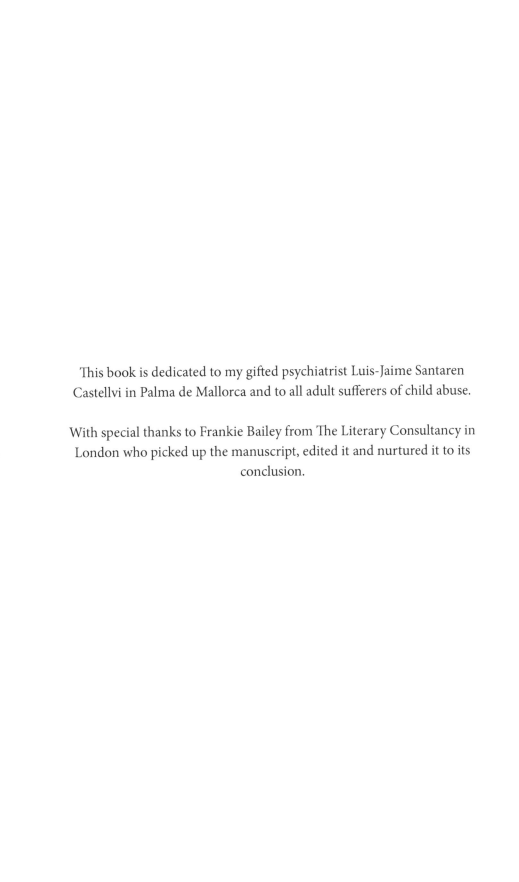

This book is dedicated to my gifted psychiatrist Luis-Jaime Santaren Castellvi in Palma de Mallorca and to all adult sufferers of child abuse.

With special thanks to Frankie Bailey from The Literary Consultancy in London who picked up the manuscript, edited it and nurtured it to its conclusion.

It is an age-old observation that in every human group there is a predestined victim; one who inspires contempt, whom all mock, about whom stupid malignant gossip grows, upon whom by some mysterious agreement, all unload their bad tempers and their desire to hurt.

If This Is a Man by Primo Levi

A slave is a person who cannot speak his thoughts.

Euripides

PART ONE

1

SURVIVING DANIEL

She is dreading the arrival. Since boarding the plane in London, like a dog pulling against a lead, she has felt she is going the wrong way – sucked back into a past she thought she had escaped forever. Freedom isn't the price of a plane ticket, she thinks, as we take ourselves wherever we go. Her apprehension has no effect on the big Boeing that, landing with a thud, sways from side to side in a series of kangaroo hops before the mighty brakes tether the beast and bring it to heel. A spontaneous uproar of cheers and clapping explodes in the cabin as the sensation of rolling smoothly on terra firma signals the turbulent flight is at an end. The uproar is tempered when passengers are advised to remain in their seats. Two burly Bermuda-shorted men are enacting the Australian ritual of disinfecting the plane by moving through the aisles to spray the cabin from high-held aerosol cans. When the red-headed one pauses near her aisle seat, his freckly lower arms seem familiar. But, she realises, it is the odour of hair oil, fermented with alcohol-impregnated upper-body sweat, that is resurrecting her long-dead father. The father who holds her from the grave. Who traps her in troubled, hard, blue eyes –before vanishing.

A deep foreboding amplifies the resistance she is experiencing. All is then quickly swept into the noisy hubbub of movement and chatter that follows the signal to disembark. She is delayed by the act of searching under the seat for a book called *Families and How to Survive Them*. She has scoured it for clues during the long flight, in preparation for returning to the place where she was born and grew up.

The delay means that, when she finally gets to the overhead locker across the aisle, she sees a red-gloved hand at the end of a crane-like arm snatch her stashed duty-free bag and dash away with it through the cabin. She is left with a blurred image of a tall woman with curly auburn hair, merging like a film fade into the avalanche of disembarking passengers. The woman might have been wearing a grey tracksuit, but she cannot be sure. The red glove, however, sticks in her mind. She imagines herself screaming THIEF! THIEF! as she has seen in the movies but, instead, simply stands there in disbelief, opening and closing her mouth like a fish.

Conditioned from childhood not to make a fuss when it comes to anything untoward, she doesn't react like other people. Subterfuge and evasion are old friends. Like a lizard changing colour, she feels safe blending into the background. She never screams. Not that she can remember anyway. Perhaps the potential was killed off in her before it got started. Once or twice, she has contemplated buying a battery-operated 'screamer alarm' for her handbag but, because so rarely conscious of her safety, the idea would waft away from her when the threat that provoked it abated.

All the carefully chosen presents during the stopover in Singapore gone! What can she do? The evidence is flimsy: tall woman, a mass of curly hair that could well be a wig, and an easily removed red glove. Even if she apprehends the thief, it would be no use as, by the time she spots her, the stolen goods would have been transferred and the plastic bag discarded in a convenient bin.

Agnes bites her lip. Tears sting the back of her eyes, then slither like sluggish raindrops down her cheeks. She is struggling to get a grip. After all you've been through in recent years this is a minor blip, she tells herself. For God's sake just put it out of your mind. It's not the end of the world.

A popular quote, attributed to Albert Einstein, and read in a magazine she browsed on the plane, sticks in her mind: 'Insanity is doing the same thing over and over and expecting different results.' Her two marriages, and most of her romantic liaisons, had ended in similar fashion. On her knees and seriously out of pocket. If the Einstein quote was accurate, it was a definite confirmation of her insanity. But *what* is she repeating, over and over? *What* is it that she cannot see?

Agnes closes teary eyes and sinks back into the padded comfort of the aeroplane seat to take stock. The plane is almost empty of passengers. She is annoyed she didn't put the bag with the duty free under the seat in front her. But an over-vigilant steward had whisked it off her lap and put it in that locker across the aisle because there was no room in the one above her head. She is catapulted straight into an all-too-familiar fugue state. This can manifest out of the blue. Someone may be speaking directly to her, but it is as if they are contacting her from a great distance. In books, when someone has something to say, there are useful little speech marks to signpost the way. Conveniently placed to assist. These days, there are no such helpful little clues popping up in Agnes's head:

Can I help you Madam?

She looks up into the beautiful face of a Singapore Airline hostess. Not the girl who served her during the flight, but one she is seeing for the first time. Petite and impeccably groomed, her soft touch on Agnes's arm, her radiant smile, seem like visitations from an angel. All the SA hostesses wear differently coloured patterned sarongs, and this woman's version is a vibrant aqua shot through with turquoise, like the Mediterranean Sea close to the shore on a perfect sunny day. Her shiny jet hair is scooped into a neat bun that shouts – "rescue". Agnes melts under her gaze and starts describing what has happened, a life of loss impregnating the tale. Her speech is clumsy – the more she babbles, the more she ends up in knots. She feels she is floating outside her body – unable to find her way back. Gently interrupting her endless ramble, the hostess advises:

Report it at our office in the airport Madam.

The hostess accompanies Agnes, with professional care, through the cabin. She then bids her farewell with a heart breaking smile that propels Agnes forward to float through the corridors ahead like an astronaut bouncing in space. But the sweet reprieve is short-lived. With the view of passport control looming, her apprehension returns. Get over it, she mumbles to herself, as she burrows in an overstuffed handbag to locate her passport, making the decision to neither report the stolen goods nor think about the duty-free thief ever again.

The Australian passport she renewed in Madrid arouses the suspicion of a thin Asian Passport Officer. Dressed in spotless white, and sporting golden shoulder epaulettes, he turns the document over at arm's length as if it is potentially radioactive. His narrow eyes contract even further as they dart backwards and forwards from Agnes to her photo. The photo is seven years old. Hard to gauge how much older she must look after the dreadful time in London. He speaks:

How long time you not been Australia?

He demands this of her sharply, desecrating the name of the country into jumbled vowels and consonants. The question surprises her. She responds:

Twelve years. More or less.

He snaps like an interrogator:

Why twelve years since last trip?

She is goaded into impatience:

Well, it just is. Any stipulated time allowed to be away? No offense to the nation.

He stares at her. Attempting to smooth out the earlier sarcasm, she adds:

The years get away and now it's lovely to be back.

She has replied awkwardly. What did she expect from an official she has never laid eyes on before? A rowdy welcome? Her eyes fill with tears yet again. She rummages once more in the ridiculously overstuffed bag for a pair of sunglasses. Her passport is now being shown to a burly fellow officer who is as scruffy and unkempt as his abrupt colleague is starched. She jams her glasses in front of her eyes with such force, she bruises her nose. The emotional waterworks keep coming like a leaking tap and she surreptitiously dabs at them with a bit of shirt sleeve hanging out of the arm of her mink coat. She is drowning in an overwhelming sense of failure. Now, at sixty-four, when those of her generation are retiring, she is getting started – yet again – and for the umpteenth time. All she can think of is that it took Napoleon twelve years five months and four weeks to conquer Europe. A fact she read recently on the internet. And here she is, after *thirty* years, still marooned in the dark. *Why* do those she trusts exploit her? How is it possible she doesn't see what is so obvious to everyone else?

The memory of that summer morning spent at the notary's office in Mallorca forces its way back, along with the dread she had felt as she dug her fingers into the leather seat, closed her eyes and held her breath as she waited for Daniel to sign the separation agreement. The notary, a grave, formal man, had frowned as he let out an uncharacteristic sigh of exasperation. Having maintained a cordial relationship with him, signing deeds in front of him for the houses she had bought and sold in the area over the years, Agnes had wished she had chosen a lawyer to represent her at this signing who was less irritable. Someone with more patience than Francisca, who had prompted Daniel through gritted teeth:

'*Por los buenos*' means 'for the good'. Whatever you bring to the marriage you take away from it.

Francisca had spelled this out as if addressing a dim child, pausing between each word in heavily accented English, her dark eyes smouldering. Agnes's own frustration was certainly reasonable too, given she had translated the legal term '*por los buenos*' into English for Daniel dozens of times before. This was the second attempt at an official signing and Agnes had felt compelled to speak:

It couldn't be fairer, Daniel. Right up your alley. I know you wouldn't settle for anything less.

She had enjoyed repeating this latter phrase – one he had once tacked on to the heavenly revelation he alleged he had received back in early1994.

'Agnes, my darling, I can't settle for anything less.' He had insisted that he had heard a voice in his ear whilst captivated by the glorious hues of an evening sunset as he drove home, a soothing Chopin nocturne on the car radio. The voice had apparently urged: 'You must marry this woman.'

At the time it had swept her away. The declaration being divinely inspired. A prompting from the heavens to marry her. And, to her eternal shame, her naïve schoolgirl heart had led her to a fairy-tale Catholic church wedding with a reception in a picturesque ancient monastery in Mallorca.

Eight years later, in the notary's office, she had gambled on beating Daniel at his own game by invoking his false invention of himself as an upright, moral Englishman to coax him into signing the agreement. She knew this well-worn performance by heart. The theatrical upper-class Englishness that permeated everything he did. Indeed, it was doubtful there was anything much else to him. She had met him at a party in London. It was hard not to notice him as he waved his arms around and shouted with unabashed confidence. He made people laugh. Made them notice him. Agnes always felt awkward at parties. The only part she really enjoyed was getting dressed to go.

Agnes, her lawyer, and the notary had all been formally dressed for the occasion. She had cringed when Daniel strode confidently into the office. A prototype of a silly Englishman on holiday, he wore a blue T-shirt depicting three white swans standing on one leg. She had forced herself to look at him closely, the dome of his bald head shining as he occupied a seat beside her at a table positioned beneath an unforgiving overhead light. A chest nipple had protruded beneath the beady eye of one of the swans. His bony knees stuck out below a pair of shorts that should have been discarded long ago. His feet resided in sandstone-coloured *alpargatas*. Agnes had imagined the long, big toes she had come to loathe wriggling with sweaty annoyance on top of the straw soles:

My wife is insisting that we do this today.

He had announced this with pure arrogance. Agnes had said nothing, only glad the notary did not speak English. She had fixed her eyes on an enlarged map of the area on the wall behind him and steeled herself for the fray.

Nearly a year had gone by since, upon seeing a corporate tenant safely installed in their London duplex, she had subjugated herself to final odious sex with Daniel in a nearby flat. A flat he had bought with her money for his now deceased mother. When he had gone out the following morning, she had phoned her son who dutifully arrived with the suitcase she had secretly packed. He had driven her to the airport where she had caught a flight to Mallorca and, upon arrival, called Daniel to say she wouldn't be coming back. It was cowardly, but what can a tree do when it is being sucked dry by a parasite?

The separation hadn't altered the way he went on addressing her as 'My Darling Wife'. The cloying salutation peppered the letters he wrote to her from Rome, whence he had subsequently disappeared to rent an apartment. Long hand written pages arrived regularly, describing sculptures, paintings, and churches he had seen, along with discursive excerpts from Roman history and random translations of Latin inscriptions. He had repeatedly told her how he had been praised at his public school for his grasp of Latin. Despite the salutation, these letters were impersonal enough to have been written to anyone.

Given her acceptance of his cultural superiority perhaps he had thought all this overblown erudition would win her back, but instead it reminded her of the way he had constantly humiliated her, quoting Suetonius, Tacitus and other Roman historians as a means to exclude her from conversations. During her time with him she had lost the connection – if she had ever firmly had a grip on it – that knowledge was attained through learning, settling into the notion that some people were chosen to know, and she wasn't one of them. But, in the notary's office, fighting to survive, her ignorance of

Tacitus and Suetonius no longer had any relevance. His pomposity comic, she had known Daniel for precisely what he was – a mere parrot. Empty of substance. A man with no profound grasp of anything more than how to bring her down.

But what wasn't impersonal in the endless letters from Rome was Daniel's spitefulness. The merciless criticism of old acquaintances he had recently got in touch with. A whole page had been devoted to trashing a couple he stayed with on weekends in Umbria to alleviate the loneliness he apparently felt in Rome. No one she knew tore people apart with teeth as sharp as his. She detested his hypocrisy. Had loathed the snide comments about those he had initially dazzled with his gigantic, piano-tooth smile. When with him, she had gradually given up on defending others. Felt ashamed of having let herself be drawn in like a conspirator.

Although she never replied, the letters just kept coming, along with postcards also addressed to 'My Darling Wife' or 'Dearest Beloved Wife', and all with accompanying hugs and kisses. It made Agnes wonder if others had also seen Daniel as ridiculous. A phony.

Even the London real estate agent had seemed to see through him. She knew the agent admired the way she had single-handedly organised the rental of the London duplex. Talking about Daniel with him, she had felt as she imagined a prisoner must feel stepping into the light from solitary confinement. No need for discretion now she had left him.

But Daniel's attempts at contact had persisted. The local florist had managed to locate the flat she rented in the Port of Soller to deliver red roses from him on Valentine's Day, but no amount of flowers could compensate for the way he had cheated and defamed her after she had extended him a helping hand. A fact he would probably never acknowledge.

The tension had been palpable on that day in the notary's office. Agnes now recalls how Francisca had turned to Daniel with a forced smile, willing him to sign, the purr of the air conditioning the only sound in the room as they all waited for what had seemed to Agnes to be an eternity. So much so that she had felt compelled to speak:

The notary is waiting to go on holiday, Daniel, and Francisca has another appointment.

She had leaned towards him, aware that inconveniencing others had always been one of his lowest priorities. He had exclaimed:

Oh, if it *must* be done today pass me the form!

He had been childishly petulant, his lips quivering.

Espero que no te sientas presionado?

Francisca had repeated the notary's polite enquiry in English:

You don't feel under duress, do you?

Oh, for *God's* sake! Just give me the wretched paper!

And abruptly, with a dramatic flurry of the pen, he had scrawled his signature in the square marked X.

It had appeared that Agnes's long-standing Spanish residency would save her from a messy and costly English divorce. The notary and lawyer having evaporated, she and Daniel had stood outside the office on an empty street. Shops and offices in Mallorca, like the rest of Spain, closed for lunch at 1pm and it was already nearing 2pm. She had looked at him and imagined he might now be regretting renting a house for the summer just up the road from her current building project. She had been undertaking a complicated renovation of an antique village house, initiating the project simply to entice him to Mallorca and extract him from their joint London home where she had invested the bulk of her capital. Standing beside him in the relentless lunchtime heat, she had wondered why, despite the relief that had initially flooded over her, she still felt responsible for him:

Can I invite you for lunch by the sea at the Port?

She had offered this more out of awkwardness than through any desire to be with him. Perverse, wasn't it, how she had felt she owed him compensation for her present triumph?

He had no time for lunch, he had told her, but nonetheless extracted what he could from her by getting her to drive him to a supermarket and wait while he shopped. Then she had driven him home. Seemingly unfazed by her lack of response as he slid out of the car with his parcels, he had smiled the piano-tooth smile and said:

Must dash. I'm meeting John and Jenny at the beach for a late lunch.

Agnes had felt sick as she pictured him sitting in the café at the beach with her friends. Not only had he cheated her, emotionally abused her, but now he was infiltrating her established friendships with others.

Now, as she stands at the passport desk, the shock of the night before the wedding seeps back into Agnes's consciousness. She had just discovered that Daniel had grossly overcharged her on the purchase of a fifty per cent share in the upper two floors of his house in Notting Hill. She had done the deal as a favour because he needed her investment to provide the full funds to enable him to buy a flat for his mother, having claimed he couldn't live with her one moment longer. But it had all been achieved too quickly and she had come to the realisation she might be well and truly stuck. So why marry someone she patently couldn't trust? Oh God! The noose was tightening around her neck. How could she cancel? Kenny and Mary had come all the way from Australia! So had Ben and Rose! Faces of guests from New York and Europe, not to mention the embarrassment in front of local people whom she had invited to the reception to repay their kindness whilst living amongst them those past years. And the treasured local next-door neighbours who had all chipped in and bought her a gold necklace – claiming her as one of their family. And the builder, the architect, and the tradesmen. They, too, she had invited to show her gratitude through hospitality.

And then there were Daniel's friends. They called themselves *The Big Chill* after the characters in the 1983 film. All had reliably shown up, many from other countries, to celebrate Daniel's nuptials. Her heart had raced like a trapped bird, fighting to get out. Her renewal of faith. Her baptism and confirmation certificates sent from Sydney. The endless paperwork. The dresses for the bridesmaids who were all to wear, like her, white lace-up wedge espadrilles simply because Daniel found them sexy. And then there was the vintage Daimler that an English friend had kindly spruced up to drive the newly married couple from the church to the reception.

And she herself had splashed out like never before for, after years of hardship, she was now being showered with gold. Thanks to the proceeds of one summer hit tune: 'Ritmo de Medianoche', a German musician, out of the blue, had purchased the village home in which she had brought up her son and which she had been trying, unsuccessfully, to sell for years. She had even thrown in one of her voluptuous, clay lady sculptures for good measure and invited the musician to the wedding. In fact, this was her second property sale, as she had already started looking for a London flat to buy from the proceeds of a house that she had put her heart into renovating, and which she had sold on to an English PR lady.

Her advent into property dealing was something she had originally pursued in Sydney, where she had run a successful real estate and design business in her twenties. It was precipitated by the desire to send her son to a boarding school in England. Up until then, she had lived modestly in a mountain village where she earned a living making art, maintaining properties for absent landlords and renting them out to people for holidays.

She planned on living in London for her son's last school year. She wanted him to experience a bigger world, beyond the confines of a small expatriate community of artists – a world where people had recognisable jobs.

That awful day before the wedding, reeling in shock and overwhelmed with conflict, she had paced up and down in bare feet on the tiled floor in the bedroom of the now ill-fated building site. Watching her intently from the end of the bed with a fixed expression was Daniel. She had tried not to look at him. A voice in her head kept cautioning her against going ahead with the marriage. To walk away. But then she was instantly swamped with the fear of disappointing the guests. How she hated herself for always putting the needs of others in front of her own. But she had already moved in with him. Her things were in his London house. Her antique chests of drawers already shared bedroom space with his William and Mary piece. Her books were arranged in bookshelves alongside his high-minded literature in serried rows. He had even purchased a new mattress for the antique double bed she had sent from Mallorca. The one with the inlaid pewter bedhead. She had paid out a fortune for the reception. This had to be the worst mess her compulsion to problem-solve had ever landed her in. She was going mad. She wanted to die.

She had gazed at her wedding dress and his morning suit, hanging side by side over a bamboo rail, temporarily supported at either end from ropes attached to the ceiling. She was fifty-two. She had believed she would at last be loved and cherished. That she would be supported and no longer be forced to battle on alone in the world. And then he had spoken, his tone calm:

My darling wife-to-be. Don't fret. Believe me, it's all been an honest mistake. I swear on my son's life. Please forgive me. I love you. Here. Take this cheque.

And he had torn the offering out of the cheque book on his lap. £10,000. It was the lifeline she was looking for and she clutched it with relief, failing to weigh up the numbers. Failing to think it through properly. Then he had thrown his arms around her, and she had let herself relax into his body.

The trauma of the previous night had already slipped away when she glided in flowing white silk down the aisle of the village church she knew so well, on the arm of her teenage son.

Then the honeymoon, and the wonder of seeing Venice together for the first time. Daniel had organised a spectacular sojourn. Knowing she loved walking, he had hired a car and driven them up through Italy from Venice to spend a week hiking in the Dolomite mountains.

It was a credit to his carefully crafted machinations that Agnes still has no memory of exactly how, let alone why, she had abruptly abandoned the flat she had committed to purchase in Belsize Park in order to buy that fateful fifty per cent share in the two floors of the Notting Hill house. Especially after the financial losses that had followed her first marriage, when she had made a solemn vow never to mix love and money again. Perhaps that intention was expunged during the long Bank Holiday weekend she spent with Daniel at a hotel in Cornwall? She did recall a brief fight in the car shortly before they arrived at the hotel, but not what the altercation was about. She had demanded he stop by the side of the road. Then she had escaped the car and fled into an open field, crying her eyes out.

Daniel had followed her, and now, as she waits in a trance at Sydney airport, tears glistening on her cheeks, she remembers how her spirit had lifted at the sight of a lark he had pointed out. As the bird soared higher and higher into the vastness above, he had held her tight in the gusting wind and she had felt, once again, safe – the discord between them seeming to float away with the tiny singing creature as it spiralled upwards. Then they had wandered, hand in hand, through a woodland pet cemetery filled with bluebells, reading as they went the dedications carved on rocks and small granite slabs to long-departed dogs and cats with simple evocative names: Chuck, Fluff, Billy, Patches, Tipsy.

Chunks of her life with Daniel start to organise themselves in her brain like the pieces of a challenging puzzle she would far prefer to throw straight out of a convenient window.

THE DEAL: It had been agreed between them that after the small outlay of funds to buy his mother a flat, Daniel would use a portion of what was left of Agnes's purchase money to finance the merger of his, and his mother's, separate living quarters into a luxury four-bedroom residence which they would then sell on at a profit. Then, they would buy a small flat for the two of them and Agnes would be reimbursed. No ambiguity. It could not be clearer.

Alongside the conveyance, wills were drawn up leaving their respective half shares to each other. And here lay the rub, as Hamlet reflects in Shakespeare's play. The sudden heavy paperwork did not include their verbal agreement. When Agnes suggested it should, along with an independent valuation, her beloved had argued persuasively about 'trust'. If there was no trust, where was the love? How could she sully the beauty of their forthcoming marriage with yet more ugly legality?

Her insistence had smouldered, smoked for a bit, before being extinguished under layers of gift-wrapping: satin knickers, naughty nighties, drop earrings, and the lovely gold wedding band (By Appointment To) they chose together. Agnes had gulped it all down like a starving child. What remained of good sense had been drowned in a whirlwind of music after midnight and the flicker of candles reflected on the glossy walls of fancy restaurants.

THE MOTHER: Agnes's first exposure to Daniel's mother was a revelation. Daniel had been entertaining Agnes over coffee on market day in the Portobello Road. He was mimicking his mother mercilessly:

And you wouldn't *believe* what she did a few weeks back in the supermarket! 'I'm blind, I'm blind, I'm blind!' she squawks! She was wearing some ridiculous dark glasses, wielding a white stick across the floor! Then she clutched at some young man's arm as he advanced to the fish counter. 'Good grief!' she cries. *Look* at the price of that mackerel!' Then she pokes the unsuspecting stranger in the ribs! I thought he was going to keel over. 'Sorry! Forgot her pills!' I tell him, swinging her around in the opposite direction, the white stick narrowly missing felling a stray toddler!

Daniel's tales of his mother's shenanigans would, in the early days, invariably have Agnes in fits of laughter. It wasn't just the blind act, however. Peeping though the open bedroom door, she had recently witnessed Daniel attend to his shrieking parent as she writhed around under a flowery bedspread:

I'm dying! I'm dying! I'm dying!

Beyond the bed Agnes could view the beauty of a giant cherry tree in blossom, framed in the window at the end of the room. The sight of it had bewitched her for a minute or two but then it occurred to her that perhaps she should offer some help by ringing an ambulance. Daniel had shaken his head:

No. Madame Butterfly will be back with us soon. Ready for her next performance.

He was attempting to soothe his mother's forehead, but she was persistently pushing away the insistent fleshy hand. As he turned his head, Agnes had noticed how strangely calm he seemed:

Don't worry. Off you go upstairs. I'll join you when I've settled her down with a pill and a cup of hot cocoa.

But Agnes, far from calm herself, was tremulous when she reached the upstairs apartment. There was something sinister about the way Daniel had looked at her in those moments that made her fearful for the old lady's well-being. Nonetheless, she had felt herself being drawn in against her will. Why? Because she felt sorry for him. One of the reasons she had chosen to live nine thousand miles away from where she grew up was that she herself had a domineering, demanding mother.

'Who will rid me of this troublesome woman!' Daniel had lamented like King Henry in the cathedral while they sat over dinner, as if gifting Agnes the potential future honour.

THE HOUSE: The merger of man and brick had begun when, as a young man, Daniel had rented the upper half of a run-down four-storey property and then sublet rooms. His tenacity in clinging on over the years was rewarded when his lease expired, and he couldn't be evicted. Aspirations to buy the upstairs space from the elderly owner downstairs had been thwarted when she died and left it to her deceased husband's family. But Daniel's long wait to purchase was finally rewarded when an easy-going, ex-hippy couple, replaced meditation in an Indian Ashram with the successful importation into the UK of Indian clothes. They used the financial proceeds to buy the house from the dead woman's beneficiaries. As the small 'fixed rent' from upstairs barely covered the maintenance costs, they sold him the two upper floors with forty per cent of the freehold at a bargain price. Their downstairs being bigger, and including the overgrown garden, they retained sixty per cent for themselves – filling a space in the weeds with a discarded Christmas tree every year as a testament to their presence. The huge pile of accumulated Christmas trees in the garden departed on a rubbish truck soon after a trendy banking couple became the new sixty per cent owners, prior to Agnes's arrival. This couple executed a speedy interior conversion. And the instigated repairs to the crumbling exterior were already nearing completion during Agnes's first weeks in residence so, in addition to the potential dilemma of being outlived by his mother, Daniel urgently now needed funds for his forty per cent of the external works bill. A problem-solver by nature, it had given Agnes pleasure to alleviate his concerns, although he had already started to diminish, rather than celebrate, her contribution as insignificant.

The rationale for the split house project was clear-cut and logical. After his father's death, Daniel had persuaded his mother to put her money into converting his run-down property into two self-contained apartments: a loft conversion above for him and a spacious two-bedroom space below for her. They shared an entrance and telephone. Recently diagnosed with a chronic illness, 'Mother' wasn't expected to live long. Yet, despite illness, she had successfully appointed herself as unofficial receptionist for her son's custom-made upholstered chairs and sofas – a business which was run from his upstairs kitchen.

In one sense, it struck Agnes that 'Mother' was quite an asset, for Daniel often entertained clients, friends and acquaintances with anecdotes about her unorthodox behaviour. It was a kind of eccentricity that went comfortably hand in hand with his pedigree Englishness. Public school, beneficiary of a personal batman during National Service in Scotland, Trinity College Oxford (sent down after six months – yet never mentioned) world traveller, fantastic mimic, fluent in several languages, splendid cook, wine connoisseur, rubber of shoulders with the rich and famous and a dedicated collector of art and antiques. But what Agnes had not twigged at the time was the importance of the background setting for his presentation. Daniel's house was his stage and integral to his performance. He was the house, and the house was him. He would be naked without it.

By the time Agnes was being secretly courted on the top floor, Daniel had grown old waiting for Mother's promised early demise and was joking about pushing her down the stairs. A sense of the thwarted plan was evidenced by the way he would check the share portfolio he would inherit as though he had already done the evil deed. Agnes still remembers the amounts, the banks, the list of company names. Chatting about who would get what was common between Daniel and his younger sister, Carmen, who was instructed about the ins and outs of it all by her impressive big brother. It was glaringly obvious to Agnes that Carmen looked up to Daniel, emulating his interest in becoming a collector of sorts – just like him.

And Mother, too, revelled in talk of her estate. She used it as a form of control. Gillian Holloway was a dramatic, domineering and remarkably handsome woman. Slim, smartly dressed, and brimming with energy, it didn't look to Agnes as if Gillian would be leaving the spacious first floor – with its lovely Georgian windows and gracious plaster wall mouldings – for anywhere more important than the supermarket, and yet more outrageous outbursts. Although never having been an actress, Gillian was as theatrical as a grand duchess in a panto. Simply a hard-working woman at the side of her husband in a small seaside department store, she had nonetheless managed to send her children to private schools.

It had occurred to Agnes that perhaps it was Daniel's blatant rejection of the meal his mother had cooked for him on that first night in their shared home, and his grim determination to maintain a strict bachelor existence above, which caused her to adopt a more cosmopolitan notice-me demeanour. She was, after all, a stranger in London. Sure enough, Gillian did attract some admirers through the local Anglican church. Nelson, a tall, thin, effeminate man with a tentative manner, and about half Gillian's age, was clearly impressed by her stately command. He worked locally in a soft furnishing shop and appeared to fill the void of domesticity opted out of by her son. Agnes once heard him declaim:

Oh Gillian, you are *so* beautiful!

She had overheard Nelson deliver this nasally high-pitched compliment during one of the in-depth discussions between he and Gillian about how to cook the vegetables for dinner.

And, happily awaiting Gillian's orders each morning was Holly – a rosy-cheeked local cleaner, whose straight grey hair clung to her head like a bathing cap. Other lady retirees visited Gillian too, as did the straight-backed pastor of the church.

Daniel's wedding announcement had left Gillian Holloway and her admirers flummoxed in disbelief. Seated around a tea tray in her pink lounge one afternoon, the conversation combusted:

How can he be *marrying*? He doesn't *know* anyone!

Agnes had overheard Gillian shrieking in astonishment, as if her own presence in the house was invisible. And, as she didn't attend the wedding – which Agnes had changed from a quick, registry office 'Yes I do' in London, to a grand spectacle in Mallorca – Gillian had decided to deny the nuptials had ever happened, choosing to completely ignore her new daughter-in-law's existence.

Henceforth, Agnes would watch Gillian in action like an episode in a TV soap. Years later, still waiting at the Passport Desk, she can still see the silver-framed photo image of Gillian in her mind's eye – looking sensational at seventy in a clinging black swimsuit – dedicated to her only son on his birthday.

But it was the announcement that Gillian would be moving out that had evoked undiluted hysteria: 'I *won't* be evicted from my beautiful home!'

She had cried out in vexation, stamping a satin slipper. She was no wilting violet, and she may well have dealt with the public in the store alongside her husband for years, but she obviously had no idea that the life tenancy she signed was protected by law. Tantrums and outrage – stoically borne by a son entrusted with her affairs – only strengthened his cause for eviction. The coterie from the church were in and out. The bishop was summoned. Her doctor hid in a broom cupboard when she forced entry into his surgery. Gillian became a human storm. Nelson was ordered to keep his underpants on and comfort her in bed that night. But neither the heightened octave of his nasality or the well-meaning supportive buzz of her acquaintances made a scintilla of difference.

It was all settled when her youngest daughter and husband, as instructed by big brother Daniel, flew in from New York. The daughter, Agnes noted, had her mother's luminous almond eyes. A late arrival to the family, she had grown up weaving a spell, like a ballet dancer on a music box, rigidly performing to please.

Although the new one-bedroom flat intended for Gillian was only a few streets away, and one of the church retirees lived in the same block, it was barely half the size of what she called 'My Beautiful House'. Agnes had thought warily at the time that Daniel might later come to regret economising on this purchase. Observing mother and son's high-octane encounters came to make her feel increasingly uncomfortable. Obvious to her now is the sinister way Daniel had encouraged, rather than dampened, Agnes's demonisation as the Jezebel who had facilitated his mother's eviction. Whenever the subject came up, he behaved like an innocent bystander. Yet, she had continued to submerge these doubts and suspicions by consoling herself that the business relationship between them was only temporary.

She had let the natural designer in her take over, throwing her energy into contemplating the reconversion of the house with its wonderful wide-open staircase, big airy rooms, high ceilings and beautiful roof terrace. Situated on a corner in fashionable inner London, it would be an easy job, with a quick sale assured – after which she and Daniel would create a life together on equal terms.

'Prediction is difficult as it involves the future', said Niels Bohr. Agnes could never have foreseen what happened next. Daniel kept delaying getting started on the project. Meetings with architect and builder were continually cancelled. She found herself gradually ground down. Days of being thwarted spun into weeks, months and then years. She became desperate, any pleas for action being twisted into personal attacks against her. Daniel would rant at her, leaving her dazed, confused, and often sobbing on the floor: You're *so* greedy! It wouldn't matter *how* much money you had – it would never be enough. They all said you were a hard-headed businesswoman and how much softer you are since you met me. You should thank me for saving you.

He would gloat and carp as if she was an undesirable undergoing rehabilitation. And then, like the purveyor of some form of perverted consolation, face distorted with false sympathy: Oh, you poor thing! We didn't get you an engagement ring!

It was unimaginable madness that something as trivial as a ring, which didn't interest her anyway, was supposed to make up for his criminal deception. She didn't care about rings. In fact, she was longing to remove the gold band – 'By Appointment To' – that bound her to his coercive presence. He expunged her name from his vocabulary. He now addressed her exclusively as My Wife, or just Wife. He loved saying it. And, as if this term was sufficient compensation, he would introduce her on the street as My Wife and then stand in front of her. She would hear him on the phone to friends, saying – My Wife said this, and My Wife said that, and she would think – what is he *talking* about? I never said any such thing! And yet, she would dismiss it.

You *know* what you're like! This pronouncement of his became a daily rebuke that she accepted in confusion like a wimp.

Nothing was what it was originally about, and Agnes had started to doubt if the agreement they made had ever happened. The capital she had worked so hard to rebuild since the nervous breakdown that followed her first marriage was starting to resemble a dowry – a 'payment received' for agreeing to marry her.

At first, she had delighted in the short trips they made to various European cities to celebrate their birthdays: Paris, Rome, Prague, Florence. And then there was the annual long-haul jaunt to New York to visit his sister and brother-in-law in September to celebrate their wedding anniversary. Now their empty time together was padded with excessive celebrations of past events. When he ran out of the personal, there was Christmas, New Year, Valentine's Day, Burn's Night, Easter, St Georges Day, and so it went on. He orchestrated the calendar like a cowboy pulling a steer on a rope, dragging her from one event to the next – a terrified animal dazzled by a bright light.

Agnes does remember trying to assert herself and re-establish reality on one particularly challenging day:

Daniel, I bumped into John and Geraldine as I was coming in the gate and John said he bought the downstairs part of the house for £400,000!

He had shouted in her face: We're *not* going through all this again! I *told* you. Their purchase was a forced sale because the McPhersons had split up!

Well, how come buying a half share in a property where your mother had a life tenancy wasn't a forced sale?

She had held her ground and he didn't like it. He had roared in her face:

I gave you back £10,000 the night before the wedding when you behaved like a fishwife!

Yes… yes… of course you did. Sorry. It's just that I've got such a poor memory of it all.

He had, yet again, managed to make her feel awkward about bringing the topic up. His tone towards her shifted into wheedling mode:

You don't realise, Darling Wife, how much softer and more attractive you've become since you got married. *Everyone* says so. Look here. Let's put this behind us for good, shall we?

She had relented: Well, I suppose it will all improve when we finally get on with the work here and sell the place on. I so look forward to buying a smaller flat. Just for the two of us, like we agreed, and then getting some money back. We'll be free of the years of baggage that swamp this place.

And Agnes, with a strained gaiety, had put her arms around his waist as he swirled some olive oil around in a pan ready to fry some fish:

I'm very lucky to have married such a wonderful cook.

She had whispered this compliment, kissing the back of his neck. But his body had suddenly stiffened, and he threw her off with his elbows. She had felt sick then. Sick in the knowledge that he would always ignore her, reject her, if she ever said anything he didn't like.

As she squints down at her own likeness in her passport from her vantage point at the Passport Desk, she recalls a framed photograph which once occupied pride of place on her coffee table. In it, she held her dog in her arms and was being blessed by a priest at the feast of St Anthony in Mallorca. Next to it stood an oyster dish Daniel was 'looking after for a friend'.

Agnes had gradually noticed how things he looked after for friends gently slipped into his ownership. She presumed he had similar plans for the oyster dish. The table was covered in trophies he had squirrelled away from others. The initial novelty of sitting at his feet on the floor, leaning her back against the '60s sofa in front of this table, had changed from companionship to servitude. She now felt like a pet dog at her master's feet. Her senses had shut down so completely she could barely hear the old jazz and classical records he liked to play. In fact, she was finding it impossible to concentrate on anything. Reading a book was beyond her. Daniel's ban on having a television in the house only added to her isolation. This ridiculous cultural snobbishness of his often being parroted by him as a virtue, she had gradually lost contact with the world. War in the former Yugoslavia and the troubles in Northern Ireland barely registered. What is more, she had degenerated from employing a cleaner to becoming one.

THE TRAP: One day, overhearing Daniel on the phone finally made Agnes realise that she had to get out of there. He was stating that he didn't understand why she had insisted on buying into his house when she 'would have got it anyway'. Constantly at the doctor's surgery undergoing tests for stomach and chest pains, she had realised that she had become powerless to counteract his constant manipulation and lies.

She still does not know what prompted her to buy Daniel a camel-hair overcoat that final Christmas. She didn't realise at the time that it was exactly like the one her father used to wear for trophy presentation in Australia – after a polo match. Like so much she had offered to her father in a vain attempt to win his heart. The snug beige wool kept Daniel warm when, on a bone-cold winter afternoon, they had driven in a taxi to Heathrow. They were due to catch a flight to join Daniel's sister and brother in-law in Baja California, Mexico – to celebrate the Millennium.

It was in Mexico when she realised that she was in serious danger. Her health run down by the torturous existence at home, she had picked up a bug that forced her to stay in bed. For several days she ran a fever that turned the giant cactuses outside the window into distorted demons capable of attack. But it was what she had overheard outside the bedroom door that frightened her more:

She's definitely a hypochondriac. Something not right going on in her head.

Sister and brother-in-law had apparently joined Daniel in a rear-guard action. Haunting voices devoid of sympathy. She was an interloper in enemy territory. Her Valentine-loving husband's effusive concern for My Wife had run out of steam.

Back in London, still weak, she envisaged herself exiting the upper floors in a body bag. She wished she could take her dog in her arms and walk back through the photo on the coffee table into another world. After all, with his mother rehoused, she was the only impediment to his complete ownership.

As he gained more control over her, he liked to show off as Lord of the Manor by throwing lavish dinner parties. After the meal he would lounge back at the head of the table – seated in one of the luxury gold brocade upholstered chairs out of the business brochure – and pontificate. Listening to the same old stories repeatedly had become unbearable to her. And, if she ever had the temerity to venture an opinion, he would either talk over her or choose to offer a plate of petit fours to a guest to distract their attention from her.

Overshadowed, her voice would echo back at her, and she would find herself stumbling with words and stopping short. The admiration she once had for the master of celebrations had turned to outright disgust. She stopped listening.

Her glumness was obviously getting him down. Blatant overtures to other women made Agnes realise she might well be on the list for replacement. He had recently flirted outrageously with a friend of hers who stayed briefly from Australia. She had no words to excuse this behaviour. It seemed her fifty per cent share on the deed meant nothing, as Daniel had the bulk of her money and there was no way of forcing him to do the renovation work, or of achieving a sale without the work done, or of getting him out of the house. Her plaintive insistences to get started now barely elicited a response. She would weep, cajole, shout. All to no avail. He had metamorphosed into a monster. A monster masquerading as an English gentleman, with My Wife cringing beside him.

He managed to stop her buying a car and insisted upon driving her everywhere. To escape him, she joined a health club and swam furiously up and down the pool till the contortion in her neck temporarily released. At the exercise classes she met busy working women and lusted after becoming one of them again. She would sit in a cloud of steam in the sauna and feed on the talk around her. It was a way of orientating herself back into a half-normal world.

When she finally had to admit to herself that he had no intention of renovating the house and selling it, she stopped spending any more of the small savings she had left and quietly invested them in the purchase of a studio flat, situated within walking distance of where they lived. Then she rented it out. But she should have kept its existence secret. That was foolish. Daniel, as always sticking his controlling nose in anything she did, insisted she cede him a small share. And, although she knew it was more than unwise, she found herself unable to refuse. His audacious declaration at the next dinner party, uttered with a self-congratulatory smirk, was a masterclass in phoney magnanimity in letting her keep all the rent:

I want My Wife to have an income of her own.

She thought of getting a job but felt incapable of managing even a checkout counter in a supermarket. She did, however, manage to supplement her income one summer by advertising holiday lets in a local magazine for the primitive, but liveable, house she still owned in Mallorca. The house that, one day, she planned to turn into a small hotel.

It was a complete myth that Daniel was supporting her, as he liked to pretend. She had long started to wonder whether the furniture business she saw floundering from month to month had ever been worth the £30,000 a year he claimed. Okay, he paid the bills on the house and their food, or at least some of it, but it had never crossed her mind to think what he had *actually* done with the thousands left over after the relatively small amount spent to buy his mother's flat. Then it dawned on her – healthy 1990's rates of interest secured on *her* money! She, in contrast, had become the impoverished one – buying her clothes at charity shops.

She doubted he had ever worked hard. His habit of going to the supermarket for a single item smacked of filling in time. In fact, the hardware shop owner had once informed her that Daniel was the only customer he remembered who had come in and bought *one* screw.

Events had suddenly swung in her favour when Gillian died. She had held out well into her eighties. When she became enfeebled, she had received help from the local authorities, but the lack of a second bedroom had meant there was nowhere for a carer to stay overnight.

And she had become even more isolated when the friend who lived upstairs died. Even the old gang from the church had gradually fallen away, and as for Nasal Nelson, he was lost to her long before she had moved there. Agnes had overheard the harsh way Gillian rebuffed him long ago from the top step of the staircase, for Nelson had chosen the moment when he and Gillian were discussing how to cook the roast to rashly confide his homosexuality:

How *could* you have led me on *all* this time, you dirty pervert! You even slept in my bed in your *underpants*! A boyfriend! How *disgusting*! Deceitful wretch! Whimpering filth! Poisonous queer! Coming out you say? The best you can do is GET OUT!

Instead of the friendly understanding he anticipated, poor Nelson had ended up wearing the uncooked roast as he escaped down the stairs – never to be seen again.

But Holly the cleaner had remained loyal. It was when Gillian unexpectedly couldn't cope and went to stay in Holly's flat that the search for a retirement home became inevitable. Indeed, her splashy entrance into a selected care home on the coast had been followed by a showy ride down the stairlift in a veiled red hat with matching heels. The uniformed manager had expressed her admiration:

What a glamour queen!

Gillian had assiduously ignored her:

She's taken a vow of silence.

Agnes had to smother a smile. Daniel could still be very droll. A group of grey-haired die-hards, seated at a table and bent over a game of bridge, looked up with disinterest as Gillian glared at them with disdain. Her show of elegance that day belied a weariness of heart that made Agnes think of the iconic line in *Sunset Boulevard* – 'I'm ready for my close-up, Mr DeMille'. She sensed Gillian was nearing a final performance. Therefore, it didn't surprise her to hear that, before her mother-in-law had a chance to make any lasting impression at the seaside home, she fell ill. Within days she was rushed with a stomach infection to Brighton hospital, where she gradually went downhill. Agnes remembers how she and Daniel had set off in the car on an icy evening, the hospital having contacted them to say they didn't think Gillian would last the night.

Daniel had approached his mother's bed. He was wearing his camel-hair coat. The only sign of affection between them, Agnes noticed, was the way Gillian had stroked the soft wool of his sleeve. She ignored Agnes to her very last breath. Agnes remained the Jezebel who had evicted her from her beautiful home. But what they had in common, of course, was that they had both been deceived by Daniel.

Agnes had watched as, after several clumsy attempts with the phone at Gillian's bedside, Daniel finally managed to connect with his sister in New York and held the phone to his mother's mouth:

I'm dying… I'm dying… I'm *dying*!

Gillian chanted this familiar mantra down the line in the amazingly energetic high pitch, emblematic of all the theatrical death scenes Agnes had witnessed in the floral bedroom. It must have left her youngest daughter dumbfounded.

Agnes could see the pain in Gillian's eyes. The blue hue of her exposed flesh. Death was creeping in. The scene was so undignified. Where was the declaration from the soul which Agnes had imagined all were blessed with in their final moments? She had sincerely wanted a better ending for this woman. She didn't see the male nurse administer the injection but watched the effect as Gillian's eyes slowly closed, and her body relaxed. The grave-faced nurse then turned to Daniel:

Don't mind me asking. Some families like to be notified when…

Daniel interrupted him. No. He definitely *didn't* want to be woken up to come to the hospital in the early hours. Which was when the nurse calculated Gillian's spirit would leave her body.

Gillian was unconscious when they left. The cold was bitter out on the street as they trudged from hotel to hotel, looking for somewhere to stay. Because the Conservative Party Conference was being held, there wasn't a bed to be had in the whole of Brighton. They ended up in separate rooms in a home for post-operative care patients. Agnes hardly slept as the woman in the next room was screaming for help all night.

Confronting a stripped-back, empty bed the next morning at the hospital had left Agnes sick at heart, as did the sight of Gillian's deceased body in the small chapel of repose. The woman lay like a marble queen atop a church monument. Although Agnes suspected she would probably have disapproved of the purple, gold-trimmed, velvet-hooded cloak draped loosely around her head and body. The white satin full-length gown beneath, however, might have been to her liking. Daniel and Agnes didn't speak. But then they hadn't spoken for days. She couldn't gauge how he felt. Or *if* he felt anything. Numbness, she suspected. And so, she left him alone with the body of his mother and floated around a small neighbouring park like a zombie.

The cheerful eldest daughter, who had chosen years ago to sever contact with her mother, arrived the following week from Canada for the funeral, accompanied by her two daughters. A retired hockey player, she was robust and natural. Her plump face was frank and open. Her loose grey curls glowed in the early slanting sunlight shining through the glass doors of the roof terrace. The friendly warm grasp of her hand contrasted with the indifference Agnes was accustomed to from the younger sister. It had long been decided between New York and London that the elder of Daniel's two sisters 'didn't deserve' a share of the estate. It was obvious to Agnes that this pleasant older sibling knew very well she had been cut out and therefore had no false expectations.

Daniel disappeared. In his absence, Agnes served coffee with a basket of fresh, out-of-the-oven almond croissants that she had been thrilled to find in the bakery that morning. When Daniel returned, he handed his eldest sister, and both her daughters, a cheque each for £3000. The presentation followed an irksome speech, delivered with ridiculous formality. As he had doubtless anticipated, they were all taken aback. On recovering, they thanked him profusely, beaming broad smiles. Of course, infused as she was with growing cynicism, Agnes had started to assess the motive behind her husband's every action. His eldest sister's lingering shame in rejecting her mother must have blinded her to any suspicion of her brother's double dealing. Aware of how hugely Daniel was benefitting, these small financial tokens looked to Agnes like offering beads to the natives.

Like snapshots in an album, to this day, Agnes retains only a few blurred images of Gillian's funeral – a quick service with a handful of platitudes to a small congregation. After a certain age, few are left behind to mourn. Daniel and his sisters had seemed as disinterested as the rest. Loyal Holly was the only person deeply affected by Gillian's departure but, sadly, unable to attend the funeral because of an asthma attack.

Gillian's coffin had rolled towards the furnace smoothly, as if indifferent to its fate. Agnes had pictured the ferocious jaws of a devouring dragon-mouth snapping suddenly shut and swallowing – along with Daniel's mother – a multitude of secrets Agnes would never know. There were no tears. In fact, Gillian's departure had a strengthening effect upon Agnes, jolting her to start scheming about how to regain control. It was so very easy to spot the bad guys in the movies. Then why the resistance to counteracting the less-than-subtle bad guy under her very nose?

Concurrent with Gillian's demise, the furniture orders dried up and the upholsterers announced their retirement. Regardless, Daniel was flushed with the success of everything he had planned and now had his mother's flat at his disposal. Agnes's moment to strike back had finally arrived. She clasped her shaking hands together behind her back and calmly suggested modernising her old house in Mallorca for them to retire to. Why not now renovate this house as planned and then rent it out? We can live like kings on a healthy income from it in sunny Spain! Your mother's flat can be your pied-à-terre in London!

All this, admittedly, would be at her own expense and, as a business proposition it was in fact a disastrous idea for her to convert the big rambling Mallorca house into a single luxury residence. But a prisoner does what she can to escape. So, the long-protracted London renovation, although much scaled down, finally went ahead. Agnes quickly had plans drawn up with an architect for the retirement house in Mallorca and, as Daniel refused to let her borrow on their house, she took out a mortgage on her studio flat and got started. A future goal in mind, she no longer cared about Daniel stinting on the work.

Miraculously, after months of high drama, the London works were finally completed and it was no surprise on completion to overhear Daniel indirectly claim credit for her efforts, whilst pointing out the concealed hall ceiling light:

My wife had the idea for this small detail.

Implying, naturally, that this was the sum-total of her contribution, whereas in fact most of the interior design was down to her.

The day they packed up their stuff and put it into storage, Agnes felt as if she was walking on air. A relocation agent had rented the two floors for the summer to an acting couple who would be shooting a film in London. Agnes went ahead to Mallorca and Daniel stayed behind to prepare for the tenants. After sending out a printed relocation notice to the old crowd, Daniel joined her in early summer in a house she had rented. Their supposed 'retirement home' remained a construction in progress. If she still harboured any doubts about leaving him, they completely evaporated when Daniel joined her adversaries to scoff at her when the local authorities had shut down her renovation. Because of a building infraction, the site was now cordoned off with a barrier of black and yellow striped tape. How he had sneered at her misfortune:

You crash around without knowing what you're doing. *Everyone* knows what you're like!

Overcome with disgust and fury, she had punched him on the arm as hard as she could. She had initially aimed for a spot he would never forget but changed her trajectory upwards at the last minute. A cowardly retreat followed, then his return from the bathroom to dangle the bruised limb under her noise, whining like a whimpering girl:

They all say you Australians are a rough bunch!

I'll show you how rough we can get if you don't get out of my sight!

But this unfamiliar fighting spirit had quickly ebbed away. With so much at stake Agnes soon regretted the outburst. Nonetheless, it had changed matters. After the 'stop work' order, a hardened distance developed between them. Ever gregarious, Daniel had quickly fallen in with the frivolous good-time crowd who descended every summer upon the resort, strolling along the seaside promenade and thronging the waterfront cafés and restaurants.

Knowing she had only ever been a means to an end, she had figured he wouldn't miss her – especially with so much more interesting company on offer – and so she locked herself in another room and went to bed when he left for the night's carousing. It was the heavenly life he had longed for: poolside parties in gardens, soothing guitars, scantily clad women, and lots of booze. She would rise early – when he was going to bed – and eventually no longer met him at the beach for lunch but would take off into the mountains to wander through the olive tree-lined paths she knew so well. Struggling with crippling anxiety, these early-morning adventures spent walking ahead of the August sun probably saved her life. When the afternoon temperatures climbed, and the garden floated in a heat haze, and the stone path outside burned the soles of her bare feet, she turned on the air conditioning in her solitary space and ironed clothes, losing herself in smoothing crumpled cloth. Her pent-up angst would burst forth with the first flow of steam and the fresh, crisp smell lifted her spirit. She hoped the pile of clean ironed clothes on his bed would smother any suspicion Daniel might have about her behaviour. It was what a woman did, after all. There was no indication to the contrary. He remained confident he had her securely on the leash.

And then, suddenly, the long-planned moment arrived. With Daniel immersed in the holiday gaiety in Mallorca, she went to the airport and flew to London the day after the three-month tenants moved out. Alone for the first time in a house where she had been held hostage for nearly seven years, she had to act swiftly. Like an unexpected blessing, a neighbour she met in the street offered her £8000 to rent the place for a month while he did up his kitchen. She instantly accepted and went to live the month out in Gillian's empty flat. An additional bonus followed for, whilst in residence at the house, the same neighbour agreed to allow the agents to show potential long-term renters around and, when one prospect phoned to make an offer on behalf of an American corporate tenant, Agnes was able to use the £8000 to pay for the new carpets and wardrobes required to clinch the deal.

It was during those months alone in London that Agnes had realised the only human kindness she now experienced was out on the street walking her dog. There was the encounter with the lady from the spiritual centre who had lost her daughter in a car accident – and owned two brown and white Jack Russell terriers. And then there was the pleasant single black mother in the rooming house next door, who regularly took her young daughter in a pushchair to a nursery on her way to work. There were also the busy professional women she met at the regular exercise class at the gym.

At this point, Agnes accepted as 'normal' the way Daniel singularly claimed the success of finding the new corporate tenants. It was completely in keeping with the way he had taken over her past and her present as if they were his own. To assert control, he faxed endless, unnecessary changes to the lease. But at this stage, what did she care? Potential liberation was on the horizon with Daniel arriving back in London at the end of September to sign the lease with an option to renew for a second year. And so, the day finally arrived when Corporate America would change her life.

But the option to renew the tenancy a year later would never be taken up. The terrorist attack on the World Trade Centre in New York on 11th September 2001 sent most of Corporate America rushing home from overseas locations – their own London tenants included.

Mejor sola que mal acompañada – Better alone than in the wrong company – Agnes would repeat to herself as she struggled with the complicated building project that, under normal circumstances, she would never have contemplated.

2

SYDNEY, MOTHER, AND AUNT MARNIE

A call from her youngest brother in Queensland had started the pull back to Australia. He and his wife were in financial difficulties, living out their retirement dream of breeding horses on a Brisbane farm. Mysteriously, shortly after, a gift-wrapped parcel had arrived from her mother. After thirty years of not even a card in the post – an astonishing revelation. The sight of a nightdress with baby smocking and bows in her mother's favourite pink and yellow, a matching dressing gown and fluffy peep-toe slippers with feathers and satin piping – stuff she would never dream of wearing – made her wonder if her mother wasn't suffering from a form of Alzheimer's that causes her to muddle her daughter with herself. She had rung Tammy Hailstone, a near neighbour, for a long-winded explanation:

Oh, Agnes, your mother is in her element! When it was clear she needed domestic help, I contacted the local council. They didn't just send one girl, but three or four. I can see a couple of them across the road right now – tripping over themselves to look after her. She's a real favourite. They take her shopping, to the hairdresser's, the doctor's, clean the house and organise the food from meals on wheels. She's particularly fond of the English girls – the ones on a working holiday. She gives them orders like a headmistress, but none of them mind. She never stops talking about her clever daughter overseas. She recruits them for parcel duty – to help lure you back. There are more treats in store. You know how effusive and convincing she is!

Tammy had rambled on affectionately, before ringing off. More likely, old Madge was showing the carers she cares, Agnes had thought – irritated that Tammy had presumed she shared her sentiments. Tammy's call had explained the youthful handwriting on the flowery gift card inside the beautifully wrapped parcel, ending with love you, miss you, longing to see you, come home soon. A carer had obliged. She, yet again, felt like a helpless target of conspiracy. The last time she had spoken to Madge, she had been ordered never to ring again – a commitment she had not found difficult to obey.

Struggling for stability after finally escaping Daniel, she had flown back to London from Mallorca to seek help at a three-day personal development program, run by the Landmark Forum. Based in a grubby part of Euston, it had taken place in a huge bare-walled room which resembled an aircraft hangar – more like a rescue shelter after a disaster than a pathway to higher understanding. Shelving misgivings, she settled into one of the hard, uncomfortable chairs. The high stage had seemed like a strange cavernous mirage. It dwarfed those assembled below. To her surprise, she had found herself unexpectedly swept into the mass dynamic. A featureless speaker, who was like a cross between a marketing manager and hellfire preacher, was rousing the group to action:

It's time to open your minds to heal past rifts! Go back! Revisit the past! Heal all resentment and estrangement! Now is the moment for reconciliation and closure!

Buoyed up by the messages vibrating through the hall, yet without being aware of making a tangible decision, Agnes had found herself in a phone box, contacting her mother:

It's me, Agnes. I'm ringing to ask you what went wrong between us and open a new dialogue.

Are you completely crazy!?

We need to heal the past.

What past?! It's the early hours of the morning and you're getting me all churned up.

Click – and the phone had gone dead.

The monitors on the Landmark course had encouraged 'persistence', so Agnes had tried again. But hardly had she stated her name before the embargo fell like a guillotine: NEVER RING AGAIN!

Listening to some of the 150 other attendees' joyous accounts of reconciliation on a distorted microphone, Agnes had realised that not only were her memories of the past frayed and shrouded in mist, but there were complete blanks in her existence – with no attached memory at all. Her problem with her mother was clearly beyond the boundaries of a few days' self-improvement in an uncomfortable echo chamber.

Back in Mallorca, she followed the Landmark experience with different kinds of healing therapy: massage, reflexology, guided imagery, crystals to balance chakras. She abandoned herself to crooning jargon-filled practitioners with enigmatic smiles who inhabited soft-lit rooms clouded with incense and bedecked with Eastern religious statues. Traversing the landscape of healing had become as challenging as the problem.

Once, a demented woman in a small mountain village had tapped the muscles around her neck and shoulders with her knuckles and thanked her absent mother for 'spiriting in' to listen to the complaints against her. When not tapping, the woman apparently divided her time between moving energy from the top to the bottom of the village.

Then there was the mystical specialist in the back room of a health food shop, dressed in an Indian print, painted with heavy black eye make-up, who had gasped at the sight of Agnes's tongue. With the hypnotic sound of a sitar in the background, Agnes had been treated to a glimpse of the specialist's own heathy pink tongue as an example of what to aim for. The ransom for this assessment was embedded in the extra mandatory purchase of a pile of vitamins and healing potions that had cost the earth.

On yet another occasion, she had mistaken Reiki therapy for Reiki massage as she lay, bemused, in a dark, silent room, her eyes closed, waiting for the masseuse's hands to whirl into action. When she eventually opened her eyes to enquire what was wrong, she saw the white-clad practitioner with arms outstretched, hovering her palms over her chest like Jesus's prelude to the loaves and fishes. The girl had spoken in honeyed tones: Your father is inside you.

As Agnes had been focusing on her mother's ruinous behaviour during her childhood, her father's appearance – out of the blue – had come as somewhat of a surprise. But she had taken no notice, paid what she considered an inflated fee, and never went back. With the sole exception of a straightforward relaxing massage, alternative healing had felt as practical as a damp squib. She decided that exploitation of the vulnerable was equivalent to an unregulated licence to print money.

Her next adventure clearly bore this resolution out in spades. She had confided how bad she was feeling to an eccentric woman she had come to know as they both regularly emerged at the same time from an early morning swim.

A scientific approach was recommended as they towelled themselves dry on a deserted Mallorcan beach, and Agnes was subsequently put in touch with a middle-aged English psychologist.

The expat psychologist – a woman – lived in a dark, run-down stone terrace in an obscure rural village. On the wall by the front door was a brass plaque, like something one would see in Harley Street, stating the practitioner's profession, her membership of the British Psychological Society, and trailing a line of abbreviated degrees. She managed to make such an accurate diagnosis that Agnes ended up doing her shopping, taking her to London for the treatment of some mysterious infirmity, and supporting her financially down to her underpants. Agnes had never been in any doubt that she was a suitable case for treatment, but this protracted relationship only turned out to be yet another descent into hell.

But solutions can often appear in the oddest places and, lo and behold, a casual comment from one of the girls who worked in the local branch of her bank led her to the psychiatrist she had been searching for all her life. He didn't speak English and she certainly wasn't confident of her grasp of Spanish – but then she had never really been confident about anything. He had advised her candidly:

The chances of being able to change reduce with age but, if you like, we can try and see how the transference goes.

Working with this man in a different language, and with an uncertain outcome, paled into insignificance beside the task of extricating herself from the charlatan psychologist. Facing the loss of generous twice-weekly payments, and easy access to loans, the woman with the formal brass plaque upped the pressure. Agnes attempted to ignore the stream of letters and emails that followed her dismissal note – sent by registered post. She would quiver like a tiny bird hiding from a cat as she listened to the phone ringing, once managing to go without answering it for over a week, during which time she would continually watch a film DVD of *The Servant* – Pinter's '60's masterpiece about a manipulative reversal of roles which, on some level, she knew without doubt reflected her toxic relationship with the psychologist.

But it wasn't until Agnes's new psychiatrist gently explained that she was suffering from a chronic level of fear that she finally understood. It explained her pathological fear of Daniel, her fear of the domineering psychologist and, yes, of so many others. She had finally found a safe harbour with a consummate professional. Agnes would enter psychotherapy whole-heartedly, coming to greatly admire the 'father of analysis' – Sigmund Freud. Long accustomed to listening to the problems of others, she had always grappled to find a voice to express her own. She was 'neurotic' – a pejorative word she had heard so often used as a complaint, but usually without the user understanding its true and indelible meaning. Her therapist had reassured her: You are here for yourself. This time is for you.

Initially, Agnes did not feel there *was* a self. She could *speak* of herself all right, running on and on, but who she *truly* was behind the words remained a mystery. When the specified fifty minutes of her session was up, and the expectation was to be quiet, she managed to train herself to stop talking. At first, she had found this imposed discipline offensive, but had gradually come to cherish the containment. Additionally, her analyst's extensive knowledge of five-thousand-plus years of civilisation stimulated her to enjoy an education that early anxiety had denied her.

After each session, as she left him, she would repeat her mantra:

Mejor sola que mal acompañada. And he would nod in affirmation.

A middle-aged Australian woman in analysis, in Spanish, with a Catalan psychiatrist. She had treasured all those precious sessions and had never disclosed her relationship with him to anyone.

Hardly had she put down the phone to Tammy than parcels from her mother had arrived at her door with accelerated zeal. Frills had been replaced by gifts that grew exponentially in size. Following in the wake of a silver lipstick-holder, matching compact, soft handbag, small drawings of Federation houses in Hill End, came huge coffee table books that weighed a ton and must have cost a bomb to send: *Australia Today, Australia Then and Now, Sydney Waterfronts, Australian Bushrangers, Australian Islands and Coastlines.* All showed up at regular intervals over the months ahead. It was after struggling home from the Post Office with the *Complete Works of Banjo Paterson* that Agnes had decided to call her mother and put a stop to it:

Did you get the parcels, Agnes? Why didn't you ring sooner? When are you coming home, darling? I need to see you! You'll be sorry when I die if you don't come!

As Agnes put the phone down, Al Pacino's lament in *The Godfather* vibrated in her ear:

Just when I thought I was out – They Pull Me Back In.

This outreach from Madge was clearly suspicious. However, the therapy sessions seemed to have prompted a growing desire in Agnes to investigate her past and had, eventually, propelled her to book a flight to Sydney. She and her youngest brother would hire a car and they would drive to see their mother in the town where she lived – an hour from Sydney. This would then be followed by a trip into the country to visit the small country hamlet where her father was born and grew up. As brother Jim had a photographic memory, Agnes had hoped he could help her reclaim lost childhood memories. Not just the odd memory. Whole chunks of total amnesia.

Memory. And its tricks and traps. Someone is talking to her. Agnes attempts to pull herself together. She is aware that the dishevelled consulting passport officer is giving her a nod and smiling. For some reason, his pride in his new nationality irritates her. She suspects it is envy, as she has never felt her nationality is really her own but is somehow on loan. She equates having to go through her family in order to 'belong' to Australia with going through a priest to get to God.

As if reading her mind, the young Asian assumes the breezy tone of his fellow officer:

Come to see family I suppose?

Yes, that's right.

She is trying to sound upbeat yet is cringing inside. He hands her the passport with a smile, and she finds herself joining a boisterous crowd as they stampede past toy koalas and kangaroos, boomerangs, Akubra hats, Australian wines, and a conglomeration of locally produced shampoos, shower gels and bubble baths. She grabs her blue suitcase, which she has spotted spinning on the dizzy round of the carousel, then stops at a phone counter to collect a pay-as-you-go mobile to save the cost of calls via Spain. This time there will be nobody picking her up at the airport.

She feels sad as she watches the effusive family reunions in the grand exit hall. Forget the marshmallow nostalgia she tells herself – it got you nowhere. Along with birthdays, Valentines, Christmas, Anniversaries, and all the rest of it: *Mejor sola que mal acompañada.* The mantra comes to rescue and enfold her like a security blanket.

Outside the airport, as she joins a fast-moving queue at a taxi rank, she can smell the sea from nearby Botany Bay. 'Captain Cook chased a chook all around my library book!' – the kids used to chant at school. The late afternoon sun is blinding and so she is glad when a taxi door opens, and she can tumble in with her stuff. Speeding below ground, the rhythmic sound of tyres over a smooth surface and punctuated by bumps to slow the traffic, is soothing. She is on the Eastern Distributor – a brightly lit, but unfamiliar, two-lane highway which transports her in and out of a series of tunnels. She feels as if she is in a homogenised bubble that could be anywhere in the world. Then the taxi suddenly rises above ground, and her heart leaps at the sight of Moore Park Golf Course and the roads around it, which she knows so well.

The cheery voice of the solid-necked driver breaks into her reverie: Okay back there, love?

He is wearing a leather cap and she notices a tattoo on the muscular arm below his short sleeve. It depicts Popeye the sailor man, captured just after he downs a can of spinach. The tattoo bobs up and down in animated motion as the driver turns the wheel through the heavy traffic in Darlinghurst. She feels compelled to speak:

I've never been on that freeway from the airport before. I was initially wondering if I'd landed in the wrong place.

Well, let me assure you, unless I've lost my marbles, you've landed in Sydney and the wonder of it all lies before you.

She notes the expression of pride on his face reflected in the rear-vision mirror as he slides a pair of sunglasses over his eyes. They combine with the cap to make him resemble Marlon Brando in *The Wild One*. She wonders if he is an actor 'between jobs' but decides not to ask.

He croons with an irresistible grin: Sit back and relax. Next stop Potts Point.

She sinks into the soft upholstery in the back seat, as instructed, and feels the tension of the arrival leave her. It's not madness, she whispers to herself. It's the anxiety that trips you up. She prompts herself that part of being in analysis is learning to train her mind to reflect on her reactions.

The car pulls up at Number 1 Grantham Street off Macleay Street. She had been to the area many times in the past, yet today, shrouded by the veil of absent years, it looks mysterious. The driver jumps out and opens the boot with a thud. In awe, she watches from the back of the taxi as, in one continuous muscular movement, he manages to settle her suitcases at the entrance door of the apartment block; his provocative swagger demands attention.

No – keep the change, she protests, grateful for the smooth ride and the cases at the door. In fact, she feels so grateful she would like to hug him – but controls the urge. He calls out the window: Enjoy your stay!

He tips the front of his cap like a professional chauffeur, before driving off. She reflects on the small vignettes in life that unexpectedly lift one up. The on-board 'Singapore Girl' and the cheerful driver have already filled her with more warmth than any family member she can think of. She resolves to give more importance to moments such as these that come, unsolicited, like surprise gifts.

The entrance door to the serviced apartments is under a low awning which is masked by the thick branch of a silver gum tree. The main trunk is so gigantic she reckons it could have been present years before the first settlement. A gust of wind blows a pile of leaves in with her through the door and her arrival interrupts a heated discussion at the reception desk. The confrontation is between a girl with streaked fair hair and a woman in a maid's uniform with Slavic features, who is built like a wrestler. The latter puts two fingers up before storming off.

The receptionist's young cheeks are flushed as she busies herself with the booking sheet under the counter. As Agnes leans on the desk, she can smell the girl's lavender perfume. She exudes freshness as if she is not long out of the shower. Perhaps she has just started her shift. Her eyelids are painted green, and she has pencilled a perfect dark line which extends out beyond thick lashes. It makes her look like a blonde Cleopatra.

Agnes sees that the girl's hands are shaking with pent-up emotion. She feels sorry for her. She would like to comfort her. She takes stock. Aware of the need to curb a reckless tendency to empathy, she stands appropriately silent. In the long pause that follows, the green eyelids remind her of a line from a 7th-century Chinese poem she has heard somewhere: 'Eyebrows painted green are a fine sight in young moonlight'. She speaks to the girl:

Agnes Keen. I booked a one-bedroom serviced apartment for eight weeks at the front of the building with a sofa bed in the living room. My brother will be joining me during my stay for a night or two.

She glances at a drinks dispenser behind the girl and thinks it lowers the tone of an otherwise discreet decor. The receptionist bites her lip as she concentrates on locating Agnes's name on the list. As Agnes waits, fatigue starts to distort her surroundings and she struggles to fill in the squares on the registration form with a biro that only works intermittently. The sleeping pill she had taken after the on-board meal out of Singapore has had no effect – until now. Her vision is swimming, and she starts to panic when she can't find her passport in the overstuffed handbag. It is jammed with so many sundry items it could be a lucky dip. But there it is! Hiding in the pocket of her coat.

The lift stops on the sixth floor. Apart from a large suitcase, she is certainly hauling too many other bits and pieces: a carry-on, an assortment of bags containing books and magazines, a make-up purse she hasn't managed to stuff back into her handbag, a half-drunk bottle of water and a plastic bag full of items she has scavenged from the food trays on the flight. She struggles to get it all out of the lift, before being impaled by the sudden closure of the door.

She staggers down a corridor, feeling like a bag lady, in search of her room. But her angst falls away when she opens the door and sees the view. She has arrived in Paradise. Unfamiliar skyscrapers, like giant guards in shiny new uniforms, fill old gaps in the Sydney skyline across the water. It is as if they are protecting the carpet of green that is the Botanical Gardens, which rolls down to the harbour's edge. She can see the back of the art gallery: a classical building that echoes Greece and Rome. For years, the grandest building she knew. Behind is The Domain – hidden under a canopy of enormous Moreton Bay fig trees. It is the Australian equivalent of Speaker's Corner in London, and where anyone can stand on a soap box and declaim to anyone else who is prepared to listen.

The white sails of the Opera House are shimmering in all their pristine purity to the right of the balcony. She is old enough to have seen it being built, and she recalls now joining in the street protest in support of the architect, Jørn Utzon, when he was dismissed by local government. The harbour bridge far behind, which joins the northern suburbs to the city, has always been in her life. Once, long ago, she had wandered across it with the intention of jumping off but, for want of finding a place to launch herself, walked on.

But this isn't the right time to think of that event. Or is it? She drops everything on the floor, closes the curtain, sheds the coats, and staggers into the bedroom, where she flings herself onto the freshly made bed, still fully clothed, and falls asleep.

* * *

She wakes with a start, her heart pounding and her arms clutching a pillow as if it is the side of a life raft. She is full of anguish. The surge upwards, from the depth of the sea to the surface, is over. She made it. She didn't drown. She's in a bedroom in Sydney and can see a thin beam of sunlight through the closed curtains. It is illuminating stains on the carpet outside the door. She grapples to make sense of the rest of the disturbing dream about her mother and her Aunt Marnie. Wearing sun hats and summer frocks, they were sitting together on the edge of Elizabeth Bay Wharf – a harbour marina within walking distance of where she is now staying. She seemed to recognise the big-brimmed straw hat with its black band that her mother wore when Agnes was in her early teens. Before her mother's hair was cut and permed. In the dream, dishevelled, long strands, the colour of shiny crow's feathers, fall to her shoulders. Agnes had loved the colour of that hair and wished she had inherited it instead of her own ginger mop that makes her feel like she belongs to an alien tribe. The rosy-hued dried flowers around the brim of Marnie's hat had also seemed familiar. Younger than her mother and married to her brother, Parry, Marnie is her mother's only ally in a large feuding family. In this early waking state, Agnes isn't sure of the style and colour of their frocks. The shapes and shades curl away like a stream of smoke as she wrestles to hold on to the images. Probably Marnie was in blue and her mother in pink or yellow, for they are the colours Agnes associates with them. The sunglasses both women were wearing denied her a glimpse of the expression in their eyes. From a distance, they were a snapshot of languid serenity, framed by rows of anchored sailing boats nudging each other gently in a soft breeze. Up close, their mouths were contorted, and Agnes now knows they were absorbed in the gossip she hates. They were naming and shaming trollops, harlots and hussies. Brazen, saucy, wanton females who steal good women's husbands.

As a teenager, Agnes had imagined these 'bad women' wearing red and purple like Belle in *Gone with the Wind*. Decades ago, an Armenian neighbour, a few years older than Agnes, and who wore a thirty-four-inch bra when she, Agnes, was still flat-chested, had read her racy bits from Mitchell's novel whilst perched up a mulberry tree in her backyard. Curiosity and wonder had been satisfied beyond dreams when they sneaked off to see the picture at the cinema. In fact, Agnes has seen it so often over the years, she almost knows the dialogue by heart.

The scathing damnation of Marnie and her mother was not only reserved for women of questionable morals, but all single women until safely married.

It had caused Agnes to equate the single state before marriage with the stain of original sin on the soul before baptism. Their talk must surely have been exaggerated but, as her mother would swerve between extremes, it became hard to gauge. Indeed, it seems to Agnes, even now, that her mother's only true motivation in life back then was to dress in expensive clothes and to air her outdoor personality, hobnobbing with the socially superior. Who was she? And who is she now?

A glimpse of memory surfaces. She is around ten. Her mother sinks into a bubble bath – her face as expressionless as the full moon as she swoons over the eggshell-blue underskirt which once shimmered like fragments of sky through the fine silk of Marnie's wedding dress. Just a smattering of blue to lift the white, her mother recalls, as Agnes listens in rapt attention. Her mother is in love with that dress, for she has always pined after a big fancy wedding, her own having been a hurried affair before Agnes's father went to war. Her mother imagines, she says, her young daughter one day wearing the same gown when she floats down the aisle. But this is no ordinary mother. She has a contradictory nature. Her marriageable daughter wearing a touch of blue is easily cancelled out by: 'You'll never get a man with a face full of freckles like that!'

The unexpected morning dream continues to unsettle Agnes. In it, Agnes was rowing a small boat up and down in front of the two women who intermittently dipped bare feet in the cool water as they talked. The metal fixings that held the oars squeaked whenever Agnes exerted pressure and she had tried to row smoothly, so as not to disturb them. Her mother was smoking a Capstan cigarette, intermittently picking bits of tobacco off her tongue. Now she can see the red cigarette pack on her mother's dressing table in the long ago. The self-same red she painted her toe nails.

What had woken her in a panic is that, in the dream, she drowned. Or disappeared. She's uncertain now, in the light of day. It's hard to fathom. She was – and wasn't – drowned at the same time. She was simply not there anymore. The boat was empty. And the horror of it was that neither her mother nor Aunt Marnie appeared to notice. They were blind to the empty vessel bobbing adrift inches from their feet. Blind to the fact she had evaporated.

At home, when Agnes was growing up, she had claimed an old art book as her own because no one else ever looked at it. Pictures in the book now drift into her mind. The dream seems to have connected her with 'The Fall of Icarus'. In the mythical story that inspired the painting, Icarus fell to earth after his wax wings burned. He had flown too close to the sun. Bruegel paints his Icarus as he slips into the sea with a tiny splash, unnoticed by either a farmer or the crew of a nearby ship.

What does the dream mean? Her mother would have blamed her for hallucinating – 'seeing ghosts' as she used to complain. This maternal influence is so potent in her life it can still make Agnes doubt what she sees with her own eyes.

Thirst drives her back into the here and now. Drops like tiny diamonds are covering her forehead. The mirror on the bedroom wall shows curvy lines from the pillowcase stamped on the side of her cheek. The skirt and stockings she slept in are clinging to her like a second skin. She has experienced four seasons in a week. Leaving Mallorca on a hot spring day to land in a freezing cold snap in London. On a whim. There is no one to tell her not to. She had bought a mink coat from a stall in the Portobello Road. A nuisance to lug around in tropical Singapore on the layover, but why not? And here she now is – in glorious, warm, autumn Sydney sunshine.

This really is a raging thirst. Drinks stored in the ugly dispensing machine at the reception desk come to mind. Then she remembers the half bottle of water she salvaged from the plane. Gulping it fast brings on a fit of coughing. She jogs on the spot to make it go down.

Then, sliding through the thick, grey pile carpet in stocking feet, she discovers, to her delight, a mini kitchen in the living room: an electric kettle on a tray with teabags, powdered chocolate, coffee sachets and brown and white granulated sugars. On a granite countertop: a hotplate, microwave, cupboards with crockery and cutlery and a small fridge with milk and a minibar. How wonderful to be in a place of her own and not be staying with friends or relatives!

The water pressure is fabulous. She revels in a delicious long shower. Sitting out on the balcony afterwards, scenting the early morning air, she feels revived. She sips a hot mug of tea and is wearing a crisp new blue patterned cotton kimono – purchased in Singapore and safely hidden in the suitcase out of reach of the thieving red-gloved hand. The croissant and biscuits taste all the better for being squirrelled off the aeroplane trays. The fabulous view is ever fascinating. Fitting the new into the familiar absorbs her like a jigsaw puzzle and helps pacify the feeling of being a stranger in the land of her birth.

'Aurora Australis'. She identifies the icebreaker through a pair of binoculars. It seems it has only just docked on the wharf at Woolloomooloo below. The ship is generating a mass of movement on the street in front. Then she spots Harry's Café on Wheels – the hamburger joint she remembers from her youth. It must be over fifty years old. Groups of sailors from the ship are heading there in droves. Its reputation as rough and sleazy, where the uncouth hang out and refined women don't venture, looks to be intact. Over sixty years old as she is, she can now venture exactly where she pleases. She's anonymous. No one will notice her. No waterside worker is going to whistle and make a spectacle of her. Gripped with a sudden desire for a meat pie, she decides to venture down there.

She unpacks her clothes. She has chosen outfits which she hopes will impress her aunts. Insane as it seems, after decades, she still yearns for their acceptance as an equal. She knows she is stuck in a time warp. But it is not only her. She will subsequently recognise that the aunts also have not moved on. She puts on a crushed black linen dress under a black and white striped jacket. Crushed linen is a fashion statement and, conveniently, no need to iron. She slips her feet into a pair of black leather thongs and does up the strap behind the heel. They are identical copies of sandals worn by her Aunt Charlotte back in the late fifties when she left on an ocean liner for a honeymoon in Europe. Head-girl Charlotte. University Honours graduate Charlotte. Her grandmother's favourite daughter who married a wealthy grazier – which was the icing on the family cake, apparently. Amazing how, when so much else is forgotten, the sight of those prim neat feet in sandals lives on in Agnes's mind.

The recognition from the aunts that she longs for conflicts with loyalty to her mother who hates the lot of them and has always expected her daughter to follow suit. Hatred is a strong word, but no other could adequately express a mother´s sentiment that never goes off the boil. Her hope, after all these years, is that the aunts may have transcended the notion that 'daughter is like mother' and are open-minded enough to see her for what she truly is – her mother's complete opposite.

Aunt Charlotte's fairy-tale romance with her country grazier was the desirable prototype – the route to happiness Madge believed should have been her own rite of passage to matrimony – many years earlier. As a young woman, Madge O'Connor had tried hard to put herself in the way of it by working as a nanny in the homestead of a grand property in the hills of the Great Dividing Range of New South Wales. It was the era before synthetic fabrics when fortunes were shorn off a sheep's back. Her boss's husband was one of four brothers, their names forever synonymous with Australian polo. They soared to fame not only in their own country, but also attained unheard-of heights on the international circuit.

As a boy, Agnes's father – a second-generation son of Irish immigrants – started work at the brothers' stables and, by the age of eighteen, was invited to travel abroad with the ponies as one of the grooms. Eric Keen had grown up in the saddle. Rode to school. Rode to the shops. Rode to collect firewood. Rode to his work at the polo stables. He and his father, the overseer of the grand property, rode the boundaries of the vast acreage together. He knew every tree and dam. He was as comfortable in the saddle as a city kid on a bike. His talent as a horseman being recognised by the polo brothers, they taught him how to refine his seat in the saddle and, via their instruction and his own pin-sharp observation, he mastered the game until he was good enough to fill in at Sunday practice matches on the homestead field. He not only learned the game, but all the techniques the brothers used to train a novice horse. This would be a skill he would later adopt independently, along with the brothers' lucrative practice of selling trained ponies after a tournament, to cover expenses.

Agnes's mother would speak of her own former employers with adoration. As a child, Agnes imagined them like royalty. The enticing, vivid description of their fabulous house and garden become part of her imaginary world. Relaxing in a hot bath, Madge's mind inevitably drifted to musing on her halcyon times at 'Pink Dale'. Black and white photos attested to her youthfully intoxicating black-eyed beauty. Adding to her glamour was a grandiose 'Presentation' dripping with every conceivable upper-class flourish. How could the young groom, just back from tending the brothers' ponies at a tournament with a maharajah in India, not believe that the vivacious and well-dressed new employee was anything less than an heiress, working as a nanny to the owner's children for some character-building pocket money?

As for Madge Anne O'Connor, there can be only one outcome to the first sighting of Eric Keen – the well-built blue-eyed man with the film-star looks. Watching him in his tight white jodhpurs and high leather boots as he cantered across the field at a Sunday practice match. Admiring the flawless under-the-neck cross shot which scored a perfect goal. And if there was any doubt about the electricity between them when their eyes met on the side-line, a further encounter under a pergola dripping with blue wisteria flowers in the famous garden would seal the promise of eternal love. Transported by the power of youthful attraction in the perfumed moonlight, it was easy for the two young people to envisage that earthly manna would flow from the wonder of it all, along with countless other blessings to sanctify their union.

The stark reality after their wedding in Sydney – that neither bride nor groom had struck gold – took some time, if ever, to assimilate. This realisation, and one that neither of them seemed to arrive at, was hampered by the fact that the pursuit of the truth was never a priority for either of them.

Agnes's father's expectations were further blighted when he found out he was a bastard.

There was no way around the damning euphemism printed in black and white on the birth certificate he needed for the wedding. **Father: not known.** It also answered the mysterious disappearance of his 'sister' at sixteen to work as a dressmaker in Sydney. He would never forgive his grandparents for passing him off as their son. How could he continue to face the small country town where he grew up? They all knew what he didn't. Without a backward glance, he cut the betrayers out of his life and adopted his soon-to-be wife's family.

His burgeoning talent on the polo field, which once led to the plausible expectation of becoming part of an international team, ended abruptly when, after the invasion of Poland, Australia followed Britain in declaring war on Germany. Eric Keen joined the Australian Air Force and was married in uniform. Things could not have turned out worse for Madge. Hard on the heels of the bombshell of a lost fortune came the Japanese attack on the Pearl Harbour US Naval Base in the Pacific on 7th December 1941 with no warning.

Early the following year, when she was heavily pregnant with her only daughter and her husband had been posted to New Guinea, US defence units started arriving in Sydney. Within months, the town was crawling with American servicemen with disposable incomes, nylon stockings, cigarettes and free access to every fashionable article ever manufactured. It was a further unforgivable climbdown for Agnes's mother, after boasting of socialising with wealthy graziers at the magnificent property in the Great Dividing Range, to have to live with her own mother in an overcrowded flat with her five sisters. Women of her age were dating generous Yankee boyfriends. Even Madge's own oldest sister, Sill, was constantly dolling herself up to be whisked out the door by yet another American suitor.

But what inflamed Madge almost beyond endurance was spotting, one crushing day in Ocean Avenue, her oldest sister's best friend, Patricia Murphy, flaunting the spoils of the Australian/American alliance. When Patricia's American Sergeant returned to the States, he sent her a Schiaparelli black and shocking-pink tight-wasted suit with embroidered arrows, along with a rosy pillbox hat and, to top it off, a pair of black wedge sandals by Lotus. What was more, Patricia was permanently soaked in enough Chanel No. 5 to send the neighbours rushing for a gas mask.

Agnes's father was already decoding enemy messages in Darwin. He needed no degree in counter espionage to understand the confetti of printed messages ejected from Japanese planes that fluttered around him in the jungle. They informed the enlisted men in New Guinea that the Yanks in Aussie were getting off with their women. If knowledge of the influx of male flesh bearing cigarettes and nylons made him feel insecure, he had no need to be. His daughter was doggedly at her post, pushing out his wife's belly to keep the suitors away.

The unhappy wife could have committed mass murder. The doe-eyed wonder of the romance under the wisteria in the fabulous garden was under threat. Madge was raging. Her schoolgirl heart – formerly the absolute property of country graziers with double-barrelled names and quadruple-figure acreages – had betrayed the home-grown for the imported. She yearned to have her own Yank like her sister and Patricia Murphy. Yet all she could do was to imagine what she was missing out on. A bad habit that became the norm. Consequently, the first words that rang in baby Agnes's ears were not Mamma or Dada or Bubba or Nanna, but:

If only I hadn't *had* you!

To be joined later by:

Look what you made me do!

The arrival of the only redhead in the family elicited no fanfare of trumpets. Agnes was christened Helen Agnes. However, not long after the ceremony at the local Catholic church, her mother, holding a baby daughter looking like a visiting fairy in a flowing white gown, will change her name. It will happen after the hated Patricia Murphy, bosom pal of eldest sister Sill, all dolled up in American imports, has the temerity – bloody slut that she is – to stand by the cot and call Agnes 'Little Hell'. Madge never forgot a slight. She could call her daughter whatever she liked, but anyone else did so at their peril. No longer Helen, Agnes became Agnes Helen Keen, which she remains. The new name legally registered, mother and daughter moved to live out the war alongside other Royal Australian Air Force wives in houses the government allocated near the Air Force Base in Dubbo. When the Yanks disappeared, Agnes's mother's only recourse was to return to the idealisation of the double-barrelled names on the quadruple-figure acreages.

After such an unwelcoming arrival into the world, Agnes soon figured out that leaving home was only sensible. Why stay where you're not wanted? She has no memory of her first three-year-old effort to run away, but the desire to escape that started as a toddler has continued for what now seems forever. Madge has never tired of recounting how a famous Aboriginal tracker had found her tear-stained daughter asleep on the banks of the mighty Macquarie River that ran through Dubbo. The photo on the front page of the local newspaper of little Agnes, cradled in the arms of her native rescuer, immortalised the event. The safety of permanent walkabout obviously held an early appeal. Agnes's mother, when recounting the anecdote, would complain about having to drag her small red-headed daughter from the smiling tracker's arms. The inference being inescapable, Agnes is in no doubt where the reluctance to be returned to Madge came from.

Agnes's first *actual* memory is of her mother running away from *her*. Just four years old, she is propped up in a bed on the veranda of a Dubbo hospital. She is feeling sick and confused. Later she will learn she is in isolation because she is suffering from infectious scarlet fever. In time, she becomes familiar with the irritable expression on her mother's face when she looks up at her lonely child from the paddock below. Little Agnes wants to run to her, or wave at her, but she can't move.

Madge turns swiftly, without acknowledging her daughter, and Agnes watches the back of her mother's lovely silky jet hair – tucked in a neat Victory Roll. She watches the wobbling heads of tall grass and wildflowers brush the hem of her mother's tweed skirt as she gets smaller and smaller before disappearing into the distance. And the bereft child is plunged into a deep sadness. A sadness that, to this day, still seems to be lodged permanently inside her.

3

WOOLLOOMOOLOO WHARF

The reception area at the Grantham is deserted when Agnes sets off for Harry's Café to satisfy her meat pie craving. She finds her way to Embarkation Park with its moving commemoration of the soldiers who once passed through the gate of Woolloomooloo wharf to go off to the Great War. When she looks down the steep flight of stairs that lead to the wharf, she regrets not wearing jeans. She is decked out in one of the outfits bought simply to impress the aunts. The pencil skirt restricts her movement. The Aunt Charlotte sandals are not ideal either. She clutches the side of the rail and lowers herself from one high stone tread to the next. A vertigo sufferer, she tries not to look down. When she arrives at the bottom, the sun is directly overhead. It burns into the top of her head like a knife slicing through butter. She wishes she had worn a hat. Freckly redheads should never go out in the midday sun without a hat.

The glare is blinding. She is standing in the middle of a wide grey street. Wide enough to be an airport runway. She is at the intersection with Cowper's Wharf. Cars whizz around her. She is disoriented. She tries to figure out which side of the grey expanse to gravitate to, as neither offers shade. She opts for the wharf side, where she clings to a flimsy strip of shadow which survives under an overhang on the fence of the naval base. The crowd of sailors she saw earlier from the icebreaker have disappeared – presumably now back with their families, sharing adventures of their voyage in the snow-capped Antarctic. Their rosy-red painted ship is thawing out in the sunshine. The colour looks joyous, and Agnes imagines it glowing like red cheeks on white skin against the snowfields. She looks up to see a helicopter, painted the same rosy colour, as it lands on the helipad at the back of the ship with a flurry and churn of blades. It is like an enormous bee discovering the right flower.

After the solid presence of the ship, Harry's Café looks like an enlarged doll's house. The garbage next to it hasn't been collected. One bin on the car park side is full to overflowing. Seagulls tear at half-eaten hamburgers and hot dogs disintegrate on stained cardboard trays. The black lettering on the narrow board below the roof, advertising coffee, Coke, hot dogs, chilli dogs, bacon and egg rolls, is faded. The middle of the day is all wrong for Harry's. She remembers it alive in a rainbow of neon, late into the night. A corpulent man in a black cap is the lone customer under the low, dark awning. An incongruous electric wall light hasn't been turned off above his head. His fleshy backside takes up two bar stools and obscures the wall of photos of famous people who have eaten there. She would like to peruse the headshots at leisure, but his odious presence keeps her at a distance. He has a mouth like a predator and sinks his shark teeth into a meat pie, held in a hand that looks like it has just been pulled out of the sump of a car. But it is the gravy oozing from the sides of his mouth that finally puts her off approaching the counter. She decides to forego the pie and walk on.

She crosses the road and follows the pavement beside a set of run-down abandoned shops. The walls are covered in graffiti: 'Come home, Mary, all is forgiven.' 'It was only a rash.' 'They've got our oil under their sands!' The tags stand out in huge zigzag letters. On the half-demolished wall of a toilet, further along, she reads words as old as her school days: 'Here I sit broken-hearted, paid my penny and only farted.'

The traffic disappears at the end of the road in the distance into two distinct left-hand tunnels. The straight trajectory in front of her stops like a dead end at the grassy hill below the art gallery. Her sight blurs in the heat haze as she tries to orient herself. She catches sight of an old-style pub on the corner of Bourke Street. Alone on an otherwise deserted patch, it looks as if it is marooned in the past. The full volume, urgent voice of a radio race commentator obliterates the distant hum of traffic entering the tunnels. It is coming from the front terrace of the Bells Hotel. As the horses come into the straight, the crescendo of garbled static intensifies towards the frenzy of the finishing line. The style of the pub is distastefully familiar. She associates it with much that went wrong when she was growing up.

She approaches the two-storey red-brick structure with a morbid curiosity. Two swinging doors are set in the brown tiled wall on the Bourke Street side. Three palm trees, taller than the building, stand on the pavement looking listless. Opposite is a new luxury wharf conversion hotel which she has never seen before. A sign in front advertises the inclusion of expensive floating apartments. She has read about them. One had sold to a famous Australian actor. 'Foster's Lager' appears in big letters under the pub awning and through the open door she can see 'Toohey's Old' and 'Toohey's New' labelling the beer taps on the counter of the bar. She cannot count the number of times she has sat outside pubs that looked like this as a child – waiting in the back seat of the car for her father to emerge. He would suddenly pull the Holden into the curb with an air of urgency and splutter: I'll be right back. Then hours would tick by with no sign of him.

Now, in this minute, she recalls one particular afternoon. She was waiting with her brothers, in silence, outside the Royal Exchange in Gresham Street near Circular Quay. For three long hours. In addition to the tedious waiting, she had disliked the strange way her father had looked at her when he finally approached the car. It was how he often became when inebriated. A glazed-eyed, gormless stare would dominate his face – like a dog about to smell another dog's backside.

The sight of the Bells Hotel on this day also brings back to Agnes the sweltering summer when she used to visit a similar style of pub in a derelict part of Newtown. She would go there with Uncle Parry – Aunt Marnie's husband. She had just turned sixteen when her parents suddenly upped sticks and moved to the country. Without her. Made welcome in a friend's home for the summer, she had never understood why her Uncle Parry had dragged her out of this sanctuary and forced her to live with him and his wife – a house in an area where she knew no one and was decidedly *not* welcome.

How strange to have dreamed about her mother and Aunt Marnie last night and to now have these old memories of her father and Uncle Parry suddenly resurface outside this rank old pub. She tries to recall more and yet knows that much of the unwelcome time with her aunt and uncle resists resurrection.

But events still return that refuse to deny memory. The painful, lonely tram rides from Parry and Marnie's house in Maroubra to the city and back. The feeling of being desperately cold and hungry. The walk across the bridge to finally end it all – her heart a cornered bat fluttering around in her chest and attaching itself to time. A gap. Then the following morning when she had woken up in a boarding house for old people with no idea how she got there. And hovering above it all, out of reach, like a deep red sunset on a mountaintop, the fire in the house. A fire she has always felt responsible for. A fire her aunt and uncle said didn't happen, and yet a fire that goes on burning inside her.

Agnes crosses Bourke Street to get a better look at the full side façade of the Bells Hotel. The sight of a shiny metal barrel leaning against the brown tiled wall makes her shudder. Her stomach turns over. She's dizzy now and feels like throwing up. Worse is the constriction in her throat. It must be the sun on her head without a hat. She can't stay there. She has to move on. She runs through the metallic haze of traffic as if carried on wings, back up the street towards Cowper Wharf. A rush of adrenaline sweeps her up the steep stone staircase. As she climbs, she rips the back of her skirt. It's open halfway up her leg but she doesn't care. Amazing how much less effort it takes to get to the top, compared to the quivering, tentative struggle down.

Safely delivered, she grasps the iron bars of a railing at the top to get her breath. She's in Victoria Street. Standing under the mottled light of a row of huge shady plain trees, she has moved back in time. The lovely Victorian terrace houses that line the street exude a past grandeur her grandmother would have known. Once, long ago, Agnes sold a three-storey house just like these – with fine wrought-iron lace work and views of the city to the rear. It was during her heady real estate days in the city. The familiarity of it all is an unexpected comfort and she notices that many of the beautiful old-town structures around her have been converted into small hotels and backpacker lodgings which add a cosmopolitan air to this quietly elegant street, with little through traffic, and a cool sea breeze drifting up from below.

A young Spanish couple come down the steps of a pale blue painted building – the hue, she imagines, of the azure sheen shimmering under Marnie's wedding dress. They are carrying a bunch of brochures. She can see that the walls in the reception area of their hotel are painted a rosy pink – not unlike the icebreaker on the wharf. They chatter: *Que bien, super-economico y limpio – la situación es perfecto.* They are happy to find a clean, cheap place to stay. Agnes bumps into them when they stop unexpectedly and hug each other in front of her:

Tienes dano? The girl enquires. She has eager dark eyes.

No, no pasa nada. Estoy bien. Agnes replies, unaware for a moment she is not in Mallorca.

You speak Spanish?

Un poco, puedo defender me.

Well, *that* isn't true. She *doesn't* feel she can defend herself. It's a Spanish cliché – something she says so often she's never really considered its actual meaning. The girl lingers, keen to chat:

Are you Australian then?

A voice in Agnes's head says the moment is over. Now move on. Take control:

Yes, I'm an Australian currently living in Mallorca.

She wants to add 'and in therapy' as the psychiatrist in Palma now profoundly anchors her there, but that would be ridiculously inappropriate.

I can't imagine how you could leave a lovely city like Sydney!

The young woman speaks with a strong accent and is looking at Agnes in such a quizzical way that she immediately feels guilty for abandoning her hometown and her country. She wants – despite its inappropriateness – to explain further. But 'MOVE ON' comes the inner instruction. 'Don't get lost in trying to defend where you're living or why.' So, Agnes smiles and says:

Sorry, but I'm in a hurry! Enjoy your trip!

Dragging her eyes away from the couple, she dashes forward at breakneck speed. She is definitely unstable. She cringes now to think how she babbled on to the curly-haired toy salesman who sat next to her on the flight out of London. Now, in her head, she hears herself apologise to him for being on her own. As if it is something to be ashamed of. Having scanned the plane in vain for the possibility of another seat, he had mumbled:

You'll have to excuse me. I'm desperate to shut my eyes.

She is like an over excited puppy, jumping up at people's feet and then getting offended when they try to push her away. Even now the hurt persists, hours after the gruff man who did the credit card transaction in the Avis car rental office had answered her smile with a scowl. Why had she gone to that office so early in the scheme of things? There were still two months till the planned road trip with Jim! The voice in her head regales her. Whenever you feel hurt, Agnes, you blame yourself for being in the wrong place at the wrong time. *Why* do you care about the reactions of others? *Why* do you care what people think of you? People who have no meaning in your life. People you'll never *see* again!

The dizziness and choking sensation that overtook her outside the Bells Hotel returns. Has she been sleepwalking through this life? Trapped in a frozen mist for years and years and only now, like the great ship back from the Antarctic, starting to thaw out?

Trying to outstep the gloom, she strides up William Street at a pace. Traffic whizzes by. This is the main artery into the city from the Eastern Suburbs and it pulses with motorbikes, cars, buses and trucks day and night. She rounds the corner into Darlinghurst Road and sees the sign on the side of the Crescent hotel – 'Ginseng Korean Bathhouse'. On impulse, she dashes up the beige carpet stairs.

The hypnotic melody of an Eastern string instrument, floating mesmerically through the sound of waves washing to shore, is compelling. The Chinese receptionist wears a gold satin Chong Sam and has seashells nestling in the folds of the long shiny black hair curled up on her head. She thinks of the soothing air hostess and muses on the manner of Asian women in general, for whom service is an art form. She gazes into the fathomless, Eastern eyes in utter bewilderment, unable to speak:

I just tore my skirt – she finally exclaims, turning her head to look at the split that almost reaches her bottom. The woman advises her with a gentle smile:

Turn it around waist to side and it look like fashion.

That makes sense. Good idea.

Agnes struggles with the waistband:

You like massage? The woman smiles invitingly.

Yes, what a good idea! I'd like a shiatsu relaxation massage please.

Agnes has replied eagerly, having read what's on offer from a gold-framed list at the desk:

Someone cancel. Svetlana do it right away.

But I don't have anything with me.

We give robe, towel, locker for things and everything in shower room after bath.

Agnes floats down a low-lit carpeted corridor under dangling chimes and enters a dressing room, where she slips out of the Aunt Charlotte sandals, undresses, and puts her clothes into the designated locker. She washes and dries her dusty feet in the shower room and slips them into dainty white slippers. Her body nestles into the white towelling robe provided and she follows the signs to the massage rooms with her overstuffed handbag under her arm.

Svetlana isn't the muscular Russian woman she has envisaged, but a short, fine-featured, auburn-haired Croatian woman who, Agnes will shortly discover, has fled the war in her country over a decade ago and settled in Sydney with her daughter. Eager to get started, to alleviate her distress, Agnes speaks to Svetlana:

I'm familiar with the routine. We breathe together and each time I exhale, you push down on my contorted back.

Yes. We breathe together in harmony. As one.

It is during the second part of the treatment, when the masseuse is running oiled hands firmly down Agnes's thighs to her toes with a deep exhalation, that her mother's obsession returns, for Svetlana has just remarked: What fine shaped legs you have.

Everything about Agnes annoyed her mother, but the mere sight of her legs would provoke an inexplicable level of vexation:

You've got your grandmother's legs!

Madge would use this rebuke as if the sight of her daughter's teenaged calves in nylon stockings was equivalent to the discovery of stolen goods. As if Agnes had wilfully misappropriated, a generation down the line, that which was meant for her. In fact, her mother was so permanently peeved by this that, years later, when the surgeon amputated Agnes's grandmother's right leg below the knee to stop the advance of bone cancer, it provoked in her small brain a reconnection with the old resentment. There and then, outside Grandma's room, on the ground floor of St Vincent's Private Hospital in Darlinghurst Sydney, where the patient lay in bed surrounded by flowers and with a tent over her stump, complaining of pain in toes she no longer had, Madge had returned to familiar territory:

You've got her legs, Agnes, *you'll* see. Enough said. This might be *you* one day.

This direct frontal assault on a day of terrible loss for Grandma had caught Agnes entirely unprepared. In fact, she had never learned to prepare for – or anticipate – Madge, because she was always responding to a mother she had invented.

Now, prone on the masseuse's table, Agnes remembers with precision. Standing in the hospital corridor. An adult. Earning her own living, and yet effortlessly pulled back into childhood, where she was stranded. Defenceless. There had been no mistaking the glee in her mother's eyes. Unjustly attacked, Agnes recalls now how she had dissolved into pathetic tears.

Madge could get to her every time. You might even say she played her like a musical instrument. A handkerchief had been thrust at her in annoyance at her tears. Triumph had given way to intolerance – her daughter's emotional response obviously being more than Madge had bargained for. The ensuing sobbing then drove Madge to further cruelty:

Stop your blubbering! Stop your blubbering at once!

The hissed sneer had slid through clenched teeth. Agnes recalls being grateful they were in a public place. If it had happened at home when she was a teenager, her mother would have knocked her head against the dining-room wall, where most of her brains had already joined the plaster.

After the operation, Grandma had all the courage in the world. She learned to walk with an artificial leg and to drive an automatic car. The leg squeaked, which was particularly embarrassing when she hobbled up the stairs to the dress circle where she liked to sit for her evenings at the ballet. Agnes would organise these outings to cheer her up. A few drops of oil or a mechanical adjustment might have helped, but no one ever made such practical suggestions to Grandma. She offered up her leg to God. Agnes always imagined it clad in a sensible, well-made shoe winging its way to heaven.

The rest of Grandma followed her leg a few years later. News of her death arrived when Agnes was in Bruges, having just sent her a white tablecloth adorned with delicate patterned hand-made lace. It was what you bought in that part of Belgium. In an effort to prove her worth, Agnes had regularly sent Grandma quality souvenirs from all over Europe. She had always craved her recognition just as she craved that of the aunts. She wanted to join what she imagined was their exclusive club. She had hoped that lavishing money and gifts on Grandma would bring her the love she sought: a touch, a smile, just one little word would have meant everything. But it had been pointless. Praise, encouragement, even gratitude, might give a girl a big head. Anyway, Agnes's substantial financial gains in her twenties, in Grandma's opinion, would have been better invested in financing the university studies of her intelligent male cousins. As for Agnes's own academic achievements, she had never been able to defend her consistent failure at school, or her mysterious inability to concentrate on the written word. The Beatles sang out in the sixties about money not buying you love. Agnes had heard the words, but not grasped the meaning. Not only did she not belong but, on occasion, she used to ponder whether her mother might have been given the wrong baby. She figured not belonging was equivalent to feeling you had arrived with the wrongly allocated sex. But she had never had a problem feeling like a girl, even though Grandma shamelessly favoured the men in the family over the women.

Now, lying prone in the treatment room of the Ginseng Korean Bathhouse, she has decided that she has always felt not only alienated from family, but from the world.

Once she had surprised Uncle Ben, Parry's brother, when as a child she exclaimed:

It must be wonderful to be an O'Connor.

He had replied in astonishment: But you are one!

Agnes lies on her back, staring at the ceiling of the treatment room. *Why* didn't she belong? *Was* she abnormal, as they constantly inferred? She would do it. She would consult Uncle Ben as part of her planned family investigation. Uncle Parry had joined Grandma in heaven long ago, but Aunt Jean, who offered to help, advised her in a letter that Parry's widow, Marnie, is willing to see her.

4

ROSEMONT

A gnes floats down the steps of the bathhouse, smelling as if she has been steam cleaned. The afternoon light is creeping westward. Temporary relief is enhanced by the sensation of freshly washed hair swinging like a silk curtain around her head. The distress provoked by the sight of the pub beer barrels has subsided. Was she hallucinating? Perhaps her ordeal is just beginning? It isn't the discovery at the end of the journey that frightens her as much as the nature of the road ahead. In the weeks to come she will regularly crawl up the discreetly lit carpeted stairs with the musical patterned waves, longing for Svetlana's healing hands.

Back at the Grantham, the blonde receptionist with the green eyeshadow hands her a note with a curt look. Agnes wonders whether inadvertently witnessing Cleopatra's weakness after the altercation on her windswept arrival might have singled her out as a *persona non grata*. The note reads:

Darling Agnes,

Sorry to have missed you. Hope you've recovered from jet lag.

Marnie can see you on Friday afternoon at 3.30. You have the address and know she had a stroke. She got her speech back but still slurs her words. She's in a wheelchair but on the whole manages remarkably well.

I didn't have to persuade her as she was keen to see you again. If you can't make it ring and let her know. I told her if she didn't hear, to expect you.

Longing to see you. Come and eat with me at Rosemont on Saturday night at 7.30. I'm still settling in but will push the boxes aside and make space for the two of us at the dining table. Look forward to hearing how you get on with Marnie when we meet on Saturday.

Love

Jean

The note gives welcome structure. She'll see Marnie on Friday and Jean on Saturday night. Younger than her mother and around ten years older than 'Super Aunt Charlotte' Jean seems to have taken an interest in Agnes's effort to recover the past. Jean has recently purchased the family apartment from her widowed oldest sister who, in her late eighties, no longer wishes to travel to Sydney from Melbourne – where she has lived half her life.

Back on the balcony, as Agnes munches a piece of spicy cooked chicken from the local deli and sips a glass of red wine, she is blessed with a magnificent sunset – gold, pink and violet hues are expanding in streamers to fill the evening sky. The city appears to stand still as twilight mutes the range of colours into pale smoky lines above it. Light from the skyscrapers reflects rivers of rainbow pastels on the surface of the harbour. As she suspects it would, Harry's Bar emerges in glimmering neon, like a huge psychedelic glow-worm. Below the safety lights of the cranes on the wharf, the hamburger joint is pulsing like a spaceship about to lift off. The warm night air gradually fills with the sound of revellers.

She finds herself repeating the name 'Rosemont' like the line of a song. During her growing up, all decisions about their lives were made there by her maternal grandmother. Rosemont. She enjoys rolling the letters around her tongue. She sees the name as it once shimmered in pale amber letters on a glass panel above the entrance door of the red-brick apartment block. When a child, she was in awe of this building – especially the red carpet and honey mahogany panelling that lined the vestibule. But it was the lift next to the staircase that enthralled. That spoke to her of European cities where famous composers and writers lived and died tragically, where Impressionism was born, and scientific discoveries made. She loved the Bakelite lift indicator numbers, set in a brass panel inside the wire metal doors. And there was something so tantalising about the way the rope mechanism clanged upwards that always excited her. She would envisage herself in one of the luxury apartments she had seen in fifties American films, where lift doors were a symphony of movement, opening directly into spacious apartments. She would picture herself sitting at a piano next to George Gershwin who would be singing: 'The One and Only You' – a song he wrote for his only sister.

But that song would have been considered an aberration at Rosemont, where children were never special and were certainly no novelty. The tribe of offspring fought for a teaspoon of attention. Staunch Catholic Grandma gave birth to thirteen of them, of which eleven survived. By the time grandchild Agnes came along, Rosemont was an all-female establishment comprising Grandma, her eldest daughter Sill, and her three younger sisters: the fabulous Aunt Charlotte, Aunt Carol (the kind one in the middle) and Aunt Tina who was only three years old when Agnes was born.

Aunt Sill acted as surrogate mother to her younger sisters whenever they were home on holiday from a convent boarding school. She administered decrees on taste, manners, skincare, and the dark art of thought control. In exactly the way the Inquisition pasted over texts in astrological works deemed blasphemous to Catholic doctrine, she banned any talk not in keeping with the tableware. In fact, when Agnes, aged seven, visited Rosemont, 'Pass the butter, please' was the start and end of what she was allowed to say. Aunt Sill monitored the past and kept it firmly under lock and key. Keeping up appearances in the family was everything. Family wheels were oiled on proverbs:

> Don't wash your dirty linen in public.
> Cleanliness is next to godliness.
> Children should be seen and not heard.
> You can't have your cake and eat it too.
> Blood is thicker than water.
> Beggars can't be choosers.
> The one that pays the piper calls the tune

It all boiled down to sticking with the family, changing your underpants every day in case you had an accident, and whatever was in your head, to *keep* it there.

Sill presided over the evening meal around a cedarwood dining table which was hidden under layers of protective cloths. Placed in the very centre of the dining room, the table was overlooked by a tall shiny mahogany sideboard set against the right-hand wall. The sideboard shelves were studded with glittering cut-glass bowls, a polished silver teapot and coffee pot, various trays, an ice bucket, as well as beautiful porcelain dishes. The crested silver-plated cutlery that would be adopted by other family members as an identifying symbol of the clan, lived in velvet-lined drawers alongside a variety of large silver serving spoons.

Meals were beautifully presented on lovely serving plates. Aunt Sill was addressed formally as Miss O'Connor and her mother as Mrs O'Connor. Nobody would ever dream of violating the established order.

As Agnes gazes down on the iridescent water, she remembers. The pinnacle of her short training in table manners had been learning to eat a peach with one of the crested knives and forks. She was being tutored to be a lady at Rosemont, all the while acting at home as lady's maid to her domestically lazy mother. Meals were eaten from plates resting on placemats printed with different scenes of historic London: Buckingham Palace, Horse Guards Parade, St James's Palace, London Bridge, The Tower of London, and Dickens' Old Curiosity Shop. Agnes always made sure, when she set the table, that her plate would land on the intriguing Old Curiosity Shop.

On a summer's day, from Rosemont's front windows, you could see the sun sparkling like thousands of diamonds on the sea in Sydney Harbour. Apart from learning how to correctly eat a peach, the only other thing Agnes can recall is 'Aunt Carol the Kind' who, safely away from the others, let her look through binoculars to see the tiny tugboats welcome the big ships inside the Heads, guiding them through the deep waters of the harbour to safe moorings at Darling Harbour and Circular Quay. As the flotilla had slowly disappeared out of sight of the windows, Carol had whispered:

You see? You can be small and strong like a tugboat.

Then she had kissed her.

This aunt would never speak in that talking-down-to-children way, like the others did. There was a painting in the family art book that Agnes claimed as her own, entitled 'The Fighting Temeraire'. It was a Turner, and it depicted a grand warship that stood in the front line at the Battle of Trafalgar. The once-mighty ship is being towed by a small feisty tug to the wreckers' yard, and the moving imagery has forever reminded Agnes of that rare and magical moment at the window with Carol the Kind.

Grandma's intimate contract with the Almighty had been all-consuming, and all the family offspring were turned by her into devout Catholics. For Agnes, as her first born grandchild, being part of the divine plan to propel Grandma safely into the arms of her maker was a good deal more noble than being blamed for a mother's thwarted expectations and so Agnes always felt safe with Grandma. And, as Grandma's disinterest was devoid of conflict, this religious woman was, by default, trustworthy. She secretly wanted to be Grandma's child and live at Rosemont with her three young aunts. She had embraced Grandma's belief in sacrifice and would do God's work in a leper colony when she grew up. Any lost fingers, toes, and thumbs from contact with the disease would be offered up to God. The little seven-year-old was ready to be spiked with swords, eaten by lions, stoned, flayed alive, beheaded, or burnt at the stake like the early Christian martyrs.

Agnes will later wonder if, along with Grandma's legs, she has inherited Grandma's madness as, according to her mother (never a reliable witness) a few years before her first grandchild's birth, Grandma once spent time in the padded cell of a psychiatric hospital. When residing in the country, a beloved teenage daughter had apparently died of a ruptured appendix, and it seemed that Grandma had sincerely believed God had taken her as a punishment for her sinful use of contraception. Her psychotic episode had been attributed to grief. Grandma had even lamented to little Agnes in a rare intimate moment: 'He took my Bess, my angel, the kindest, sweetest most helpful child'.

Perhaps constant childbearing had continued to affect Grandma's mental health, for it appeared that, one morning, Aunt Sill's eyes had been prised from the printed word by the sound of frantic chirping. She had run to release what she thought was a trapped, winged creature in a closed room but instead had found her mother, clothed in a white nightdress, balanced on the ledge of an open window, preparing to fly down to the branches of a Moreton Bay fig tree below. Aunt Sill's nursing training had certainly not prepared her for a case of metamorphosis. But miraculous powers often arrive in a crisis. Just the week before, a newspaper had reported that a country-dwelling mother had lifted a tractor off a son who was pinned underneath, and that same superhuman strength was gifted to Aunt Sill in the critical moment. She had hauled her mother from the window to safety, locked it, and phoned for help.

Perhaps also in sympathy, or because she also secretly wanted to escape, Aunt Sill will develop a bird-like twittering stutter that remains with her for life. Her speech becomes hesitant and clipped, giving the impression that, as soon as the words are out, she wants them back. With her emaciated parent valuing the laugh of a kookaburra over the spoken word, Sill – the young bookworm – had dutifully taken on her mother's responsibilities alongside her father, and the children were farmed out to various institutions. It is at this precise moment in the history of the family that Madge O'Connor came to take up her position in the grand property homestead in the Great Dividing Range of New South Wales in order to better herself.

News that her husband was dying of cancer had jolted Grandma back to sanity. Her husband, an extraordinary man famous for pioneering cars and aeroplanes, died two years and seven months before Agnes was born and his emboldened wife took control of the profitable cotton factory he had established in Sydney when the Depression had forced the family to leave a farm in the country. Taking the place of her deceased spouse had given Grandma the right to rule. It was an established norm that a woman could only govern by default, unlike on the dance floor when a girl must always let the man lead. Thus, Grandma elected to replace insanity with rigid conventionality. Presumably, her sons were valued over her daughters because Eve gave the apple to Adam. With the exception of Aunt Sill (who worked as her mother's secretary) sons went to work in the family business, while those daughters who didn't become nuns (none did) were encouraged to join the caring professions: nursing, physiotherapy, speech therapy or social work, while they waited to find husbands.

Grandma deferred to nobody: her one and only absolute master, to whom she prostrated herself entirely, was God the Father. His location was never clear: here, there and everywhere, but you always looked up to find him. His fingers were the rays of light that exploded through the clouds with the sun.

The anguish of struggling against a backward evolutionary slide had pushed Grandma prematurely to old age, where she remained suspended like a specimen in formaldehyde. Nothing, however, decreased the strength of her presence. The widow who now ruled the clan was a Prometheus, a

Pygmalion, a Caesar, and was as infallible as the Pope. Extraordinary tales abounded of her brave feats in the country before the Depression: how she nailed a black snake's tail to the floorboards, blasted the heads off several others with a shotgun, and chased a thieving pet kangaroo – who stole the bread out of the wood oven – all around the garden.

Little Agnes wrapped the stories about Grandma around her and made them her own. She caught on to another family tale at this time – that the predominance of raven hair and dark eyes in the family was an inheritance from a distant relative on the father's side: an Englishman who married a Tahitian princess while captaining a ship in the South Pacific. She, of course, was not a beneficiary of this desirably exotic magic.

Whenever Agnes stayed over at Rosemont, she slept in a single bed in the corner of Grandma's large bedroom which, given the superfluity of offspring, was dotted with beds like a dormitory in a boarding school. Grandma limited bedtime stories to the descriptions of Christian martyrdom. It was probably why, when the light went out, the silent, still authority of death loomed large enough to fill the whole room and Agnes was too afraid to go to sleep in case she didn't wake up. During the long fight against drowsiness, she would watch car headlights flash across the white walls in the darkened room as they swished up and down Edgecliff Road, in front of the building, all night. She wanted to jump into Grandma's bed, or at least hide under it, but knew such behaviour wouldn't be welcome. Eventually, the comfort of Grandma's snoring would lull her to sleep. She would wake exhausted, but glad to be alive. Her compensation for the lack of a pair of protective arms was to slip into the bottom of Grandma's wardrobe whenever she went out, and where she would sit in the foetal position, inhaling the scent from Grandma's coats and frocks.

Terrible coughing would accompany Grandma's first waking moments. Doubled over, she would reach back in her throat to shift phlegm from a damaged chest. Then she would sit, ramrod straight, spitting yellow muck into interminable tissues. Agnes would watch the vigorous grooming of thin, brown, greying hair with a silver-backed brush until electrically charged strands stood out on Grandma's head in defiance of gravity, resembling an uneven spiky halo. Daily hair brushing was a prescriptive requirement for girls at Rosemont. Slowly and methodically, and unaware of her little granddaughter's spellbound gaze, Grandma disciplined the heaven-bound, defiant strands by twisting them into a severe bun. Her long arthritic fingers pounced on any recalcitrant wisps, imprisoning them under a scaffolding of bobby pins.

Elizabeth Arden night cream and day moisturiser kept Grandma's skin soft. Cheeks and nose were dabbed with a powder puff as light as a clump of fairy floss. Red lipstick was worn on the mornings she attended the boardroom at the factory. Little Agnes mirrored her lip movement as Grandma applied the colour roughly like a dash through a word, as a careful cupid's bow would be too frivolous. For the devil could lure even the most vigilantly faithful into vanity.

The sombre grey skirts and white blouses Grandma favoured made her look like a nun. But the nun departed the convent when she pulled nylon stockings onto those famous, fabulous, shapely legs and slipped her feet into a pair of expensive English medium-heel court shoes that always looked new. The saggy flesh on her underarms would wobble like creased tissue paper in a breeze as she moved, and she would squint with concentration while securing a three-stranded set of pearls around her wrinkled neck. The acquisition of a set of cultured pearls was a prescriptive rite of passage for all O'Connor girls.

On a good morning, a red felt hunting-style hat, full of jaunty feathers, was fixed above the bun with a hatpin. A black snakeskin handbag, with a clip that snapped shut like a rat trap, was normally chosen to accompany the hat. Grandma's image flickered like a triptych painting in the three mirrors of her mahogany dressing table as she paused to dab '4711' perfume behind her ears and wrists, wiping off the excess with a delicate embroidered handkerchief. Grandma's belief in always buying 'quality' was almost as intense as her devotion to God. Clothes, handbags, shoes, cars, carpets, furniture were unfailingly discreet, subtle and expensive.

Little Agnes always cherished a rare sense of belonging whenever she was allowed to accompany Grandma in the Humber. A Saint Christopher medal on the shiny wood dashboard kept them safe from accidents, and a Black Watch tartan cashmere travel rug sat on the burgundy leather upholstery like a promise of warmth.

* * *

Agnes is woken in the middle of the night in bed at the Grantham by a nightmare about her father. She is speeding in the car with him over a slippery road. She is in the passenger seat, where her mother usually sits. Rain crashes in torrents against the windscreen like bullets trying to break the glass. A swirl of huge spidery shapes explodes in front, illuminating the oncoming traffic. They are hemmed in on either side by rows of trees. No room to pull over. The windscreen wipers are in a frenzy. The line in the middle of the road becomes dim. The high beam struggles to cut through the wash. The city lights blaze ahead. Then everything whirls out of control. Wheels skid around sharp curves. Her father is no longer at the wheel. He has disappeared. She makes a desperate effort to pull herself over into the driver's seat. But, in mid-flight, her legs freeze. The car rolls downhill, gaining speed. Terror grips her as she waits for the crash that will stop the descent. A red light looms. The car shoots through. The collision from the side is deafening and is followed by intense heat, the sound of metal twisting, and shattered glass. Blood pools in her mouth, drowning her teeth. Swirling blue lights and sirens become dim. Her body is crushed under a huge weight. Only the pain keeps her alive. And then nothing. Silence fills the void. She is in darkness. It is not death, but the end of living.

Propelled by sheer fear, Agnes rushes out onto the balcony where the loud cheers and shouts of revellers float up from the wharf. She swigs what is left of the bottle of red wine. Her heart is racing fit to take off without her. Shades of the nightmare are still with her. She knows it was her father at the wheel. She could feel him close to her, even though she could not see him. It is the first time her father has ever appeared in a dream. She knows she died in the accident. It leaves her sick at heart.

* * *

It is a year after the end of the war, and the young couple whose union began under a pergola dripping with blue wisteria flowers in a perfumed garden are the parents of three children. Their first son is conceived while Eric is home recuperating from second-degree sunburn at the Air Force base in Dubbo. The accident happened when he fell asleep in his underpants under the shade of a Ficus Benjamin tree in the New Guinea jungle and the harsh sun moved.

This child, Bert, is born eighteen months after Agnes, and a second son, Jim, arrives a year after peace is declared in 1946. Agnes is no longer the only target, for there are now two more impediments to her mother's high expectations. Agnes protests:

I'm not the only one to blame. What about the boys?

You think you're so smart, Agnes. Always the sharp tongue! And so much to say for a chip of a girl! You were the first. Before you came, the whole world lay before me. By the time the boys arrived the damage was done!

Agnes has never understood the significance of 'chip of a girl' that makes her sound like a broken cup. Madge Keen's resentment against the restriction imposed by motherhood can be triggered by something as simple as a casual glance in a magazine or newspaper where she might spot a glamorous politician's wife cutting a ribbon to declare a new bridge open, or an elegantly turned-out female launching a ship with a bottle of champagne, or a stately matron laying a condescending gloved hand on an Aboriginal child's head. What is clear is that none of her blighted expectations require physical or mental effort.

When the world said goodbye to the war, it exploded into the Keen family house behind a high wall on New South Head Road, Rose Bay. Henceforth, it will travel with them wherever they go. Eric, the returning Air Force man, has no more intention of settling down with his wife and children than his wife has of making a home for her family. His desire to return to playing polo finds a willing ear with his mother-in-law who is at her wits end fending off her eldest son Mack's demands to take over the cotton factory: a threat that is having a bad effect on Ben and Parry, his two younger brothers.

The plan to unite all three sons in a polo team, with her son-in-law as Captain, arrives like a gift from the Almighty. Polo will end the bickering. Polo will re-establish family prestige after the fall inflicted by the Depression. Her daughters' future husbands can also make up a team. A family dynasty of players passing the baton from father to son will surely follow. Eric, the saviour, is rewarded with an automatic job in the cotton factory. No qualifications, interviews or assessments are necessary: a Catholic male, married to an O'Connor girl, with nothing more to offer than an understanding of the standard plot of a romance novel, is seemingly reference enough. Protestants need not apply.

Mack and his brother-in-law Eric are around the same age. From the outset, an edgy discord exists between the two men. Mack resents the attention lavished on the handsome ex-serviceman, and especially by his strait-laced mother who turns into a butterfly whenever Eric enters the room. For the new polo team, whose good fortune depends completely on the Grand Matriarch, work is about to take a decided back seat to play. However, the saga of work financing play will continue over the decades until the balance severely nosedives firmly in favour of play on Ben's watch – and the cotton factory is no more.

For now, ponies are carefully chosen and purchased. Eric employs the training techniques he has learned from the brothers on the grand property in the Great Dividing Range. He rides the ponies patiently for hours up and down a fence till they respond automatically to the lightest pull on the reins and cease flinching when a polo stick swirls alongside their flanks.

The feuding O'Connor brothers declare a truce, uniting behind Eric as Captain to form a team. By the time they ride out onto the field together, there are enough new members of a revived post-war polo club near Mascot Airport to challenge them to high-level weekend practice matches.

The gene from the Tahitian princess that apparently fashions the O'Connor women into classical beauties has overcooked on the male side to produce men with faces like burnt toast. All share a full-faced five o'clock shadow that appears within hours of shaving. Excessive body hair and a rough demeanour makes them look more like mafia gangsters than middle-class gentlemen. But Mack and Ben's swarthiness doesn't appear in the stubble on Parry's chin, for he has inherited his mother's pale complexion and feathery brown hair.

Eldest sister, Sill O'Connor, minister of taste and keeper of family secrets, could, by consulting her book on etiquette, have provided the wherewithal to smooth out her brothers' rough edges, but they are beyond her jurisdiction. One could also be forgiven in thinking that Grandma, the Grand Matriarch, may have considered courtesy and politeness unmanly. All the brothers are afflicted with septum trouble, further complicated by excessive nasal hair. And, as if nature's assault on male O'Connor noses isn't enough, Parry has received a blow that leaves a bump in the middle of his that resembles a tiny crater. Surviving an accident-prone childhood, Parry has arrived at adulthood also having lost half a finger in a mysterious accident. It isn't just his fairer complexion and misshapen nose that make him different. He is quietly spoken and sympathetic, establishing himself as the reliable one to turn to for help in a family crisis. Eric depends on him as the peacemaker in the team when tempers between the other two hotheads flare out of control.

But broken noses, five o'clock shadows and missing fingers did not diminish the transformative effect of a man dressed for polo. For what man does not look handsome sporting a pair of white jodhpurs, long polished leather boots, a smart team shirt on his back and a helmet crowning his head? By the end of the first official polo season after the war, the new team's names are engraved on major New South Wales and interstate trophies. The international circuit is within their grasp. Eric can tap into contacts in India, England and America and knows how to manage polo ponies on board ship. The predicted profit from selling the trained steeds after a tournament convinces the Grand Matriarch she is making a lucrative investment. Although Mack still holds a grudge against the golden boy, he defuses the bile in his belly with an extra beer or shot of whisky and bides his time.

After a special Mass and a priest's blessing, the team sets sail for India with twenty trained ponies. It is 1947, the year India gains its independence from Great Britain. However, in stark contrast to the horrors of enforced partition, the Australian team floats above it all. They are treated like foreign dignitaries in a princely kingdom, kept safely away from civic strife and the ordinary cares of life. And there need to be no concern over the O'Connor men's lack of finesse and macho tendencies in a country where young girls are traded in marriage and a widow, considered a waste product, can be thrown onto her dead husband's funeral pile to be burned alive.

Such are the team's high spirits after the sensationally successful Indian tour that, within weeks of sailing into Sydney Harbour, they are itching to be off again. The remuneration from the sale of twenty trained ponies to the Maharajah of Jaipur is so generous that, without hesitation, the Grand Matriarch sanctions investment in a new stock of ponies.

Training of the new novices commences. Thus, when an invitation arrives to play in a tournament at the Riviera Country Club in the Palisades of California, contained within the city limit of Los Angeles, the triumphant team is perfectly prepared to accept. And so, just nine months after the return from India in April 1948 – when Prime Minister Ben Chifley launches the first Australian-made Holden car – and after a further priest's blessing at St Joseph's Catholic Church, the team sails out beyond the Heads of Sydney harbour for the second time – with a further draft of twenty trained ponies, bound for America.

If being surrounded by sumptuously draped elephants and wined and dined at banquets in the Maharajah's palace weren't dazzling experiences enough, then the treatment the team receives in California has them floating on air. After winning matches, they are elevated on a podium in the manner of Olympic medallists. The glittering gala champagne dinners go on for days. Rising above the ephemeral, the short-lived and the transient are the solid, weighty, huge sale prices for the ponies to high-profile buyers: Spencer Tracey, Walt Disney, David Selznick. The prices paid by these luminaries even outshine those paid by the Maharajah of Jaipur.

The wonder of it all comes to a shockingly abrupt end. A dramatic spiral downhill occurs, like the crash to earth from a punctured air balloon. Eldest son Mack – still nursing that huge chip on his shoulder – runs off with all the money. His teammates are left stranded. The brazen thief flies into Sydney Airport and sets about investing his ill-gotten gains into establishing a cotton factory in competition with that of his mother.

Parry O'Connor's reverse-charge call from America leaves the Grand Matriarch in a state of complete shock. But, with characteristic stoicism, she offers it up to God and sets about making arrangements to get the three stranded players home.

And, as if her eldest brother's behaviour isn't bad enough, news reaches Madge Keen, née O'Connor, that her husband has been ensnared by a Hollywood movie star and imprisoned on a ranch with a stable full of thoroughbred horses in Santa Barbara. Rosemont intelligence wastes no time in monitoring the case. Within hours of Ben and Parry O'Connor's plane landing in Sydney at Mascot Airport, Parry is on a return flight to California to rescue his brother-in-law from the thieving American trollop. The handsome blue-eyed renegade Captain of the polo team is released and delivered back to his wife in the house in Rose Bay.

Eric Keen's dreams of becoming an international polo player are shattered. Destiny has dealt him a cruel blow. An additional jolt to the already besieged O'Connor sense of dignity comes when errant eldest son, Mack, manages to lose the ill-gotten gains from the fabulous pony sale in California. The cotton factory he sets up goes broke, and he suffers the humiliation of being bought out by his mother. The Santa Barbara incident may be buried, and the file closed in the Rosemont cabinet, but Madge Keen will keep it forever alive, to accompany her ever burgeoning menagerie of gripes and resentments:

That bloody actress *bitch*! And she's a *Catholic*! Didn't she *know* he had a wife and three children?! I *told* Mother I should have gone with him! How am I supposed to defend my man against an American harlot if I'm stuck here in Sydney with *three children*! If I hadn't had *you*, Agnes, I would have been *right there*. At the Riviera Country Club. Guarding my man. If it wasn't for *you*, no predatory bitch would have got her claws into him. I'd have scratched her eyes out and booted her so hard up the bum, she wouldn't be able to sit down for *months*!

In this tone, and with an ever-changing variety of expletives, Madge Keen raves on with increasingly exaggerated versions of the same stories, repeating herself like a demented parrot. The inhabitants of Rosemont step in to soothe the beleaguered wife with a shopping trip to 'David Jones'. Herewith, a new practice is implemented that will become the norm. Opposite Hyde Park, the famous department store becomes the appointed dynasty store of choice. In the years ahead, any O'Connor (or née O'Connor) wife displaying signs of insurrection will be coaxed back to their matrimonial duties with an expensive, good-quality outfit, plus shoes and handbag, which Miss Sill O'Connor, in her role as public relations officer and minister of good taste, will help select.

At the time of the generous family gesture to appease Madge O'Connor, neither the Grand Matriarch, nor her first in command at Rosemont, could ever have imagined that an account casually opened for a deeply thwarted wife as a temporary appeasement would become the source of regular and brazen exploitation.

5

THE NORTH SHORE

Friday has dawned and with it comes Agnes's appointment to visit Aunt Marnie. The air is cool and the sky full of fast-moving clouds when she leaves the Grantham. She falls in with the quick pace of people rushing to work along Victoria Street to King's Cross railway station. Peak-hour commuters dash in all directions. She squeezes into a packed Eastern Suburbs train into the city, forced in the squash to stand next to a tall man in blue overalls with a hooked nose who reeks of body odour. To avoid further peak-hour crushes, she decides to alight at Circular Quay and catch a ferry across the harbour and then board the North Shore train at Milson's Point.

She inserts a ticket in the turnstile and runs onto the wharf as the big hand on the wall clock edges towards departure time. She is the last one on board. A uniformed man closes a chain over the entrance to the boarding ramp after her, then pulls the ramp aboard. The powerful engine churns the sea, and the ferry takes off with a flurry of soapsuds.

Agnes stands on deck beside a group of middle-aged American tourists who all wear grey tracksuits and trainers. American Express Global is emblazoned across their chests. Busy joking amongst themselves, they almost miss the spectacular view of the Opera House, pointed out by their tour leader. The glass skyscrapers at Circular Quay reflect a sudden burst of sunlight, only to be quickly eaten up by thick cloud. The sight of the dark underside of the harbour bridge in the grey light makes Agnes feel uneasy. She doubts the wisdom of the meeting ahead. She wonders if other people are as adversely affected by a sudden change of light as she is. Gusts of wind rasp the sea. She holds on to a handle on the side of the boat as it begins to bounce. The huge rosy-cheeked, pop-eyed face at the entrance to Luna Park comes into view. The amusement park is just as she remembers it – standing in full lollipop dominance of its own harbour peninsula.

The ferry pulls into the opposite wharf. Enlivened by the journey, Agnes strides up the hill with renewed purpose, combing her windswept hair into place with her fingers. She walks past the big municipal swimming pool where she used to watch swimming races and diving competitions as a child. Shortly after, she arrives at Milson's Point Station, where she would board the train as a teenager, late on a school afternoon.

As she is so early for her appointment with Marnie, she decides she might get off the train at Gordon and find Lennox Street. It had already crossed her mind to go there but, for some reason, she had resisted giving the idea the weight of a plan. The family had moved there from the Rose Bay house after her brother Jim, then a toddler, miraculously survived a fall off a high wall onto a grassy stretch beside the pavement below. This narrow escape of one of her 'souls for heaven' had caused Grandma to step in to help Agnes's parents find a safer place to live. What Grandma didn't know, however, was that nowhere was safe with a mother whose preferred occupation was staring into space, and an absent father to whom the children were invisible. After the catastrophic end of his international polo exploits, Eric had been promoted to sales manager of the cotton factory, which meant he had to constantly travel interstate in order to visit branch offices and see clients.

As Agnes's train moves further up the north shoreline, houses and gardens expand and clusters of trees thicken beside the tracks. Agnes and her school friend, Maria, once rode their bikes through the sleepy streets outside the train window, freewheeling down hills and peddling like crazy up the other side. Agnes now remembers the thrill of discovering deciduous trees – the wonder of the autumn colours and the sight of bare-bone branches. Henceforth, as she knew no other area with deciduous trees, she had associated falling leaves with money and luxury, along with flowering shrubs and trees like camellias, rhododendrons, magnolias and azaleas, which also proliferated in the suburbs of the Upper North Shore.

Gordon Station hasn't changed. It is still the leafy backwater she remembers. She heads for the left-hand exit and consults a map in the Gregory's Street Directory she had bought at King's Cross. Poor concentration makes her a bad map reader. She wishes she wasn't so muddled. She starts to feel like a spy, prying into a past that doesn't feel fully her own.

In a parallel road to the station, she connects with the map to turn right into Park Street and then left into Rosedale Road, where a rush of cool air rises up from the deep gully below. The sign on the bridge says Stony Creek. Below it, there is a sheer drop to a stream, flanked on either side by a dense tropical rainforest. The drop brings on vertigo, and she steps back to walk up the hill, dazzled by the familiarity of it all.

Lennox Street is the second parallel street after Glenview Street. She stops to photograph the sign from different angles as if it is an important monument. Which, for Agnes, it undoubtedly is. A fanfare screech of cicadas greets her entrance. She is pulled forward by unseen hands, drawn to the mottled light pattern on the ground, imprinted there by the tall trees interrupting the sun. The kaleidoscopic patterns seem to hold a deep resonance. The early morning clouds have disappeared. The sky is now a roof of cobalt blue.

As small children, Agnes and her brother Bert would walk, hand-in-hand, along the dirt paths at the sides of these slumbering streets. In contrast to the roaring traffic on New South Head Road, a passing car used to be a novelty. They would drag their gum-booted feet through puddles and watch the rain melt into the ground. They made dams and collected tadpoles. Once, Agnes made a twig bridge and lined the floor with gum leaves. She imagined a line of bull ants crossing it like she had seen illustrated in *The Complete Adventures of Snugglepot and Cuddlepie*, by May Gibbs. She and her brother were the two gum nuts in the story. Agnes was Snugglepot and Bert was Cuddlepie, and they were off on an adventure. Agnes had loved this book so much she took it to bed with her and would panic if it fell on the floor and she couldn't find it.

She had never lingered in the Lennox Street house. She would jump out of bed early in the morning and eat a bowl of rice bubbles, which she drowned in milk and sugar. Mothers in the street used to mix the cereal with chocolate and put it into paper cups to sell at fêtes. She liked the bubbles every way – even dry straight out of the packet. She would slurp down the mix in a hurry, eager to get to the tree house in the bush and see if there was a message for her in the bark post box, before rushing back to get dressed to catch the bus to school. Then she would skip down the street singing the advertising jingle: snap crackle pop, snap crackle pop, snap crackle pop.

The enormous sandstone boulder with a craggy overhang, and the deep cave underneath, still loom over the end of the street, just as they had dominated the vista for thousands of years – when Aborigines were the only inhabitants. Huge, dark, dank, their musty smell fills Agnes with sudden dread. She knows the fear has something to do with her brother Bert, but the intimation of a memory slinks away, too raw to touch.

The native wattles, dense clumps of gums and banksias trees, and the former maze of paths winding through them, have been pushed back behind new roads. She wonders if the tree house is still there. She doesn't have the right clothes to go and look, as she has worn stockings and high heels and a striped cotton dress under a white jacket in preparation to see Aunt Marnie. She decides to come back, more suitably dressed, on another occasion.

As she turns back up the street, she sees a horizontal flash of yellow and red that must have been a rosella or parrot, for she recognises the familiar squawking. The atmosphere pulses as the midday heat intensifies and the cicadas up their pitch. She can hear the calls of faraway currawongs above the treetops and wonders if the little finches and willy wagtails still chirp and bob amongst the low-lying scrub in the early morning in their search for seeds.

The street is deserted. The parked cars look as if they have been asleep forever. She knows it instantly, although the number on the caramel brick bungalow has changed from 13 to 11A and a huge L. J. Hooker sign, with 'SOLD' plastered over it, smothers the façade. Along with the other dwellings in the street, the house is built well back into the block. The wide, flat grassy strip between the low brick garden wall and the kerb of the street is still there – once the no-man's land where she had played with the other kids in the street. And she can see through the smeared glass of the bare windows that the house is empty. The dusty rooms are covered in piles of old newspapers.

She spreads a handkerchief on the step leading up to the balcony entrance so as not to dirty her clothes and sits down. She waits, suddenly despondent, unsure what to do next.

A bent-over, elderly lady with heavy frown lines and a big fleshy nose appears on the other side of the low wall. She is accompanied by an old, droopy-eyed golden Labrador on a tattered brown lead. The woman shouts. Her voice is a little shaky, yet strong:

Are you the new owner?

No, I'm not!

When the woman cups her hand around her ear, Agnes jumps up and moves towards her:

But I used to live in this house when I was a child.

My name is Beryl, and this is my dog, Aristotle.

Hello there. My name's Agnes Keen.

Well, my goodness me. I probably knew you! I've been in No 23 for sixty-six years. I moved in when I was nineteen as a young bride. Now I'm the last of the original owners. My husband, John, has gone to the angels, but nobody could persuade me to leave this earthly paradise. I've seen many come and go. The Thompsons, after thirty years. The Granges left so long ago I can't remember. Our closest friends and next-door neighbours, the Heeleys, were both killed in a car accident. The turnover of buying and selling has so accelerated in recent years that I've hardly got to know them before they're gone.

One side of Beryl's face is slightly fixed. It appears numb, giving her speech a laboured impediment. Agnes wonders if Aunt Marnie might look like that. She mumbles a response:

We were only here for a few years. It was a glorious time and then we left.

She realises she is struggling to remember. Beryl starts to quiz her:

Where you in the house when Paul Rushford picked up an electric cable?

No. We definitely weren't here then.

Agnes has replied rather too hastily, for she cannot bear to admit the fact of the matter. That they had left this house only *because* of the accident. Paul's name coming right at her from the long-distant past has really startled her. But Beryl, apparently, is on a roll:

It happened after a terrible storm in late January. The storm broke the drought. Sydney had been sweltering in a heatwave. Bush fires were raging in the Blue Mountains. The nights were stifling, dogs were panting, and cats disappeared under the houses. Steam poured out of car radiators. A section of track buckled, stopping the trains. And there was so much dust! Tar on the road melted like gravy boiling in a saucepan!

Beryl is sounding like an Old Testament prophet as she paints the scene in melodramatic tones. While Agnes stares at her, dumbfounded, Beryl continues relentlessly:

Mercifully, a Southerly buster arrived one afternoon to cool things down. I ran into the street and opened my arms to let it rush over me. It was so strong it tussled my hair and pressed my clothes to my body. Women ran to rescue clothes straining on lines in horizontal flight. We were all exhilarated!

The woman finally pauses for breath – her eyes tightly closed as she relives the experience.

Agnes is feeling deeply conflicted. She is ashamed not to remember this epic storm. Beryl waxes on lyrically:

Late in the afternoon, everything went still. The sky darkened as bruised clouds fingered together into a tight interlocking mass. Lennox Street was trapped under a giant grey lid. It was how you imagine the Last Judgement. God and the angels at any moment cutting a hole in the sky to police the traffic between heaven and hell. I had a presentiment that something awful was going to happen. Thunder exploded its authority like the stamping foot of an angry beast. Lightening cut jagged lines in the dark sky. Then another kind of wind, ushering in waves of torrential rain. Cyclonic gusts and downpours raged throughout Sydney and East Gordon all night and, the next day, the street was covered in fallen debris. A black overhead power line had come down. It was dangling from the roof of your old house like a giant snake. Right here. Fell onto the grassy stretch exactly where I am standing.

As Beryl pauses, Agnes is aware of a familiar horrible sensation, like ants crawling over her skin. She feels she might be going to be sick. But Beryl hasn't finished her tale:

Paul was a bright boy. We all loved him. The kids in the street followed him like he was the Pied Piper. He was going to be a scientist – like his father. They did experiments together in a small lab off the bunk room at the back of their house. He must have thought the overhead cable was safe to pick up. He was in bare feet. He lit up like a firecracker. They put him in an iron lung, but the shock was too severe. He died the next day in the Royal North Shore Hospital.

Agnes suddenly recalls it all. It has emerged from a dark place. Like so much past horror, it has never left her. Denial has rendered it inert. Memories come tumbling like stones crashing down a ravine. Her stomach contorts. She had been holding Paul's hand when he picked up the cable – but was saved because she was wearing gumboots.

Beryl's faded blue eyes had turned brighter with every utterance and her dog, stimulated by his mistress's mounting excitement, is now wagging his tail so vigorously that he looks like he is about to lift off the ground:

How dreadful! How dreadful! How dreadful!

Agnes hears herself saying, trying to hypnotise herself with the repetition. But there is no stopping Beryl yet:

There was a silly woman living in your house who they all blamed for not reporting the cable to the authorities. Paul's family left the area after he died. Then the next lot in your house changed the number from unlucky 13 to 11A. It must have been before your time:

Yes. Must have been.

Agnes can only murmur this response. She knows what Beryl does not. That the 'silly woman' was her neglectful mother.

When Beryl launches into how horrified all the neighbours were, Agnes knows she cannot hear any more:

It's been amazing listening to you, Beryl, but I have to rush off.

Oh, that's a pity. Well, lovely to meet you Agnus Keen. Knock on my door if you ever come back.

Beryl is looking slightly puzzled. It makes Agnes wonder if the woman has worked out that she is being deliberately evasive. She thanks Beryl, manages to collect herself, then starts to walk away on shaking legs. But Beryl calls after her:

I remember now! There was a little girl with red hair like yours. Dora Chadwick, who lived in the house opposite, was fond of her. She was quite an amazing child. She put on a shadow-play once, out the front here with Paul and the other kids, in a marquee they rigged up one Christmas. The kids all sat here – on the grass. I can still see Paul's father struggling up the street with plastic chairs for the adults:

Yes. Thank you so much, Beryl.

Agnes is aware she has replied in a rather dismissive way, but she is desperate to distance herself and establish some form of inner equilibrium. What she really wants to do is to hug Beryl tight – but knows she would only weep buckets all over her. And what on earth would the poor woman think? Aristotle is nosing at her ankles. She bends down to stroke his ears and whispers:

Goodbye, old fellow.

She turns, smiles, and waves at Beryl several times as she slowly plods down the street with heavy feet. Part of her wants to be alone. Another part wants to describe to someone the internal tearing apart she is feeling. If she had been back home, in Mallorca, she would have rung her psychiatrist and made a special appointment. It would be superfluous, unethical, to ring him from Sydney. But his last words to her now come back like a gift:

You're no longer a child, Agnes. Assimilating knowledge of the past can only make you stronger.

* * *

The other side of Gordon station is full of new shops and fancy coffee places. She enters a takeaway sandwich bar with seating at the back. A young girl with a turned-up nose and wearing a butcher's apron thrusts a menu into her hand and asks, without a pause, what she wants. The girl smells of peppermint chewing gum. It is too quick. Too abrupt. She isn't capable of reading anything:

I'll just have a sandwich and a skinny latte, please.

What do you want in the sandwich: egg mayonnaise, ham, sausage, chicken, tuna, salmon – we also have toasties and wraps?

Chicken and salad.

She has replied brusquely, desperate to get rid of the robotic waitress.

Two workmen are sinking their teeth into club sandwiches at one table and a mother, accompanied by a pair of disgruntled twelve-year-old twins, sits opposite. The kids are wearing Black Watch tartan school uniforms which Agnes instantly recognises as belonging to Presbyterian Ladies College. They are having tea and cake. The girls are sniping and arguing. The mother keeps trying to shush them, darting sharp glances at Agnes, as if she is an unwelcome eavesdropper. She rejects Agnes's vague smile with middle-class disdain. Agnes feels as if she has walked into the wrong room in someone's house. She has absolutely no appetite and, anyway, the baguette is too thick. She picks a bit of chicken out of the middle, drinks the latte and, when the server doesn't come to give her a bill, gets up and pays at the counter. She walks out onto the street with relief.

Everything has changed. Sadness infuses the clear sunny day with a strange haziness. She must cancel Aunt Marnie. She cannot possibly pretend to be nice to anyone – especially a cruel bitch she hasn't seen for thirty years. Strange that she has never before thought of her aunt's behaviour as cruel. Probably, as always, she had accepted she deserved the punishment, even though she has never known what she was supposed to have done.

She dials the number of the care home on the mobile she bought at the airport. What luck! Marnie was having a bath and couldn't come to the phone. The nurse is very understanding and would give her aunt the message. And, yes, Agnes would be in touch to arrange another visit, so goodbye for now.

She slumps onto a wooden bench at Gordon railway station and watches vacantly as trains come and go. She can't remember ever cancelling a meeting at the last minute, especially because she felt she could not cope. But she is positive she would have blundered on mindlessly and made a complete fool of herself. It is, without doubt, the right decision.

A buried memory emerges…
I am so excited when I find Paul's note under the bark in the tree house telling me to come to the experiment that day. Other kids had added their pee to Paul's own. It filled the stinking bucket that his father had boiled down into hard stones to turn into Potassium. Boys of thirteen usually shun nine-year-old girls like me, but Paul isn't like the others. When I appear at the door, he pulls me through the house with the rest of the kids. He goes barefoot like Robinson Crusoe and Lennox Street is his island. His Jewish parents came to Australia from Berlin to escape the Nazis. They love each other like the songs on the radio. The laboratory at the back of the house has a small sink, a Bunsen burner, Petri dishes and lines of glass retorts scattered along what looks like a wide kitchen bench. They have lots of books in their house: on shelves, on tables, on chairs and even in the toilet.

Paul's father's wiry, grey hair stands out like a cartoon character after a shock. One day he lifts me in his strong arms onto a stool and let me look at an insect under the lens of a microscope. He is a practical joker. When he came to ask my mother if I could go with them to Worth's Circus, he had a light bulb in his bow tie that he flashed on and off from a switch in his pocket. My mother's eyes blinked, but she never twigged. Paul and I struggled not to laugh.

I go to the pictures at Lindfield with them. In the car on the way back, we keep repeating what John Wayne said and laughing our heads off: if you know you're the fastest gun in town, don't tell anybody, as there'll always be someone wanting to prove he's faster than you.

The day the storm ends, my mother shouts at me. Paul is on the ground. There is a bald man with a metal rake trying to get the cable out of his hand. My mother brings out rubber mats from under her washing-up tray. I don't know what to do. I feel so terrible that I climb up the tall tree opposite and stay there, hidden behind the foliage. They put Paul in the back of the ambulance on a stretcher and speed off with the siren screeching. I wish I could go with him. It is nearly dark when I come down from that tree.

There is a lot of running around and shouting in Lennox Street after that. Angry-faced people bang on our front door with heavy fists, yelling, their teeth bared like growling dogs. They say bad things about my mother, but I don't understand what they mean. Two men come in a police car. It has a light on top and a siren that isn't turned on. A tall man wearing a suit sits in the back. He asks things and writes in a notebook. He can't talk to my mother because she isn't there. My little brother and I shake all the time. Nobody ever comes to our house, so it feels like we are living somewhere else.

The houses, the cars, the bicycles, the grass, the trees, the people, the bush, the wildflowers, are covered in dust after Paul died. I lose Snugglepot and Cuddlepie. I can't see the neighbours' faces. I don't recognise anyone. I keep seeing my hand pulled out of Paul's and his body light up in a purple haze. A blue glow hovers around his lips. I don't understand how it all happened and why he didn't get up. But I know my mother has blamed me.

I don't know where my father was before my mother disappeared. He wasn't at war, because there wasn't one – except in our house – and he wasn't playing polo in America because my mother said, 'Never again'. He came back just after the accident happened and fought with my mother. He told the angry people who came to the door that my mother didn't have a telephone so she could not contact anyone to tell them about the fallen electric cable. Someone, I don't know if it was the policeman or the man in the suit, said:

But the children were playing outside all morning. Any one of them could have touched it. Where was your wife?

My father never speaks to me directly. My mother explains things to him, even when he is there, like an interpreter translating a foreign language: Your father says this, or that, and your father thinks this or that – so it is a big shock when he addresses me:

Look what you've done now! Why didn't you look after your mother? Why did you bring that boy to our house?

He grips my shoulders and shakes me, repeating the same thing as if I haven't heard him.

Your mother is upset. She'll never forgive you. This time you've gone too far.

I just look at him and don't say anything because I don't know what to say. I don't understand what he means because I haven't done anything to my mother. I hardly have anything to do with her because I am always out and never at home. Someone is dead and it isn't her.

Tell me what you did, Agnes!

But I didn't do anything! I just let go of Paul's hand!

Your mother told me how you caused all this trouble!

But I didn't! I didn't!

Then my father goes away, and I cannot find my mother in the house. I know the phone number at Rosemont in my head because I used to answer it when I stayed there and would say the number down the phone like the switchboard operators at the pictures. I get some coins and go to a phone box in another street and ring the number and ask to speak to Grandma. But they say she has already left with my mother – on a sea plane for New Zealand. The voice on the other end laughs and says that right now they're probably somewhere over the Tasman Sea. It is one of the aunts speaking but I don't recognise which one, so I put the phone back on the hook.

My brother Bert arrived back after Paul died. He had gone to stay on a country property with two wealthy spinster ladies. Bert knows how to talk like the smart polo people, like he is already grown up. The old ladies say he is charming. I feel shy when I try to copy the way they speak. My voice sounds silly, and I can't go on. Bert is sniffing triumph. He puts the kids in the street onto Jim and me. They call me names. He ransacks our tree house with another gang. Paul's group don't come out anymore. I burst into tears a lot. Bert makes fun of me. They all taunt me:

Look how she's shaking. She's a cry-baby. Come on, cry-baby and we'll give you something to cry about!

Something has broken inside me. I take to hiding up the tree. But Bert finds me and forces me to stand on top of the giant boulder at the end of the street. I am terrified when I hear eerie voices chanting from below: the girl with hair the colour of wattle must die. I believe they are devils coming to get me. They chant over and over, till the sound is so loud I think my head will explode. If only Dora Chadwick was home over the road when it happened, I could have hidden in her house, but she was in England visiting her sister. Paul died just after the shadow-play we put on in the street, during the run-up to Christmas.

Dora taught me all about shadow-plays.

Some of the neighbours think Dora has a screw loose. It is because she looks odd, lives alone and never speaks to anyone. Her gaze is so direct, I think it frightens people. Her long grey hair is worn in a ponytail and curly bits twist around her ears like tendrils on a passionfruit vine. She looks so serious that, when she smiles, I feel it is for me alone like George Gershwin's song: 'You Are the One and Only'. She drives a green utility truck into a wooden garage next to her gate. Mostly she wears overalls like a workman, but sometimes she comes out of the gate in long Eastern-looking embroidered skirts with coloured wool stockings underneath in winter and lace-up school shoes.

When I first got to know her, she told me that in England, where she grew up, she would have been called eccentric, which was okay for women of a certain age. People feel uncomfortable when they can't slot others into boxes, Dora says. She once told me people see her like anything from a bag lady to a criminal in hiding. But she doesn't care what they think. I don't understand a lot of what she says, but I get the same good feeling with her as when I have my hair cut, and how I imagine a cat feels inside when it purrs.

Dora says she and her husband used to work for the British Council in Jakarta. Dora says she was so 'enraptured' with the Australian bush, she bought a house in Lennox Street and set up a workshop where she makes pottery and paints pictures. I target Dora as a potential recipient of the good deeds I trade with God to stay alive. Dear God, if I do this for you, will you let me stay alive so I can go to the birthday party on Saturday?

I am really scared, when an exciting event lies ahead, that I might die before the day arrives. Working for the Almighty makes me courageous. But Dora ignores my advances, especially after I give her a holy card of Saint Teresa. She throws a stick at me and tells me to go away. I hope you're not planning on being one of those infernal missionaries, she says. She snarls at me out of the car window. She hated the missionaries she met in Indonesia. Why on earth do they have to pester others to believe what they do, she says. I'll tell you why, Agnes. Insecurity in their own beliefs!

I know if I tell her I am going to work in a leper colony in India when I grow up, she'll only get annoyed, so I keep it to myself.

One day, her green utility pulls up yards from where I am standing. I try to have courage. I think I might as well give it another try. I dash forward and stand beside the driver's window but just find myself staring at her. I am frozen.

What – cat got your tongue, goodie two shoes? Dora says. Come on, I could do with some help.

And I become the only one in the street to get inside Dora Chadwick's gate. I help her load sacks of clay and white powders, Japanese paintbrushes, a *basket of shopping and garden tools – all piled into a wheelbarrow parked on the brick path that leads to her front door. Her house is hidden behind a row of pine trees.*

Dora has books in her house like Paul's parents but, unlike their place, all the walls are covered in colourful paintings. The hallway through the middle of the house leads to a double studio room at the back. There are glass doors looking onto a stone-paved terrace which is overhung by a giant jacaranda tree. Clay pots are dotted everywhere; honeycomb shapes, and pregnant-bellied shapes, trailing ferns and variegated leaves and tropical flowers sprout out of them. Birds splash and shake their feathers on the edge of a clay bird bath. It is the most beautiful garden I have ever seen. When I turn back to the front of the house, I notice the whole inside wall of the studio is covered in posters of Australian wildflowers.

Dora says: You must have seen these flowers in the bush?

I've seen the bottlebrush and waratah, I reply shyly. Naming things isn't my strong point. With most adults I get anxious and remember nothing. But I shall never forget what Dora has told me. She says I've fallen in love with the wildflowers: she says she supposes if you've grown up with a thing, it's not quite the same as travelling the seas to discover it. I don't know how to reply, so I shrug my shoulders and try hard to look at her with the good intentions I feel. She shows me how she distils her drawings of wildflowers into a few fluid lines that she uses to decorate big vases and the inside of ceramic bowls. She works the clay in a room with a sink off the back studio and fires the pots in a brick kiln in a garden shed. Those she is satisfied with are sold through a gallery somewhere.

One day she lifts me up in her strong hands onto a leather swivel chair in front of a white worktable and says: I've seen you skipping down the road towards the forest. I feel funny knowing I've been observed. I'm enchanted by the light here, Dora says. There is passion in her eyes. I keep blinking as I look at her like I am in a dream. Nobody ever talks to me like this. Well, Grandma had once pointed out God's fingers on the horizon, but nothing at Rosemont ever led to more exploration of such interesting things.

Dora asks: Would you like to see some tricks with light?

I have hardly nodded 'yes' before curtains are pulled, a screen comes down, and the lights are off. Dora fixes the beam on a stand and picks up a cut-out shape on a thin stick: one of a bird, then of a cat, and then a butterfly. She holds them between the source of light and the screen so that the form intercepts the light and beams the shadow onto the white screen behind: what I'm making artificially is what you see happen naturally on the ground as the trees interrupt the sun, Dora says. Then she splays her big hands in front of the light to make the shape of a bat in flight. Next, she opens her fingers to make a huge spider. A pointed fist creates the head of an ostrich, and a cupped hand with two open fingers a snail with antennae. The closer the shape to the light, the bigger the image and the further away, the smaller it becomes. I am transfixed.

I feel strange here, in the company of a woman others view with suspicion, but Dora ignores my reticence and persists in encouraging me to experiment with the shapes for myself. Once I start, I become engrossed and forget everything.

Dora exclaims with a smile – Look at all the shapes you're making! Now look at these wonders!

She pulls out papier-mâché figures she has collected on her travels in South-East Asia. There are kings and queens in gold-trimmed robes, warriors on horseback wielding swords, dancing girls with legs and arms that can be moved like puppets. She works them below the screen in front of the light, changing her voice accordingly for the different characters.

They dance, they fight, and they sing. All are calling my name. It sounds like gibberish to me, as the voices are in a foreign language, but it is thrilling all the same:

Next week I'll show you how to create your very own shadow-show, Dora says.

We make an agreement that I will help clean the studio and work in the garden in exchange for lessons every Friday afternoon after school. She also introduces me to the clay from which she forms her pots. I have a date with Dora, and I know not to tell anyone except Paul, because he knows how to keep a secret. He has been keen to see the pottery kiln for himself. But Dora is so hostile to the world outside her gate that I worry about asking her if Paul can come too. She keeps her front gate locked. I have to arrive on time as she tells me she doesn't like to wait around to let me in. But I need not have worried, as the idea of a boy who could easily do odd jobs, and with a scientific knowledge of electricity, appeals to Dora. She is delighted when he proposes we come into her garden over the fence from the street behind her house. She puts an old stool under the fence on her side so that it is easier to climb over.

Paul and I start to make a pinch pot in clay, before graduating to a coiled vase. Dora just talks and shows us things. I like listening to the straight up and *down way she speaks English. It is at Dora Chadwick's house that the idea for the shadow-play is born. Paul does the lighting and I invent a story about a dummy in the shop window of 'David Jones' who is so moved by the constant presence of a small orphan girl outside the window that she comes alive to help her. Together, they go on an adventure.*

Everyone in the street came to the show. Some of the kids even took part in the acting, and the rest watched. Everyone clapped so hard, we had to do an encore.

Before leaving the following day to join her sister in England, Dora Chadwick gives me a book: Wildflowers of Australia *by Thistle Y. Harris, which I keep for years – that is until it disappears, along with everything I own, when I am sixteen.*

Inside the cover was written:

To Dear Agnes,
Well done. Go on being yourself.
To see the world in a grain of sand
And heaven in a wildflower.
William Blake, 'Songs of Innocence'
Love Dora Chadwick.

One day we leave Lennox Street forever. Uncle Parry drives us to a children's home. Someone in the street throws a ripe tomato at the car as we drive off. I can see people staring at the stain that looks like blood on the bonnet when we drive across the harbour bridge. On the other side of the bridge, we cross the city and go south through streets I have never seen before. We don't live with adults who explain things to children, so we three sit silently in the back of the car.

The orphanage lady has a long neck like an emu and bulging eyes. She shakes our hands with a forced smile and tells us that our father will come the next day. But he never does. We don't miss him because he hasn't been a presence in our life. Anyway, he belongs to our mother and so is no good without her around to speak for him.

Jim is a fussy eater. The thing he hates most is butter. He can't stand the sight of it and throws a tantrum when a white uniformed lady with muscular arms puts it on his toast. After that he refuses to eat plate after plate of food, until the uniformed lady finally takes a stand over a bowl of pea soup. It is as *thick as glue and looks like snot. I manage to eat it without looking at it, but Jim refuses:*

I won't eat it! I won't! He whimpers – pushing it away.

The lady snaps at him: Well, you'll sit there till you do. This isn't a hotel.

Jim is incredibly stubborn. Determined not to give in, he sits in front of the thick green liquid for hours. After the dining room staff clear the room, he remains rigid, with a tiny stony face. I keep coming downstairs to see if he is alright, but he won't speak. When I attempt to take the bowl and tip the soup away in the garden, the lady catches me:

No, you don't! Put that soup back and leave the room – immediately!

I put it back. Jim is only four. It is impossible to rescue him. He is still sitting there when the lights go out for bed. I think he must have fallen asleep with his hair in the soup, as someone eventually carries him up to bed.

The emu-necked woman comes to tell us that our father will be coming on Sunday. We wait two whole hours until a girl who helps out at weekends rescues us. Her name is Jenny. She has a dimple in her chin and laughs a lot. Jenny gasps, putting her hand over her mouth in astonishment when she sees the three of us still seated in a row, just inside the front door:

Dad not come yet?! Well, you can't sit here all day looking miserable.

She scribbles a note in big letters and sticks it on the hall mirror:

11am. Taken Keen children to beach.

We are wearing jumpers, so it must be winter. There are only a few people around. The sky is overcast, and a blustery wind blows across the sand. A huge grey fish with a shiny body jumps out of the water close to the shore and smiles at us.

Then there is a mass of them leaping and Catherine-wheeling in the air, winding around each other, twisting sideways, then splashing down again like kids playing. I have never seen anything like it. Jenny pulls me down in the sand and puts her arms around my waist from behind. She nuzzles her nose into my neck and whispers in my ear:

They're called dolphins. I asked them to come and say hello.

The dolphin show goes on for ages. The world stands still as they perform for us. I feel happy for the first time in ages: They're sociable mammals just like us – and they live in groups called pods, Jenny says. There are stories from Roman times of boys riding on their backs, also tales of dolphins helping drowning sailors and rescuing swimmers from sharks by making a protective ring around them and beating their flippers. Elephants are the same, Jenny says. Sociable mammals who live in herds. Like monkeys, dolphins care for their young in groups. What's unusual about elephants is the way they visit the bones of their dead. Jenny laughs when she sees the look of surprise on my face.

I wonder where Paul is buried. If I knew, I would go and visit his bones. I wish I had been born a dolphin or an elephant.

* * *

Shadows are starting to appear when Agnes rouses herself from where she has been sitting. She has barely moved for hours, seated quietly on the bench at Gordon train station. Remembering. And remembering. Now she no longer has the station to herself. The handful of passengers coming and going during the afternoon has swelled because the first commuters are arriving home from work.

She finds herself filled with a sudden tenderness for the North Shore. She loves the way the trees and shrubs encircle the station, like a leafy green frame. And the way the unchanged wooden slats turn over to indicate which station the next train will stop at.

She jumps up suddenly, and hops on the next train bound for Wynyard. As soon as she gets back to the Grantham Apartments, Agnes phones Jean to tell her she has had to cancel Marnie because of a stomach bug. And, for the same reason, would have to cancel dinner on Saturday night. Jean was due to fly to Melbourne the following day to care for ninety-year-old Aunt Sill – former minister of taste and keeper of family secrets. Retired from this lofty position after her mother died, Sill had married her secret lover of many years after the death of his wife and lived with him in Saint Kilda until his recent death. They were together for forty years. Sill is very wealthy, and Jean, Charlotte, and Tina – who doubtless expect to inherit her money – take turns to fly to Melbourne to care for their aging sister. Agnes's trip to Rosemont would thus be indefinitely delayed.

Jean asks:

Is there anything you'd like to talk about now?

Absolutely not.

Agnes knows instantly that she has replied in a tone far too terse. She is still holding back a dangerous urge to unburden herself. There is a short pause, then Jean says:

Well, I'll be in contact when I get back and we'll choose a date for a get-together with the others.

Jean sounds suddenly formal and is obviously wounded by Agnes's sharp rebuff. The call ends.

The Lennox Street visit has left Agnes exhausted and disillusioned with the whole O'Connor clan. She looks at the clothes in the wardrobe she had carefully chosen to impress the aunts and wonders why she bothered. She cannot now imagine sitting at a table and making polite conversation with any of them.

She decides to take a swim in the pool and puts on a towelling robe she has found behind the bathroom door over her costume. She rides the lift to the lower ground floor. Guests in the apartments will be getting ready to go out for dinner and Agnes is hoping to have the pool to herself.

The pool is all hers. The over-chlorinated water makes her skin itch, but the view of the harbour lifts her spirits. She swims up and down in a mesmerising rhythm trying to tranquillise the earthquake that has taken place inside her. The temperature is caressingly warm and soothing. She towels herself off and settles on a lounger under a light. Feeling a little better, she is about to read *The Power and the Glory*, which she has found in the leftover bookcase in the foyer. It falls open on a few Graham Greene lines someone has underlined with a yellow marker:

'He had always been worried by the fate of pious women. As much as politicians, they fed on illusion. He was frightened for them. They came to death so often in a state of invincible complacency, full of un-charity. It was one's duty, if one could, to rob them of their sentimental notions of what was good.'

Yes. It was far too late to rehabilitate Grandma in her memory bank. Why on earth did she take her useless daughter to New Zealand and leave two defenceless, innocent grandchildren to face the brutal reckoning resulting from their mother's gross negligence?

Agnes knows she is slowly being taken over by a past she has, till now, assiduously resisted. It doesn't have to do with her willpower, her wanting or not wanting. She simply feels deeply uneasy, like a ship moving into uncharted waters. It is like waking from a dream into an empty space – a space that is hers alone to fill. Yes. You are alone, she tells herself. As the old saying goes, you are born alone, and you die alone. She had retained no memory of Paul when she had arrived in Lennox Street earlier that day, yet everything has flooded back. His smile. His parents. His home. The accident. The orphanage. Indeed, she realises now, in these quiet moments by the pool, that his death explains the irrational fear she has always had of electricity. Something inside her shut down a long time ago on that day. The day she let go of his hand. And survived.

Agnes resolves to stay alone in the apartment and write what she can now remember of the years that followed Paul's death. It will be a beginning.

PART TWO

'My dream stands in front of me, still warm, and although awake I am still full of its anguish: and then I remember that it is not a haphazard dream, but that I have dreamed it not once but many times since I arrived here. Why is the pain of every day translated so constantly into our dreams, in the ever-repeated scene of the un-listened-to story?'

If This Is a Man by Primo Levi

6

CHATSWOOD

The Keen family are reunited in a single-storey timber house three train stops closer to Sydney on the North Shore – far enough away to be safe from enemy fire in Lennox Street. Surrounded by dark-brick bungalows, their white-painted timber house is situated on a corner at the top of a hill and looks like a lighthouse in a sea of baked brown. An art nouveau-style glass panel of red, blue and yellow lilies above the front door suggests it dates from Federation at the turn of the century.

In her schoolbooks, Agnes writes: *Agnes Keen, The Corner of Rose and Edmond Street, Chatswood*. The address sounds posh, like living in a double-barrelled name. And, as if to compensate for the lost bushland paradise, the surrounding streets are named after flowers: Rose, Daisy, Iris, Tulip, Zinnia and Violet Street all run off the busy artery of Archer Street that cuts the suburb in two.

With a lane running parallel to Rose Street, the block would be an island but for two small brick semi-detached houses facing Archer Street at the end of the back garden. Dirty-faced children spill out of the doors and windows of the semi nearest the lane. Squawks and clouds of feathers, followed by Mrs Cleary's anguished cries, can be heard as her unruly brood persecute chickens in the galvanised iron-roofed shed that abuts against the Keen back fence. Plump, with strands of wet hair over her red face, Mrs Cleary is worn ragged with housework and changing nappies. Her kids are too young for Agnes and her brothers, and the parents deemed far too working class for Agnes's mother and father.

A thick wisteria vine in full bloom smothers the roof of a four-posted construction adjacent to the Cleary chook shed. It is where Eric Keen parks his car. Agnes feels sure her parents' choice of house must have been influenced by the sight of those trailing blue flowers under which their love was first kindled in that famous garden on the property in the Great Dividing Range. The purchase of the house, in the normal way of things, has probably been financed by Grandma.

Ignoring the Clearys, Madge Keen condescends to grace Mrs Machin – who occupies the other semi – with her upper-class monologue over the back fence whenever they chance to hang the washing out on the line at the same time. Marlene Machin's hair is eternally trapped in enormous rollers that make her head look like a maze of empty pipework. As well as politely listening to her new neighbour's boastings of connections with the social section of the *Woman's Weekly*, Mrs Machin kindly makes her phone available until the new owners get their own installed.

From the front door in Edmond Street, a hall cuts the interior of Agnes's home in two. There are three bedrooms off to the left, on the right is a den, and a living room that no one ever goes into. Agnes's parents sleep in a set of shiny wood single beds in the big front bedroom and Agnes sleeps in the small bedroom next door. Jim resides in what is left of the third small bedroom after the construction of full-length luxury wardrobes to house the parents' clothes.

A step down at the end of the hall and there is the dining room. The kitchen is off to the right and on the left a narrow hallway leads to Bert's spacious bedroom and a dilapidated bathroom. A solemn mahogany sideboard sits strategically against the left-hand dining room wall camouflaging plaster holes. Displayed on its top are polo trophies from India – and from the California debacle. The lath and plaster walls are so fragile that every time the back door in the corner of the long exterior wall is slammed, it triggers a fall of plaster snowflakes. This is exacerbated by the children's habit of dashing out as quickly as possible to avoid a confrontation with their mother. Deterioration of the walls, along with the ugly green and yellow patterned lino on the timber floor – an obstacle course for bare feet – will evidence the family's precarious existence over the next seven years. Lip service is paid to Grandma's vision of reforming the crumbling interior into a modern home, but after the installation of her parents' wardrobes, followed by the execution of a set of architect's plans for the renovation, all progress has stopped.

Unable to make the leap from word to action, Madge has, from year to year, reiterated to their few visitors (and without the least embarrassment) that the builder will be 'starting next week'. This pronouncement always precedes the ritual of displaying the architect's plans, which live in the top drawer of the sideboard. She would unfurl the detailed drawings, spreading them out on the dining room table by way of explaining the transitory nature of her family's shabby existence. Books would be used to hold down the sides of the tracing paper: *Art Treasures of the World* traps one side, and *Lust for Life*, a biography of Vincent van Gogh that had arrived in the mail with the *Reader's Digest* subscription, anchored the other. The books add gravitas to a ceremony no one escapes.

Having attended the showing of the plans and carrying the two books down the hall from the den so frequently, Agnes has eventually become so familiar with the design that she is called upon, much to her chagrin, to explain the finer details of a construction that will never be realised. In this way, the family live like supporting actors in backstage dressing rooms, preparing for the outdoor theatre where they are obliged to perform their prima donna mother's half-baked script to the world.

Madge plants a row of pines to make the frontage of the house bordering Edmond Street as private as possible, but although the trees shoot up above the roof of the house, they never succeed in blocking the sound of a passing conversation on the pavement. Public exposure is spotlighted one day when a surprised passer-by catches the full decibel level of Madge's rage. Agnes retains no memory of what provoked the outburst. Probably it was the usual vocal protest about a perceived injustice. It took little to trigger her mother's mighty fury which had returned with her, as if invigorated, from New Zealand and turned the house into a permanent combat zone. After all, offering praise and encouragement, particularly to her only daughter, would only be giving the enemy an advantage. Although Agnes has tried hard to expunge the effects of her mother's blistering tongue, the following phrases are heard so often they have become part of her DNA:

You're getting me all churned up! (Always the sign her mother's lid is about to blow.)

You think you're so smart!

You're a useless chip of a girl!

I'll whip that tongue out of your ugly head if you dare answer me back!

But it is the death threat, that day, that makes Agnes bolt for the door:

Now you've gone too far! I'm going to *kill* you!

This chilling pronouncement is declaimed like the climax of a Shakespearian tragedy.

Agnes's survival is no easy matter as only the impossible, it seems, will satisfy her mother. She still trades with God to stay alive, but since their arrival in the new house, the very sight of her is an irritant to her deranged parent. If not literal death, she is certainly in danger of being maimed for life. On the day of the ultimate threat, she had fled through the open doors of the den as her mother's hand came down to strike her. Leaping over the low gate, she had knocked over the cuckoo's nest post box – overflowing with unpaid bills – and ultimately collided with an astonished, well-dressed man in a grey suit carrying a brown attaché case. Red and shaking, she had blubbered an awkward apology. The astute man had summoned Agnes's vigorous abuser through the open door:

Come out here, you coward, and stop those threats or I'll ring the police!

Terrified that the intervention of an outsider would provoke repercussion, Agnes had taken off down the street. When she dared to stop to look back, she had seen the indignant man giving her mother a telling off at the front gate.

The incident is not mentioned again. Flight is Agnes's antidote to further violence as, within a few hours, Agnes's mother is either staring into space or involved in retribution against another enemy. But the balding gentleman's rebuke has a lasting impact, for Madge now exercises her vocal cords with the front door shut and the bedroom window firmly closed.

External interference from strangers has also caused Madge to edit out the den. She now keeps the door permanently shut as a monument to outside intrusion. Yet any form of contradiction from her only daughter is still viewed as a wilful attack. Like any tyrant, she demands total submission. Fortunate for this problematic woman – who has so little control of her temper – is the fact that across the road in Edmond Street is a sprawling bungalow which is run as an Old Age Home. Camouflaged by a jungle of tall gums and a willow that trails over the paling fence onto the pavement, its main frontage on Rose Street is set back behind a manicured lawn and garden beds full of thick shrubs. The mostly octogenarian occupants thus pose no threat. Slumbering in straw chairs on the front balcony with rugs over their legs, they can barely hear each other, let alone their ranting neighbour across the road.

Madge is also in luck with the house on the corner over the lane, as elderly twin sisters live there who have withdrawn from the world and keep to themselves. Finding good companionship in each other, they acknowledge neighbours with a polite nod. Stick thin, with identical grey perms and dressed in matching patterned frocks, they look like a pair of slender Siamese cats curled up together on their veranda in the winter sunshine. Their bygone pace reminds Agnes of the leisurely figures, dotted in poppy fields and rowing boats, peopling the impressionist paintings in *Art Treasures of the World* – or 'The Art Book', as it is now commonly known in the family.

Agnes unofficially claims the abandoned den as her private space and often sneaks in via the glass doors off the front veranda. This avoids the exposure of direct hall access. There she reads *Lust for Life* and peruses a selection of Van Gogh paintings in The Art Book. Her favourite occupation is to lie on the floor and endlessly flick through its pages. She also examines the contents of her mother's orange floral knitting bag – parked on the inside doorknob during the move and long forgotten. What she learns of world events comes from its contents. Entwined amidst a tangle of wool are *Sydney Morning Herald* front pages recording the Bombing of Pearl Harbour, The Allied D-Day Invasion, the Liberation of Paris, Peace Celebrations in Europe, the dropping of the atomic bomb on Hiroshima, and the Coronation of Queen Elizabeth.

Further down in the depths of the bag she has also discovered *Woman's Weekly* photos of the polo people her mother loves and admires as they pose at tournaments and picnic races. There are also a few American dollars – presumably left over from her father's ill-fated trip to the Riviera Club – a flying boat ticket to Auckland, and the empty stubs of Madge's old chequebooks.

Agnes is fascinated by a certain photo. It is headed 'Collaborators'. The French girlfriends of German soldiers are being paraded through Paris streets. Bare feet, heads shaved, they are wearing hessian cloth dresses that look as if they are made from grain bags. Agnes wonders if her mother and aunt would consider these women as hussies and trollops, but of course she will never dare to ask. An eavesdropper, Agnes only knows what she overhears.

Her favourite newspaper front page is of a flower-strewn army tank. Pretty girls in summer frocks hug the liberating American servicemen in front of the Arc de Triomphe. Drawn to the history of the occupation and liberation of Europe from the Nazis, Agnes wonders if peace will ever be declared in their house, so they could laugh and embrace – like the women clambering onto the tanks.

Agnes misses the bush in Lennox Street. She tries to replace it with the municipal park in a gully at the end of Rose Street, but the configuration is all wrong: wooden swings and a slippery dip cemented into the centre and surrounded by a closed ring of saplings. House fronts are packed together on three sides and seem to stare her out. It is here, in the disappointing park, swinging high in the air, that she experiences what a doctor will later identify as a panic attack. When the thin trees in the park seemed to move, bearing down on her in formation, she had bitten the side of her mouth and told herself she was imagining it. But when they had charged at her like an army, she had leapt off the swing and run up the hill to escape, the ground shaking under her feet. Was it an earthquake like the one that had happened to her mother in New Zealand?

By the time she had got to the garden on the other side of the Old Age Home, the tremors had subsided, but her mouth was so dry she could not swallow. Prostrate on the grass with a lump in her throat, she tried to engage the Almighty. And, when her heart stopped pounding, she knew that God had heard her plea as she was in a community area – an extension of the park – which included a small oval grandstand and flower beds full of rose bushes. A few minutes' walk from her house. She had found herself a secret oasis.

Shadowed now by ever more unpredictable visions, she joins Bert to kick stones and tins around as they wander the new streets looking for something to do. They team up with Richard – the son of the couple who run the Old Age Home. Richard lives with his parents in the annexe at the back. He is a weird kid who twists his body and hands like a shy girl when he speaks, and never stops grinning. Agnes had hoped he might turn into another Paul, with an experiment on the go in the annexe. But the experiments that interest Richard are anything but scientific.

Richard cements the friendship by helping brother and sister build a billy cart out of fruit boxes with old pram wheels from the dump. It has no brakes. Reins on a central moving shaft allowed them to steer the rattletrap down the hill. Agnes and Bert jump in, laughing their heads off as it speeds down the steep hill on the cement pavement. They will crash it over at the end of Edmond Street, where they will topple out onto the grass, screaming with delight. Then they will drag it back up the hill and start all over again. One day, as they lie on the grass, the billy cart will take off without them, to be converted into a pile of matchsticks under a lorry.

Richard starts luring them to abandoned buildings. He favours a burnt-out factory on the other side of the railway line, with danger lurking in every corner. The cement in the upper floors has fallen away, exposing rotting black roof beams. Richard likes to carry Agnes's underpants in his pocket, so he can command her to pee in whatever place in the factory gets him excited. She has been happy to oblige. When he dares her to tightrope walk one of the beams so he can stand underneath and look up her dress, she doesn't hesitate. Although there is a huge drop to the garbage-strewn floor below, she must do it because she said she would. It never occurs to her that she could change her mind. When she squats in the middle of the beam to urinate, as commanded, the beam starts to crack. Below, she can see a slab of broken cement with rusted metal prongs sticking out. If she fell, she would be cut in two.

Agnes can still see the look of horror suffusing Richard's face. With the beam shaking beneath her feet, she had tiptoed dexterously across to the safety of a platform on the opposite wall. It had been a miracle that she managed to keep her nerve. So keen to please others, she would take any risk.

The three of them will occasionally visit an abandoned tannery for some intimate examination of private parts but, after the scare in the factory, Richard will turn his attention to skulking under windows and watching women undress. As Madge Keen often throws off her clothes with abandon in front of her children, and Agnes and Bert are certainly not seeking out what they already find disgusting, they will abandon Richard to his perving.

One night, Richard will unfold a ladder in a patch of hydrangeas to improve his view of Madge undressing by the lighted window. The ladder will upturn and send him flying with a deafening scream. Madge, who pads barefoot up and down the hall in summer, toenails painted red like ten stop lights and wearing only a bra and pants, will behave like an indignant nun interrupted at prayers. She will not offer Richard – who has a badly injured ankle – an iota of kindness. When the police arrive in response to her call via the accommodating Mrs Machin, Richard will be identified as a serial pervert. His parents will promptly pack him off to boarding school and Madge will develop a close friendship with one of the policemen.

* * *

Agnes started having the nightmare when she was in the children's home. The same horror story, night after night, which keeps coming back. It is like a war picture – when the SS come to arrest the Jews. A fist smashes on the front door, followed by a bleary-eyed walk, in dishevelled clothes, to a car with blackened windows. As the banging increases, Agnes runs through the house searching for someone to help her. But there is no one. Uniformed men with blank faces break down the door. When she hears a stampede of boots along the hall, she slides under the bed with a blanket over her head. But they find her when they tip up the bed. She is shivering in her nightdress. She struggles into her clothes at gunpoint. Because the men have no faces, there are no eyes to appeal to. A huge searchlight shines on the outside of the house. Agnes is on trial for a crime she has not committed. She doesn't know what it is as no one ever tells her. They put a chain around one of her legs and tie her hands behind her back. Uniformed men pull her roughly down the aisle of a church past benches full of people. The tabernacle disappears. The church is a courtroom. Judges in grey wigs and wearing black robes look down on her from a bench above. She stands alone, looking up at them. They are elderly, with bushy eyebrows and pockmarked noses like turnips. Twelve men, who sit in two lines at the side, must be the jury. Their faces are covered with stockings, and they keep shaking their heads. Agnes's chain jangles when they lead her up a few steps into a box from where she can see people seated in the crowded courtroom. A bright light shines in her eyes. The judges chant together:

What is your plea? Guilty or Not Guilty?

Her heart is racing. Her hands are sweating:

NOT GUILTY. She struggles to get the words out. They stick like a piece of toast in her throat. She is choking. She struggles to deny her guilt again and again, but still no sound comes out. Her mouth has turned into a rusty trapdoor that won't open. She is crying out inside for help but is abandoned. She searches the blank-faced jury in the hope that one member will show mercy, but they all go on shaking their heads in unison like mechanical dolls.

Every night she is back in the courtroom struggling, but failing, for want of a voice, to defend herself. She is destined to be locked in a body that can never fight to defend itself. Inside, she is shrieking her lungs out till her throat aches, but no sound ever comes out.

The judges become angry waiting for the reply that never comes.

Again, she tries with all her might to scream: I'M INNOCENT.

But the hammer comes down, striking the desk in time with the words: GUILTY AS CHARGED!

She wakes in terror at the very moment the chief judge is about to announce her execution. Her body is always as cold as ice – and she is utterly unable to move.

Because of the recurrent ordeal, every evening when it starts to get dark, Agnes has started dreading going to bed. Her suffering coincides with an increase in her mother's lethargy – a lassitude so chronic that Madge now screams out to Agnes to bring the cigarettes and gold lighter that live in a cut-glass ashtray on the dressing table only a few steps from the bed in which she reclines. Madge will usually be wearing nothing but a string of cultured pearls, for Agnes's mother believes contact with the skin increases the pearls' lustre and the process, for some extraordinary reason, is more effective when horizontal rather than vertical.

One evening, overwhelmed by the horror of the relentless nightmare and desperate for help, instead of keeping her usual distance, Agnes hangs around her mother. But, upon broaching the problem, her mother cuts her off and packs her off to do the ironing. It is after being summoned to bring her mother a cup of tea in the bath that Agnes determines once again to talk to her mother about the nightly torture. But before she has a chance to speak, her mother starts raving about one of the aunts:

That simpering, conniving *bitch*!

This is Madge's response to news that Aunt Sill has taken Uncle Ben's new wife, Beth, on a trip to 'David Jones' and bought her a sinuous, black Balenciaga tunic dress, weighted at the top with a black fox collar over the shoulders. And, on top of that, the greedy wimp has apparently managed to wangle herself a veiled flowerpot hat. There are shoes and a handbag too but no descriptive details as yet. Madge is screeching like a banshee and rolling from side to side like a porpoise in a tank:

She'd suck up to the *devil* to get what she wants!

Uncle Ben and Uncle Parry's new wives, Marnie and Beth, were friends when they met the brothers. It is probably Marnie who has, in all innocence, told Madge about Beth's bonanza shopping trip. But, before long, Marnie's own grievances against the family she married into will provoke her to abandon her gentle-natured friend in favour of the acerbic and feisty Madge.

Madge's mind is jumping wildly now. She swerves from the Balenciaga tunic and unknown shoes and handbag to musing on memories of the ice-blue petticoat under Marnie's wedding dress she still imagines Agnes wearing when she gets married. The tirade culminates in the customary admonishment:

Agnes – you'll *never* get a man with a face full of freckles!

Madge's current obsession with the shopping trip denies Agnes a chance to speak of her suffering. Rosemont's enchantment with Ben's new wife, Beth, has branded her, in Madge's eyes, as a villainous interloper to be undermined at all costs. It is never clear to Agnes which of the two her mother hates more – her brother Ben, or Beth. Agnes is expected to hate in solidarity with her mother. Any attempt to defend Beth will get her a clip across the ear, so she remains silent.

It is not only Beth who has been indulged by Rosemont largesse. Ben, it seems, has been given the latest model Holden Sedan, while Eric – who drives hundreds of miles in his position as Sales Manager – must still make do with an old Ford. On top of all that, Aunt Sill's old friend, Patricia Murphy, has divorced her Yank. She is back in Sydney and about to marry a wealthy newspaper man. Plans for a spring wedding are apparently all over the *Woman's Weekly*:

That bold-faced *bitch* couldn't keep her own man and now she has the *audacity* to flounce in here and steal another man's wife!

The rotating wheel inside her mother's demented head inevitably lands on the Hollywood actress who kidnapped Eric all those years ago:

And the *nerve* of that sly bit of work in America who got her hooks into your father!

Agnes is constantly baffled by the way in which her mother regurgitates the past, triggered by the indignation of some recent event. What is it that causes her to care about lives that have nothing to do with her own?

Mercifully, the hot bathwater is starting to soothe Madge's agitation. Indoctrinated in the strictest modesty by Grandma and the nuns at school, Agnes always grapples for fixed points in the bathroom when she attends her mother's bath-side so she can avoid looking at her body. Below the maternal chin lies mortal sin. Agnes must be careful to keep her soul clean in case she dies before making a last confession. It helps that the narrow space between wall and tub oblige her to sit in the foetal position with her knees almost in her mouth and her head stretched back. Initially she focuses on the peeling paintwork on the ceiling. She keeps very still so as not to irritate her mother, until a maternal shriek over a past resentment triggers a fresh snowstorm of plaster. At such times, Agnes will leap up to catch the flakes before they hit the water, aware that she can rely on her mother ignoring anything that requires the instigation of a repair.

Still burning to talk of the recurrent nightmare, Agnes hooks her eyes onto the streaky flames that run along the metal plate below the gas heater, which are constantly reigniting to keep My Lady's water hot. A daddy-long-legs weaves a web on the small frosted-glass window positioned high up near the ceiling. Her mother's neck is perilous territory, like a lighthouse warning a ship off its course. The devil is tempting. The prospect of boiling in oil in hell is ever present. Agnes is desperate to unburden herself, but she really should leave and try another moment. She hears her mother chide:

Look at me when I'm talking to you, for Christ's sake.

Agnes's last refuge from the devil is to fix her eyes on the rusty drip marks scarred into the enamel under the taps. It is where her mother's feet surface to reveal the ten crimson stop lights on her toenails. She can't confront the whole, but dislikes the body under the water in bits, starting with the feet. Drowsy from the steam and trying not to listen, her willpower deserts her and she confronts a vision of the floating breasts. After a brief investigation, she is consoled to conclude that breasts couldn't really be a sin because there is a picture in The Art Book by Jean Forquet (French School) of the Virgin Mary holding baby Jesus with one whole breast falling out of her bodice. But, unlike the Blessed Virgin, her mother is a freak, devoid of maternal instincts, which makes her body tainted and, somehow, perverse. But what *has* to be a mortal sin is the black hairy fox, now being soaped with abandon under the water as Agnes struggles to avert her eyes. Unwanted confidences are heaped upon her as she awaits her chance to speak:

On pain of death, Agnes, close your eyes and hope to die, if you *ever* repeat a *word* I tell you!

Although she detests it, Agnes feels, in a strange way, privileged to be her mother's confidante and will henceforth equate listening to other people's problems as being allotted a special place in their hearts. What

Agnes already knows, at nine years old, is that tragedy, for her mother, does not mean premature death, war, fatal disease, accident, loss, betrayal, or hunger as in the great works of fiction, but is the redirection – the veering off unexpectedly in another direction – of money, property, or gifts she expects to come her way.

The mounting pressure of the unspoken is killing Agnes. In utter frustration, she hears herself scream at her mother:

It is *you* who are the cruel, heartless bitch! You're a *wicked* mother who *only* thinks of *herself*!

Madge rises out of the bath like Lazarus back from the dead. She hits her small daughter across the face, before falling backwards in astonishment to create a resultant flood over the bathroom floor.

Agnes is already apologising. She kneels in the swirling pool of water as if the bathtub is a sacred shrine. She no longer cares about the nudity. She holds the towel out for her mother. But she must – *must* – spill out the nightmare and beg her to stop it for her sanity's sake. She tells all. Tells of the way the judge and jury always shake their heads. Of how she is always struck dumb. Always unable to defend herself. She keeps pestering her mother. Insisting that she make everything better. She promises she will do anything she asks, if only she will help her stop the nightly horror. Her mother appears to listen, but then Agnes makes the fatal mistake of mentioning the visions that often accompany the nightmare. Visions of the electrocution. The mere mention of Paul's name pitches her mother into a deep fury:

If you don't shut up about that boy, I'm going to give you a clout that you'll remember for the rest of your *life*! He was a *troublemaker*! His father was a mad-man, and the wife wasn't much better. They should have kept him in check. They let him do *whatever* he wanted. Budding scientist?! Little genius?! He didn't know a *damn thing* about electricity or anything else. They're peculiar people, Agnes, do I need to spell it out? They're *Jews*!

Agnes is past caring about repercussions:

Well – I wish *I* could be a Jew!

You're a chip of a girl! You don't know what you're talking about!

But I feel terrible when the judge says, 'Guilty as charged' and my voice won't come out!

You *shouldn't* feel like that!

But I *do* feel like that!

Well, *STOP* feeling like that, or I'll give you such a hiding you won't be able to sit down for a *week*!

I'm going to tell Daddy! He'll understand and want to help me. He might make it go away! Someone *has* to do *something*, because I can't *bear* it!

Of course, Agnes never speaks to her father. She still vaguely remembers how, after the electrocution, he accused her outright of not looking after her mother. But she is driven to such despair by her nightly terrors she has, in the heat of the moment, decided to bypass the usual agent of contact with him – her mother – and go direct. Perhaps he really *could* help her?

But Agnes is wrong about Daddy. It's unusual for him to be home early from work as, normally, he gets home after the children are in bed. As he walks into the house, she runs to him and clings to his knees. It is a chilly evening in early spring. The back door is open, and the jasmine in bloom on the paling fence is filling the room with perfume. Eric Keen looks down in annoyance at his small daughter's hands as they clutch at the front of his treasured camel-hair coat. Agnes pleads:

Stop the nightmare, Daddy! They say I'm guilty! My voice won't come!

What's going on? Get up, Agnes, and don't be so silly.

He tries to push her aside as he calls out to tell her mother that he's just seen Alex McLeod at the Royal Automobile Club. An encounter with anyone from the polo crowd is a cause for celebration, especially a sacrosanct character like Alex McLeod.

Agnes is so crushed by her father's casual indifference that she drops to her knees, covering his shoes in hot tears. She can smell the boot polish on the leather. Eric Keen always keeps his clothes spotless and footwear shining. When Madge spins out of the kitchen, excited to hear about Alex McLeod, the sight of Agnes's supplication infuriates her. She rushes at Agnes and screams:

Let go of him! Let *go* of him, this *instant*!

When Agnes persists in clinging onto her father's coat, Madge hits her fingers with a rubber egg flip from the kitchen. Agnes looks up at her father imploringly. His swimming-pool-blue eyes are bloodshot and swirl uncertainly. He is irritated at having the conversation piece he brought home to his wife side-tracked by this vexing child's interference. Agnes is still holding on like grim death as Madge slaps her hard across the face. Agnes feels as if she's been hit by a truck. A high-pitched ringing swamps her hearing. Looking up from the floor, she sees her mother hook her eyes into those of her husband:

Smack her, Eric! She's telling lies. Going on about nightmares and that brat of a boy in Gordon who caused all that trouble. She's pestering me. Driving me crazy. I told her to shut up a *million* times, yet the same rubbish keeps pouring out of her! For Christ's *sake*, Eric, smack some *sense* into her!

Eric Keen looks bewildered, standing just inside the back door with his briefcase still in his hand as his wife goads him with a diabolical chant:

Smack her! *Smack* her! She's too strong-willed for her own good. She never stops moaning about her feelings. What right's *she* got to talk about feelings?! *She's* got no right to complain! She's lucky to have a roof over her head! Beat some sense into her, Eric! NOW!

The briefcase falls out of Eric's hands onto the cracked lino floor. Suddenly, without looking down at his daughter, he pulls the belt out of the waist of his pants and cuts Agnes hard around the legs. Agnes runs into her bedroom and shuts the door, leaning against it with all her might as there is no key. Her father follows, hot on her tail. He almost squashes her arm as she struggles to keep the door shut. He bangs on it with his fist:

Open this bloody door immediately!

She can hear the thwack of the belt striking the back of the door, imagining the pain in her legs intensifying. He temporarily hesitates. But, within seconds, she hears her mother behind him, shrieking:

Punish her! Do what I *tell* you, Eric!

The bedroom door is flung open under her parents' combined might. Agnes manages to scramble out past their feet and bolts for the back door:

Catch her, Eric, before she gets away!

Agnes is leaping over the step down into the dining room and, with a moment of undiluted joy, sees that the back door is open – her father's brown leather briefcase is leaning against it and has prevented it from closing:

Get her! Get her before she escapes!

Agnes's father tackles her like a rugby player. She comes down with a thud and feels a terrible rain of blows around her legs as his belt descends with violent force. Madge's anger has jumped into her husband, the way a bush fire jumps a road, instantly igniting the brush on the other side. His swimming-pool eyes are fixed on his wife, as he mercilessly cuts into Agnes's flesh. His carelessness leaves Agnes dumbstruck. Tangled up in their great love, she is invisible.

She knows she is in serious danger. Scurrying like a crab towards the back door, in agony, she screams for help through the gap. Her mother interrupts her escape trajectory to the street by slamming the door shut and so Agnes has no choice but to beg her for mercy:

Stop, stop, *please* stop! I'll never say anything again! I'll never talk about it again!

Blood is running down her legs. She is spreadeagled on the floor. The last thing she sees as she stares up, before she passes out, is her tabby cat, Ness, out on the veranda. Balanced on top of the canary cage, the cat is peering down at the tiny yellow bird imprisoned beneath.

The little bird could just as easily be herself, towered over and entrapped by these two enraged, unreasonable, adults.

7

PENICILLIN

gnes wonders if she has died like the little match girl in the Hans Christian Anderson fairy tale, who, after freezing to death on earth, finds a warm fire in heaven. She doesn't want to be in the house on the corner of Rose and Edmond Street, so she keeps her eyes shut. She feels peaceful, and does not feel alone, for she has her picture-show in her head. Cloud-formed balloon men, wearing black and white striped pants, somersault across the screen of her mind. They bounce around on pogo sticks. They juggle bright objects. They leap on one another's shoulders and then they are gone. Her mind-screen goes black like an intermission at the pictures. Then on comes a pod of dolphins, swivelling balls on their noses, clapping flippers and leaping through golden loops before floating off. Agnes wants them back but knows her willpower can only bring exploding ink spots and darkness. She cannot influence what arrives on the screen. Performances don't end, but merge into others. But, even in a blackout, Agnes knows new figures, animals, shapes, colours will arrive – if she waits patiently.

She is deeply immersed in a jungle landscape when she picks up a smell like toothpaste, and hears a male voice she doesn't recognise:

My pretty? Is there anyone home in there?

Gentle words float down from a peppermint tongue like a shower of stars from a magic wand. She is gazing into the kindly grey eyes of a bald, portly man with several double chins. When she tries to sit up, she falls back.

The big face distorts like a reflection in the Hall of Mirrors. She surrenders the struggle and closes her eyes. A soft, fleshy hand gently brushes strands of hair off her wet forehead. A sucking sound indicates a peppermint imprisoned behind teeth:

I'm Doctor Finnegan. How are you feeling, my pretty?

Blubbering about feelings has ended her up in the present predicament. The doctor's interest in her astonishes her, but she hesitates before replying in case her mother is listening. She tries to lift her head to see if Madge is there, but flops back on the pillow. She feels limp and dizzy and her throat hurts when she speaks:

My cat was on top of the canary cage. I have two cats, Ginger and Ness. Ness, the tabby one, insists on sleeping there. I call him Ness, like the end of my name, Agnes. When I lift him off he always comes back. Please believe me. I'm not guilty. I don't know what I did. They never say. They point fingers and say, 'Guilty as charged,' and then pass a sentence I don't hear. I can't get my voice out!

She can hear her own woozy voice, along with an internal volley of returning accusations from the nightmare:

You're not guilty of anything, my pretty. You're an innocent child. We almost lost you. We're rejoicing with the angels that you're back with us. Don't fret yourself now.

She's not talking that nonsense again is she, doctor?

The sudden harsh voice makes Agnes shudder. She closes her eyes as her mother's cautionary hand tightens on her wrist. From far away she hears the doctor's warm and friendly tone change. Amazingly, he is scolding her mother:

Severe throat infection… raging fever… mouth ulcers… care… nourishment… this child is in poor physical health…

Days and nights merge. Her picture-show goes fuzzy. Black spiders crawl over her. Snakes slither in the folds of the sheets. One minute she is on fire and the next so cold she turns to ice. She waits for the smell of peppermint and the touch of the cool pudgy hand.

Doctor Finnegan has stitched the small cut on her head, made by a sharp piece of lino sticking out of the skirting board of the dining room as she attempted to escape her attackers. He has also put a few stitches on the side of her shin bone where the buckle of her father's belt has sliced her flesh. He has given Agnes an anti-tetanus injection and now comes every day to put a penicillin injection in her bottom. She is so sleepy that she hardly feels it. Madge changes the sheets before the doctor comes and pushes and pulls her daughter's limp arms and legs into clean pyjamas. She even dabs perfume behind her ears. Agnes notices how the soft concern in the doctor's eyes turn to thistles whenever he glances up at her mother. His stethoscope gleams like a halo around his neck. Her mother is wearing her fluffy slipper expression. Her mother and the doctor both seem to have multiple sets of eyes and their clothes are covered in jumping noughts and crosses. This time, Agnes clearly hears the doctor's chiding voice. He sounds increasingly impatient, but Agnes hasn't the energy to intercede on Madge's behalf:

Your child is still chronically run-down and very seriously ill... thin as a matchstick... obvious to me she hasn't slept properly for weeks... you still haven't told me how on earth she got those deep cuts on her legs...

She's very self-willed, doctor. We can't control her.

Nonsense!

Aware the doctor favours her over her mother makes Agnes fear Madge's vengeance. So, when she feels a little stronger, she mentions the architect's plans to him. But he shows no interest in them whatsoever and so she tries another tack. She praises Madge's cooking to him. Informs him that her mother carries it into her on a tray. She doesn't have to make this up, for Madge is a good cook, and the curried eggs on toast and the kidneys and bacon in brown sauce on toast are the best flavours she has ever tasted. She is ravenously hungry now she is recovering. Bowls of strawberries and ice cream are gradually replacing visions of the gnarled face of the judge in the courtroom. What Agnes doesn't share with the doctor is the joy of eating in peace, without her mother constantly hovering behind to grab each dirty plate.

Penicillin saves her life and iron injections cure the anaemia. And, today, the physician is banging hard on the front door as if he suspects he may not be let in. When Madge rushes inside the bedroom to check the state of her daughter's sheets, Agnes sees that her face is already set in the silly, false sympathetic expression she puts on for these medical visits. Wearing a red and white chequered, freshly ironed gingham apron with a frill around the bib over her dress, her mother looks like a magazine model advertising a cleaning product. It's amazing to Agnes to see her outdoor personality self-enacted indoors. Ever since the doctor has emphasised a continuance of strict hygiene, Madge vacuums his daily visit trajectory: up the hall from the front door to the same worn green carpet around Agnes's bed. Every surface in the little bedroom receives a meticulous clean, starting with the white chest of drawers. As Madge has always disliked Dora Chadwick, describing her as an elongated scarecrow, Agnes worries she might deliberately break the ceramic roses she made in Mrs Chadwick's studio back in Lennox Street. The blooms still warm out of the kiln, the kindly potter had crossed the road for the first and only time to screw them onto the middle of each drawer on the white chest. She had even painted each tiny screwhead with pale pink paint.

As Madge also hates Jean – her own sister – Agnes is always relieved when, after a light wipe-over, there is no damage to the guardian angel (drawn by Jean's Scottish husband) that hangs above her bed. In the corner of her small bedroom, between the old Victorian fireplace and the wall, Agnes keeps the remainder of her treasures in two blue-painted shoeboxes placed on top of Dora Chadwick's book on Australian wildflowers.

She hears her mother dash down the hall to open the front door to Doctor Finnegan, who has come to take the stitches out of Agnes's forehead:

Close to the hairline, my pretty, so your beauty is secure. With a face full of lovely sun kisses, nobody will notice.

Not only do the dreaded freckles receive an upgrade, but a hairdresser in the shopping centre in Chatswood will shortly turn Agnes's carrot top into strawberry blonde. Indeed, the doctor's lovely compliment will hold up a mirror to another world.

Agnes isn't aware she suffers because it is all she has known. Living in a combat zone, she is overly vulnerable to the worth of a few crumbs of affection that need no repayment, for they are the normal expression of civilised natures.

When the day eventually arrives for her to get out of bed, the doctor will ask her mother to leave the room as he wishes to speak to her daughter in private. Madge will chide him in a haughty tone:

There is nothing you need to say to my daughter that can't be said in front of me.

Please Mrs Keen – with respect. Don't make this awkward.

Madge will reluctantly leave the room and Agnes will always remember how he closed the door firmly behind her:

Now, my pretty. I'd like you to tell me how your parents treat you. Don't be afraid, you can trust me completely.

The idea of telling on her mother and father will strike Agnes with horror. The maternal ear must surely be pressed to the door. She will feel like a worm being cut in two. Why had Doctor Finnegan put her in this position? She has never been asked for her opinion on anything. She is terrified to say the wrong thing. Yet, when he asks her about physical abuse, for a moment she will hesitate. Fear of more violence will stimulate an emphatic denial. Desperately confused, she will shout out loudly, so her eavesdropping mother can overhear:

I have no complaints against my parents!

Had she known what lay ahead, she might have acted differently.

* * *

As she slowly recovers, Agnes becomes engrossed in a radio serial called *White Coolies*. She imagines herself alongside the courageous Australian and English women prisoners in Singapore, standing up to their cruel Japanese captors. These courageous women remain obdurate after every beating, encouraging one another to keep up their spirits. Agnes's fascination with the Second World War, ignited by the knitting bag, is now fuelled by the war pictures she sees on Saturday afternoon at the local cinema. She wants to be a hero like Douglas Bader in *Reach for the Sky*. It strikes her that, instead of serving in the leper colony, she could give up her legs for her country.

Madge also closely follows a radio serial. It is called *Blue Hills* by Gwen Meredith and is a saga of life in a country town. It stimulates her fantasy of living in a grand country homestead like the one in the Great Dividing Range where she once worked. Anything to do with upper-class life on a country property, Madge gulps down uncensored. Similarly, her voice swells with emotion when she recites the opening lines of *My Country* by Dorothea Mackellar:

I love a sunburnt country,

A land of sweeping plains,

Of ragged mountain ranges,

Of droughts and flooding rains.

But Madge's nationalism does not include Aborigines, cities, suburbs, or landholdings of less than 6000 acres.

Eric Keen was away on business in Brisbane while his daughter lay fighting for her life. Neither parent mentions the beating in the dining room again, but it is merely the first of other senseless physical punishments her mother will impose and which her father will carry out. Punishments caused, if caused at all, by trumped-up stuff that has far more to do with the chemistry between the self-absorbed pair than with their daughter's behaviour.

Agnes views her father as a victim like herself. She feels sorry for him. She believes her mother has put a spell on him and he is not responsible for his actions. In Agnes's teenage years, her mother will insist in a distasteful tone:

Your father loves you.

She will say it as if it is something she would like to alter. Agnes suspects it is not normal to beat someone you love without giving them a chance to explain. Yet, whatever happens to her, whatever punishment is meted out over her growing-up years, Agnes will never blame her father.

Adding to Agnes's confusion, her mother will suddenly call her Darling, or Possum. Unexpected endearments her baffled daughter adores. But they also make her doubt if what she is experiencing is actually happening. Nothing is named and she doesn't have the complicated language to explain hypocrisy. During the weeks recovering her health, the atmosphere inside the ungainly white timber house will seem rinsed clean. Agnes will sleep soundly and wake to the sound of music on the radio and the scent of frangipani flowers floating in through the open window. The nightmare over, again, she has survived. Yet, at gut level, she will know she has been changed forever by what has happened.

She will keep out of her mother's way and be liberated from the embittered woman's ravings as, with the timely installation of a phone, Madge's gripes will be redirected to Aunt Marnie.

Henceforth, the line pulses hot for an hour a day as the two women trash the other relatives, along with all the ubiquitous trollops and harlots that have the temerity to steal other women's husbands.

8

THE FARM

I s it divine intervention? Nobody knows what prompts Grandma to leave St Joseph's church after early Mass wearing her flamboyant red hat with the feathers and, instead of returning home for breakfast, drive into the country in the Humber to buy land. In shocked amazement, Eric, Ben and Parry, corralled in the cotton factory boardroom, receive the news that a hundred acres have been purchased for a polo base. Excitement increases as they bump over potholes on the dirt road in convoy after the Humber. Up and over a hill speeds the matriarch's beast of a vehicle, kicking up a whirlwind of dust before stopping, abruptly, at the decreed site for the stables. Four years on, the dream of a polo dynasty that died with Mack's betrayal is resurrected. Rumour has it that Mack now sells encyclopaedias door to door. No one mentions his name, although Parry relays a recent call from a desperate man, vowing in a drunken slur everlasting vengeance against Eric. It is a threat that neither Parry, nor anyone else, take seriously. It's in the past. The file closed. The page turned. An hour's drive from Sydney, situated between Liverpool and Camden, the hundred acres will be known simply as – The Farm.

A workforce of family and friends mobilise to build the stables over weekends. With hard work threatening, Madge puts a picnic basket for her husband and sons in the boot of the car and remains at home. Agnes stays at Rosemont on weekends and accompanies Grandma back and forth in the Humber. It is a happy, festive time and Agnes imagines it like the communal effort of medieval towns to build the great cathedrals Dora Chadwick once told her about. Uncles, aunts, dogs, and children tumble out of cars, laughing, making faces and shouting. Most of them city kids, they revel in the space to chase each other and roll down the grassy hill above the burgeoning stables, where Grandma plans to construct the grand homestead in the country that Madge constantly pines after.

Agnes can't wait to hear the blare of the horn that announces Jean Pales and her husband Richard's arrival with their three small girls and a few friends. Scottish-born Richard will take Mack's place as the fourth member of the polo team. Alongside the rumbustious, swarthy uncles, refined Richard Pales looks straight at you calmly, and with a clear gaze. He listens patiently and can alter himself like a chameleon to match others. Agnes is in awe of the way in which he captures trees and landscapes in his sketchbook. He explains to her:

It helps me to see. That's why early man painted the bison on a cave wall, so he'd have a better aim when it came time for the kill.

Agnes watches his pencil fly over the small page. She likes his Scottish accent and is constantly aware of his presence. She will forever treasure the guardian angel he has drawn for her which hangs over her bed.

The group joins Grandma with spades and picks to clear the low-lying scrub for the stables. Bent over on hands and knees, they move like a swarm of locusts in formation until, by the end of the first morning, they can peg out the new buildings. A line of stables and a feed room will occupy one side, and an equipment room with a front porch – called the tack room – will emerge at the top of the slope. It will look down on the stables and beyond to the new polo field in the distance. The combined structure will create an L-shape that will be squared off with a fence on the other two sides. Further discussion provokes alteration of pegs and string. Uncle Ben has technical knowledge from his engineering training. Richard Pale and Eric Keen know carpentry and Uncle Parry is a competent handyman.

A contractor digs two dams – one on the paddock inside the entrance gate and another on the plateau above the stable block, where a local builder will erect a small timber house for a groom to live in and care for the horses during the week. Fleets of trucks with materials arrive in such quick succession, and the acceleration of the structure is so fast, it looks like a film on fast-forward.

Because of Madge's hostility to even a single nail being hammered in the walls at home, Agnes's excitement to be part of a construction project is palpable. Her world has come alive. She *loves* making things and will, in future, never miss a chance to look through a hole in the fence of *any* building site. She joins the other kids in painting the timbers for the new stables with a harsh-smelling wood protector that stains exposed skin iodine yellow.

Sausages, chops, hamburgers, and steaks sizzle on the barbeque grill at lunchtime. The smell is intoxicating. Potatoes in tinfoil are rolled into the hot coals, the pulpy flesh drenched in butter and pepper and eaten piping hot. The workmen are ravenous. Bottle tops fly in the air. Uncle Parry can cleverly open one top with another. The amber liquid fizzes and spills down the cold glass bottles. The group fans out around the fire to eat – some on picnic rugs on the ground, others propped on building materials. All are encouraged to savour the communal salads and delicacies from one another's picnic baskets. And then it's back to the fire for afternoon tea, where the billie is boiled for the brew, and the women hand around delicious homemade cake. They all call Agnes by name, and for a short time she feels like she belongs to a family of people who care about each other.

The exception to the general family enthusiasm is Sill O'Connor, who takes no interest in the farm. Sill is a thoroughly urban animal who shuns places with snakes, or spiders and flies. And she hates polo.

As for Grandma, and despite the exciting building initiative she has orchestrated, most of the grandchildren continue to find her aloofness intimidating. It is amazing to Agnes how little individual interest she takes in her souls for heaven, having given birth to so many herself. But, because she is used to her grandmother's silence, while the cousins hold back timidly, Agnes volunteers to work alongside her. Together, they clear the scrub off the flat site for the polo field. Agnes wears jodhpurs, elastic-side riding boots and, like Grandma, heavy gloves to protect her hands from thorns. She watches Grandma closely. Bent over and quietly concentrated on the task in hand, Agnes has never seen her so content. She doesn't seem to care about laddering her nylons or the legion of paspalum seed heads clinging to her skirt. Apart from the occasional refinement such as wiping sweat off her powdered face with a perfumed, embroidered handkerchief, her grandmother looks like a hardy pioneer in the Westerns at the pictures on a Saturday afternoon.

Scythes cut through the brush and recalcitrant roots are dug out with picks. At the end of the day, Grandma gives Agnes the honour of striking the match to set the bonfire mound of cuttings alight. Red, yellow, blue, the flames soar upwards. The evening mist descends to freeze the blurred background of tall gums into rainbow magic.

Parry ploughs the bare ground with a tractor and removes loose stones, ready to plant hardy grass seeds. The kids fight over whose turn it is to ride on the tractor and stand on the running board of the Humber whenever the uncles drive to the store for supplies. And then, one day, the work is miraculously finished. With the goalposts in place on the field, the gates hung, horses installed in the stables, the farm is ready for polo.

Madge appears like the Queen of Sheba and gives orders for a line of poplar trees to be planted and fenced in along the outside yard of the stable block. In future, the sound of rain on a corrugated iron roof, and the wind rustling through poplar leaves like women dancing in taffeta skirts, will forever take Agnes back to 'The Farm'.

Once the Sunday practice matches are in full swing, and new players gradually join the club, Grandma stops coming. The uncles' restraint in her presence degenerates into larking around like schoolboys in her absence. In particular, Parry and Ben delight in teasing their Scottish brother-in-law. They kill a black snake and pull it on fishing wire over his feet, dissolving into raucous laughter as they watch him take off like a rocket over the hill. That same hill that is earmarked for the future mansion. Putting up with the uncles is a significant downside of joining the polo team, and yet Agnes observes the artist bouncing back from their pranks with amazing good humour.

Two children's ponies arrive: a chestnut called Paddy and a grey called Snowy. Sighting Agnes slopping around in the saddle on Paddy, Uncle Ben decides to teach her to ride:

Weight on the ball of the foot… toes slightly out and heels down… reins crossed over in right hand above the pommel of the saddle. Sit straight… shoulders down and cling on with your knees. No, not like that – you look like a sack of potatoes… bottom out of the saddle when you trot. You can do it, Agnes!

No, I can't! It's too much to remember!

She yells at him in anger, having bitten her lip as she is bumped around on the trot. Then suddenly something clicks, and it becomes as natural as walking – one two, one two, up down, up down:

Wow! I've got it! I can feel it! Look I'm *doing* it!

Damn right you got it! Now off you go for some free-range practice!

Ben is running down the stable yard from the porch of the tack room to open the gate, chuckling happily to himself. His curved eye teeth seem to infuse a tenderness into what can often look like a silly grin. He is grinning now as she trots out of the yard. She is counting one two, one two, one two. But Paddy isn't keen to leave the stables. He stops dead on the other side of the gate. Agnes kicks him in the ribs, but he turns to stone. She urges him on:

Come on, Paddy! Come on, old boy!

And then they're off. She doesn't see it, but she has heard Ben's whip connect with Paddy's rump. He shouts:

Off you go, you stubborn mule!

Ben is laughing uproariously as Agnes shoots off over the hill. Paddy is so stimulated that he breaks from a trot into a canter. It's sublimely exhilarating. The wind is in Agnes's face. She merges into the animal's body – streaking forward as if in a dream. She's Elizabeth Taylor in *National Velvet* – training her rambunctious pony for the Grand National.

Once they arrive at the main farm gate, Paddy suddenly stops. Agnes pulls the right-hand rein to steer him down towards the creek in the far paddock, but her steed has a mind of his own. She increases the pressure on the reins, but Paddy turns back to stone. She wonders if he's only capable of two directions. And then, as if he has heard her thoughts, he springs to life again and charges back to the stables. She yells:

No, Paddy, no!

But Paddy defies her efforts and heads for home. The canter to the gate was fast, but now she's galloping. Paddy sprouts wings like Pegasus. She's flying. She now knows what it feels like to be a jockey moving at full pelt to a finishing line. When she arrives back at the yard, Uncle Ben booms:

Who is the master? You or the horse?

She has lost her helmet and Paddy is foaming at the mouth. She shouts:

Can't you see? The horse, of course!

Is that so, my girl? Well – we're going to change all that!

Agnes loves the way he says that, as if he is committing himself to her improvement when no one else has ever done so. And, indeed, he teaches her not only how to ride but how to jump, so she can enter the local hunt. And when she is older, Ben says, he'll teach her how to drive a car. He treats her like one of the blokes, unselfconsciously, not remotely aware of his drooling mouth as he points out to her the finer points of a female curve:

Fair crack of the old whip, get an eyeful of what's going on in the cardigan! My fanny aunt, I've never seen a pair quite like that!

As well as ogling ladies' bodies in tight clothes, Ben also delights in sniggering over dirty jokes:

Listen here, Agnes, man to man, ha-ha, nudge-nudge (with appropriate smutty wink) – ya not going to believe it but there's a nudist colony down the road a few minutes' drive away near my brother's old factory. What I wouldn't give to have a look inside! Got to be careful of Long John when they're cooking the snags on the barbie, eh?! And I'd like to see them tits flapping when they play netball. What I'd give to jump in there amongst them! Ha-ha!

Agnes is curious and would also like to have a look. As her Uncle Ben graphically imagines himself as a netball goalpost, or an athletic horse in contact with all that naked female flesh, she finds herself wondering at her obsession with this warm-hearted man. His ramblings might make him sound a bit dim-witted, but she always feels relaxed with him – never intimidated or uncomfortable in the way she feels with her father – or Uncle Parry.

She smacks Ben's hand playfully and tells him not to be rude. She doesn't have tits and wonders about all the fuss. At ten, however, she is on the same scatological level as Ben and can't wait to share a rude joke with him. His explosive, boisterous laugh is compensation for the silliest tale.

Ben plays 'back' on the polo field, sitting solidly on the big horses he favours. Unlike Eric who loves his horses, Ben has no warm feelings for his mounts, often roughly yanking and pulling on the bit till their mouths bleed. Compared to Eric's smooth seat in the saddle and riding finesse, Ben looks like an overheated steam train. Although he is eager to please, she has worked out that his blindness to the feelings of others leads them to dismiss him as a buffoon. Agnes has never understood why he favours her and ignores some of his own children. Also, how he remains unaware of Madge's antipathy towards him, no matter what diabolical trick she cooks up. He chuckles at complaints others voice about her, all the while in denial that she is anything less than a devoted sister. And yet, he certainly enjoys recounting to Agnes how a gorilla at the zoo once got his own back on Madge when they were children:

She taunts the big boy one time too many, Agnes. She's eating the bananas she peels instead of throwing them into his cage. Without warning, the great beast does a giant poo in his hand and throws it at her. Wham! Bull's eye! Splat through the bars! Ha-ha! He gets her straight in the face! The shit's everywhere – clothes, hair, ears! She has to shower in the keeper's cottage and go home in a raincoat! Ha-ha! The bugger was as big as King Kong! Imagine what he might have done to her if he wasn't in the cage!

Ben laughs uproariously whenever he recounts this episode, his eyes watering with mirth. He appears almost sick with delight at the prospect of the liberated gorilla's revenge. Then, with a recovery of composure, he turns contrite. But he doesn't desist for long. He and Agnes trade silly stories with impunity. They are conspiratorial. With his quizzical, puppy dog look, raucous voice, and eyes like frantically blinking ink blots behind thick glasses, she detects that he lacks dignity, but who is going to tell him to turn down the volume? As all the women at Rosemont are trained to humour him, he expects the world outside to treat him the same and so is confused by the disparaging looks he receives in polite company. He never gossips about other people, but his steely ambition to take over the cotton factory certainly has everyone talking about him.

Ben is in high spirits on the Sunday morning Agnes accompanies him in the utility truck to look at a horse for sale at a pony club in Camden. He rejects the horse, but convinces Roger McFarland Mead, who runs the club, to invite Agnes to join the hunt. Agnes nearly dies when Ben tells Roger what a cracking good rider she is: a judgment he has seemingly based on seeing her canter on the polo field the previous Sunday. His praise seems to be coupled to his pride in being her teacher. Roger intones in a plummy voice:

It's not a proper hunt as in England, my dear, but a drag hunt. We lay a scent for the dogs to follow. There'll be jumps, although plenty of space for unsure riders to bypass them. You're very welcome if you care to join in.

Roger is looking at her uncle from under eyebrows like pulled threads of steel wool. Ben towers over the other man, his glance intermittently flashing towards the stables. Agnes knows he is hoping for another look at Sandra, a well-endowed and pretty girl on a working holiday from Wiltshire. She is wearing a T-shirt with no bra. Ben says:

What about it, Agnes? Fancy joining in?

I'd be glad to have a go if you think I can do it.

She has replied nervously. Ben smiles down at her:

You can do it, girl, don't worry. There's a good six weeks to prepare.

That's settled then, Ben old chap. Jolly good. Splendid. Couldn't be better. I'll put her name down. Yes, I'll put her name down as soon as I go inside.

McFarland Mead seems approving, but Agnes notices that he wears a muddled look, as if he's trying to sort something out in his mind as he walks her and her uncle to the utility truck:

Well good to see you, Ben old chap. I didn't sell you the horse, but we've got ourselves another rider for the hunt. You know where to come if you change your mind.

McFarland Mead bangs Ben on his lower back, which is as high as his short arm will reach. Ben gives him a playful army salute, filling the paddock with his familiar guffaw.

Ben is impressed by McFarland Mead and the other polo people, but he doesn't deify them like Agnes's parents, nor put on another way of being around them. He is his same uncouth self with everybody. A toot of the horn, a wave, and Agnes and her uncle charge off in a tornado of dust. She feels excited and scared simultaneously. What has convinced her to have a go at the hunt, despite grave doubts, is the welcome chance to surprise her father. She pulls at Ben's shirtsleeve urgently:

Know what, Uncle Ben? I'm not going to tell anyone, so I can surprise Daddy. We'll keep the hunt a secret just between you and me. He won't believe his eyes when he sees me.

Okay, young Agnes, it's a deal. My lips are sealed.

Ben lends Agnes a horse called 'Jake' that she exercises for him on weekends. He is a nervous, finely made black gelding with a gleaming white star on his forehead – his coat so dark, it looks purple in the sunshine. Ben watches her and says:

He's too small for polo, but he'll make a perfect equestrian jumper.

Agnes replies, swelling with pride:

Yes. He'll be my Black Beauty.

If he performs well, I'll sell him to McFarland Mead. That'll be a turn-up for the books, eh? Ha-ha-ha! We go there to buy a horse and end up selling *him* one!

Ben schools Agnes in what he knows about jumping. So that she can practise, he places some recently cut saplings from the woodpile between petrol drums out in the yard. She spends hours and hours going over them, getting out of the saddle time after time to put them back in place whenever Jake kicks them off. Although no one ever comes to the back of the stables, to ensure she isn't seen Agnes pushes the petrol drums closer to the back wall, out of sight after every session. She knows she is improving because she even manages to clear the highest jumps Ben sets up for her. He applauds her efforts, and she feeds off his optimism to secure a place in her father's heart. There is a little nagging doubt, however – perhaps she should wait a bit, for she's never ridden out with a pack of riders. Yet she remains determined to prove herself.

On the morning of the big event, Ben drives Agnes to the pony club with Jake in the back of the float. He broadcasts loudly that he has sold the horse to McFarland Mead. This strikes an easy chord, as those at the farm know a deal is on the cards. Later, Ben will bring her father along in the float to the finishing line at Camden Park House so that they can all return to the farm together.

Agnes is carrying her best jodhpurs, a white shirt, and a wool tie she has nicked from her father's wardrobe. They are secreted away in a bag. She changes at the Pony Club. The long brown leather boots, pink coat and black helmet they lend her at the club fit perfectly. Well-endowed Sandra from Wiltshire plaits a black velvet ribbon through her long hair. To Agnes's delight, everyone who sees her exclaims how sensational she looks.

At the starting line, with the other horses and riders milling around her, Agnes's confidence swells. Jake looks just as good as the other mounts. It's a crisp autumn morning, the sun held back behind a thick cloud. As condensation billows out of the warm mouths of horses and riders, Agnes notices a few other girls her age. She leans forward to rub Jake's neck. He is trembling, his ears pinned back close to his neck, and his hooves are stomping. He is overstimulated. She tries to soothe him by gently repeating his name. Ben approaches, and Agnes whispers urgently:

Jake doesn't like it here.

Ben squints at her through shrewd narrowing eyes:

Nonsense. You read too much into everything. They're all frisky at the start. Once you get going, he'll be fine. Don't be scared, stay in posture, cling on with your thighs. That's it. Heels down. Toes slightly out. Don't forget elbows down, reins firm. Anticipate the jumps by getting ready to move forward.

She grasps the double reins tightly as Ben takes off his hat. Then he hits her leg in a crass gesture of good luck. At the unexpected impact, Jake flares sideways. As she struggles to control Jake, Agnes is shocked to spot Uncle

Parry, Richard the Scottish uncle, and some of the cousins dotted in the crowd at the starting line. She hopes no one has told her father and spoiled the surprise.

She could never have imagined what happens next. She wonders if it is Uncle Parry, as she is wary of his continual pranks. It might even have been Ben. In the terror that follows, a lot gets blurred. All she knows is that, suddenly, shockingly, a rogue whip came down hard on Jake's rump and he has taken off like the Indians are in pursuit behind firing arrows. She will forever be haunted by the sound of that single lash that sent him into such a frenzy. She may have felt uncomfortable about not knowing the other riders, but before too long they will *all* know about her.

Jake is flying through the undergrowth. She clings on, bending down over his mane like the cowboys at the pictures to avoid a bullet in the back. Pulling on the reins with all her might makes absolutely no impression on him. She has lost all confidence. The creature is in a flat-spin panic. She breaks all the rules of riding etiquette by hanging on to the pummel with both hands like a buck jumper. She manages to stay in the saddle over two jumps. If she had been in control, she would have gone around them, but she is in the firm grip of sheer terror.

Mercifully, the nightmare ends when Jake unseats her, and she lands, head-first, in the mud at the third water jump. She lies there, motionless, seeing it all unfurl around her in slow motion. Horses' hooves thunder perilously close. The lovely pink riding jacket, long boots, and the black velvet helmet now look like they've been lodged in a storm water channel for months. While mortified by the state of the borrowed clothes, she is grateful the ordeal is over. As Agnes has such little concern for her own well-being, it never occurs to her that she might have broken her neck.

She is carried to Camden Park House in a blanket. A lady shears away the legs of her jodhpurs below both knees where sharp branches have cut in, then gently cleans around the cuts, and bandages the wounds. Agnes cringes inside when she hears someone say:

I think she's Eric Keen's daughter.

Uncle Parry, Richard, and two of Richard's daughters arrive in an open Jeep to ferry her to hospital. Richard drives while Uncle Parry cradles Agnes in his arms in the back. They all sing silly songs to cheer her up.

Uncle Parry holds Agnes's hand while the doctor gives her a local anaesthetic and proceeds to stitch the torn flesh on her knees with black thread. The doctor puts five stitches in one knee and six in the other. Richard buys the children ice creams from a van outside the hospital and then Parry drives back with Richard sitting beside him. Agnes and the two cousins are in the back, singing: 'How Much is That Doggie in the Window?' As a prize for her bravery, Agnes gets to sing the chorus whenever Parry puts his hand up.

While aunts, uncles and cousins rally around her, the one person Agnes longs to hear from is pretending she doesn't exist. There is complete silence in the family car on the long drive back to the corner of Rose and Edmond Street. Her knees are swollen like footballs and sting like hell. She is covered in bruises and her body aches all over. She tries to explain herself:

Someone hit Jake on the rump with a whip. That's why he got a fright and took off.

Unable to tolerate the tension, she has finally blurted this out when they pull up at the house. But her parents and brothers abandon the car in silence, leaving her sitting in the back seat alone.

Despite the pain, she finds herself squatting down next to her father as he sits silent in the dining room. He is perusing the horse race form as she attempts a further explanation:

If that had happened to any of the other riders, their horse would have done the same. Jake never rode in a pack before. If I hadn't been sabotaged, Daddy, you would have been so proud of me:

Get her away from me!

Eric Keen has shouted to his wife who is in the kitchen. Agnes knows her father is avoiding addressing her directly. As usual. He carries on:

I can't hear any more of this rot, Madge! She's a disgrace. Why Ben ever let her enter the hunt is beyond me. Her performance makes fools of us all.

But Agnes persists:

Ask the others and they'll tell you how I managed to get over two jumps before I was thrown. I stayed with the horse, Daddy. That shows real courage.

At this, Madge finally emerges from the kitchen:

Go to your room, Agnes, and don't upset your father. You can't imagine the shame he felt when people he's known all his life, professional horse people, described your *ridiculous* behaviour!

Her mother is looking triumphant. It's clear Agnes's tale of truth is unwanted, and she is starting to suspect that, had she been seriously injured and, perhaps, put on life support, neither callous parent would hesitate in giving permission to turn off the oxygen. She wonders, too, if they aren't also punishing her for fraternising with Ben – who is now the well-established silent enemy.

The humiliation of the hunt will set the ball of change rolling even faster. Richard Pales' time as fourth player of the team will be brief. He and his family will depart Sydney to revive the depleted fortunes of a sheep farm miles away in the Northern Tablelands of New South Wales, an enterprise once run by the notorious Mack. Agnes will really miss the fun around the barbeque, the games, the shared picnics, and the cakes with tea, for the farm will feel horribly deserted when they leave. And, within another year, Eric Keen will lose the ameliorating influence of Uncle Parry. Weary of brother Ben's scheming for ultimate control of the factory and having to further put up with him at weekend polo meets, Parry will resign his job, sell his horses, and never come back. He will join his wife's family in the pub business, buy a boat, and take up golf.

Losing Parry's support will deal a serious blow to Eric Keen's stability. Devoid of the relief of airing his frustration over Ben's misrepresentation at work with Parry, his exasperation will pierce the silence of the early morning hours in Agnes's parents' bedroom. Night after night she will be woken by her father's impassioned lament. How, she will hear him demand, can he deal with the lies that Ben constantly drips into his mother-in-law's ear:

Why don't we break away like Parry?!

He will endlessly implore his wife in a voice so saturated with despair it will tug at Agnes's heart. While assiduously ignoring his proposal, Madge will swear everlasting vengeance:

First thing at nine sharp, tomorrow – on the *dot* – I'll ring Mother and have it out. Without fail tomorrow. The old lady's eyes will be opened to the skulduggery around her.

This vitriolic pledge to action finally soothes her husband into sleep and, before long, loud snores will replace the anxiety.

The following day, Agnes will wait expectantly for her mother to make the promised call. But she never will. Nine o'clock will come and go and her mother will remain in bed, humming to herself while she cooks her pearls against her skin.

One morning, after a further heartbreaking outburst in the room next door, Agnes will confront her:

When are you going to ring Grandma?

Why do you want me to ring her?

But, as Agnes can't possibly divulge what she has overheard, she will make no reply.

* * *

Back at the farm, Agnes watches her father associating with Ben around the stables with utter astonishment. The animosity that regularly shakes the front bedroom at night is nowhere in evidence. The two men behave with perfect civility as they discuss an increase in club membership fees or choose players for the team. Agnes starts to doubt what she has overheard, until the tortured pleas for help, once again, explode out of Eric from the depths of his bedroom. It appears that night and day are disconnected. It is also strange that her father never asks his wife if she has made the promised call. His plea and her pledge seem to Agnes like the flame on a damp fuse that fizzles out before it reaches the explosion point. She reckons you couldn't have a story like that at the pictures because it doesn't go anywhere.

News of sibling benefits derived from Grandma, and from which she is excluded, turns usurped Madge militant. She decides to conquer the farm for herself, treating family members who dare to turn up to watch a Sunday polo match with such hostility that they never come back. However, the one person she fails to dislodge is Ben, who remains devoted to his mother's dream of a polo dynasty. And who is impossible to insult.

Marginalised after the hunt, Agnes comes to dread Sundays at the farm. Her brothers helping her father at the stables, she is now left to her own devices. Ben having sold Jake to Roger McFarland Mead, the children's ponies – once in big demand – are left out in the paddock. Agnes feels free to claim Snowy – the part-Shetland pony – for herself. He may fart all the way over the hill in time with the rising trot, but he is hers. She tries to make him swim in the dam like the cowboys at the pictures, but stubborn old Snowy will have none of it.

Increasingly listless, Agnes defies the strictly forbidden activity of swinging on the front gate. She imagines herself performing in the Hollywood musicals she loves. She's the lead in *Annie Get Your Gun*, she's Doris Day in *Calamity Jane* and Shirley Jones in *Oklahoma*. She teaches herself all the song and dance routines, especially those delivered on tops of gates and wooden fences. She sings and dances her heart out, while Snowy swishes the flies off his back with his tail, watching her with indifference.

When not acting in a musical, Agnes indulges in imagining herself as a Regency heroine in a novel who is escaping abuse in an English Country House by fleeing on horseback, disguised as a boy.

She starts riding out the front gate to a small Gothic Revival Anglican church. It stands like a stone oasis in a hamlet of run-down single-storey houses. Their broken corrugated-iron front verandas are like rusty teeth. Further up the road from the church, on recently created five-acre blocks, small fibro houses have sprung up like mushrooms to be instantly surrounded by old tank stands, wrecked cars, baby prams, motorbikes, and various leftover building materials. The once virgin landscape has been desecrated. To Agnes, it looks as if the lovingly constructed 'Church of the Innocents' has flown off course and landed in a garbage dump.

She loves reading the headstones in the old graveyard. Some date back to the early settlement, and a few inhabitants were even born twenty years before Captain Cook sailed into Botany Bay – probably all convicts sent to the colony for stealing a loaf of bread when they were starving. Grandma wouldn't have approved of her hanging around with dead Protestants, but Grandma isn't there.

Late one afternoon, after leaving the church and entering the farm gate, she hears the pitiful whinnying of a distressed horse. Close up, she recognises it is Paddy, the pony she learned to ride on. He is bleeding from a gunshot wound to the leg. Some idiot must have used him as target practice. She canters back to the stables for help. Only Uncle Ben and her older brother, Bert, are at the stables. Ben is in a bad mood as, that morning, he had arrived to find the Aboriginal resident groom had left. There was a scribbled note to say the fella had gone walkabout. Not only had the groom upped sticks, but he had burned the timber floor in the house for firewood. Madge and Eric had driven off to Camden to interview a potential replacement.

Ben, Bert and Agnes manage between them to hobble the injured pony to the fence next to the back paddock and Ben ties a long rope onto metal rings either side of a halter that he fixes to Paddy's head. Then he hands Bert and Agnes the end of the rope on either side. He attaches a further rope from a strap under the horse's neck to the fence post in front. Paddy's enormous brown eyes are watering in pain. Ben orders:

Hold tight to the end of the ropes and stand well back.

With the usual lack of an explanation, he puts the barrel of a shotgun to the white patch between the injured horse's eyes and pulls the trigger. The deafening shot blows a crater in Paddy's head. Brother and sister both lose their grip on the rope as Paddy upturns with a mighty thud – all four legs vibrating in a violent spasm. Agnes and Bert are covered in fragments of flesh, fur, and splintered bone. One of Paddy's eyes has lodged in the loose threads of Agnes's jumper.

Both children look at their uncle in dazed disbelief. He shouts at them in response to their silent criticism. Sometimes Agnes wonders if Ben was ever young, as he seems to have absolutely no awareness of a child's fear response. She waits now for a Rosemont proverb. By way of making up for his inadequacy, he often spouts them. 'The one that pays the piper calls the tune' was a favourite that gave him the illusion of complete control. And a work-related bunch were uttered around various jobs at the stables: 'A bad workman always blames his tools', 'Never put off till tomorrow what you can do today'. And, usually trotted out to justify an increase in female cardigan ogling – 'Variety is the spice of life'.

But no proverb could possibly fit the smell of the gun and the huge hole in Paddy's head, which is now fast filling with insects. Agnes keeps looking down at Paddy's eye, still stuck fast in her jumper. She is unable to speak. When Ben spots it, he flicks it away without comment as if it is yet another insect. Agnes and Bert mechanically obey the Piper's order – to fetch dry wood, which they carefully stack around the carcase. Ben brings rotten fence posts and dumps them onto the funeral pyre, which he douses with petrol. He leaps back from the lighted taper. Huge flames erupt, merging with the hot evening air and scattering the thousands of flies that have settled on the dead pony. It will take days for the giant mound to disappear.

After Paddy is shot, Agnes loses interest in telling Uncle Ben jokes, and stops being one of the blokes. She will start to hate the long return drive through heavy traffic from the farm on a Sunday night, as her hostile parents seethe about something Ben said or did. The only highlight of the day will be when she and Bert steal corn-on-the-cob from the silo of the dairy farm next door. The friendly owner knows they do it but doesn't seem to mind. Bert and Agnes will climb down the stepladder into the depth of the spherical storage container and collect enough for everyone.

The anticipation of eating hot corn soaked in butter and covered in black pepper will be what sustains Agnes during the drive home, as does singing along with the hit parade on the radio. Particular favourites being 'This Old House', sung by Rosemary Clooney, 'Mr Sandman' by The Corvettes,

'In the Chapel in the Moonlight' and 'You're Nobody Till Somebody Loves You'. And the crooning recordings of 'Autumn Leaves' and 'Love is a Many Splendored Thing', which invariably send her into an unbearable swoon.

But the radio hit parade will grate on the ear the night the motorcyclist dies. It will not be uncommon, on these Sunday evenings, to pass a car accident. It might even be the same day Ben shot Paddy. Agnes has always coupled both incidents together, as she has never forgotten either. Her father will usually avoid highway traffic jams by taking a shortcut through backstreets, but there is a section through Ryde that offers no alternative. Having crawled for a while at a snail's pace, the police will stop the car. A mangled motorbike will be lying on its side and a river of blood will run down the gutter from the head of its sprawled rider. Her father's car will be so close that Agnes will clearly see the empty stare in the young man's eyes. The police will oblige them to remain stationary as they sort out the traffic to allow an ambulance through. In the front passenger seat, Madge will be nearest to the dead man but, if she notices him, she will make no comment. Nor will her husband.

As the car's headlights illuminate the terrible spectacle, Agnes will wait for the expression of some sentiment from her parents, if not to their children, then at least between themselves. But no communication or acknowledgement will take place. The motorbike accident will demonstrate, in horrible detail, that her parents are not only disconnected from their children, but from each other.

9

REDBACK SPIDER

gnes refuses to use the only toilet in the house on the corner of Rose and Edmond Street after she is bitten on the bottom by a spider. Faded cornflowers, still visible around the top of the old ceramic pan, have been obliterated at the bottom where solids linger before being flushed to oblivion at the activation of an excessively long chain. It strikes her that the size of the bowl would be more appropriate in a kindergarten and, given the long chain, concludes that it may have been installed in error. This mistake – and that is how she thinks of it – lives in a lean-to which hangs off the outside corner of the house near the lane. Gaping cracks between the white-painted planks of wood allow spiders to enter without knocking and a bent frame makes it hard to close the door. Mostly, Agnes is in and out like a flash. What had made her mark time that fateful day was the sight of her mother's angry face at the kitchen window when she came through the gate after school.

She sits, lingering there on the bowl, hoping the delay would alter her mother's mood. As soon as the fangs puncture her skin, she springs out of the door with her pants around her ankles. Since the persecution over the nightmare, Agnes has tried to avoid bringing any distress indoors as her mother has exclusive rights to suffering and doesn't relish competition. The best moment to approach her seems to be when she is drowsy after her afternoon nap. Then, Madge would always light a cigarette to go with the tea Agnes normally brought to her bedside. The smoke would curl up like a peace signal. But, on the day of the spider, her mother is already up and on the warpath.

Agnes circles the garden in mindless despair, clutching her painful bottom, and weighing up the fear of her mother against the fear of dying. Names and faces of neighbours flash into her head, but she would be exposing her mother if she appealed to them for help. The persecuted Cleary chickens are squawking in alarm as usual, feathers flying over the fence, much to the children's delight. Forget them, she thinks. And Mrs Machin is in awe of her mother, so would instantly make a beeline for Madge's back door. Plus, the placid, elderly twin sisters over the lane are beyond dealing with an emergency. Agnes has bothered them a few times to do God's work, hoping they might turn into another Dora Chadwick, but all they have in common with Dora is a shared skill at keeping the world at a safe distance.

And so, with no port in the storm, she lies on the grass trying to cool her bottom and evoking the help of the Almighty. Increasingly groggy, she must have passed out. When she comes to, she has no idea how long she has been lying there. She suddenly feels horribly nauseous. Struggling to stand, she makes it as far as the flower bed at the Rose Street entrance. She assumes it must have been about 3.30pm, because she always finishes school at the convent in Archer Street at 3.00pm and walks straight home.

Agnes rarely vomits. She has assiduously trained her body to expel only as a last resort. But, today, she has no control over herself, and is shocked by the force with which her desiccated school lunch lands, in a disgusting mess, over a patch of nasturtiums. Startled, Ginger Cat screeches and leaps off the grass where she has been sunning herself.

But spilling her guts near the Rose Street gate has attracted the attention of Natasha, an Armenian girl, who is a few years older than Agnes. Her parents rent rooms out to Chinese students in the house opposite. The girl's mother, Petra, dashes down the cement steps into the garden and gently squeezes both Agnes's shoulders, crooning soothing words to her in her own language. Agnes instantly declaims dramatically:

I've been bitten by something – and am dying of poison!

Petra's English classes are not quite up to this level yet, but the wonderfully chiselled face that seems as if it has been fashioned on an anvil has melted into an amazing softness, and the sharp eagle eyes are wide with compassion as Natasha translates to her mother. Agnes explains that she stepped out of her underpants and left them on the path because her burning bottom hurt so much that she didn't care. The sight of her rear end sets off gasps and incomprehensible foreign exclamations. Natasha shrieks:

My God, you should *see* it, Agnes! One cheek is swollen like a giant strawberry jelly! We'd better get you to hospital. Where is your mother?

This, a normal question from any near stranger, could prove fatal for her. Fearful they will abandon her to Madge, Agnes mumbles a falsehood:

Inside the house, but she's not very well.

She pleads with Natasha, looking deeply into the girl's beautiful dark velvet eyes, which are framed by lashes so dense that they shadow her face:

Can *you* help me?

Yes – of course I'll help. Stay there with my mother.

Agnes knows that Petra had given birth to Natasha late in life, so that is why she seems more like her grandmother. The Armenian woman's rough paw, full of knobbly joints, is stroking her brow. It is sheer heaven. But now Agnes's nose and eyes are starting to run as waves of bitter-tasting bile rise into her oesophagus. She buries her burning face in a black scarf, covered in bright red and yellow flowers, which Petra has pushed into her hand. Agnes also knows, and trusts, that Natasha is mature for her age, as she alone in the family speaks fluent English. And it had duly proved to be so for, in a matter of minutes, Natasha has the trip to the hospital efficiently organised.

Time has seemed to shrink to a pinpoint as Agnes opens swollen eyes to see Madge sitting stiffly in the front seat of the taxi. She is looking resentful at being given orders by foreign ladies. On a pillow, safely cushioned between the Armenians in the back seat, however, Agnes can at last relax. She has spotted the sign – Royal North Shore Hospital – as she passes under it on a stretcher, into Casualty, while lying on her side. It occurs to her that this place had been the very location where Paul, the boy her mother always referred to as THAT BOY, had died in an iron lung.

The doctor confirms from the shape of the puncture that Agnes has been bitten by a redback. The nurse produces a consent form, giving the hospital permission to treat Agnes with an anti-venom. Madge Keen loathes hospitals and does everything she can to avoid entering one. Even in her distressed state, Agnes remains cognisant of the drama her mother manages to create over simply signing that form. Don't make a meal of it, just *concentrate*, she thinks to herself as she hears the nurse patiently explain for the umpteenth time where on the form her mother should place her signature. Then, when the agony of suspense is over, Madge manages to spill the coffee the nurse offers her all over it and it all has to be done again.

Although in current use, the anti-venom shot is still officially in trial stage. The doctor explains that it is a bureaucratic hitch but thanks God they have it. It is miraculous, he says, the way the burning sensation neutralises after the injection. The swelling will eventually follow suit.

The specialist who has just spoken – the 'poison doctor' as Agnes will always refer to him in future – wears an oversized white coat that only emphasises his shortness. Perhaps only the big sizes were clean that day. His long thin head is disproportionately large for his body and his short, curly hair resembles Nero's close-cut style in *Quo Vadis*. Dark-rimmed thick spectacles enlarge his eyes and make him resemble an anxious grasshopper. DR JOHN JENKINS is written in capital letters on a tag pinned to the lapel of his coat. He tells Agnes she was lucky she wasn't bitten by a funnel-web or a tiger snake.

Agnes didn't mean to say 'yes' when he asks her if she would like to see a specimen of the spider that bit her. But she is keen to delay the maternal anger that surely awaits her. Feeling much better and more relaxed, she annunciates clearly as she addresses him formally:

Yes. And thank you, Doctor Jenkins, for making me better.

He ushers her into his office. Agnes still doesn't know exactly why she challenges the doctor, but she has been taken over by the random wildness that, whenever there was an audience, would often grip her. Especially at school. She continues:

There are a lot of dangerous creatures that might have bitten me – sharks, crocodiles, piranhas, wolves, rabid dogs, etcetera, but perhaps real luck is not being bitten by anything at all.

Hah! Quite right, quite right!

Doctor Jenkins is laughing cheerfully at her boldness and Agnes feels pleased with herself. She watches him closely as he picks out two jars from a line of containers on a shelf at the far wall of the small office. He motions her to sit down, forgetting she has a swollen bottom so, instead, she leans against the corner of a large desk covered in papers, bottles of pills and a cardboard model of a body depicting the nervous system.

Doctor Jenkins sets down a jar on a clear patch of the desktop. The vigorously wrestling, spherical black body in the jar has a prominent red stripe on the upper side of its abdomen and six or seven thin black legs that seem out of proportion with the rest. She watches the doctor's bug eyes expand in wonder as he gazes into the jar's depths:

The redback is one of the few venomous spiders indigenous to Australia that, like the black widow, display sexual cannibalism whilst mating…

This little lecture sounds as matter of fact to Agnes as a shopping list. In fairness, one spider eating another was a bit too close to Agnes's daily existence to elicit any scientific wonder. Wrapped up in his lesson, the enthusiast continues:

The male in the other jar with no red stripe is a quarter the size of the female. He lies spreadeagled on the bottom of the jar, fully aware of what awaits him. And you can't go without seeing a funnel-web – one of the most dangerous spiders in the world. They proliferate on the North Shore. But don't worry – you'd never find one in an outside toilet as they prefer damp soil.

Aghast, Agnes catches her breath. This combative, hairy creature in a double-sized jar makes the redback look like an ant. But it appears the doctor is only just warming up:

Observe the large mating spur projecting from the middle of the second pair of legs. Opposite to the redback, the male we have here is highly aggressive if disturbed. Those powerful fangs can penetrate fingernails and soft shoes.

For once, Agnes is grateful to her mother for bringing the show to an abrupt end. For, reliably impatient and uncouth, Madge is now banging on the glass door of the doctor's office with her fist. Jealous of male attention to a fault, her mother quickly embarks upon informing him that they have a doctor in 'our polo team' – as if, by association, it makes her an honorary member of the medical profession. But as soon as the name-dropping begins, the doctor points to his watch and makes his escape.

Madge pushes Agnes into a taxi with her usual urgency to get home in time to do nothing more than wait for her husband's unpredictable arrival. Agnes ventures to ask:

What happened to Natasha and Petra?

Oh, they caught a train back as they wanted to shop on the way home. I don't know what they were doing with us in the first place! Why you drag every Tom, Dick and Harry into our garden, I'll *never* know. Didn't you see Natasha's mother has a gold tooth? They're common! It's enough to have to put up with those Chink Chong Chinamen they house, all taking photos of each other draped over my pine trees. *Surely*, I don't have to put up sharing a taxi with peasants as *well*!

Madge spits out her vitriol, ending with the usual long exhalation that follows such an outburst, then pulls her eyes into a slant with her fingers and puts on a stupid grin.

Agnes will come to learn that the Chinese were not only derided by her mother but feared by the whole nation. It had been the era of 'The Yellow Peril' – a popular myth bandied about by the Western powers since the Communist takeover of mainland China in 1949. News media had efficiently fanned the primal fear that the Chinese were on the brink of rowing down to Australia in sampans to take over. Never could they have conceived that, fifty years on, they would be buying clothes made in China and those they derided would own huge chunks of Australian land and purchase eighty per cent of its mineral reserves.

A fumigation of the dunny does nothing to alleviate Agnes's fears. The vision of all the poisonous creatures in jars plays on her mind, influencing her to plan her bodily expulsions elsewhere. On the upside, the danger of further redback attacks, or worse, provokes a renewal of discussion with the architect. The plans, yet again, lie in state on the dining room table weighted down, as usual, by The Art Book and *Lust for Life*.

An additional incentive to keep the plans on show is the fact that Eric and Madge have become friendly with a couple at a local tennis club. The wife, Jacqueline St Paul, is an interior designer who is taking an interest in the Keen house reformation. Following Lew Hoad and Ken Rosewall's tennis stardom, Agnes's parents have been lured by the tennis fever that now grips the nation to don whites and take to the court. And tennis is the spur by which these two very different couples pair up in a doubles match and maintain a brief acquaintance. Agnes prays that Jacqueline will be the catalyst who pushes the house project forward. But, one day soon, the plans will disappear forever and, with them, the hope of a new bathroom with indoor toilet.

A second fumigation doesn't restore Agnes's confidence in the dunny and she vows never to enter that dismal hole again. A space for private peeing is accidentally freed up under the overgrown wisteria vine when her young brother, Jim, lets the handbrake off in her father's car while it is parked in the garden. The car had rolled down the slope and hit one of the garage posts, thus twisting and lowering the roof. Henceforth, her father parks in the street, for he takes no interest in repairs to the house, reserving his building skills exclusively for the farm. When the wisteria loses its leaves in winter, a wild choko vine festooning the top of the Cleary's chook shed appears miraculously to continue to screen Agnes off from any onlookers. Nonetheless, she trains her bowels to save the important number of the day for the flush toilets at school.

Fear of the dunny has also stimulated her to reach out to neighbours. She develops a route map of loos in the near vicinity – often finding herself struggling with polite conversation en route to a neighbour's bathroom. The nearest toilets are at Natasha's house, or at the Old Age Home, where Agnes still does God's work with the residents in order to stay alive. There is also a toilet under the grandstand at Trumper Park, down Rose Street, where she often hides out – but it is mostly locked.

She is forced to revise her map after her bladder collapses one day in a phone box in Victoria Street shopping centre, and she suffers the humiliation of watching the river that runs down her legs spill out the door, waterfall over the step and streak past a line of astonished waiting telephone users, before finally meandering into the municipal gutter.

The message of being an unwanted impediment is never so obvious to Madge's three children as during the evening meal, when they line up in a row at a red Formica breakfast bar in the kitchen. Eating is done in silence, while their mother breathes down their necks waiting for each dirty plate. Pots, pan, knives, forks, glasses, and plates must be washed, dried, and put back in the cupboards of a spotless kitchen before her husband's car pulls up outside, after which Madge chases them all off to bed.

Agnes has always deemed it a pity her mother contaminates good flavours with bad grace, because Madge is a competent cook, with good attention to detail, and they eat well: chops, steak, cutlets, mashed potatoes, boiled potatoes or baked in their jackets along with generous servings of peas, beans, cauliflower in white sauce or carrots garnished with butter and honey. Agnes's favourite dish is baked sausages in an onion gravy. She can't contain a gasp of 'How good!' whenever she sees them steaming off the plate, but her mother never acknowledges the compliment as her eyes are riveted to the kitchen clock.

Jacqueline St Paul from the Tennis Club shows Agnes how happy family life can be. She and her husband Edward have two daughters: Madeleine, who is six months older than Agnes, and Colette, who is a few years younger.

Agnes falls in love with everything about them. She writes herself into their lives and imagines the four of them will be friends forever. Agnes will learn later that her own parents have a bad reputation for fobbing their children off onto friends and relatives so they can go to polo tournaments together. This is probably how, in the first flush of the new friendship, Madge imposes on Jacqueline's generosity and Agnes gets to stay in the St Paul family house during the school holidays. Agnes and Madeleine become firm friends, but it is Jacqueline with whom Agnes falls in love.

The St Pauls live in a beautiful house, nestling below a jungle of trees at Castlereagh. Walter Burley Griffin, the same architect who designed Canberra, had designed the lovely two-storey property. Full-length glass doors opened off the living area onto a balcony as wide as the house, from where occupants could view Middle Harbour through the lush surrounding greenery. A sea breeze cooled the interior in summer. Built with local quarried stone, it is like a magazine advertisement for a house, and possesses the first open-plan kitchen Agnes has ever seen. The parents' bedroom on the top floor has an attached bathroom, and there is a second generous bathroom for the children, a guest toilet and hand basin off the living room, and even one in the garage downstairs. The internal walls are made of clinker bricks, so no falling plaster.

Today, Jacqueline is working at a drawing board at the end of the living room. She tells Agnes that the house follows the humanising ideas of Arts and Crafts. It all sounds grand, but Agnes has no idea what Jacqueline means. The lovely woman is warm and affectionate. She kisses and hugs Agnes as nobody has ever done before. Agnes asks Jacqueline if she can help her in the kitchen just to be near her, because being close to her is like being in heaven.

Edward St Paul is a barrister with chambers in Philip Street, from where he can walk to the law courts. As a professional man, Eric and Madge have placed him on a pedestal, although occupying a lower rung on the social ladder than the polo people – who reign supreme. To Agnes, Mr St Paul behaves like a proper dad does at the pictures.

Jacqueline speaks English with a French accent because she grew up in Paris. Her talk brims with enthusiasm. It doesn't matter what she says, Agnes cradles her every syllable as if it is sacred. Agnes doesn't call Jacqueline 'Mrs St Paul' and, although Jacqueline has told her to call her by her first name, Agnes feels awkward, and so she doesn't call her anything.

Agnes is so accustomed to listening to her mother's so-called woes that she is comfortable listening to adult problems. Today, while helping Jacqueline in the kitchen Agnes is startled to see the lovely woman start to cry. At first, Agnes isn't sure if the tears are caused by the onions Jacqueline is slicing for the beef bourguignon dinner that night. But, as she washes and dries her hands, Agnes notices teardrops are still cascading down her cheeks. She feels embarrassed observing this grief yet feels bad ignoring it. Madge never cries. Jacqueline is the first adult she has ever seen openly weep. Agnes asks Jacqueline, without using her name, if she can make her a cup of tea. Jacqueline sighs, looking down at her with a sorrowful expression:

Oh, ma petite cherie...

With her light brown hair cut in a thick fringe across her forehead, her small full lips, long sharp nose, to Agnes, Jacqueline looks just like the woman behind the bar of the Folies Bergère in The Art Book painting by Edouard Manet. What makes the resemblance even more striking is that, today, she is wearing a black velvet ribbon around her neck with an elaborate silver pendant – just like the woman in the image. Agnes wants to bring the book from home to show Jacqueline but fears she might not like being compared to a bar lady.

Jacqueline bends to hold Agnes's head between her hands and gently kisses the top of her head. Agnes swoons as Jacqueline murmurs:

You're very sweet to be concerned, my little Agnes. Today is the anniversary of the day we escaped from Paris... so long ago, but like yesterday...

You mean you weren't there for the liberation?

Agnes doesn't want to sound disappointed, but she has always imagined Jacqueline reclining on an American tank in a summer dress covered in flowers, the Champs Elysée outlined in the background, exactly like the newspaper photo in her mother's knitting bag. Jacqueline obviously feels the need to unburden herself:

No. We left the city after a young Polish Jew, vaguely related to my father, shot the German Ambassador in November 1938. It was a reprisal against the Nazis expelling his parents from Germany. Suddenly every Polish Jew, even those born in Germany, was in danger. And then, later that month, SS thugs smashed the windows of thousands of Jewish shops and burned hundreds of synagogues across Germany. Both my parents are Jewish. My mother, a French violinist who played in an orchestra in Paris. My father, a Polish architect who was supervising the construction of a new school there. Nazi spies started hunting down all Polish Jews in Paris. It happened fast, Agnes. My father was in serious danger. My mother insisted he and I leave immediately, and she would follow. She wanted to see her sick father before he died, you see. When we left for London, she and my brother drove to her family home in Burgundy. A friend of my father's drove the two of us through the night to Calais where we caught a boat to England. From there we sailed to Sydney and joined my father's brother. He ran a busy architectural practice in the city. I worked with them after finishing my training. Horrified by the religious strife in Europe, my uncle joined a group of people who believed in a union of all religions – called the Theosophical Society. They gathered in the local community hall not far from here. It's where I met Edward. At a meeting. He'd just returned from his studies in England. When war finally broke out, he joined up and was sent out to Palestine. We got married quickly before he left, then months later, I found I was pregnant with Madeleine…

The fascinating story is paused as Jacqueline dabs at her eyes, then:

I really wanted to get married after my mother had safely arrived here… but after her father died then her mother got sick and so she stayed on. Then war was declared, and it was too late, little Agnes, too late…

Agnes is left wondering what happened to Jacqueline's mother and brother but knows she cannot ask.

She also knows that Jaqueline hadn't meant to tell her all this for, when Madeleine interrupts, she quickly dries her eyes and doesn't go back to it. Agnes supposes she could ask Madeleine for more details, but doesn't like to, as she heard Mr St Paul say that it was disrespectful to pry into the affairs of others. Agnes doesn't have to pry at home, as it all falls into her ears unwanted. She thinks, perhaps, that people tell her things because she appears not to belong to anyone, especially in the way all the St Pauls belong to each other.

Instead of children being chased off to bed as they are in Agnes's house, Mr St Paul's fatherly homecoming is a real celebration. As his car drives into the garage under the house, the three girls hide in the living room, ready to jump out and surprise him when he walks up the stairs. There is plenty of time to prepare because they have a steep drive, and the silence outside guarantees no false alarms.

This, the night of the beef bourguignon, is Mr St Paul's birthday. Agnes squeezes in next to Madeleine behind the sofa to hide, and Colette conceals herself in the broom cupboard. All the girls struggle to stifle their laughter when the father enters the room. He pretends to be surprised when they leap out. Agnes wavers between pleasure and self-consciousness. She can't help, sometimes, feeling like an intruder. But Mr St Paul acts surprised, even though he knows it's her:

And who have we got here? Well, if it isn't our darling Agnes!

Madeleine and Colette shout out clues to the treasure hunt they have laid with Jacqueline around the living room for their father to find his birthday presents. He locates a pair of leather gloves, a red cashmere scarf and a book, which he unwraps with excitement. Then he hugs them all. So that Agnes won't feel excluded, Jacqueline has hidden a box of handkerchiefs with Mr St Paul's initials on them, as if gifted from her. Then Madeleine and Colette set the table with special long-stemmed glasses and lovely red cloth napkins.

Agnes will never forget the taste of the exotic starter of hot canapés stuffed with creamed lobster. The three girls join in the toast for Mr St Paul's birthday with half a glass of champagne, which makes Agnes woozy. Then they all sing 'Happy Birthday' in English, and French, after which Madeleine plays 'The Moonlight Sonata' on the piano.

Jacqueline's enthusiasm for the Keen house transformation grows in fervour. During the brief friendship with Agnes's parents, she consults the plans on the dining room table and sketches out additional ideas for the interior. As Agnes only has a small bedroom, she can never ask anyone to stay with her. But even if she'd had two beds in her room, the primitive facilities in her home, and her parents' unpredictable behaviour, make the prospect of Madeleine staying there unthinkable.

One day, she plucks up the courage to ask her mother if she knows what happened to Jacqueline's mother and brother. Madge responds:

Oh – they died in a concentration camp. But you shouldn't know things like that.

Agnes is not certain what a concentration camp is. But it is terrible to know for sure that they died. When she tells her mother that Madeleine is the top of her class at school, Madge replies dismissively:

Just as well she's clever. With a nose like that, she'll never get a man.

The friendship with the St Pauls will end abruptly when they drop Agnes home. It is the same evening Uncle Mack comes to the house to kill her father.

The sound of her mother's heavy steps on the way to the front door will spell trouble. In the darkness shrouding the front of the house, Madge will fail to see the kind couple from Castlereagh standing behind Agnes and will declare:

Your Uncle Mack just tried to kill your father!

She will blurt this out at her daughter as if she is somehow responsible. And then will be taken aback when she catches sight of the St Pauls. Jacqueline will gasp in shock:

Oh, my goodness! Is Eric all right?

Madge will quickly regain her composure:

Yes, he's all right. A bit bruised and bloodied, but his injuries are minor. Worse was the shock of having the wretch, out of the blue, burst in the back door. I rang the police, who arrived within minutes. When Mack heard the siren, he dashed to his car and drove off. The police took Eric to the hospital. My brother Parry will be bringing him home any minute.

Edward St Paul will offer his assistance, but Madge will decline. She will then summarily dismiss the St Pauls by closing the door to the house behind her and walking them to their car. Here, Jacqueline will kiss Agnes and hand her a copy of *The Diary of Anne Frank*. But Madge's proximity will cause Agnes to pull away from Jacqueline's proffered embrace, for she will not want her mother to see the affection between them. Heart sinking, she will watch the St Pauls drive away and down the hill.

Her reaction might as well be a premonition of doom, for it will all end that evening. Madge will never return to the tennis club and there will be no further contact with the St Pauls. Six months later, Mr St Paul will phone Madge to say Jacqueline had committed suicide by taking an overdose:

Clearly unstable. A lot of those French types of women are!

Madge will pronounce this judgement without a second thought. Agnes simply will not be able to understand it and will wish profoundly that she hadn't pushed Jacqueline away when she tried to hug her after giving her the book.

Sometime later, her mother will mention in passing that Edward St Paul has put his two daughters into boarding school and is marrying 'a sensible woman'. Agnes will wonder what a sensible woman is like. And, many years down the line, she will discover Madeleine living near her in Notting Hill Gate, after a book Madeleine has authored is shortlisted for a prestigious London literary prize. During their brief reunion, Madeleine will confide to Agnes the devastating effect on her life of being packed off rapidly to boarding school and so denied a chance to grieve her mother's death. Agnes will invite Madeleine to the ballet at the Royal Opera House in Covent Garden. She will have to organise a car to drop them off directly in front of the theatre and pick them up afterwards, as Madeleine has difficulty breathing. In fact, she does not have long to live, but will remain just as alert and sharp that evening as Agnes has always remembered her – eyes darting with pleasure over the faces of every new arrival in the theatre foyer.

After the St Pauls' car disappears that awful night, when the streetlights have fluttered and gone out, and mother and daughter found themselves plunged into total darkness, Madge will grab Agnes's arm, hissing:

This must be your uncle's doing.

Working the municipal electricity! You must be joking!

Madge will flash a torchlight in her daughter's face:

I don't need any lip from you at a time like this!

You're blinding me!

Watch your step! You think you're so clever now you've wormed your way in with the St Pauls!

Why do you say such horrible things?!

Agnes will know her mother isn't about to attack her physically because she is clinging on to her daughter as if her life depends on it. It will be one of those familiar double-edged moments when Madge cleaves close, while simultaneously blaming her daughter for her dependent need. Then the electricity will surge back on, the Armenian garden opposite lighting up like a funfair with familiar human shapes outlined behind the pink curtains in the front living room. Light will filter reassuringly through the green tangle at the side of the Old Age Home, and Agnes will see the twin sisters in their house, illuminated behind white curtains, like performers in a shadow-play. They will have calmly resumed their sewing on either side of a work-table – their spectacles on their noses. She will long to be spirited away to sit next to them in peace.

Given Madge's habit to overdramatise, Agnes won't really take seriously what she has been told about Mack and her father until she enters the dining room and sees the smashed venetian blinds and the huge cracks in the big pane of glass behind them. The lower slats will look like strips of kindling for the fire, while the ones above are concertinaed together. As the blinds are always closed against prying eyes, it will surprise Agnes to see the semis twinkling at the end of garden and the spidery leaf formation of the willow tree on Rose Street under the streetlight.

Bloodstains will be evident on fallen chunks of plaster and under broken glass on the old lino floor. Madge will hand her daughter a broom and watch Agnes sweep the debris into a pile, scoop it into a dustpan, and tip it into a big garbage bin her mother has carried in from the laundry. Through the broken pane, Agnes will spot Tabby Cat Ness on the veranda, curled as usual on top of the birdcage, totally unperturbed by the happenings on the other side of the wall:

How dare *your* uncle destroy *my* furniture! *Look* at this!

Madge will thrust a broken chair leg in Agnes's face:

See why I'm so upset?! Mother gave us this dining set as a wedding present!

Then Madge will notice that the purple and white Regency-striped cover on another chair is split down the middle:

Look at *this*!

She will tear out a clump of course hair from the split and thrust it toward her daughter, but Agnes will gasp aloud at a larger crime and bend down to retrieve the crumpled tracing paper and torn pieces of Jacqueline's drawings from under the dining table:

Oh, my God. The architect's plans!

Desperate to find The Art Book, Agnes will be relieved as she manages to locate it still in one piece near the kitchen door. *Lust for Life* lies face down in the bathroom passage minus its cover and a chunk of front pages. Agnes will cradle The Art Book and carry it reverently back to the den as her mother rants:

YOUR uncle had the *hide* to come here and blame YOUR father for what *he* did all those years ago at the California polo club! He stole *all* of it! Mother would have got a good return, like she did after the India trip, if he hadn't run off with that money! That's how that actress bitch slipped in to steal YOUR father!

Agnes will, decades later, be able to clearly picture Madge as she tosses the ravaged building plans and what is left of *Lust for Life* in the garbage bin with complete indifference. Will still clearly picture her stack the bigger broken slats of the venetian blind in the corner of the room and barricade the locked door with the ironing board. Will still hear her rail, and rail, and rail. Extra emphasis on the personal pronoun 'your' can still make Agnes squirm to this day.

Then Eric will arrive home with a swollen and bloodied face and leaning on Parry's arm, his features merging as if they have been rubbed out with an eraser. Two black stitches standing out on his shaved, iodine-painted hairline. His sad, shrunken eyes reduced to two blue beads of glass hiding beneath a shelf of puffed eyebrows. The delicate skin beneath his eyes puffy and ringed in violet and vermilion that will turn black in the days ahead. His upper lip split, caked blood clinging to the inside of his nostrils. Agnes will see, through the half-open hospital gown, wide bandages strapping what she will shortly learn are two broken ribs. He will limp into the bedroom clutching his chest, letting out a deep groan when Parry helps him up onto the bed. Collapsing back onto the pillows, which are covered in freshly ironed crisp white pillow slips, he will whisper:

Don't fuss, please…

Eric Keen, hoarse with pain and aspirin, will moan aloud as Madge leans forward to straighten the pillow behind his head. Agnes will observe that she appears oblivious to her husband's physical distress. In fact, when Parry outlines his brother-in-law's injuries, she will change the subject and shriek:

You should have seen the venetian blinds! The broken glass! Look at the mutilated furniture! Mack has destroyed my house!

Parry will put a stop to her tirade:

Enough! Don't raise your voice. They can all be fixed. Eric is the priority. He needs to rest in peace and quiet.

And Madge will leave the room in a huff, making it completely clear where *her* priorities lie.

Parry will bring a chair from the den and seat himself beside Eric's bed. Pulling Agnes down to sit awkwardly on his knee he will tighten his grip when she struggles to get up and she will protest:

It's too hot, let me go.

And Parry, reluctantly, will release her.

* * *

Madge heats up an Irish stew. Parry retrieves the ironing board from the back door, carries the garbage bin down the back stairs, puts the broken chairs under the house and tapes up the cracks in the glass. Agnes helps him pull the dining table out. The family normally only eat at the table on Christmas day, so sitting together eating the delicious stew is a rare event.

Parry sleeps the night with them on a camp bed Madge has prepared beside the back door in case Mack returns. But he never does, and few ever see him again. He may have been the victor of the fight but, defeated by life, Mack will drift along a path of drunken deterioration that leads to an early death.

Parry acts as a go-between, bringing papers from the factory for Eric to sign, and keeping him supplied with whisky. He organises a glazier to replace the broken glass in the back window, sends a man to measure the new venetian blinds and has a second telephone extension put in the den for Eric. But, even after the new blinds are in place, Madge goes on complaining like a cracked record about the destruction of the old ones. Even a new set of dining room chairs from Rosemont fails to pacify her. Agnes knows her mother, as ever, is longing for revenge.

Having her husband at home convalescing is a serious disruption to Madge's lethargy. With people coming to see Eric, she no longer stamps up the hall barefoot in bra and pants. Forced into the role of housewife, she directs her aggression onto dirty clothes. Her red-painted toenails are hidden in a pair of slingback sandals, and she wears simple short-sleeved cotton frocks. Normally, in school holidays, the children wear whatever they like, but exposed as they now are to the gaze of visitors, Madge scrutinises every bit of cloth on their bodies – viewing stains and spots as a personal affront, and her children as their allies.

The boys take off each day and, when home, keep out of sight. The laundry floor is covered in clothes soaking in buckets of bleach and detergent and the washing machine keeps turning. Eric is regularly issued with freshly ironed cotton pyjamas and, much to his annoyance, Madge insists on changing the sheets on the bed every two days. Her uncharacteristic domesticity is aimed at showing her man the hardship of keeping the home fires burning. But, like her, he is in another world and hardly notices what she does.

Relieved of her usual laundry duties, Agnes determines during this rare period of access to her father to convert him into a loving parent like Edward St Paul. She is initiated into preparing the exact proportions of whisky and milk with ice – which he likes to drink with slices of raw potato and celery covered in salt. She goes to the shop for him each day to buy the newspaper that has the horse-racing form on the back pages and which he studies assiduously. There is always a race on somewhere. After hours of intense scrutiny, Eric shuffles into the den to ring the SP bookmaker and place his bets. But Agnes mourns the loss of the den as her private space. She suggests they put the second telephone handset in her parents' bedroom, but her father is a light sleeper and, once he has nodded off, hates to be woken.

Christmas comes and goes without the relief of a Southerly buster. Agnes retains no memory of it being celebrated. Now Mack's threat to kill them has subsided, they can relax and open the doors and windows to let the fresh air in. At the front of the house, where Eric alternates between lying in bed and talking on the phone in the den, Agnes can hear what is happening on the street outside: the Chinese students jabber in Mandarin as they take photos of each other in front of the pine trees, and Don, the postman, calls to her to come and collect the mail from the front fence because the cuckoo letter box is already stuffed full.

As she carries the post to her father, she can hear the postman telling the elderly twin sisters from across the lane how he has just seen *From Here to Eternity* at the pictures:

Everyone's talking about Burt Lancaster and Deborah Kerr on the seashore. Kissing with the waves breaking over them. It was so bloody hot in the cinema, I felt like jumping into the surf with them!

He is laughing and the two ladies both titter at him coquettishly. Zelda, the slightly taller one, giggles:

We haven't been to the pictures for years. We might wander down and see the film to cool off. Or heat up, as the waves take us!

Agnes presumes her father has overheard the entertaining conversation and mentions it to him. But he looks at her oddly, clearly unaware of what she is talking about. He never greets the neighbours. She doubts he even knows they exist. Nor does he share his interest in horse racing with his wife. It is his secret world. Agnes presumes he discusses the races with his mates at the pub. She never knows if his horse wins, as he shows neither excitement nor disappointment while listening to a race unfold. He continues to look at her strangely, but she ignores it. She tells him how Mr St Paul reads plays with his girls and they all take different parts. She suggests she and the boys could do the same with him. He nods his head, but she can tell by his blank watery eyes that he is somewhere else.

But what brings Eric Keen, and the whole country, to life is the final of the Davis Cup between Australia and America in the last week of December 1953. Luckily, the weather cools down south in time for the start. Agnes and her father listen to the coverage from Melbourne on the radio in the front bedroom. She is glued to a spot on the faded carpet and can rest her head against the wooden frame of her father's bed. She is elated. She can hardly move for excitement – intent on listening to the radio commentator's every word. From the moment the America team arrive in Australia, the nation's excitement is palpable. The newspaper reports that 17,000 people have purchased tickets to watch the first singles match.

The Americans win the toss to serve first. Lew Hoad hits good strokes: a volley, a forehand passing shot and then he generally mixes the returns. He is dominating play. He can hardly put a foot wrong. There is an early break of serve.

Good on you Lew! The boy is smashing the most sensational serves of his life!

The commentator is roaring, breathless with the thrill. Then suddenly it's over – game, set and match. Hoad wins in straight sets in just under an hour.

During the match, Agnes's father keeps asking her to come and sit beside him on the bed, but she refuses as it's too hot and she is too enthralled in the match.

Rosewell's singles match in the afternoon is disappointing. He appears disorientated and, at times, can hardly hit the ball over the net. Agnes feels sorry for him. He is missing easy shots and hitting others wide of the line and high over the baseline. Agnes worries that he might be jinxed just because she is listening to the commentary, so she leaves the room hoping that free of her presence, he will make a comeback. When she returns a minute or two later, she hears that her absence has made no difference. Rosewall never gets back into the match. The American player wins in straight sets.

The selectors decide to replace Rosewall and pair Hoad with another player for the doubles the following day. Eric and Agnes join the commentator in considering it a mistake, as Hoad and Rosewall have been winning doubles tournaments together since they were twelve years old. Hoad and his new partner lose the doubles, as predicted. All expectation is on the final day's play when the pair swap singles opponents and must win their games for Australia to take the Cup. The commentator enthuses:

The Hoad match is a titanic struggle. The standard of play is high.

Eric and Agnes are beside themselves:

Come on, Hoad! You can do it! That's the boy!

Eric is shouting at the radio and grinning at Agnes, his voice going up an octave with every new gulp of whisky and milk. Then, suddenly, he lets out a plaintive cry and grabs his chest as if he is having a mock heart attack. His rare high spirits infect Agnes. They are both there on the tennis court with the players – living every shot:

Come and sit beside me.

He has asked her again to join him on the bed. When Agnes shakes her head, he pleads:

Don't you like being next to your old dad?

He is already slurring his words and sweating – the bruised eyes and face further puffed with alcohol. She slides up onto the bed beside him. Her awkwardness is soon eclipsed by the triumphs of Rosewall's four-set win. It's a rapturous conclusion. Australia has *won* the Davis Cup and Agnes basks in the pride of belonging to the winning nation. She lingers on the bed, listening to the discussions between trainers and commentators, savouring the glory.

As she waits for her father to dismiss her, she feels his rough hand slide up under her dress. She is stunned when he caresses the soft skin inside her thigh. Then he pokes a finger into the crack under her panties. She can't believe it. She freezes. The finger goes on moving up in there. She surreptitiously slides off the bed. Her father is looking the other way, like his hand and head are disconnected. The ceiling crashes down, the walls of the room crush in on her.

When she leaves the room, she can see her father's reflection in the dressing table mirror, his head lolling back on the pillow, his eyes shut as if he is asleep.

10

ROSEVILLE BATHS

gnes develops the habit of going to Roseville Baths on the bus on her own. A rectangle of submerged wooden planks cordons off a section of Middle Harbour to protect swimmers from the great whites, bronze whalers, bull and tiger sharks that roam the waters. The entrance is through a turnstile with a sloping roof. It is a miniature replica of the roof on the bandstand, on top of the building below. A steep wooden stair leads from the entrance on Babbage Road to the changing room facilities under the bandstand, near the water's edge.

The pool is submerged in a national park surrounded by native bushland. Tall red gums, shaped like prehistoric creatures, cover the hill above where Agnes gets off the bus at the last stop on Babbage Road. A mixture of banksias, wattles and scribbly gums – so-called because of the pattern left by burrowing insects – grow in pockets along the shoreline. This display is interspersed with low-lying vegetation that shades striking rock formations covered in rich green moss. Roseville Bridge, which links the peninsula with the rest of Sydney, is the only man-made structure in sight.

Agnes likes to get there early in the morning so she can gaze over the water from the timber platform that circles the perimeter of the pool. She has figured the path northwards would join the national park area at the end of Lennox Street. Magpies, parrots, honeyeaters and wrens swoop by her. They may well have perched on the self-same trees she used to climb near their old house. Early sunbeams break through the mist from across the water at French's Forest.

The smell of salt in the air and the chatter of feeding birds make her feel close to God – through his creation. She begs Him to change all that is ugly and unhappy at home. Squinting through the blinding glare, she marvels at the illusion of thousands of shimmering, white-feathered creatures flapping their golden wings as they skid over stars and under diamonds. She could just as well be back on the St Pauls' family balcony on that marvellous birthday night of the beef bourguignon.

Why did someone who loves life want to die? She can't imagine the St Paul family house without Jacqueline and the girls. Why did the father put the girls into boarding school? Could it be the new influence of the 'sensible woman'? Stepmothers in fairy tales are notoriously cruel to children not their own.

Each day, Agnes understands less. She can still feel the touch of Jacqueline's hand on hers when she gave her *The Diary of Anne Frank* and deeply regrets not showing her how much she cared about her, instead of frantically hiding the affection between them from her mother. She remembers the gardenia-scented perfume on Jacqueline's bare neck when, once, she bent down to help her tie her shoelaces. Jacqueline dances in the sunlight on the sea and lives on in everything that is gentle and refined.

It is the school holidays and, as the morning progresses, the pool gradually fills with shrieking kids who, clinging to the railing, tumble down the steep stairs. They abandon their bags on the grass at ground level and dash into the water – dive-bombing, running, jumping, and doing mad, twisting gyrations. Some older kids, with no money, sneak down the steep rock face under the wooden slats behind the stairs, get a toe hold in the cracks and climb over the wire fence. Free entrance being small compensation for the perilous efforts to avoid paying, nobody seems to mind.

Agnes can't remember how she learned to swim. She had taught herself to dog paddle in the snag-infested creek at the farm, where the muddy water was a minefield of unseen danger. And kids at the pool show her stuff which she copies. Today, she settles on swimming breaststroke because she can't master the breathing that goes with the crawl.

Having watched a middle-aged bald man – whose head sits on a long neck between startlingly wide shoulders – give a group of boys a diving lesson, she develops a sudden fierce desire to learn to dive. The instructor has a whistle around his neck and wears a pair of lime-green sunglasses. She has a premonition about him. Then he speaks:

Okay you lot! Rule Number One! Never, never, *never* dive into shallow water! I know a kid who broke his neck doing just that. I'm not here to scare you, but to underline the importance of calculating the depth of the water before you dive. Don't take *anything* for granted. Always – and I mean *always* – check for yourself that the water's deep enough. I'm not nurturing sheep. I want you to think for yourselves and make your own decisions. All clear so far?

He concludes his orders, searching each boy's face for a reaction. His deep voice sounds as if it's coming up from his toes. The boys nod in unison. A couple of them murmur:

Yes, Mr Lawson.

Okay! Now! On with the show! What is the most unnatural thing in the whole world?

The boys are looking at each other and shrugging their shoulders:

I'll *tell* you what's unnatural! It's completely unnatural to do *anything* headfirst. We don't dive out of bed, or onto the school bus, or into the classroom or onto the football field, *do* we? The body moves feet first in most of what we do – *except* diving into water! So, my young friends, we're going to train our bodies to do what goes against the grain. Chins in, hands together, like you're saying a prayer. Arms in the air, lean forward, legs slightly apart, knees bent and toes over the edge.

Mr Lawson assumes the diving position so they can all copy him. But he hasn't finished:

Important point! Imagine your trajectory before you hit the water! Understood?!

He goes down the line checking the position of each boy before giving each a gentle push into the water from behind.

A dizzying assembly line follows. Each boy dives when Mr Lawson blows the whistle, swims back, pulls himself out of the water and re-joins the line. Agnes observes that three boys, although ungainly, all get the idea quickly, but a curly-headed, plump boy balks at the last minute and ends up doing one massive bellyflop after another, until his grazed stomach stings so much he obviously can't go on. She watches the boy, who is called 'Dan', slump down with his feet dangling over the edge of the platform. He looks very sorry for himself:

Okay, kiddo! You get the prize for the biggest splash, but don't give up, we're going to get there together!

Mr Lawson encourages 'Dan', wrapping a red fluffy towel tightly around his shaking shoulders and ruffling his hair. Then he reaches into his shorts pocket and hands him a bottle of pink liquid:

Rub this lotion on your tummy, lad. It'll take the bite out of the sting.

Another casualty of the lesson that Agnes observes is a thin, scraggy blonde-haired boy who masters the dive reasonably well, but with a weird jerky style. He ends up with red-rimmed eyes. Mr Lawson soaks cotton wool in water from the tap and gently bathes them. An endless supply of medications and lotions seem to spill from the pockets of Mr Lawson's shorts. Then, the lesson over, eyedrops administered to those who request them, he leaves the pool with one arm around 'Dan' and the other around the blonde boy's shoulders. It's impossible not to be struck by his kindness.

That night, in bed, Agnes goes over the diving instructions in her head. She is almost the first one at the pool the following day, intent on putting the borrowed tuition into action. Like the fat boy yesterday, she loses her nerve, hesitates at the last minute, and goes splat on her face from the poolside. Despite the protection of her Speedo top, her chest stings like hell. Gradually though, as her body relaxes, she succeeds in dominating the jangling nerves that habitually strangle her whenever she tries to learn anything new. She improves. Then, resolved to test herself, she climbs the steps to the diving board. From the top, the water below looks like the distance between the deck and the level of the sea on an aircraft carrier in the war pictures she loves so much. She almost loses her nerve, but she can't possibly go back now. No way of chickening out – not with a bunch of kids already lining up behind her. Taking the chance pays off. Cutting into the water headfirst feels so sensational that she's instantly back in the queue to prove she's not a 'one-dive wonder'.

She copies the little jump the boy in front of her executes and, after the second or third time, absorbs the practical use of invoking the spring in the board that gives those extra few seconds to tighten the stomach and point the toes before moving off. She also adopts the practice of swinging her arms up with the jump, which adds more lift-off.

From the steps, on his way down to the pool, Mr Lawson watches her complete one of her best dives. Agnes desperately hopes that they will connect one day. She likes him so much:

That dive you did was a bobby dazzler!

Mr Lawson *was* watching and is tapping her on the shoulder. He carries on:

My only comment is push further out from the diving board like you're flying against gravity *before* letting the descent take hold. But, well done, girl! You look like a natural!

Agnes melts when he pats her on the head. He smiles at her:

By the way – what's your name?

Agnes Keen.

Well, Agnes, I'm John Lawson.

I know. I saw you give a lesson here yesterday.

She wants to tell him how he has inspired her but thinks she might get lost in the telling and sound stupid. He scratches his bristly chin:

Well now, Agnes. If you can repeat what I just saw, I think you can learn all sorts of tricks.

They are standing at the side of the pool under the diving board. To make his impression concrete, Agnes is overcome with an urge to run up the mounting steps and do it again:

Can I do another dive for you, Mr Lawson?

Sure, go right ahead. I'm watching.

Her knees start to shake as she mounts the board. No… no… don't mess it up, she cautions herself. The horror of the accident at the hunt comes back. With each step she climbs she is assaulted by the almighty fall, the cold terror of mud, tangled stirrups, sullied pink coat, spattered riding boots, and the agony of humiliation that followed. She always feels jinxed when seeking adult approval. She closes her eyes at the top of the board to try and calm down and, when she opens them, is assailed by hundreds of colliding multicoloured dots that swim across her vision.

Take your time, don't rush it!

A slightly authoritarian tone in Mr Lawson's voice further unnerves her. He sounds a bit accusatory but, worse, she senses he may be feeling sorry for her.

Agnes is in the water, knowing the distractions have made her bungle her effort. She has hit the surface in a loose-leg splash. She is so disappointed that she feels like drowning herself. She pictures Mr Lawson walking off in disgust. Struggling with a lump in her throat, she decides to run to the changing room and catch the next bus home. How embarrassing, after all the false bravado! She wants to slither away from the baths and never come back.

She's already dripping her way in the direction of the changing rooms with her head down, when she feels another tap on the shoulder:

Agnes? Where are you off to? You're not abandoning ship after one go, are you?!

She is so amazed and delighted that she runs back up the stairs to the diving board. The kids in line smell her urgency. She moves like a car with a blaring siren through traffic, and they step aside to let her pass. Running along the board with a new sense of freedom, she sets the bounce with one foot and surges forward. Nothing else exists but this dive. When she surfaces, she hears clapping. She looks up from the water and sees Mr Lawson's heartbreaking grin. He is waiting for her when she climbs from the pool:

Try and keep your chin in.

Full of renewed vigour, she giggles at him:

I know, I know, I try, but it feels awkward – like I'm imitating a turkey.

Well, Agnes, you don't look like a turkey to me. Let's have another crack at it. Lengthen the body, grow arms and legs. Let's see what you're made of.

He stays and gives her loads of helpful pointers for at least twenty minutes, as if he has all the time in the world. His enthusiasm is contagious. Diving fever grips the pool. Now all the kids want to learn. She knows he teaches for money but doesn't know how that works. She chooses to see his presence there that day as divine intervention – as she does anything good that happens to her.

It seems that God has not only sent Mr Lawson to the swimming pool but installed him a short walk from Agnes's house. They're neighbours. A left turn at the bottom of Edmond Street and there he is in Nicholson Street in a big two-storey square brick house – on the corner with Havilah Street overlooking Beauchamp Park. She has walked past his place hundreds of times on the alternative route to school. She remembers the house because all the windows are always open and the garden full of the sound of children. He and Mrs Lawson have five kids – three of their own and two adopted. She discovers that not only does Mr Lawson live nearby but owns a sports shop in Victoria Street. He has even swum freestyle for Australia in his youth.

With school about to start, Agnes regrets only getting to know Mr Lawson halfway through the summer holidays. Before leaving the pool on their last day, she goes over to thank him. It comes out sounding a bit stilted, like anything she rehearses too much, but he puts her out of her misery:

Delighted to hear we're neighbours, Agnes. I'll tell you what. Now school's about to start and I've got to work in the shop, we'll be coming here early morning to swim. There's a place in the van if you'd like to join in. You're ready to learn some advanced dives. We could start with a jack-knife, if you like that idea?

Learning to do a jack-knife! Who would believe it! But, on the appointed morning, Agnes is overcome with doubt. It's been a week since she saw Mr Lawson so he may have forgotten. Children, business, teaching – he's got a lot on his plate. Maybe he didn't mean it. Just saying it to be nice. As nothing happens in her house without a good deal of shouting, his casual manner had felt insubstantial to her. He had said the van was due to set off at 6am. The more doubts that take hold, the more Agnes dallies but, to her amazement, when she walks down Edmond Street half-heartedly, she sees they're all in the van – waiting for her:

Oh, Mr Lawson I'm so sorry! I didn't know if you really meant it!

What do you take me for, girl! Of course, I meant it! Now hop in – and if you're not on time tomorrow we'll go without you!

The following day she was there by the kerbside before they all tumbled out of the house. The eldest boy, Matt, was fifteen. He was a very good swimmer, already entering competitions. There were twin girls about Agnes's age called Sadie and Rose and two boys – John and Alan – twelve and thirteen, who the Lawsons had fostered before adopting them into the family. Agnes thinks how good it would be to live with them all.

Mr Lawson teaches Agnes to dive from a run along the diving board making a one-legged jump to gain even more height. The van goes every morning except Sunday. They can stay later each Saturday morning as Mr Lawson has a man helping him out in the sports shop. The best time to learn to dive is between the early morning swimmers leaving and the weekend families arriving. Agnes stays behind to practise and is thrilled, one Saturday morning, to show Mr Lawson how she has improved the jack-knife. Emerging from the water, he pats her on the head, exclaiming:

You're a star!

For days afterwards, Agnes is walking on air. The desire to show her father what she can do in the pool grows inside her. She can expunge, once and for all, the bad impression from the hunt. Gratifyingly, Eric does seem quite enthusiastic at the prospect of a regular swim. He's an early riser, so says he can easily adapt to a quick morning trip to the pool before he leaves for the cotton factory. It'll help him get back in shape, now he's up and about after the Mack event.

The early summer mornings become full of joy and promise. Agnes is happy to unite the family and proud to show Mr Lawson she belongs to one. Entrance to the baths is free until the talkative blonde lady arrives at 9am to take the money. She is proud, too, to discover that her father is a good swimmer, and enjoys introducing him to Mr Lawson, who winks at her encouragingly:

Show your dad what you can do on the diving boards, Agnes.

Although she is nervous, she dives, and feels she has dived well.

Her father's reaction – and what happens next – fragments. She knows she is drying herself on the grass away from the others, after a shower at the poolside. Her father's face is blocked out by a late shaft of sunlight. She doesn't need to see him to recognise that familiar rough hand moving between her thighs and the same finger, under her Speedo, pushing up inside her and starting to twirl around. She can't remember exactly but supposes he must have pulled his hand away. She knows he says nothing. She knows he walks off.

Her stomach is turning over. Her mind reels in confusion. What does it mean? The sky darkens. Her skin crawls. In the car on the way home he is acting as if nothing has happened. He even whistles as he drives.

The next morning, she says she has a headache, so her father and brothers go swimming without her. She never goes back to the baths – or dives – again.

Agnes has always been haunted by her father's act at the pool. It did – and didn't – happen. Was – and wasn't – his hand. She reasons that, as he is a good man and all fathers are good, there must be something bad in her that has provoked it. It is – and isn't – a concrete fact. And what does it mean anyway? Thoughts splinter apart. She can't unite the Davis Cup bed incident with the incident at the baths. She can't categorise them as similar as she can't grasp either. Any effort at recall leaves her crippled with doubt.

Her father returns to ignoring her. She hears her mother tell Aunt Marnie:

Agnes sees things that aren't there all the time.

Is this a trick to undermine her credibility? But something *has* happened because, in the pit of her stomach, she feels bad and dirty in a way she never did before. Why didn't God protect her? Is it because she's not worthy?

One day she bumps into Mr Lawson in Victoria Avenue. She hardly recognises him as he is dressed in a suit. The shirt and tie swallow his neck:

Agnes! Good to see you!

He keeps repeating her name and smiling at her warmly, while patting her on the head.

Why are you dressed like that, Mr Lawson?

He replies with a laugh:

I'm in a suit, Agnes, because I've been to see the bank manager. You should never go to the bank looking as if you need money.

Agnes's insides churn as she anticipates his next question, but he doesn't chastise her for not coming back to the pool. She wonders if he knows something. Mr Lawson says:

I'm delighted to go on teaching you, you know. There's always a place in the van for you. And, by the way, you're welcome at the Lawson madhouse any time. Or come by the shop if you want.

He is squeezing her shoulder in a gesture of reassurance. Agnes keeps thanking him. She knows she is grinning awkwardly. But the whole diving adventure is tainted. She wants to tell Mr Lawson what happened to her. She has never wanted to tell something so badly to anybody but knows she can never breathe a word of it. She is ashamed for somehow provoking the whole thing. She even blames the Roseville Baths. She goes on seeing herself in the wet green Speedo against a black sky. Now, when she wakes early out of habit, she goes to 7am Mass and takes communion at the parish church in Archer Street.

Once her father is fully recovered and back to work, the house returns to the past. Madge abandons her domestic frenzy and returns to cooking her pearls in bed. Agnes brings her mother her tea before she leaves for school. Back home after school means more tea in bed, then back down Archer Street with a note, money, and string bag to do the shopping. Madge orders the heavy items by phone for delivery. Agnes then returns to do the ironing. The drama of clock-watching, dirty-plate hovering and agitated pillow talk returns.

Agnes never knows whether her brothers are aware of her father's continual angst, as she never confides in them. She presumes that, like her, they try not to listen and keep their distance. However, it amuses her brother Bert to challenge the Mad Woman – as he calls his mother. Avoiding the whole Lennox Street tragedy somehow gifts him with the power that is denied Agnes and Jim to defend themselves. Thus, the beatings Agnes endures bypass Bert and land on six-year-old Jim.

Agnes only knows that something terrible must have happened at home to make Jim steal £10 from Madge's purse and run away. She does not know what it is. He had caught a train to Hornsby but, when he tried to cash the £10 note in a shop, the attendant rang the police. Agnes had not been at home when two social workers brought him back.

One day, Jim will be rushed in an ambulance to the children's hospital at Randwick. He will be bleeding to death. His spleen will have stopped producing platelets – an essential ingredient for blood clotting. Blood transfusions will eventually save his life, but Jim will remain seriously ill in hospital for several months. His mother, who likely caused this severe damage, will relate events outside the house and bathe in sympathetic responses from family and neighbours. However, inside the house, the subject will be forever taboo. Which is why, when neighbours ask Agnes for updates, she will have none to give.

In the days that follow Jim's admittance to hospital the phone will constantly ring, and the new post box will be crammed with Get Well cards – none of which will reach Jim as his parents don't visit him. When Agnes reveals a plan to go by train to Town Hall Station and, from there, to catch a bus to Randwick to see her little brother, Madge will clip her across the ear with such force that she will never dare to broach the subject again.

The powers-that-be at Rosemont will enrol both of Agnes's brothers in boarding school, and Jim will be liberated from further beatings when the doctors at the hospital send a warning that, under no circumstances, is he to be hit – either at home or at school. Nor should he be allowed to play sport for the foreseeable future. Completely recovered a year or two later, Jim will achieve victory over circumstances by managing to excel in the rough and tumble as a rugby player in the school team.

Rosemont will decide to sacrifice Agnes on the family altar. She is to keep her mother company when her father is away on business. The formal decree being: SHE IS TO REMAIN A DAY GIRL AT SCHOOL.

11
DAVID JONES

Nurtured by a few wise young nuns, Agnes has enjoyed three good years at Our Lady of Mercy Convent.

The sight of a beautiful woman gliding down the school path, wearing a lipstick-pink halter-neck dress, turns heads in the playground. Agnes realises, with pride, that it is her mother. Slim, imperiously erect, Madge looks bewitchingly glamorous. Agnes is playing basketball on the court at the far end of the school ground when Madge arrives, and she manages to score a goal – much to the delight of the team. Her mother has shown up just before half-time. Agnes hopes she will look over at the court and see how well she is playing. But, if Madge does glance across at the court, she never mentions it.

One of the girls in the team hands around a plate of orange segments. Madge raises a manicured hand in disdainful refusal – a gesture that displays her exquisitely painted pink fingernails. Agnes worries her mother might be rude to someone, as she has no sympathy for the least blemish or human oddity. And so, she stands in front of a girl in the team who has a face full of explosive pimples lest the unwholesome sight robs Agnes of a rare moment in the spotlight. Thankfully, although utterly indifferent to her surroundings, her mother appears to be on her best behaviour. In fact, she is leaving a dazzling trail of glitter in the impressionable minds of Agnes's schoolmates:

Is that really your mother? God – she's *gorgeous*!

Agnes keeps hearing it repeated around her:

God – she's gorgeous.

God – she's gorgeous.

God – she's gorgeous.

It makes Agnes feel guilty for ever hating her. She instantly forgives her mother for not coming to any school she has ever attended until now. Agnes is constantly searching for the least fragment of evidence to excuse both parents. She has single-handedly invented their great love – an all-consuming passion for each other – that justifies their neglect. This one-off appearance serves to intensify her mother's exoticism and makes it all the more memorable for never being repeated.

One of the young nuns rushes up to Madge. She is gushing with enthusiasm:

I never saw such a miracle, Mrs Keen! When she first arrived here, she was like a limp rag. Such a sad little face. Lips pressed together, eyes on the floor. The least angry word would bring tears to her eyes. She just stared out the window in a kind of a trance. I decided that discipline would be a further burden on a soul in pain, so I left her to come around of her own accord. So *wonderful* to see her blossom! She pays attention in class. She's one of our best basketball players, you know! She likes Botany and English, does lovely needlework, and recently got 100% in Religious Knowledge!

Such praise might have pleased Grandma but is of no interest whatsoever to Madge. She doesn't need an earnest nun bothering her with talk of improvement. Her children's unread school reports keep company with unpaid bills in the drawer that once housed the architect's plans. She hasn't visited the school for a progress report, but to tell the nuns she'll be taking Agnes out a day early for the Easter holidays. But Agnes will not be going to the dentist – as Madge has deliberately misinformed the nuns. Instead, she will be accompanying her mother to 'David Jones' department store where Madge hopes to bump into all the polo wives who are due in town for the Royal Show. For two weeks every Easter, town and country dwellers rub shoulders in a miniature walled city at Moore Park on the edge of the city. Agnes's attendance at 'David Jones' is intended to be a kind of backhanded rite of passage. She is to be presented as a well-educated daughter in a new frock.

Madge wakes Agnes the following morning. She is holding up a coat hanger which is draped with a sleeveless green cotton dress. It has a white lace collar, like a decorative nun's bib. A new pair of black patent leather strap-over court shoes, and a pair of short white socks with a frill on top, are displayed on the white chest of drawers with the ceramic roses. Agnes finds herself pulled and pushed into the dress and her hair is pinned into kiss curls around her face and sprayed with lacquer. At this last indignity, Agnes protests:

I'm *not* going looking like a kewpie doll!

Don't get me churned up with your likes and dislikes on an important day like this, Agnes!

Arguing is futile. Agnes decides her mother will soon forget about the curls, which she surreptitiously straightens with her fingers as they move along the street towards 'David Jones'.

The ground floor of the store is a shimmering wonderland. Agnes's head spins with the large silver baubles as they swirl in mesmerising circles from the ceiling. The cosmetic concession counters – Max Factor, Elizabeth Arden, Helena Rubenstein, Yardley – are attended by well-groomed, glamorous shop assistants radiating elegance from every skin pore. Enlarged photos of on-screen idols – Bridget Bardot, Elizabeth Taylor, Sophia Loren, Lauren Bacall – dominate each counter.

Dressed in a ravishing, well-cut, pleated yellow linen dress under a yellow and white striped linen jacket, Madge could easily take her place with the stars. Agnes observes her mother's inherent irritation evaporate as she drifts dreamily from counter to counter, fondling the latest skincare and make-up product, pausing to spray her wrists with a new fragrance. She sees the tightness around her mother's mouth soften and her heavy, dictatorial step become carefree and dainty. Agnes tags along behind her, not sure what to do. She's on tenterhooks like a maid waiting for instructions from a temperamental mistress. The buzz of the ground floor is soothed by the sound of a Chopin Polonaise being played on a grand piano by a lady dressed in black. The performer is raised on a dais in the centre of the floor.

Madge settles her preferred custom on the Elizabeth Arden counter, choosing three or four items for which she signs the account. Purchases completed, she then dashes for the lift – forgetting Agnes, who runs behind and just manages to squeeze in behind her mother before the door closes. A short, tubby lift driver, with hair growing out of his ears, announces the availability of goods on each floor in a sing-song voice, before opening the lift door:

Fourth Floor: Furniture, barbeques, venetian blinds, curtains, etcetera…
Fifth floor: Electric domestics, including washing machines, stoves, fridges, radios, and gramophones, etcetera…

He opens the doors to the sixth floor in silence. Agnes thinks he must have lost his voice.

Then she twigs that the sixth floor is so exclusive that any direct reference to barter would be offensive to the pedigree ladies who alight here. The sixth floor is no place for casual browsers. Only the initiates sink their high heels into these acres of plush red carpet.

Nose in the air, Madge strides into her favourite playground, with Agnes making a snail track in her wake, dragging the new patent leather shoes through the deep carpet pile. Compared to the ground-floor bustle, the hush on the sixth floor is ecclesiastical. It wouldn't have surprised Agnes to see a holy water font appear from behind one of the bedecked mannequins. No other space, apart from the sideline at polo matches, appears to tranquillise her mother so effectively.

Feeling rather like a stray cat, Agnes watches a few well-dressed women survey the latest imports from Paris, London and New York and marvels at how secure her mother seems amongst them. Madge would normally treat shop assistants with contempt, but here she bows to them as if they are sanctified beings dwelling in a heavenly cloud. One so anointed spots Madge and sails forward. Regulars luxuriate in hearing themselves addressed by name. In no time, all three ladies who swanned in from the lift are claimed in person:

How are you, Mrs Keen? It's been too long since we've seen you. I must say, you're looking radiant in that lovely yellow linen. I remember parcelling it up for you last year.

'Valerie' clasps the gloved hand Madge extends, holding her gaze in mascara-hooded emerald eyes as she draws her close and intones the words Madge has longed to hear:

Wait till you see what we have for you!

En route to the promised speciality, which awaits Madge in a wardrobe at the far end of the store, 'Valerie' pauses briefly to straighten a black jersey knit with a cowl collar back onto a wine-red satin coat hanger. As she turns to collect Madge, who is admiring a pink wool dress on a store mannequin, she catches sight of Agnes, who is hiding behind a fluted pedestal that supports a Grecian vase containing a bunch of long-stem red roses:

And who have we got here?

Madge, anticipating this eventuality, steps forward on cue:

This is my daughter, Agnes!

What lovely red hair! How are *you*, Agnes?

Very well, thanks.

I seem to remember your mother told me you play the piano.

Madge quickly chips in:

She could end up performing. Mrs Grierson says she shows great promise. The problem is, she has to practise at school as we don't have a piano in the house. As we're spoiled for space, I said to my husband, we *must* buy the girl a piano. Nothing lovelier than piano music in the home. But, for now, all plans are on hold as Eric is playing polo at the show and what with the horses currently stabled at the ground, I can't think of *anything* else.

Agnes is always dumbstruck by her mother's shameless outdoor personality. She wishes the floor would open and swallow her up. She manages to muster a limp smile for 'Valerie' as she winds her non-musical fingers awkwardly around the clasp of a cheap white plastic handbag. She is praying this torture will soon end. She has had a mere handful of piano lessons at the convent and knows nothing more than the position of Middle C and a few scales. What is more, her mother has never heard her sound a note – Madge's non-existent interest in music is further evidenced by not even noticing the Polonaise pervading the ground floor:

You'll be in seventh heaven, Mrs Keen, when you see what I've hidden away for you…

Valerie's velvet tone seems to have mesmerised the normally tyrannical woman like a magician's pendulum. The astute shop assistant moves on, gently guiding her captive towards the treasure. Superlatives flow in admiration of her client, who is soon parading in a Norman Parkinson fine pleated wool and silk dress in pale grey and pink tartan, with a short tailored matching jacket lined in pink satin.

The next purchase to be swaddled in tissue paper is a fine Charles Creed yellow and blue tweed pencil skirt with matching three-quarter jacket, pockets and collar trimmed with blue velvet. Valerie deftly prolongs the banked purchase of the two outfits by extending Madge's passion further. Agnes observes her besotted mother as Valerie trails an Emilio Pucci short crêpe evening dress in gold with a flowing skirt, long sleeves, and a crossover bodice along the spotlessly clean carpet. Valerie keeps repeating bewitchingly:

It's got your name *all* over it…

It truly is a perfect fit, and the colour a wonderful complement to Madge's raven hair and searing dark eyes. As Madge signs her name to the last docket without even glancing at the price, Agnes is already anticipating her father's fury when the extortionate bill arrives. Immune to the reality of cause and effect, Madge has no fear of the consequences of her actions.

Upon completing her final purchase, Madge's longed-for social cachet moment arrives, for there is Janie, the polo wife she adores: Mrs Janie Marble Flood, wife of the Captain of the Goulburn polo team, is floating out of the lift and heading towards her. Madge drops the carrier bags and flings her arms around her idol. The serene country beauty appears startled, rather as if she has just been hit by a truck. But she quickly regains her composure and beams a perfectly restrained white-teethed smile at Madge. Agnes watches as her mother gushes:

When did you get here?!

We drove down yesterday morning. We're staying at the Australia Hotel. Dan's at the showground helping stable the horses. I've just snuck off to get my hair done upstairs and I wanted to try something on that 'Grace' put away for me yesterday afternoon.

As the elegant woman speaks, she discreetly gesticulates to a tailored woman in black with a blonde beehive who looks up and nods from her island desk sanctuary in the middle of the room.

Agnes is in as much awe of Janie Marble Flood's appearance as her mother. The woman's smooth, lightly tanned complexion melts into a natural pink blush over high, rounded cheeks. A sprinkle of tiny dark freckles across a pert nose adds an impish touch to her classical beauty. She seems to be a woman who never has a hair out of place, for Agnes can attest to having seen the thick, naturally curly brown mane unruffled in all conditions. Whilst other women wrestled with scarves on the windy polo field sidelines, Mrs Janie Marble Flood's curls would remain unfazed. Agnes knows all too well that her husband, Mr Dan Marble Flood, is the fourth generation of the family to live in a stately country house, with its very own ballroom, and dating back to the original land grant.

Madge's adoration of Janie has the intensity of a schoolgirl crush. She is as possessive of her as she is of her husband, surreptitiously intercepting approaches to her by any outside intruder. She even takes exception to her sisters and sisters-in-law daring to stand near Janie at the polo. Such impertinences could provoke a spiteful pinch, or a shove in the ribs. Where this woman is concerned, Madge abases herself without encouragement. Her obsession extends to Janie's three children, upon whom she lavishes the breadth of attention of which her own offspring can only dream.

As a grown woman, years hence, Agnes will encounter Janie's daughter, Sarah, at the Bank of New South Wales in London, and will still be curious as to what evoked her mother's unabandoned affection for this person, when all she herself ever got was a clip across the ear.

Now Janie utters the words Agnes dreads hearing. Words that stab her with guilt for harbouring hateful thoughts:

Oh, Agnes, how lucky you are to have such a *wonderful* mother!

Struck dumb, Agnes can only nod. Janie continues:

You'll need strong arms to carry that bundle home. It looks like you've been enjoying yourselves!

Madge takes this as an invitation to embark upon a monologue, detailing each purchase, along with what she said to 'Valerie' and what 'Valerie' said to her. Agnes watches the underside of Janie's crocodile high heel poised for a quick getaway, but Madge cannot stop talking – her mouth gallops like a racehorse to a finishing line that never comes. Janie is beginning to look desperate, and Agnes can't stand it. Her mother never knows when to stop with people she puts on a pedestal. She lacks any awareness of others and, just like Uncle Ben, is utterly insensitive to a snub. She's even oblivious to the subtle exasperation exhibited by Janie that is now causing Agnes so much pain on her behalf.

Agnes courageously finds her voice:

'Mummy, Janie's short of time. You'll see her tonight.

After this unexpected intervention, her mother looks more bewildered than angry.

Janie flashes another toothpaste smile before dashing away. There are no repercussions for Agnes finding her voice. Since the Rosemont decree that Agnes was to be sacrificed to care for her mother, she has dutifully acted as prompter and interventionist lest Madge put the wrong foot in the wrong fiction. She knows people laugh at her mother behind her back but, although painfully shy, manages to defend her with a boldness she could never exert on her own behalf.

Back home, Madge transfers the tissue-paper-shrouded dresses onto satin hangers, hiding them at the back of the wardrobe. She orders Agnes to dispose of the telltale carrier bags in a bin in another street, as the mere sight of them has the potential to turn her husband into a raging bull. Eric never comments on what his wife wears, although he's clearly proud of her appearance. Agnes suspects he maintains an out-of-sight-out-of-mind attitude to what lies behind the wardrobe door. Tonight, under floodlights, he is to play in a high goal polo team at the showground – a pinnacle in his polo career – and is consequently in an above-average temperamental state when he dashes in the back door. He ignores Agnes, as usual, settling on the back step to clean his long riding boots until they shine like tinted glass. He showers in the tub, cleans his teeth, greases his fine hair, and puts on the standard white jodhpurs and club T-shirt under a tweed coat with a member's tag displayed in the lapel.

Although Madge is itching to show off her new clothes, she exercises restraint, aware the sight of an expensive new outfit could ruin the whole evening. Bathed, hair done, made up and perfumed, she wriggles into a coral pink wool suit.

Fully aware they don't want to take her along Agnes hears herself insisting she will be fine at home. She is trapped yet again in the horrible cycle of having her mother cling to her in her father's absence, and then resent her presence when he returns. Now she overhears a brief exchange that horrifies her:

Does she *have* to come?

Mother said we must take her with us.

And it seems Aunt Sill had rung up the day before to cancel Agnes's planned stay with Grandma over Easter. Another blow.

When Agnes falters outside the car, her mother gets annoyed:

For *Christ's* sake, Agnes, just *get* in and don't make us late! You're enough of a nuisance as it is! Your father's got a *lot* on his plate!

Feeling utterly wretched, Agnes sinks down into the back seat.

Eric drives fast, swerving around corners, shooting daggers at Agnes whenever their eyes meet in the rear-view mirror as if she is the source of his present frustration. When he turns off the engine in the showground car park, he jumps out of the driver's seat, gets his stuff out of the boot, and slams the lid. To her astonishment, he and her mother run off – like two robbers leaving the scene of a crime. It feels pre-planned. Agnes knows her father will be heading to the stables and that Madge will be joining Janie and the other idols in a small exclusive members' stand. But why did they just suddenly desert her, and without even saying anything? Do they expect her to wait in the car? She watches them emerge out of the dark distance and into the brightly lit street without looking back. In these moments she fervently hates them and wishes they would die. In numb despair, she clings to the door handle outside the car to steady herself.

The car park is filling up. Doors are slamming shut and voices are swirling around as people walk away from parked vehicles. Agnes is feeling cold. She didn't bring a coat. Her green jumper is thin and her legs under the tartan skirt are bare. She had expected to be with her mother in the Special Members stand, where she would be protected from the weather.

Her mouth is dry. She can't swallow. She is abandoned by prayer, too, as she can't seem to remember the words of the 'Our Father' or the 'Hail Mary' that she parrots at school every day. Sudden memory loss will, from this point, become a permanent disability in Agnes's life.

A bearded man with bulging eyes walks between the cars. He is shining a powerful torch on the ground as he picks up litter with a spike and puts it in a plastic bag. He is suddenly alongside Agnes and is forcing his cracked lips onto hers. The putrid smell of his foul breath is nauseating. She runs from the car park, dashing wildly towards the crowd on the brightly lit street, her eyes blurred with tears. She collides with another man who shouts at her. She is swept along like the ballerina in *The Red Shoes*, compelled to keep moving. She floats through display halls with intricate carpets of vegetables, woven tapestries of fruit and fabulous displays of plants, crafts, cakes, fabrics, and flowers. Men wearing official badges are standing around chatting. She snuggles up close to family groups, pretending she belongs to them, but panics when someone suddenly turns and stares. She can't bear anyone to know she's not wanted.

Chips of wood fly in the air and sweat rolls down the faces of muscular men in blue singlets as they split posts in a line in the woodchopper competition. At the back of her mind, Agnes wishes she could pause and enjoy the surroundings, but she needs to keep moving to maintain a cover.

The mounted police pass in formation on the road, followed by horses and riders, cows, Shetland ponies, goats, sheep, dogs, and pigs, graded in size, and led by attendants wearing long dustcoats. Purple, blue, and yellow ribbons are draped around the necks of the winning animals. She's aware, from previous visits to the show, that this is the Grand Parade exiting the main ground but, tonight, she sees it all in a blur, just as she does the buck jumping and bull dogging.

She's afraid to return to the car. Her parents will attend a drinks party in the exclusive stand after the match, but she doesn't know where it's located, let alone have the heart to chase after them. And so, she watches the polo match alone in a crowded stand, hardly seeing a thing.

Exiting the stand, she is pushed along in a thick crowd, like one of a herd of sheep, and finds herself in the middle of the dazzling lights and loud music of the entertainment area. Shrieks, cries, screams, and laughter saturate the cold air as pleasure seekers jostle each other at the wheels of dodgem cars. People are spinning in the big dipper or riding up and down on the horses and chariots of the carousel. She looks on from the street, as she has no money to buy a ticket for a ride, or a sideshow. Promoters fight to lure customers to see a woman cut in two or to gaze at acrobatic midgets. There are freaks with two heads and contortionists who lick their own backs. Hysterical laughter leaks out of the entrance to the ghost train. She passes shooting galleries, dart throwers and contestants rolling balls into the rotating mouths of brightly painted clowns.

A motley line of Aboriginal boxers, dressed in white singlets and shabby satin shorts beneath worn silk dressing gowns, bounce up and down in thin lace-up boots. They are punching right and left hooks mindlessly into the air. A fat-bellied man with a pork-pie hat and vacant stare bangs a huge drum that sounds like the accompaniment to an execution, while a short tubby fellow in a check suit, with a friendly weather-beaten face, shouts in a monotonous voice into a blurred microphone:

Roll up, roll up, roll up! Come on, gentlemen! On with the gloves to challenge our boys! Roll up, roll up, roll up! On with the gloves to try your luck!

Agnes is mesmerised by these sad boxers on the elevated stand. It is an intensely dark night, with no moon and, standing still now, she realises she is freezing cold.

A rumble of thunder explodes in the sky, followed by huge spidery arms of lightening extending out like the roots of great trees. People gasp and scream as a lightning bolt hits a huge wooden post near the boxing troop. The boxers leap up and people stampede for cover. The strike has cut a line in the post, which explodes into sparks like a firecracker. Numb with horror, Agnes feels as if she is living the Lennox Street electrocution all over again.

As if programmed to put out the fire, the heavens open and rain pours down. The remaining intact floodlights illuminate knife-like raindrops and

Agnes runs towards a road that looks familiar. Tripping up in her haste, she lands, spreadeagled, on the ground.

Strong hands lift her up by the waist and she finds herself looking into the concerned face of a policeman. She gasps:

I'm *so* cold…

He carries her gently, wrapped in an army blanket, to a tent full of people where she gulps down a hot cup of tea with lots of sugar. As she dozes under a pile of blankets on a camp bed, feeling comfortably warm for the first time that night, she hears the police report that an ambulance has taken a few injured people from the lightning strike to hospital. It seems there were no fatalities.

She is fully woken by another voice; the voice she does – and does not – want to hear:

Darling! What on *earth* are you doing? Your father and I have been *frantic*… looking *all* over the ground for you! *Thank* you, Officer! We've been worried *sick*! I'm *so* glad you found her!

Mercifully, the next night of the show, her parents let her stay at home. Alone, she seeks comfort in her mother's wardrobe, curling up in the foetal position under the illicit clothes. She imbibes the perfume in the fabric as she had once done in Grandma's wardrobe at Rosemont. The inside of her mother's wardrobe is a constant wonder. It could easily be a display cabinet in an expensive women's boutique: satin underwear and nylon stockings in cloth envelopes, woollen jumpers kept like new in plastic bags, drawers with jewellery in boxes wrapped in cotton wool, creams and perfumes with unopened reserves – worthy of a Hollywood star. Agnes knows the clothes in her mother's wardrobe so well that, if they had been a subject on the school syllabus, she would get a hundred per cent – to match her score in Religious Knowledge.

The bill from 'David Jones' arrives in the first mail after Easter. The familiar houndstooth check logo on the envelope inevitably incites tension between husband and wife. Along with other bills addressed to Eric, the longer it sits on the dining table, the more this tension grows.

On the day Eric Keen summons up the courage to rip the envelope open, he is already trembling. The amounts stated on the account inside send him into a predictable frenzy:

I can't believe it! How could you do this! We can't afford it! Where the *hell* am I going to find the money? Just when I'm getting ahead, you throw me back into debt! Always the same story! It's *unendurable*!

He smashes his fist into the top of the walnut table:

Can't I *ever* get *through* to you?!

Madge's continued silence incites him to further fury:

Well?! *Say* something woman! You promised your mother you'd exercise restraint, but you bloody well *double* the spending! I'm ruined and you don't give a *damn*!

Despite the cold evening air, sweat is pouring down his red face. He kicks a chair, causing the leg – glued back after the fight with Mack – to permanently join the junk under the house. Agnes knows her father was defeated before he even began. She searches her mother's face for some relief – an apology, contrition, empathy. But there is nothing of the kind available there. What Agnes does see, however, is the angelic look of a ham actress, masking a bare wisp of a triumphant smirk.

Eric Keen tears the account statement to pieces like a petulant child, throws them in the air, grabs the car keys on the table and creates a fresh snowstorm of plaster as he smashes the back door behind him. A screech of tyres indicates that he is off to find solace at the pub. But his daughter knows that he doesn't need a 'David Jones' bill as an excuse to indulge in a drinking binge. Any pub is more of a home to him than the ugly rooming house his fractured family rattle around in.

Agnes will feel sorry for her father for the rest of the day. She will already be in bed when he staggers up the hall to a restless sleep. He will leave the house early the next morning, seemingly ashamed of losing his temper the day before. She knows that Eric Keen is a proud man. And it is clear Rosemont contributes to his dilemma. His wife's unruly spending forces mother and son-in-law into conspiratorial huddles, like the parents of a delinquent child. Agnes has watched him flirt with all the Rosemont women and Grandma is no exception. It is, she deduces, almost as if he could be married to Grandma, rather than to her vexatious daughter.

12

THE DRESSMAKER

The matronly local woman in garish florals who sews.

This is how Agnes hears her mother refer to their new dressmaker during one of the marathon character assassinations by phone with Aunt Marnie. The three children are being fitted for new clothes to wear to the wedding of the oldest of the three young aunts – the fabulous Charlotte. Charlotte – the Rosemont daughter who has done everything right: school head girl, university degree, engagement to a wealthy country grazier, planned European honeymoon. It will be the only family wedding Agnes ever attends and, today, she can hardly contain her excitement.

Rosemont's last-minute decision to include the Keen children as guests has caused a rush to find a dressmaker and Mrs Ryder is the only one in the area prepared to accept the tight deadline. Two further fittings follow the initial measurement day and then, miraculously, the wedding outfits are ready to go. Mrs Ryder never makes clothes for Madge. There is no way Agnes's mother can be weaned off the designer labels on the exclusive sixth floor of 'David Jones'. Agnes overhears her mother tell Marnie:

I'd never contemplate having cloth draped around my body by the likes of a woman who grew up in an English bed and breakfast next to a common funfair in Blackpool.

It amazes Agnes how someone so ignorant of the world finds ammunition to feed her snobbery in a chance remark about a town, and a country, which she has never seen.

From the front, the Ryders' wine-red brick bungalow looks uninhabited. On entering the garden, the first sight is a set of closed dark curtains behind insect-spattered glass porch doors. These double doors have been closed long enough for spiders to weave webs around the joins in the middle, and for mushrooms to sprout on a pile of uncleared damp leaves on the porch floor. The stained window on the other side of the frontage blocks out the world with identical closed curtains. Any traffic in and out follows a well-trodden path around the right-hand corner of the building and up a set of wooden steps which lead to the dressmaker's workroom.

You would have thought that the Keen family lived in a mansion, the way Madge scorns the Ryder house. Starting with the broken entrance gate held permanently open by the tentacles of a morning glory vine, she spills out her bile:

Be careful! Stay away from the gate! You children will get a good clip across the ear if you catch your school uniforms on those spikes! Why doesn't Mr Ryder do something about that gate? I'll tell you why – because he's in *bed* all day! They're a dirty bunch, these Poms! *Never* shower! They leave their squalid tenements in England to sail here on luxury liners for ten pounds and expect to have it all laid on – gates and all! They live like *pigs*!

This is crisp talk coming from someone who has never fixed anything in her life and spends a good part of the day comatose in bed. The wooden gate to Madge's own side entrance had long ago disintegrated into a pile of broken bits that the council removed from the pavement without either she or Eric even noticing. The proverb 'people in glass houses shouldn't throw stones' obviously didn't feature high on the Rosemont list.

The dirt path through the Ryders' overgrown front garden is flanked on the roadside by a thick wall of woody hedge decked with red berries. A hidden hole at the far end of this hedge leads to a cavernous interior space. On the other side of the path, a tangle of vigorous brown weeds stands to attention like an army, having killed off whatever used to be in the flower beds beside them. Remnants of dry bamboo supports testify to annuals which once grew in an orderly line. For Agnes, the wild garden, the broken gate, and the dark hiding place in the thick berry hedge all add to the delicious mystery of the inhabitants, who are made the more intriguing for being both foreign *and* non-Catholics. It is when seated on the earth floor and hidden from view in the front hedge that Agnes, and Mrs Ryder's daughter, Rita, will hug each other and vow eternal friendship. The mingling of the blood on their arms will signify nothing can ever part them. Through Rita, Agnes will fall in love with the ballet and for the next few years the two girls will remain inseparable. Agnes will also develop an all-consuming interest in Mrs Ryder's skill as a dressmaker – from the first cut of the material to the production of the final article.

When Agnes first surveyed the intriguing interior of the Ryder premises, where rows of completed garments hung on a moveable metal rail, ready for collection, she had recalled how Dora Chadwick created ceramics and painted pictures and it had occurred to her that women could make their own living instead of waiting for the uncertain arrival of an inebriated husband.

Like the form within the clay, potential resided in every roll of cloth. Her fascination with Mrs Ryder's dressmaking creations is at odds, however, with the indifference of their creator, who only receives payment on completion and always seems to be short of money. This is the reason that the dressmaker accepts any imposed deadlines as, apart from supporting herself, her child, and an elusive husband, she must find the money for twice-weekly ballet classes in preparation for Rita to become a prima ballerina.

In contrast to the moribund face of the Ryder house that frowns at the street, the rear extension shouts welcome from every timber plank. Overlooking a wide strip of land, and supported on a brick foundation, it runs the full length of the house. From the first day Agnes entered Mrs Ryder's workroom, a place flooded in light from a line of glass louvre windows, the atmosphere drenched in the perfume of the honeysuckle flowers from the fence opposite, she had sensed the start of something new. This long narrow space of endless creativity opened into a new back extension with an open-plan kitchen and living area from whence glass doors led to a timber deck the width of the house.

Agnes has also spotted that the original side door on the inside of the workroom was screened off with a white sheet which was covered in magazine cuttings, tailor's patterns, and bits of sample material. She suspected the door was locked. In this new world of female industry an unspoken prohibition existed against mentioning Mr Ryder, the mysterious husband, who, Agnes comes to discover, inhabits the front of the house, and works at night. Thus, the noise of falling objects, or shuffling furniture behind the mysterious curtain during fitting visits, will pass without comment. So much so that those present end up wondering if they have imagined it.

Today, the final day of the fittings, 'Gypsy' – Mrs Ryder's torpedo-shaped black mongrel – is lying, as usual, on a mat beneath one of the two tailor's mannequins.

There is an apple-green dress with a Chinese collar fitted on one mannequin. Draped over the other, and reminiscent of Hawaii, is a white cotton print dress resplendent with framed poinsettia flowers, coconuts, and seashells on a sandy beach.

Sartorially speaking, Mrs Ryder does always look somewhat dishevelled to Agnes. Springy strands of fair hair escape the victory roll at the back of her head – a war-years style she still clings to. Whenever Agnes tells the dressmaker she admires her hairdo, she laughs good-naturedly and says:

There is a certain age when a woman stops bothering about fashion and settles for the familiar.

A quick natural smile makes Mrs Ryder's tired green eyes sparkle, while pink cheeks appear to question the dark circles under them. She is dignified in manner and, Agnes notices over the ensuing visits, rarely irritable. The pressure of deadlines may mean she has little time to attend to her appearance, yet there is a beauty in the fine-featured, unblemished skin, and the dimple in the centre of her fleshy chin gives her an air of cheeky defiance.

Madge's mindless name-dropping will reach new heights when she locates a *Woman's Weekly* photo of Janie Marble Flood, and other similarly adored personages, at a picnic race meeting. Mrs Ryder will nod politely as Madge gushes, but Agnes will see that the dressmaker is clueless as to who her mother is talking about. Interestingly, she will feel less embarrassed about her mother in front of Mrs Ryder, who shoots her the occasional knowing look over a pair of pink batwing glasses. A look as if to say – there are lots of silly people in this world, Agnes, and that is *their* problem, not ours. Boredom with these fitting sessions will get the better of Madge, who will avoid further contamination with the Blackpool Poms by issuing instructions by phone, using Agnes as go-between.

Agnes senses that she and Mrs Ryder share an unspoken way of seeing things. She loves the dressmaker's funny mannerisms: the way she twitches her nose when she pushes the flamboyant glasses up to her eyes, sighs, and looks heavenwards, as if attempting to engage a passing angel.

A wooden cutting table dominates the middle of the workroom. On top are packets of patterns, scissors, bowls of pins and chalk and, at one end, a Singer treadle sewing machine with a wooden straight-backed chair.

Today, Agnes and her brothers are waiting, seated on an old beige lounger that leans against the wall behind which Mr Ryder bumps bewilderingly around. 'Gypsy', alert to Mrs Ryder's every movement, sits with half-closed eyes, nose resting on long paws as her mistress fits the children one at a time. Agnes is to wear a blue taffeta dress, blissfully unaware now that there will be a mighty *shindig* on the actual day of Charlotte's wedding, when her mother will insist that she remove the petticoats under the skirt that make her 'look like a bluebell'. On that day, Agnes will refuse to give in and will thus enter the reception, held at a fashionable Rose Bay harbour restaurant – Caprice – alone.

What jolts the three children into the present moment on this, their final morning, is the sudden arrival of a smelly fart too potent to ignore. Agnes elbows her brother who shrugs, protesting innocence. Then Bert catches the odour and looks around at the others as Mrs Ryder, on her knees, pins up the length of his pants. Agnes and Jim shake their heads. Jim and Agnes are struggling not to laugh when Mrs Ryder identifies the culprit:

Gypsy out! Out! Oh, Gypsy, you *dirty* dog! Get out of here!

'Gypsy' wearily heaves herself up on all fours and slinks away like a misshapen lizard, pushing open the door into the kitchen with her long nose, then disappearing onto the back terrace. Meanwhile, Mrs Ryder ferociously chases the smell as if it is a living entity, flapping it out of the entrance door until it dissolves into the fresh air.

In the preceding weeks, Agnes has come to know that the serial farter wasn't 'Gypsy' at all, but Mrs Ryder herself. Rita had secretly confided her mother's problem – set off, apparently, by a stomach injury sustained in the war. 'Gypsy', it seems, is the perfect foil. Dog and owner are complicit. Rita respects the alliance but, at times, her family loyalty will collapse, and she and Agnes will explode with laughter in the sanctuary of the front hedge.

Future blood will be spilt in Agnes's commitment to become a ballerina with Rita – the only soulmate she will ever have. But, as Agnes has missed out on basic parental instruction specifically identifying north and south, and left and right, she will struggle when Rita initiates her into the five basic ballet positions. Finally eliminating the need to make the sign of the cross to differentiate her left from her right, these two directions will magically enter her feet and arms.

Rita has such a large bedroom that the girls can twirl freely, without bumping into anything. They jump on the beds, stand on their heads, roll over and spin around holding hands till they're sick with happiness. Mother and daughter's bedrooms are alongside each other in the old section of the house. Agnes guesses there is a connection into Mr Ryder's domain through a wardrobe in Mrs Ryder's bedroom, although she has never actually seen it. Mother and daughter also share an internal bathroom with a skylight, situated at the back of the workroom.

One night soon, Agnes will fall asleep in Rita's spare bed. Drenched in flowery scent wafting in from the open window, she will feel as if she has landed in paradise.

The real wonder in the house is the ballet studio on the ground floor. It is situated alongside a spare room with attached bathroom that opens onto the back garden. It is called 'George's Room', as Rita's Uncle George apparently paid for the whole extension. A full-length mirror covers the back wall of the studio, with a ballet barre in front and a sprung wood floor – considered essential for ballet – compliments also of Uncle George, who plans on visiting one day before too long.

Rita attends her ballet lessons in the 'School of Arts' building in Victoria Street, next to Chatswood Town Hall and has already reached an advanced level in the Trinity College London exams, which are held in Pitt Street, Sydney. Margot Fonteyn is Rita's idol. Ballet posters, sent from London by Uncle George, cover one whole wall of the studio: Margot as Chloe in *Daphnis and Chloe*, as Aurora in *Sleeping Beauty*, as 'Giselle', as Odette and Odile in *Swan Lake* and in a stunning full-skirted black lace dress in Frederick Ashton's *Apparitions*. Agnes falls in love with all these images. Perhaps most stunning for its pure physicality is a depiction of a blonde-wigged Margot flying through the air in Ballet Imperial's choreography by Balanchine. Behind the door are yet more posters of Moira Shearer and Margot Fonteyn in *Symphonic Variations* choreographed by Frederick Ashton.

Agnes has decided that her favourite dancer is Moira Shearer. She stares for minutes on end at the wonderful photos of Shearer dancing the first act of *Cinderella*, complete with headscarf and broom, and spends hours in front of the mirror practising her foot positions before moving into *pliés* and *battement*, which are designed, Mrs Ryder tells her, to give strength and flexibility to the whole body. Rita shows Agnes how to fix a point to return to when doing a *pirouette*. Slowly, gradually, Agnes even manages to do the splits. After hours of excruciating practice, she performs in front of Rita and her mother for correction.

Rita willingly shares the space with Agnes, but there is a limit to the diversion of her mother's attention from herself before Agnes spots a note of sarcasm creeping into Rita's voice. Yet, Agnes knows that when she has done well, a kind of raw joint enthusiasm succeeds in sweeping the two friends back together. Thus, the better part of Rita's nature usually triumphs, and both mother and daughter clap and cheer as Agnes takes her bows at the end of her demonstration. Her weak point will always be her hands. Unravelling her fingers, long constricted in anxious fists, is a challenge. Gradually, the music persuades these rigid muscles to open like reluctant buds coming into flower.

Rita is a few years older than Agnes and lives in fear of outgrowing the petite physique of a ballet dancer. She constantly fights a mop of unruly blonde curls. Sharp features – apparently inherited from her father – are softened by heavy-lidded green eyes, polished rosy cheeks and full lips that are identical to her mother's. Rita is the most sophisticated, self-assured girl Agnes has ever met. She can toss off criticism that cripples Agnes, as if swatting a fly off a windowsill, but can also make Agnes feel that no challenge is insurmountable. Rita can mimic English accents and the speech and mannerisms of American screen stars like Lauren Bacall and Veronica Lake. Cloistered in the red berry hedge hole she and Agnes decide they will, one fine day, tantalise audiences with their extraordinary balletic talents. Agnes will resolve to be talked *about*, instead of *doing* the talking about – like her mother and aunt.

As for Mrs Ryder, she is delighted to find a sister for her daughter, particularly one who is besotted with ballet. One day, she hands Agnes a pair of pink ballet shoes which fit perfectly. Agnes loves them so much she keeps them close in her school bag. In return, Agnes persuades Mrs Ryder to let her help her with the hand-sewing in the workroom. Henceforth, many a hem goes out the morning glory gate happily sewn by Agnes.

Whilst sewing companionably, Mrs Ryder tells Agnes about her time making costumes for some Sadler's Wells' productions, along with describing in detail the guest dancers who performed at the Royal Opera House before the war. She has an in-depth knowledge of the history of dance. Agnes becomes increasingly fascinated to hear about Diaghilev and his influence on European ballet. According to Mrs Ryder, for twenty-nine years of the 20th century, whatever Diaghilev felt, or thought, was transferred to the stage. She confides to Agnes how much she regrets missing out on the re-establishment of English ballet, with Markova and De Valois, as she had emigrated to Australia straight after the war. Mrs Ryder avoids talking about the war. At some point Rita will confide to Agnes in the hedge that after a bombing raid in Germany, her father sustained burn injuries when his Spitfire crashed and caught fire in a badly lit English airfield. It will be a subject Agnes instinctively knows not to mention again. She will discover too, over time, that Mrs Ryder has even more reason to feel sad, as her parents were both killed in a German bombing raid in London. She and her brother were saved by a street warden who shepherded them into an underground railway station, miraculous minutes before the raid began. Agnes will think it strange the way mother, father and daughter live in the split-up house, but gathers that they seem happy. When his wife and daughter do visit him through the secret entrance, Agnes hears Mr Ryder's big belly laugh and his lusty baritone banging out popular war songs on an out-of-tune piano. His timetable is clearly organised to avoid people. He apparently leaves for work in the late afternoon and returns home in the early morning before anyone is up.

Any doubts Agnes might have harboured about devoting her life to ballet will be swept away when she accompanies the Ryders to a production of *The Nutcracker* at Her Majesty's Theatre in the city. In the afterglow of the performance, Mrs Ryder declares Agnes is destined to be a red-headed ballerina like Moira Shearer. Thoughts of working in a leper colony instantly vanish; Agnes will do God's work by training the body he has given her. But she can't ask her mother for money to buy toe shoes, as Madge knows nothing about her daughter's clandestine ballet training and wouldn't approve. And asking her father would be out of the question, as months continue to go by without him even acknowledging her existence.

And so, Agnes hits on an idea to make money. After spotting pictures for front-door Christmas adornments in the *Woman's Weekly*, she is thrilled with Mrs Ryder's positive reaction when she consults her about making their own decorations and selling them door to door:

Great idea, Agnes! How enterprising! Of course I'll help you!

Agnes will set off with a list to a haberdashery shop at the top of Victoria Street that supplies dressmakers and milliners. She will buy different coloured ribbons and bows, a roll of red felt, dried sheaves of wheat, hatpins, and a mixture of dried flowers, Mrs Ryder having agreed to authorise the purchases to go on her account. Returning to the dressmaker's house to get started, she stops at the hardware shop for a roll of soft, bendy wire.

On the calendar day that marks three weeks till Christmas, the shops will already be spilling over with decorations and Agnes and Mrs Ryder will have already completed three models: one, called 'Bows', is comprised of a red felt bow surrounded by pine cones painted silver, and sprays of red berries gleaned from the hidey hole in the front garden. The second is called 'Spruce' and combines holly, dried spruce, silver and red baubles. Number Three is dubbed 'Beads' – its miniature sheaves of dry wheat, billowing thin red ribbon and coils of wooden beads redolent of a snowy English village. As she lines the inside of a straw basket with silver paper in which to transport her products, Mrs Ryder will advise Agnes that a selection of goods will help her to engage the buyer. Thus, Agnes will carry two of each design. Six being a bit of squash in the basket, she will set out with four to start, as she can easily come back for the others if she gets lucky.

Knowing she must pluck up the courage to knock on doors Agnes will march up Archer Street drawing on all the determination she can muster. The flower-named streets feeling friendly, she'll start in Violet Street and move on to Tulip and Daisy. Initially, she will choose a well-kept house with a pretty garden, deliberately missing out the unkempt one next door. When footsteps respond to the ring of the bell, she will struggle with an urge to run.

A droopy-faced, sleepy-eyed woman who looks like a basset hound will open the door and grin at her with yellow teeth. She will speak in a gravelly smoker's drawl:

Well, if it isn't Little Red Riding Hood! Come and take a look at this, John!

The woman has shouted out over her shoulder to summon 'John' from behind her. Agnes will open her mouth, but nothing will come out. Struggling for composure, her words will evaporate. Dumb. Yet again trapped in the wretched wordless nightmare.

John will appear. He will be wearing a white singlet, baggy undershorts, and flip-flops. He will scrutinise the basket and save the day:

Selling these for the front door, are you, love?

Yes. Yes, I am.

Right. Which one would you like, Angel?

I like this one, John. 'Spruce'. It's full of Christmas cheer.

Here we go, love. This should cover it.

Quite a generous amount of change is pressed into her hand and Agnes will ring the next bell with confidence. She knows the acceptable price now and has change from John if she needs it. Within half an hour, she will have sold all four displays in her basket. A few sour faces have closed the door in her face, but most are genuinely captivated by the product.

Mr Lawson buys a holly arrangement and commissions a bigger version for the window of the sports shop. One of her best arrangements will soon enliven the front door of the Old Age Home and Natasha and her mother will choose 'Beads', which she gives them as a Christmas present. Mrs Ryder will not stop smiling when Agnes drags her up Archer Street to marvel at the wonder of their work adorning so many doors. This will be designated, in Agnes's memory, a happy time.

Convinced that God must be behind her success, Agnes will be careful not to neglect good works for him. She will also continue to run home after school to get the note and string bag for her mother's shopping. But, one day, Madge will leave her daughter dumbfounded when she tells her to stay at the Ryders and not bother coming home. Agnes will suspect that the policeman who came to the house way back when Peeping Tom Richard O'Sullivan fell off the ladder, and who visited them again after Mack tried to kill her father, is keeping her mother company. She will notice that Madge has taken to having her afternoon nap in Bert's back bedroom next to the bathroom and that there is a strange smell emerging from the sheets beneath which her mother dreamily reclines when Agnes takes her a cup of tea after school.

One day soon, when Agnes spots a policeman's helmet on the dining room table through the venetian blind, she will retrace her steps and go straight to the Ryders without going into the house. From that point, if she ever sees a police car parked nearby, she will stay away. She will be forever grateful to that policeman for taking care of her mother, as it gives her more time to help Mrs Ryder in the workroom and to practise her ballet in the studio.

When Madge ignores the fact that her daughter doesn't turn up at home at the usual time, Agnes will know she has done the right thing. She also knows never to mention the policeman, in the way that she never mentions Mr Ryder. Encouraged by her mother's prevailing good mood, she will ask her to buy her a ballet book for Christmas and reserves a copy of *Barron at the Ballet* at the bookshop in Victoria Street. As her mother never remembers a promise, Agnes will remind her continually and so, one day, upon finding the policeman in the dining room, she will mention it in front of him to evoke his support and force her mother's hand:

Oh! Hello! They can only hold *Barron at the Ballet* for another week. Mummy's buying it for me for Christmas!

Then she will beat a hasty retreat.

Agnes will not have needed to be quite so vigilant in hiding her ballet passion from her mother as Madge will be showing less interest in what her daughter gets up to than usual. This maternal good mood will last long enough for Agnes to get not only *Barron at the Ballet* for Christmas but *Barron Encore* – three months later – for her birthday. And, when the moment to buy some new toe shoes arrives, Mrs Ryder will take Agnes to a shop in Imperial Arcade and Agnes will, for quite some time, consider this to be the best year of her life.

Not only toe shoes and *Barron at the Ballet* but that Christmas Agnes and her brothers are given a small record player. And, to top it off, Mrs Ryder will hand her a record of Prokofiev's *Cinderella*. When her brothers return to school, she will have the record player all to herself and she will never have felt so rich. After paying Mrs Ryder back for the materials bought on her account, and buying Christmas presents for the family, and for Rita and her mother, she will have enough leftover money to buy a record of Tchaikovsky's *The Nutcracker* and *Swan Lake*.

When Eric Keen returns from interstate business, instead of going to the farm on Sundays, Agnes will stay home and convert the dining room into a ballet studio where she will dance to her records. As the yellow and green lino has been thrown out, she will have the advantage of a wood floor to dance on. She will imagine her audience seated on the other side of the big window where the cat and canary continue to conduct their absurd relationship. The dining table is the low barre and the sideboard the high barre. She will cover the dining table in a blanket to avoid scratches. After her workout, she will plug in the little record player and the room will fill with Prokofiev. With a scarf around her hair and broom in hand like Moira Shearer, she will immerse herself in the dance and lose all sense of time. Exhausted, she will flop on the old carpet in the hallway and float up to heaven. She will work hard to improve. No need to dig deep to conjure up the character of Cinderella for, after all, Agnes *is* Cinderella.

* * *

With the arrival of a small Japanese piano for Christmas from Uncle George, Rita's time is absorbed during the summer holiday with piano and singing lessons. Mrs Ryder maintains that a girl can never have enough strings to her bow and, as her daughter is shooting up like a well-watered bamboo in the monsoon rains, she can always aim for a career in music should she exceed the corps de ballet required height.

Rita has been working hard for the Trinity College ballet exams scheduled for the coming autumn and her dedication pays off. She is cast by Odette, her French ballet teacher, to dance the part of 'Swanhilda' in the second act of *Coppelia*. Odette's husband, René, is to dance the part of the toymaker 'Doctor Coppelius', and the corps de ballet is to be made up of student dancers. The performance will be organised to raise money for crippled children. Cinderella's solo dance in Act One, after the ugly sisters go to the ball, will also be included in the programme.

Rita persuades the ballet teachers to let Agnes sit in on rehearsals for the gala. Initially they had said 'no', but Agnes knows God must have intervened as she is now sitting on a bench piled high with bags and coats and is drinking it all in. She is completely enthralled as she watches initial separate steps emerge into a fluid routine. She longs to have lessons at the ballet school, but her mother categorically refuses to pay for them. Rosemont forbids all stage activity, sanctioning only what forms of education lead to university, the caring professions, teachers' training college, or secretarial training – all the approved stopgaps for girls before marriage.

As the big night advances, every usable space in Mrs Ryder's workroom is covered in material to be made into costumes. As Swanhilda, Rita will wear flamboyant red satin to symbolise her jealousy when her fiancé, Franz, falls in love with the motionless girl on the balcony. Agnes knows that Swanhilda will sneak into the toyshop. Trapped inside, she will discover the truth about the doll and will change into Coppelia's blue dress with its marvellous puff sleeves and gleaming satin sash. Seeing his doll dance, the toymaker will believe he has brought his creation to life.

Rita follows the custom of the great Diaghilev, who made his soloists saturate themselves in the music of any upcoming performance. Leo Delibes's score for *Coppelia* constantly reverberates through every corner of the Ryder house. Rita's flair for comic acting enables her to master to perfection Swanhilda's deceptive pretence. With her abrupt, stiff, staccato head and doll movements, together with her startled blinking eyes, she uncannily resembles the tiny ballerina in the music box in Mrs Ryder's living room.

Agnes never misses a rehearsal of *Cinderella*. She masters the choreography in her mind during her solitary Sunday vigils. And, at the end of each day's dancing practice at home, her imaginary veranda audience clap and cheer as she takes her final bow, after which she rushes to put the room back in order before her parents return from the farm.

It happens on a stormy night. Violent thunder and huge seizures of lightning herald sheets of rain that lash at the glass louvres of the Ryder home. Unaffected, 'Gypsy' snores in her basket on the workroom floor, Rita is playing cards through the wardrobe with her father, and Madge is at home being looked after by the policeman. It is a week before the gala. Mrs Ryder and Agnes are sewing costumes when Odette bursts through the workroom door, sobbing. Black curls dripping, lipstick smeared across her cheek, streaks of mascara under her eyes, she can hardly speak. Cup of hot tea in hand, seated at Mrs Ryder's kitchen table, Odette finally confides what has brought her low:

Janet 'as ze measles. Her *maman* rang me 'alf an hour ago. *Absolument no* Cinderella for le gala! And *no* time to teach anyone else. *What* are we going to do?!

Mrs Ryder looks at Agnes, whose heart is thundering when she hears her say:

Agnes can dance the role! I've seen her do it! She is your understudy, par excellence!

And this is how Odette comes to work with Agnes in the dance studio over the weekend, and then every afternoon after school before Saturday's performance. The teacher will struggle to cope with her anger. Several times she will even hit Agnes. The woman is as changeable as her mother – one minute it's, '*Magnifique*, darling!' with hugs and kisses, and the next it's, 'Stupid girl! 'ow many times do I *tell* you!'

Mrs Ryder will alter the dark blue satin dress to fit Agnes. And, on Saturday night, when her parents are dining with Parry and Marnie, with scarf around head and broom in hand, Agnes will leap onto the stage in blue toe shoes to match the satin costume. Sick with nerves in the wings, her body on stage will feed on the confidence of knowing the part well. That night, intoxicated by the beauty of the music, Agnes will become 'Cinderella'. The applause – when it comes – will no longer be imagined, but real and thunderous. The Lawson family will be there in full, as will Natasha and her mother, and the reformed Peeping Tom, Richard Sullivan, who has driven the elderly twin sisters across the lane to the performance in his new car.

The beautiful bouquet of flowers they will hand Agnes will send her rocketing to the moon and she will whisper her thanks directly to God who, she believes, has granted her the greatest night of her life.

* * *

There's no one living in the house opposite.

Rita has announced this to Agnes in an urgent, serious tone.

How do you know?

Remember I told you, I've been keeping an eye on it. Now I'm convinced it's deserted.

Rita and Agnes are tucking into thick slices of crusty fresh bread covered in lashings of peanut butter and honey, as is their custom, before starting ballet practice in the studio. Rita's attitude towards Agnes has altered since the gala. Although Rita's Swanhilda was a raging success, she has found herself struggling over Agnes's own triumph as Cinderella. Agnes suspects that she is no longer viewed as the pathetic waif desperate to learn. Still, she tells herself – all friendships have their ups and downs. But what appears to annoy Rita most is the fact that she has grown taller, and that Agnes's height is unchanged. Agnes feels sad when her friend narrows her eyes at her, or suddenly shoves her in the back, or occasionally trips her up, but she can't be held responsible for programming her friend's hormones.

Agnes responds to the observation about the house opposite:

I don't remember you saying anything about that house.

What's the matter with you? I told you last week. You get this faraway look in those big blue eyes, like you've gone a bit soft in the head!

Agnes is aware that something strange is happening. She does struggle to listen, certainly, and things often don't stay in her head. She must be looking downcast because Rita, knowing she has hurt her, tries to make amends:

Come on, don't be glum. Blow the ballet. Let's go across the road!

She is putting her arm around Agnes's shoulder and squeezing it. Still in their leotards, they run out of the morning glory gate, holding hands. It is a dull afternoon. A cap of bruised clouds hangs low in the sky after an early downpour. Rita says:

Everyone's indoors. Perfect timing. Look – the street's deserted!

Rita has jumped sideways, clicking her feet together like a Russian dancer. She is pulling Agnes along behind her:

Come on!

But Agnes is still lingering outside when Rita kicks the gate to the deserted house open. She decides to follow her cautiously down the narrow side passage of the house. The passage is towered over by a line of tall pine trees that runs along the back fence of Agnes's school. Rita climbs onto a meter box and pushes open a leaf of the front sash window. As she clambers into the house, Agnes stares after her, wondering what to do. A few seconds later, Rita pokes her tongue out at her from the window and wiggles her fingers either side of her ears. She chants:

The working class can kiss my arse I've got the boss's job at last! Come on, don't be a scaredy-cat. There's no one here. I'm conquering for England!

Once inside, Agnes wanders tentatively from room to room. She calls out:

Is there anyone here?

But no one answers. The interior of the single-storey house smells musty as if it's been shut up for a long time. There is mould in the kitchen sink. The one bedroom contains an enormous brass double-bed, and to Agnes's delight there is a modern bathroom with every luxury. The living room, facing front towards the street, is stuffed with loungers draped in sumptuous pieces of patterned brocade and lace. The shades on the table lamps are hidden under exotic brightly coloured scarves with embroidered moons, stars, and little mirrors in the shape of the signs of the zodiac. A green three-seater lounger wears a layer of coffee-coloured lace around its back and shoulders with matching antimacassars draped to the floor. Dusty ceramic ducks and birds stare at them from every corner: a mother duck leads her ducklings along the shelf above the fireplace, three geese fly in formation on the end wall between the windows, a gaggle of farmyard fowl waddle over the coffee table, and a pair of tall storks stand upright in a corner – exactly like schoolteachers about to address the class.

Their feet are sinking into high-piled patterned green rugs. Mobiles of white cut glass hang from the kitchen ceiling. A sudden beam of sun from the back window shines through, setting off a rainbow that dances on the pale walls. Agnes turns a key in the lock of the back door and jumps back when it springs open. A carpet of blue flowers shed from an overhead jacaranda tree covers the brick-paved courtyard. The fallen blooms float in puddles left by the rain. Agnes twirls around outside with her arms open. A light fairy rain is falling. She opens her mouth to catch the drops falling on her hair and down her back from the tree. Then Rita grabs at Agnes's arm and they spin around laughing. In that moment, all fear of losing her friend's affection vanishes. They truly will be soulmates forever.

The sound of a dog barking sends them scurrying back indoors, but the covert exploration of the house continues, and they're captivated by a bedroom wardrobe overflowing with exotic clothes. There is a silver-framed photo of a regal, long-faced woman with violet eyes on the dressing table. She wears a gold turban and holds a crystal ball. The photo sits in the midst of an array of glittering, costume jewellery. Perhaps the owner of the house is a fortune teller or, as Rita now points out, she might be posing in fancy dress.

Rita puts on a loose silver lamé jacket from the wardrobe and slips her leotard legs into a short silver skirt with side splits. She fixes a headband with three white feathers and a diamond brooch in the centre round her blonde curls and launches into the Charleston, twisting her feet and flinging them sideways. They burrow deeper into the wardrobe, putting on clothes and discarding them with abandon on the red satin bedspread. Agnes teams a green velvet coat with a black feather boa and drowns her neck in masses of glass beads. There is an amazing collection of shoes, encrusted with bows and jewels, all too big for Agnes, but which do fit the feet Rita so despises for ignoring her command to stop growing.

Dressing up in the abandoned house will become a favourite activity. Sharing its secrets will bring the friends even closer together. And, as the weeks roll on, the familiarity they develop will make them feel as if they own the place. They will meet at the house most afternoons, but the wonder of it all will be doomed to end abruptly. Agnes will be perched on the meter box, with Rita close behind her, when it happens. She will nearly fall sideways in shock when she finds herself staring through the window into the hooded, smoky eyes of her mother's policeman. He has clearly been waiting for the criminals who have broken in to emerge. His thick dark hair and sharply chiselled features make him resemble the calm Marlboro man but, at that moment, his expression will be anything but serene. He will look annoyed, and she will detect that he sincerely wished the culprit was not her. He will smile at her in the way that people do who feel uncomfortable with children:

You girls can't come here again. This is a deceased's estate. We're blocking off access.

Have you found anything?!

It is another male voice, calling from inside the premises. Her mother's policeman will reply:

No, nothing, mate! Nothing at all! Just talking to a cat on the windowsill!

Then he will give the girls a signal with his hand to run. The girls will flee into the back garden and slither through the hole in the paling fence, scramble through heavy bushes on the convent side, scratching arms and legs as they go. Agnes will remain in control of herself this time. Reassuring Rita there is no chance of running into any nuns as they would all be in the church opposite for Benediction, she will carefully guide Rita around the perimeter of the playground to the entrance gate. Safely emerging on Archer Street, they will both burst out laughing with sheer relief.

Agnes will live in fear that the policeman might say something to her mother or come looking for the jewellery that she has taken from the house and hidden in her room. She doesn't consider it stolen, for she has every intention of putting it back, but it will now be too late to do that safely. She will have to get rid of it.

With trembling hands, she will tip the bracelets, necklaces, beads and jewelled hair clips out of the shoebox under her bed and hide them in a paper bag under her pillow. Lying in bed fully dressed, waiting till her parents are breathing heavily in the next room, she will tiptoe out the back door with her ill-gotten gains. Creeping down Rose Street to the circular rose garden in Beauchamp Park, she will dig a hole by the light of the moon, deep down under the topsoil, with a small spade. She will choose a spot not far from where she had buried her cat, Ness, who had been run over by a car several months earlier. Bluebell, the canary, must have missed her constant companion because, a few days later, Agnes had found the tiny bird, its feet stiff in the air, on the floor of the cage. She had wrapped Bluebell in mulberry leaves and interred her close to Ness. She liked to think of them together in death, as they had been in life. She could have buried them in the back garden, but preferred the secure, unchanging tranquillity of the rose garden at night when the world slept.

Slipping the bag of jewellery into the deep hole, as the pungent smell of the newly deceased animals filtered upward, it will occur to Agnes that, just like the Egyptians' cats and birds thousands of years ago, Ness and Bluebell now had precious jewels to pay their way wherever they were headed. Losing the light of the pale moon behind a cloud, she will quickly cover the hole in the pitch black and run home.

Once safely back in bed in her nightdress, something strange will happen. Her father will appear beside her bed in his pyjamas. He will just stand there, staring down at her. He will look like a ghost, and she will wonder if he is sleepwalking. It will feel creepy. Closing her eyes tight, she will pretend to be asleep and, when she finally opens them, he will have disappeared.

* * *

Rita's insistence to see the second *Barron at the Ballet* book that Agnes received for her birthday pushes Agnes close to breaking her long-running embargo of letting friends come to her house. Yet she knows it is still a bad idea and has decided to put a stop to it. And so, as she and Rita walk out of the morning glory gate and down the road towards the Lawsons' house, Agnes declares:

No. I'll run ahead and bring you the book. Please, Rita – you can't go home with me. My mother's sick.

The excuse of mother being sick in bed is no novelty. But, Agnes realises, even if she said Madge was highly infectious with mumps, Rita would not be deterred, for Rita knows all too well that Agnes lies about her mother:

You're *always* saying that. You make her sound chronically bedridden!

I tell you what. Wait outside my house and I'll bring you the book and you can take it home with you!

This is a good compromise and seems to work. It would be a huge mistake to let anyone she knows come into the house. A maternal grenade or bomb could explode any minute and what would Rita think? Agnes's mind is buzzing. Rita still hasn't got over her friend's triumph as Cinderella but, mostly, she's furious about having outgrown the stipulated height for ballet by several inches. Mrs Ryder has constantly cited the example of Beryl Grey (who was well over the stipulated height when she made her debut during the war at the Royal Opera House and went on to dance all the classical roles) but this has done nothing to console her daughter. Agnes is frustrated for her best friend, but it isn't her fault that Rita is too tall. If they could only return to the happy times in the deserted house.

Rita is being horribly persistent:

You've stayed *hundreds* of times at my house, and I've never spent more than a few *minutes* in yours. Wouldn't you say that's a bit out of proportion, Agnes?

Rita's hands are on her hips. It's the pose she adopts when she is determined to get her own way:

You think its's all about *you* now that you're Odette's little pet! She plans to persuade your parents to let you come to the ballet school. If they won't pay, she's going to try and get you a scholarship.

Rita's nasty sing-song tone is frightening Agnes. As is Odette's plan. Neither of her parents has any clue she has danced 'Cinderella'. She implores her:

Please, Rita, I beg you, tell Odette not to do that. They'll never agree to me having ballet lessons, with or without a scholarship!

Agnes could not explain her parents' hostility to outside interference, nor how her mother would fire up her father to bring his belt down on her for the most minor indiscretion. She couldn't explain it because she didn't understand it herself. But Rita was not about to be dissuaded:

Wait till they hear what a little *star* you are! They'll be applauding like everyone else!

Please don't talk like that, Rita. I *hate* it when you talk like that. Aren't we friends anymore?

Instead of replying, Rita runs up the hill and Agnes rushes after her in a panic. On reaching the top of Edmond Street, she is momentarily distracted by the Chinese students from the boarding house who are taking yet more photos. She turns the corner. No sign of Rita. She runs to the Rose Street entrance and there, standing in the fifth ballet position by the steps to Agnes's back door, is her smirking best friend. Her blonde hair is pushed behind one ear like Veronica Lake. Weak with relief, Agnes is suddenly annoyed with herself for reacting so intensely when she's obviously just being teased. Agnes instructs:

Wait there and I'll come back with the book!

But then Madge suddenly appears on the veranda above. She is wearing an extremely figure-hugging frock. Amazingly, she is waving at Rita to come in! Agnes has never seen her in a dress like that before. The colour's right but not the shape. She guesses her father must have arrived home early afternoon from his last trip, but she spends so little time at home these days, she must have lost track.

Agnes finds herself standing next to Rita in the dining room. Suddenly, her father runs out of the bathroom with only a towel around his waist. He grins at them and opens the towel, so they can see his sausage dancing from side to side with the movement of his gait. Madge, who is leaning against the sideboard, lets out a brief, humourless laugh. The flasher turns on the step up the hall and wiggles his hips, giving a final wave of the sausage before disappearing into the bedroom.

Rita and Agnes fall into each other's arms, giggling. Unsure what to do next, Agnes can only think to drag her friend by the hand into her bedroom, where they lie on the floor and flick through the ballet book. Neither mention the wiggling sausage. They come to a whole section on Beryl Grey, the tall dancer Rita's mother constantly cites as an inspiration for her beanpole daughter. Agnes reads excitedly out loud to her friend:

A foreign critic said of Beryl Grey, 'watching her gives the sense of spaciousness one gets when looking at a view from a high mountain in the cool clear air'. Imagine, Rita! By fifteen she was a star! You can do the same! Your mother will take you to London, you'll see!

The two friends lie on the floor chatting and laughing. In moments such as this, Agnes believes, regardless of their spats, that nothing will ever destroy their friendship.

But change will strike hard and without warning when Grandma enrols Agnes in a prestigious big convent school. It will be goodbye to the glorious days of running down Archer Street to the local Mercy Convent. Henceforth, she will travel each day by train to Milson's Point and will be wearing a new grey check uniform. It is the school where she will spend the next five torturous years.

After a heated period between Agnes's parents of fierce arguments and sly remarks, her father will temporarily suspend his interstate travelling and, coincidentally, the policeman will stop coming. Her new school day will include a train trip, which means that Agnes will arrive home a lot later. But this will not deter her mother from reasserting her demand for help in the house.

* * *

Three weeks of the enforced changes have gone by when Agnes runs down Archer Street on a Saturday morning and turns left into Malvern Avenue.

She has finally found some time to see those dearest to her in the whole world. She can hardly contain her excitement. But the frontage of the Ryder house is completely transformed. She hardly recognises it. Totally confused, she walks up and down the street outside.

The morning glory has disappeared. Gone, too, is the high hedge and with it the cubby house where she and Rita once swore eternal friendship. In its place is a new fence and gate with a padlock, too high to climb over. Agnes is locked out. The front garden has been cleaned up. A line of orderly shrubs stands in place of the former mess of tangled weeds – each bush neatly attached to one of the old bamboo supports. No more mulching leaves with sprouting mushrooms. The porch, along with the glass in the front doors and the windows either side, are so clean they look like they've just been installed. Freshly washed curtains open out and swing in the breeze. The sun shines, birds sing and the air smells of fresh-cut grass. Surely nothing terrible can happen on a lovely day like this?

As Agnes looks closer, she notices new straw chairs on the porch and realises the recently painted clean door is partly open. She stands up on a rung of the new gate and calls Rita's name. And she keeps calling for her until the porch door opens further and a tall, slim man, leaning on a stick, slowly comes towards her. This must be Mr Ryder! His twisted face looks as if it has been caught in a door. Lifeless, plastic, cobbled skin distorts his right eye, forcing his nose upwards and exposing a pair of flat nostrils like a pig's snout.

Agnes now remembers what Rita said about a plastic surgeon in England grafting skin onto burnt noses to grow down like an elephant's trunk, which is then cut and remodelled into a new nose. It seemed too extraordinary at the time to be true. Mr Ryder's remodelled nose looks like putty crudely stuck on with glue. His upwardly twisting mouth is set in a permanent sneer. The left side of the face he seems to favour putting forward, apart from a flickering scared eye, looks almost normal. When he turns his head to tell 'Gypsy' to sit, Agnes notices the hair on the back of his head is growing around a ring of scar tissue, like grass around a pond. The awful story Agnes has heard in snippets now comes together. Burning fuel had disfigured him when he crash-landed his Spitfire after a bombing raid in Germany. She is spellbound. She can't look away. She stares at his face, trying to find the handsome young officer in the photo on the sideboard in Mrs Ryder's living room underneath the scars. But what comes out of his twisted mouth chills her more than his appearance:

You must never come here again.

But why? Her head is spinning. She wonders if her mother's policeman had come to see the Ryders about the missing jewellery in the abandoned house. He elaborates slightly:

Dear Agnes – Rita and Mrs Ryder can't see you anymore.

Tears well up in her eyes. She struggles to be strong. She can hardly swallow for the lump in her throat. Her only consolation in these terrible moments is 'Gypsy', who keeps jumping up at the gate and wagging her tail at her:

But what did I do, Mr Ryder?

No more, Agnes. The friendship is over.

The proclamation from the twisted lips is low and determined. But she cannot grasp it:

But it *can't* be! Rita and I made a vow to be friends forever! We exchanged blood and everything! We made a pledge!

My dear girl, you will find other friends. So off you go now and please don't come back.

There is a softness of a kind in his tone. Agnes detects a Scottish accent, like the men in *Whisky Galore*. She persists:

Is it because Rita and I broke into the house across the road? Is that why you don't want me here anymore?

Mr Ryder shakes his head:

No. It's not because of anything you said or did. My wife and daughter remain fond of you, but things change. Your adventure together is over. Life is like that. One door closes and another opens.

Agnes feels a searing pain in the area of her heart:

But I don't want to open and close doors! Please, please, *please* let me come in and see them just one more time!

She is sobbing uncontrollably. But instead of responding, Mr Ryder turns his back on her and hobbles away back into the house. He closes the door firmly. Agnes is shattered. Could the new fence and gate really have been put there to keep her out? She stands there, stock-still, going over it. A horrible possibility occurs to her. Is this terrible banishment because her father showed off his sausage? Had Rita told her parents about it? About how her mother had laughed and said nothing? She is glued to the spot, lost in her frantic thoughts. Minutes pass and she cannot move. The war hero returns to the porch and orders her in a loud voice to leave or he will ring the police.

For the next few days, when Agnes arrives home from her new school, she will drop her bag, do the shopping for her mother, and sit on the wall of her old school opposite the Ryder house. She will wait for Rita and Mrs Ryder to come out. Everyone else in the neighbourhood will pass her but the Ryder mother and daughter will not be seen. Mr Lawson will jog by in a tracksuit. He will pause to tell Agnes how his eldest son, Matt, is training to compete in the freestyle race for Australia in the Olympic Games. And that his sports shop is doing good business and, would you believe, that Mrs Lawson is pregnant? He tells her jovially that this will *definitely* be their last child because there are no more seats in the van. By the way, if she ever fancies coming back to the pool, he could always make room for her. When he messes up her hair affectionately with his big hand, she has to look away. Has to fight the urge not to fall into his arms and weep buckets.

In Mr Lawson's wake, the bent-over old man with cirrhosis of the liver who lives further up the street will shuffle by, his wrinkled face as yellow as a buttercup and Agnes will wonder if this deterioration awaits her father.

Even Richard will greet her with a hug. Having spotted her from Archer Street, he has made a special detour. He seems all grown up – his hair oiled and puffed like Elvis. He will say:

Hey, you're a *fantastic* dancer, Agnes! That was one hell of a performance. I'm studying art in Sydney. We do life drawing from models. I could do a drawing of you in your ballet clobber like Degas did, one day, if you'd like?

But, before she has a chance to answer, he will look at his watch and run from her, blowing her a kiss, and Agnes will allow herself a little smile to think how his window perving is now legitimised.

The two elderly sisters in different coloured flowery dresses will appear, Zelda pushing Hilda in a wheelchair. When they stop on the corner of Archer Street, Agnes will run up the street to say hello. Hilda will see her coming:

If it isn't our sweet Agnes. Where have you been? We haven't seen you for ages!

I've changed schools.

Of course! You must be in senior school now. How lovely you look with your red hair in a ponytail. Congratulations on your performance. We wouldn't have missed it for the world. You'll be a famous ballerina one day I just know it.

Zelda will turn in her chair and snap at her sister:

191

Ask her if she's still making door decorations!

Ask her yourself, you silly woman. Don't mind her, Agnes. She's turned bolshie since she broke her leg, giving me orders like I'm a footman. We kept the wreath you made permanently in the hall, so you'll have to make us something new next Christmas.

Knowing she will never fulfil the order Agnes will meekly reply that it will be no trouble. Then she will ask politely:

Does your leg hurt, Hilda?

Clean break. Nothing to worry about, dear. If you promise me a new Christmas creation, I'll let you write on my plaster cast.

Agnes will take the proffered biro and scrawl on the creamy plaster: Please God let Rita and Mrs Ryder be my friends again.

Hilda squeezes her hand:

I'm sure your wish will come true, Agnes.

At one point, used to seeing her at her lonely post, the Chinese students will wave to Agnes as they cross Archer Street. Sometimes, no one comes for ages. It will be on the fourth day of her vigil that the two people she yearns for emerge from their front gate: Mrs Ryder will put her hand up in a stop sign and Rita will hang her head as they accelerate their pace to avoid her. Agnes will run after them, frantically calling their names as they cross the road to avoid her. There will be a screech of brakes and Agnes will find herself sitting in the gutter. A wild-eyed man who has swerved to avoid hitting her will scream out of the driver's window:

You stupid little bitch! You almost got yourself killed!

Agnes will stare at him as he drives off, shaking his head, and she will realise that Rita and Mrs Ryder have disappeared from her life. Their rejection having hurt her so deeply, she will stop her vigil. It will be years before she fully absorbs the profound effect that Rita's fulsome description of the showing of the sausage must have had on Mr and Mrs Ryder.

As a last resort to regain some happiness, Agnes will plead with her mother to let her have ballet lessons, but it will be to no avail. After consulting Rosemont, it will be decided that elocution lessons would be more appropriate. But nobody will ever tell Agnes *why* it would be appropriate. And so, she will put the ballet shoes and the Cinderella dress into a painted shoebox, and they will join the graveyard of dead dreams she keeps under her bed.

PART THREE

If you repeat a lie often enough it becomes the truth.
Nineteen Eighty-Four by George Orwell

13

MOTHER MIRIAM

The head nun bellows:

A child of the devil walks amongst us!

Agnes's name is obsolete. Everyone knows it is her. From the top step of a veranda that leads to the classrooms, Mother Miriam, the school Superior, scrutinises her pupils – like cells under a microscope – in the courtyard below. A nudge, a smirk, a raised eyebrow or even a frown can provoke the head nun to swoop down from her perch, grip her unsuspecting victim's shoulders, and shake her like a washing machine on spin dry.

Mother Miriam is on Satan's trail and so can't be careful enough, for any moment he could slip by unnoticed. Constant vigilance is therefore imperative: broom cupboards, storage areas, dark annexes, basements, boiler rooms, behind blackboards, even the narrow gap between the walls of the school and the classrooms, the location matters not. Like a gardener searching for snails, she has even been seen scouring the bushes alongside the main drive. Diabolic innuendos cling to the tail of any sudden, unexplainable flash of light. The innate goodness of the middle-class girls from comfortable families who attend the school only pressurises her to delve deeper into darkness. It is not clear what she plans to do with the devil when she does apprehend him.

Mother Miriam has the habit of abruptly changing tack, like a sailing boat, in mid-sentence, but nothing alters the mean curl of her upper lip, nor the twitching pulse in the right reptilian eye. Now Agnes is exposed, she proceeds, in a less strident tone, to discuss preparations for Sports Day and a fête to raise money for the black babies in India. The sudden change of subject heightens rather than alleviates the group discomfort. Girls shuffle their feet and look bewildered. Agnes bends her knees and tries to hide behind a tall girl with a head full of black curls like a maze of miniature caves. She wishes she could disappear. It is a bad beginning. Formerly, school had been her respite from the combat zone at home. Now, her whole world has turned into a theatre of war, and any chance of escaping the front line looks remote.

She struggles for reasons. If not for her devil-red hair, then did Mother Miriam single her out because she slunk in alone after the beginning of term like a stray dog? Or is it because, unable to concentrate in class, she throws caution to the wind by constantly amusing her classmates? But the mad avenging nun hasn't finished with her yet:

Look at her cringing in shame and so she *should*! There'll be no more disruptive shenanigans around *here*! I'll say no more other than Agnes Keen is a *bad* influence. Heed my warning, you gullible girls, and stay *away* from her. One rotten apple in a box can contaminate the *lot*!

Agnes dreads those around her will move and expose her. But nobody does. To her relief, some of her new mates from the North Shore inch imperceptibly closer. As she braces herself for the nun to swoop, a young novice taps the Mother Superior on the shoulder and whispers something in her ear:

I'm called away to the telephone, girls! That will be all! DISMISSED!

With the nun's disappearance, the torture is over for another day. At the sound of the school bell Agnes shuffles into class with the others. The classroom. A place where she is finding it increasingly hard to listen, absorb, and comprehend what is going on around her. At this new school she feels defeated before she has even begun, struggling to navigate the labyrinth of corridors in a huge building that resembles Government House, and slowly finding her way through the enormous grounds that eventually lead to tennis courts and playing fields. Yet, as if granting her a reward for her endeavours, she will shortly discover that the grounds are blessed with dazzling views of the northern harbour, which will help.

The furthest school outpost is the sports field where, every week, the school divides into four teams, identified by colours, to compete in the forthcoming Sports Day. Agnes is part of the 'green' cohort. Experienced in quick getaways, she excels as a runner. The sports field is hidden from outside view by a row of huge Moreton Bay fig trees yet is close enough to the harbour for Agnes to hear the wind singing in the rigging of the sailing boats moored in a small bay below. The tang of salt impregnates the air. In the silence, at dusk, she can hear the roar of lions across the water from Taranga Park Zoo. This invariably reminds her of Uncle Ben's gorilla story. The only one of God's creatures who had managed to inflict revenge upon her mother.

Mother Miriam is seemingly unaware of the nervous tic that sabotages her tall, gangly frame. The whites of her eyes enlarge as she rocks backwards and forwards in her worn lace-up black shoes and Agnes watches, fascinated, as the frenetic pace accelerates until the woman is rocking so fast her face blurs. At this point, the relentless shuddering converts Mother Miriam's stovepipe body into a series of reptilian gyrations like a loose hosepipe receiving a sudden gush of water. It occurs to Agnes that perhaps the devil is closer than she thought.

Agnes's classmates decide that the mad nun 'has a set on her', which seems to mean that Agnes provokes an inexplicable irritation. This is not hard for her to grasp, as she has always had the same effect on her mother. It is hard to know if the nun is singling her out because she happens to be the first unfortunate face the woman sees, or whether she has unwittingly committed a specific offence.

The first assault had happened at morning break, whilst Agnes had been eating play lunch with her friends. As they lounged around, striking sophisticated poses on a bench in the courtyard, Agnes had suddenly found herself submerged in a mass of black cloth as if someone had put a bag over her head. In the process of taking a bite of her sandwich, she had found herself in danger of crunching into one of the wooden rosary beads around Mother Miriam's waist. Thin, sinewy fingers clamped down on her upper arm, the nun had dragged her across the quadrangle without explanation and plonked her into the middle of a bunch of startled youngsters from the junior school. Then the savage voice had sieved through long, discoloured teeth:

Stay *there* and eat! *Impudent* girl!

Giggling girls had fallen silent as they moved apart to accommodate the order. Then they had wriggled away awkwardly in an attempt not to look at the culprit. Agnes had stayed put, though yearning to be back with her group, especially as she could now see their doe-eyed prefect – who all, including Agnes, had a crush on – had just sat down with them.

But none of the teenagers had looked her way. She had felt glad of this, as recognition would only have added to her humiliation. Several girls from her group had then disappeared down the steps behind the railing to the toilet block in the basement. It was the route past the locker rooms they followed at midday in order to ascend the chapel steps for rosary. Agnes had watched in growing dismay as Mother Miriam put an arm round the prefect's shoulder and smiled at her. The intimate gesture had felt like a further slap.

Marooned in purdah, Agnes had watched as nuns flew in and out of the mysterious door to the convent at the end of the veranda. This was firmly designated 'out of bounds' and, consequently, the girls were hugely curious to see inside. Talk of underground tunnels leading from the convent to the Jesuit priests – streets away at St Aloysius Boys' School, kept the girls fascinated. Aware of the pupils' obsession, the nuns only succeeded in adding to the intrigue by snapping the mysterious door shut, like the release of a mousetrap, behind them.

That morning, through the line of smudged glass windows in the dilapidated science block, Agnes could view some older girls hovering over a lighted Bunsen burner. Increasingly, she had found herself staring intently at her surroundings to enable herself to manage a wave of sadness that constantly threatens to engulf her. It had been another bad day all round – her mother screaming for another cup of tea that morning when Agnes was already running late for the train. She had looked up at the two-storey block of classrooms that ran parallel to the boundary wall with the street, too sick to the stomach to eat her sandwich. It was tasteless anyway, for she had thrown a piece of sausage meat between the bread – the butter having been too hard to use because she had forgotten to take it out of the fridge. And, as she stared down at the inedible sandwich, she had tried to comprehend the humiliation of being plonked down by Mother Miriam in the middle of six small girls with milk teeth, like a grown bird in a nest of small chicks.

Unable to bear it any longer, as soon as Mother Miriam released the prefect from her grim embrace and disappeared from view, Agnes had run around the corner, up the stairs, and straight out of the school gate. Her chest had collapsed into such forceful sobs, they had racked her body. She had clung on to the outside wall of the school to stop herself from falling, grief-stricken, to the ground. Then moving on, eyes blinded with tears, she had sent a pile of empty garbage bins scattering in all directions. The clang had been deafening. She had to chase one of the bins down the hill to catch it and, as she rearranged them back into a neat row at the main gate, she had felt the sky darken and fall upon her, like when Jesus asked his father why he had forsaken him in the Garden of Gethsemane.

Unlike Jesus, Agnes knows she can't be forsaken, because she's never been claimed. That morning, when she had been ejected from her own group of new friends, had not been the first time she had thought of leaving home – and school – but she doesn't know where to go. And so, Agnes has decided that her faith is being tested. The devil can assume any guise, after all. Could he be cunning enough to tempt her to lose her faith by inhabiting the hosepipe body of the Mother Superior? She doesn't know *what* to think anymore.

She decides to keep out of Mother Miriam's way, ducking around corners, standing behind others, and sliding surreptitiously under the desk if she ever comes into the classroom. Agnes can hear her imminent arrival – the swirl of the long black habit sending the beads clanking against the strap around her waist and amplifying her step. But what she can't avoid is the uniform inspection, conducted before the pupils leave the school. Agnes tries to tell herself she is exaggerating this madwoman's grudge against her, but just the way she waves the others on with scant interest, settling instead on Agnes's uniform, makes it hard to deny. There always seems to be something to engage her predatory eye. Regularly forced to stay behind to darn a hole in a glove, or sew up a hem, she frequently misses the train and is forced to catch a later one, all alone.

Agnes remains as resilient as she can in the face of this onslaught by falling over, doing hare-brained tricks, balancing on one leg, jumping like a monkey, and generally being silly to amuse the others. When not held back at school, the train ride is, in fact, the highlight of her day. At least half of her class live on the North Shore and get on and off at different stations, starting with those furthest up the line who live in big houses with leafy gardens, swimming pools and tennis courts. Not that the kind of house a person lives in makes any difference, thinks Agnes, for they are equal and united in Catholicism. It's the Protestants who are inferior. In the mornings, by the time Agnes steps onto the train with two other girls, there's a rowdy group congregated near the door of the carriage where they huddle together, chatting and laughing in a circle. Agnes absorbs her classmates' anecdotes: family outings and holidays, older siblings' tennis and pool parties, birthday surprises, practical jokes, endearing parental idiosyncrasies, menageries of animals, and descriptions of shows from those who possess TV sets. She cobbles together what she hears and invents a life in tune with her peers. She makes up fictitious visits to see her brothers at boarding school on their birthdays, bearing her beloved siblings cakes mother and daughter have slaved over together. She invents a loving father, who saddles her pony and calls her pet names like Pumpkin and Precious.

Even Grandma is reinvented. Ever keen on the sensational, Agnes elevates her parents' great love to a fictional level – equivalent to that of Anthony and Cleopatra, Paris and Helen, Queen Victoria and Albert, Jane Eyre and Rochester, Bogart and Bacall, or Grace Kelly and Prince Rainier.

Imitating her teachers is the only benefit available to Agnes from their efforts to educate her. Her impersonations provoke spasms of laughter from the other girls, Agnes having learned that nobody argues with a person who makes them laugh. The train carriage has become her stage. Striding to the station each morning, she edits her inventions, honing bits of her script. She never disappoints her audience, and their pleasure transports her every time. An impersonation of Mother Miriam is her greatest hit – she has even mastered the nervous tic. Her only problem is to get through the performance without collapsing with laughter herself.

Agnes's urge to ingratiate herself with her new classmates transcends caution, which is why, when Ellen forgets her train pass, Agnes jumps in to save the day:

Don't worry! I'll go through and show my pass and then hand it to you at the side grille and you can use mine! The ticket master never looks at them anyway!

But instead of the usual ticket collector studying the horse-racing form with one hand and waving passengers through with the other, the Station Master is officiating at the exit. Ellen and Agnes are caught in the act. Mr Fog is well known for his working-class chip on the shoulder and his overblown ideas of how the other half live. He imagines the private school children who pass through the turnstile are extruded from opulent palaces up the line, with butlers and footmen catering to their every whim. He grabs Ellen and Agnes roughly by their shoulders:

A ripe pair of crooks! I got the 'andle on yas! Eyes as sharp as a tack I 'as, and there's a few Japs limping today to prove it! So, who've we got here? Let's see that pass. Agnes Keen, born in March 1942. And what's *your* name, bright eyes?

I'm Ellen.

Is that the only name ya got, Bean Pole?

Ellen winces at the reference to her height:

No. Ellen Carey. I live near Agnes.

Ellen is blubbering now and fixing her eyes on Agnes, as if the proximity of their houses will save her. But tears do not move Mr Fog:

I don't care if ya live next to the Prime Minister. The two of yas broke the law and it's incumbent on me as 'ead man 'ere to report yas.

I'm so sorry, Mr Fog!

Ellen has spotted his name on a badge pinned to his shirt. But Agnes is not about to be shamed by the likes of Mr Fog:

We come through here *every* day and so you *know* we all have passes. She left hers at home, but she'll bring it and show you tomorrow. It can't be *that* serious!

And just who da ya think *you're* talking to, Miss High and Mighty?

I'm talking to *you*, Mr Fog, because I think you're making a mountain out of a molehill.

And *do* you now, bluey?!

Agnes knows she's provoking him, but given the captive audience, she can't stop. Here is a golden chance to upgrade her reputation and wipe away the stain of being a bad influence.

When Mr Fog is distracted by collecting tickets from another arrival, Ellen nudges her to shush up, hissing:

Don't be such a smart arse… just say you're sorry!

Then their usual short-sighted ticket collector is running up to the gate, puffing heavily, a newspaper tucked under his arm. He waves at Mr Fog:

Sorry, Stan! Emergency at the dentist!

Agnes's heart sinks a little. If only they had been ten minutes later, then none of this nonsense would have happened. Mr Fog isn't swayed:

Okay you two crims – follow me!

He announces the order triumphantly as he waves the other girls through, all of whom could have forgotten their passes for all he knew. Agnes sees clearly that he intends to squeeze every last drop out of, feasibly, the only alert moment he has had in years.

The Station Master's complaint to the school will send Mother Miriam into a self-righteous frenzy. A day later, bestriding the veranda, Mother Miriam will straighten her veil and launch forth her damnation, deliberately keeping her feet well apart so that neither can contaminate the other and set off the uncontrollable physical spasm:

Two girls have disgraced the good name of this school! A respected 'Blue Sodality' member led astray by the notorious troublemaker I have *warned* you about! If you wish to advance through the Sodality of The Blessed Virgin Mary, *avoid* the pernicious girl in question!

Agnes and Ellen will hang their heads. Ellen will stroke the blue sodality ribbon around her neck in a show of preening goodness that Agnes will find nauseating. Advancement through the sodality depends on good behaviour and Agnes already knows for certain that she will leave the school with the first stage narrow green ribbon she started with. Public disgrace will be followed by line-writing punishment, and effusive apology letters to Mr Fog, as well as to high-ranking members of the Sydney Railway Department, who must have wondered at the sanity levels of the school. To keep her spirits up, Agnes will make jokes about Ellen being the bad influence – brushing specks of wickedness off her uniform. She will mock the embargo but, despite her strategies, it will get to her.

Mother Miriam's persecution will come to an end abruptly one day, after the rosary service in the chapel. Given Agnes has pride of place in the nun's crazed state of mind, she knows she really should be more careful but, instead she will hand Mother Miriam the perfect gift by winking at a friend on the opposite aisle of the chapel while they await the signal to file into the pews. Mother Miriam will spot the transgression instantly, drag her roughly by the arm out of the row of girls, and fling her into a prayer chair at the back of the chapel – recently vacated by a deceased nun:

Disrespect in a holy place, Agnes Keen!

It will be a Friday – when benediction follows the rosary. The priest, wearing sumptuous gold and green vestments, will glide out of the sacristy and cross to the altar to officiate. The scent of incense combined with the singing of 'O Salutaris Hostia' at the top of her voice have never failed to lift Agnes's spirits, and this day will be no exception. But the respite will be brief. The service over, Mother Miriam will attack from behind, ordering Agnes to stand next to the stair-rail where maximum humiliation can be guaranteed as pupils walk past when exiting the door of the chapel. Agnes will stare defiantly ahead. Most girls will avert their eyes. As the last voices fade and Agnes waits to be dismissed, Mother Miriam will wage another assault. Grabbing at Agnes's arms, she will start to shake her violently, and Agnes will feel a cold fear rise inside as the nun hisses:

Why do you persist in this boldness?! And in the house of the *Lord*!

The nun will continue to rant – her face scarlet. The frantic muscular movement behind the heightened complexion will look to Agnes like the internal workings of a clock. An explosion is imminent. Anything might happen – and does. The madwoman will push Agnes's head back over the stair rail. Aware of the three-storey drop looming below, Agnes will see the ceiling above whirling as long thin fingers close around her neck. She will think: She is going to kill me.

In a reflex action, she will bring her arms up and jerk the sinuous fingers from her neck, duck low, and race down the stairs, Mother Miriam hot on her tail:

Come *back* you impudent, *wicked* child!

Agnes will hear rosary beads and leather strap clash together like an African tribal dance as the nun follows her. On the ground floor, she will run into the school and, turning hard into the toilet block, lock herself into a cubicle. Mother Miriam's fist will hit the wood of the cubicle door with a resounding thud:

Wicked, *evil* daughter of Satan, come out at *once*!

Agnes will inadvertently think of the gorilla at Taronga Park Zoo, but something more grown up will happen next. From the depths of her being will emerge a commanding and unwavering voice:

Go away, Mother! You've gone *too* far! This is *madness*!

There will be a pause, and upon hearing receding footsteps Agnes will be utterly astonished to realise the nun has left. After a short time, to make sure, and still trembling a little, she will dry her eyes, wash her face and run to the lunch-room, where she will collect her tray, sit down at a table on her own and eat in silence. For some reason she will resist confiding in the comfortable goodness of those seated around her. She is confused about who she is and who they are. She yearns for sympathy yet keeps her distance. Her energy at school has been dissipated into continually showing these girls she is just like them, and so worthy of being part of the group. But the truth is she has never formed a close friendship, like the one with Rita Ryder, with any of them. The inner turmoil of her life has left no space for anything more than a struggle to survive.

But perhaps meagre miracles exist on occasion for, after naming Mother Miriam's erratic behaviour out loud as madness, it will miraculously cease. The nun will, henceforth, ignore her completely. And then, one day, the psychotic Mother Superior will no longer dominate the school. Nobody will mention her disappearance.

Agnes's colourful reputation as 'a naughty girl', however, will be further established and, in the hopeless years that follow, no humiliation meted out by Mother Miriam will compete with the agony of the consistent non-appearance of her parents at prize-giving, and at every other school function.

* * *

The weekly elocution lessons commanded by Rosemont are coinciding with Agnes losing concentration. Gradually, relentlessly, comprehension of the various texts she is obliged to read diminishes. For one horrendous hour, she finds herself scrutinised by a series of bemused voice teachers as she degenerates into mouthing words, without meaning, like a parrot. Words, once dear companions, have turned against her – hovering, smudging, and vanishing from her reach. The downward slide at school coincides with strange levitations in bed at night, when her body rises to join the guardian angel in the treasured drawing that hangs above her bed. She can no longer read fluently and, to avoid ridicule during sessions of reading by turns aloud in class, she tries to calculate in advance the paragraph she will be designated so she can rehearse it. Sometimes this works but, more often than not, she anticipates her turn incorrectly and is left stuttering and tripping over unfamiliar words like a small child with a severe handicap.

God in his mercy organises a teacher to make Agnes feel better about herself. This octogenarian nun, who teaches English, possesses less power of concentration than Agnes. Unpinned starched wimple seriously skew-whiff, she shuffles into class looking as if she is wearing a broken white box on her head. Age has drained her lips of elasticity and her gaping mouth no longer closes properly. A cruel addition to what is already an ugly appearance is the proliferation of hair around her chin. If a passion for literature ever burned inside this woman, it has long been extinguished as the syllabus sends her to sleep within minutes. As each girl reads in turn, her eyes begin to droop and, gradually, her head flops forward until her own open book becomes a pillow. Once cushioned comfortably, a light snore is audible. The English class waits, motionless, until she suddenly raises her head like a jack-in-the-box and point an arthritic finger at a non-specific face:

Next, next, *next*!

As the teacher's desk is on a raised podium, Agnes takes advantage of the decrepit nun's bad eyesight to sink low over her own desk and so avoid reading altogether. After all, there are enough girls more than keen to oblige, so by abstaining she is giving them a chance to take another turn. Agnes's classmates remain loyal, for nobody ever points out to the teacher she is being missed out.

Yet, regardless of her deteriorating ability to read, Agnes still loves to hear a story. The one book she can't forgive the teacher for desecrating with snores is *Great Expectations*. Unlike the soporific crash-landing guaranteed with Shakespeare's *Twelfth Night*, it takes a little longer for Dickens to send the old nun off to sleep. Consequently, as the class are burning with curiosity to know what happens next to Pip and Estella, they gradually edit out their snoring teacher and go on reading. When she returns to consciousness and sits bolt upright, often just before the bell that heralds the end of class, she will invariably declaim:

Such a good plot! *Such* a range of unforgettable characters!

At the end of the story, when Pip recognises his pretentions, makes amends and embraces Joe Gargery's love, Agnes always wonders if her parents will eventually have a change of heart and value her as much as they do the polo crowd. Yet, she knows in her soul that her educational development is in decline, for she increasingly seeks refuge in the passing clouds and is grasping less and less of what happens around her.

One day, fortunately not in class, the nameless old nun will drop her head onto the New Testament – open at Saint Paul's Epistle to the Romans – and never lift it again.

Along with Ancient History, English Literature is resurrected by an enthusiastic lay teacher called Mrs Burton who, to Agnes's delight, reinstates *Great Expectations*. Her reading simply crackles with verve. She knows just where to pause and change the timbre of her voice and has a wonderful talent for stepping into character. Agnes's disability is safely concealed as, instead of asking the girls to read in turn, Mrs Burton appoints a handful of favourites and leaves Agnes in peace, skulking at a desk at the back of the class. However, when Mrs Burton's ambitious stage production of *Twelfth Night* – to be enacted for parents and friends – proves a great success,

Agnes feels sadness, for she loves to act. After all, she does it all the time, having invented an entire new family and home life. But her poor reading at auditions always prevents her from getting parts in school productions that, with practice, she feels she could surely manage. And, sadly, Mrs Burton's *Twelfth Night* audition is no exception.

Nature has fashioned Mrs Burton in the shape of an upside-down triangle. Two giant melons live in her bodice, dominating a narrow waist with small hips. The whole structure is poised precariously on short sparrow legs. It is a body perilously out of balance and is a continuous fascination for all who gaze upon it. Yet there is style in the scarves, jewellery, and exotic belts she wears, only eclipsed by the startling range of flamboyant hats stabbed through with huge ornamental hatpins, which she often keeps on while teaching – or leaves, to be admired, at the front of the desk.

Mrs Burton's bodily proportions will be seriously tested when she bursts into the classroom one fatal morning. Displaying a disconcerting rigor-mortis grin, she will caper around like a clown in a circus:

Good morning, my lovelies! Why are my babies so hesitant this morning? Do you want to make Mrs Burton sad?

Ignoring the want of a reply, she starts clapping her hands, massaging her knees, and bending over to pat her own shapely bottom:

Hands, knees, and *bums-a-daisy*!

She will chant this refrain as she continues her perilous gyrations. Although accustomed to her eccentricity, the class will soon realise, from all the slurring and swaying, that she's drunk as a newt. So, when she finally topples over with a crash, one of the girls in the front row of the class will slip out and grab a passing nun. Two strong members of the sacred order will pull the wayward teacher to her feet and gently guide her out of the classroom. For the last time. Speculation will ensue as to the nature of the tragedy that drove Mrs Burton to drink that day. Was there a Mr Burton? And, if so, had he been stolen by another woman? Later, at recess, Agnes and her classmates will watch with sadness the final act of the calamity – a crestfallen Mrs Burton being helped into the back of a black car at the main entrance to the convent. Seated in a corner of the car, their last view of the unfortunate teacher will be the daisy chain of cloth strawberries and white snowdrops that adorn the crown of the vibrant red straw hat screening her bloodshot eyes.

Agnes will miss Mrs Burton and will be ever grateful for her vivid telling of the adventures of Hannibal and his Carthaginian army as they crossed the

Alps, as well as her fantastic reading of *Great Expectations* – performances to be eclipsed only by the teacher's spectacular final curtain call.

Mother Miriam may have been the tallest nun Agnes has ever encountered, but her reluctant successor – Mother Jude – is the polar opposite. Closer in size to a midget, she seems to swim inside her capacious habit. Not only is she physically diminutive, but everything about her – from her delicate white skin to the pink blush on her cheeks – resembles a saint on a holy card. The devil-crazed tyrant has been replaced by an angel! But this allure of sanctity is reduced when Mother Jude dons a pair of oversized beige glasses. They magnify her pale eyes to the point of cartoon comedy, all the while reducing her tiny nose to a knob.

Agnes comes to like everything about Mother Jude's manner: she puts the girls at ease and doesn't play one off against the other. Named after the patron saint of lost causes, the little nun's soft voice and shy, retiring demeanour can't help but give the impression that she herself may soon be in need of assistance from the very saint whose name she has taken. But her gentle aspect is not confined to voice or nature. Instead of rousing assemblies and public humiliation, Mother Jude favours the noticeboard and personal consultation. She makes it known to the pupils that she is always available to listen to their concerns, privately, in her office. Naturally, Agnes is desperate to talk to someone. And so, she hovers outside the new Mother Superior's office with longing. More than once, she resists the temptation to unburden herself for fear any complaints will inevitably reach her mother.

In less than a year, however, Mother Jude will no longer be the head of the convent. It will be decided that her saintly complexion and sensitive demeanour are more suitable for teaching the subject of Art. Decades later, all Agnes will remember of her brief initiation into art studies with Mother Jude is the gentle nun's prudish defilement of the school's art books. His delicate masculinity hidden under a toga of pink tissue paper, Michelangelo's 'David' will look like a marcher in a gay parade, and countless will be the variegated tissue clumps adorning the timeline of marble and bronze sausages from the Renaissance to Rodin.

Although she has no technical knowledge of art, after her years as the self-appointed keeper of The Art Book, Agnes will be further distressed to discover works she has long admired with added extras – particularly Rubens' 'Three Graces' who, under Mother Jude's auspices, now sport clumsy white tissue nappies. And the relaxed fold between the legs of various reclining nudes will be stamped with a single gold star, as if Mother Jude has elevated Giorgione and Titian to the top of the class.

Agnes will long imagine Mother Jude, alone in the privacy of her chaste cell with her tissue paper, like the shy professor in the Marlene Dietrich film *The Blue Angel* when he blew on a postcard of Lola – secretly titillated by a sudden glimpse of what lay underneath.

By the time Miss Josephine comes into her life, Agnes will be weary of authority. A recent graduate of psychology, now working as a lay teacher, Miss Josephine will have a target: that of improving Agnes's deteriorating ability to read. At heart, Agnes desperately wants to be like everyone else, so can Miss Josephine really perform wonders when she asks:

Are you happy at home, Agnes?

Miss Josephine will fix Agnes with her piercing sapphire eyes. Although hopeful, Agnes will feel awkward being plucked from the back of the class for experimentation. It will be impossible for her to answer sincerely, as the invented life has fast taken over. There will be no option but to go on lying:

Oh, yes, I'm *very* happy at home.

She will try to be diplomatic, for her parents still haven't got over the social worker's questions after little Jim ran away all those years ago. When summoned to the school by Miss Josephine, Madge will taunt her daughter:

I'm going to ring and *cancel*!

But, like the promised pillow-talk call to Grandma, she will never activate her threat. The call to come to the school will have Madge cornered. She will waver, but her vanity will not be able to resist a golden opportunity to give the yellow mohair coat – the one she has knitted specially to take to the Scone polo tournament – its first social outing.

On the appointed morning of the assessment, Agnes will fervently wish she could turn the clock back. This will be her mother's first and last visit to this school and, unlike her deceptive trip to the Mercy Convent, will end in disaster.

Madge will arrive, looking gorgeous in her daughter's eyes. Having had her hair done, her nails will be painted coral pink and the soft yellow mohair will perfectly complement her shiny dark hair. Hovering in the doorway, Agnes will watch as her mother engages in animated chatter with Miss Josephine. A young, nuggety, bright-eyed nun – also studying the impact of learning difficulties – will be in attendance too.

Agnes will enter the room, sliding awkwardly onto the seat beside her mother and, as the experts talk briefly between themselves, Miss Josephine will turn to address Madge:

We think Agnes 'sees' words differently to other children. It's a disability that impairs a child's reading fluency and comprehension. Words look 'different' to Agnes.

Miss Josephine will repeat this sentence in an effort to elevate Agnes from difficulty to uniqueness. If, at this stage in her young life, Agnes knows one thing for certain, it will be that she sees more than the *words* in her world differently. She will keep a close eye on her mother for any sign of irritation as Miss Josephine presses on. And then, soon, very soon, the eruption Agnes accurately predicts will come:

What are you *talking* about! She's a *perfectly normal* child!

Yes, indeed that's true, and absolutely not in question. You'll perhaps recall what I pointed out on the school report – about Agnes's short attention span.

As Madge never reads school reports, she will dismiss this with a wave of a manicured hand and reply sharply:

Probably a bad day. It's likely she didn't sleep well.

Miss Josephine, unaware of the deadly heat building under the mohair, will plough on:

Let me point out the three cognitive subtypes – auditory, visual, and intentional.

She will go on to explain these categories in depth, assuming the listener's interest. The one thing Agnes has always been able to read, without impairment, is her mother's moods. Her survival has depended on it. On this day, as she observes Madge's lips tighten and her voice become strident, Agnes will brace herself.

The tipping point reached, Madge will spring to her feet and, staring daggers at Miss Josephine, yell:

No child of *mine* is retarded! How *dare* you insult my daughter and I!

Then Madge will flounce from the room, the assembled experts watching her departure in shocked amazement. When Agnes runs after her outraged mother as she struts indignantly up the drive, Madge will turn on her and snarl:

I'll deal with you *later*, young lady!

What Agnes will remember most of this precarious time in her school life, and with affection, is the camaraderie of her peer group and their unflinching commitment to the unwritten rule of never telling on a mate. As she has continued to spiral downhill with increasing momentum, they have felt nothing but sympathy for her and have laughed amiably at her inevitable blunders.

14

THE ANGEL OF DEATH

The nuns have chosen a priest from the Redemptorist order to officiate at the school retreat. This event runs for a full week on the school calendar and is set aside for spiritual contemplation – to be observed in silence. Unlike the customary slow build-up of solemnity that the pupils are accustomed to, Father McBride leaps into the pulpit on the first morning like someone jumping on a bus. An audible sigh precedes a bug-eyed stare at his congregation, before he embarks on a thunderous sermon about the arbitrary nature of death:

The angel of death strikes suddenly. He comes at *any* time. Night or day. You *can't* trick him. He issues *no* warning. There is no preferred year, no preferred month or moment. *Nothing* you can calculate in advance, *nothing* you can prevent. Death swoops down when you *least* expect him! Yes, he does! He *swoops* down from heaven in a flash of light and taps you on the shoulder and says: Your... time... is... up... come... along... with ME!

Father McBride's voice, which had softened into a sinister whisper, has just exploded into a shattering crescendo:

You are chosen for *death*. And no-no-no, you have *no* choice! When the call is given, you are dragged from earth. No pleading. No sidestepping. No way to prevaricate or hide. Take stock, my children, and remember these words. If your soul is stained with mortal sin, you are destined to burn in the never-ending FIRES OF HELL!

Concluding his terrifying address, he slumps forward over the rail like a tenor taking a bow. Spikes of oily, grey-streaked hair, dislodged by the violent movement of his head, stand erect like a series of small radio antennae. The chapel walls seem to vibrate. The tranquil doves that habitually fly in and out of the high windows won't be seen again until he departs.

The helpless, hopeless finality of his sermon hangs heavily on the shoulders of the young girls as they stumble out of the chapel and descend the stairs, tightly clutching at the rail. The bewildered group which emerges into the sunlight in the courtyard have little appetite for play lunch. They shuffle in a trance, nibbling despondently on their sandwiches and biscuits with bowed heads, contemplating the arbitrary nature of the grim reaper.

Nuns move like shadows amongst them, ready to counsel any girl struggling with sin shaken into conscience by the priest's address. Agnes feels as if she is sleepwalking through the ruins of a city after an earthquake because, absent at this year's retreat, is the usual light-hearted hand language, exaggerated lip movements and pupils rushing to give friends last-minute holy cards to wish them a happy and holy retreat. Father McBride has succeeded in quenching the spring of youthful happiness with his hellfire.

The next day, his hair neatly combed, he jumps back into the pulpit. Exercising the same vocal acrobatics, he keeps repeating the word 'PURITY' as if struggling to find the answer to a riddle:

Purity is freedom from adulteration, from contamination, from immorality. Now my children. The loss of purity is like… a… white… sheet… splattered… with… MUD!

Again, each word is vocalised between pauses in an ascending crescendo. Then he pulls open a white handkerchief and holds it up, like a magician about to do a trick. Next, he uncaps a fountain pen and squirts ink on the surface. Pen recapped and popped back under his cassock, he holds the soiled cloth up to the congregation, moving it around and above his head so that everyone can imbibe the desecrating spatter:

What you see here, young ladies, is a VIOLATION OF PURITY! Those of you who are sceptical – any of those Doubting Thomas's amongst you – take heed. This is not a game or an idle experiment. This is an image of a soul stained with MORTAL SIN! Mark my words! Here, in front of you, you see, the loss of purity as clearly as if the walls in this chapel were COVERED IN MUD!

Agnes is deeply troubled after the retreat. The lightest touch on the shoulder makes her jump. She focuses on the state of her parents' souls, for it is her duty as a Catholic daughter to bring them back to God. Her father, for instance, would have gone straight to hell had he died when he recently fell asleep at the wheel while driving home drunk. He had crashed into the wall of a railway underpass at St Leonards Station. She pictures the potential carnage. The image of the river of blood from the motorcyclist's head that long-ago Sunday evening has never left her.

She hears Eric Keen late at night – when only cats stalk the pavements. He slams the back door and lumbers up the hall as he bounces off the walls on the way to the front bedroom. He is usually mumbling to himself these days. Concern for her father's well-being has stimulated in her close observation of drunks in the street. What drives them to drink? And, lately, the incoherent, dead-of-night pillow talk is sounding even more frantic:

Let's make the break, Madge, before, it's too late. Let's split with the family, like Parry. Buy our own place in the country. Why not? What's stopping us? Work for ourselves. No bastard telling us what to do. I know sheep and cattle, Madge. I could train horses. Sell them. Get a polo team together. Go to America. I've still got contacts. We'd be free. What do you think?

Madge's reply is, as usual, inaudible, and Agnes knows, as heavy breathing fills the small space between their rooms, that the sorrowful pleas in the next room will be swept away with the morning light.

Her chances of rehabilitating her father become even more remote on the day he ignores her in front of her classmates. It happens on the sideline before he is about to play polo as a member of the NSW's team at Warwick Farm. They are up against a visiting English side that includes the Duke of Edinburgh. Agnes strolls towards her father, where he is signing autographs surrounded by fans – some of whom are her school pals who have unexpectedly turned up to watch the match. She stands with these girls on the outer circle.

They all see Eric Keen turn his head and look straight at his daughter, without showing her any recognition whatsoever. No acknowledgement. The empty connection with his eyes is indisputable, along with the snub. The pain is so intense, Agnes feels as if she has been stabbed through the heart. She stays, riveted to the spot, until she fully realises that he really does have no intention of greeting her, or of meeting her school chums, who remain standing uncomfortably beside her.

Shrugging her shoulders in front of them, she tries to cover it up by telling them that she and her father had a fight that morning and that he obviously has not forgiven her. They nod kindly, yet she senses they smell a rat. Perhaps they even doubt he really *is* her father, and not just someone she has invented – like everything else.

The agonising pain lingers, but she cannot hate someone she wants to save. The priest's ink-stained handkerchief is etched into her father's troubled face. The more isolated she feels, the more intensely religious she becomes. She lives and breathes saints and miracles and prays constantly and fervently to the Blessed Virgin to send her a sign. Her efforts are gratified when the Virgin Mary obligingly appears on top of the flowering wisteria vine in the back garden as Agnes kneels on the rough ground below, saying the rosary. Wearing a blue mantle over a white robe, Our Lady matches the blooms perfectly. Agnes offers the pain in her knees up to Our Lady and asks her to save her parents.

This apparition had occurred at twilight, precisely when day merges into night. All around Agnes had been silent, as the disruptive Cleary children were indoors getting ready for bed. Ribbons of thin white clouds, like hundreds of merged feathers, had swirled above the vine. As the perfume from the flowers intensified in the evening calm, Agnes had been filled with a wave of pure joy, for Our Lady was whispering to her: 'Have courage. Trust in God and you will find the grace to intercede.'

And, of course, there were the levitations. Although keeping these events to herself at school, she has started to reveal her nightly experiences to Monsignor Harrington in the confessional at the Parish church. When he had revealed to her how Saint Teresa of Avila had such powerful levitations that the nuns in the order had to hold her down, Agnes had replied eagerly:

In my case, Father, one minute I'm in bed asleep and then the next, I'm leaving my body. It's not imagined, but real. I float up to join the guardian angel in the picture above my bed. Is God calling me to bring my parents back to the faith? I'm worried they'll go to hell. They don't go to Mass on Sunday. My mother has forgotten it's a sin to eat meat on Friday. She is so furious when I remind her. I leave the meat on my plate and just eat the vegetables. What's the matter with you, wasting good food? she says. You should be shot. She chastises me, Father, but I remain silent. My mother goes crazy at the *mention* of sin.

Agnes had felt disloyal telling on her parents. But Monsignor Harrington had reassured her that it was an act of love – not betrayal:

We'll work together to restore them to God, my child. A surprise call on the victim of the devil is the first step.

Thus, the fatal die was cast. Agnes and the priest had discussed an afternoon for him to come and see her mother when her father was away on business. There was no threat of the policeman dropping in on Madge unexpectedly either as, ever since a heated argument in the kitchen between her parents – in the course of which she had heard the officer's name mentioned – there had been no helmet on the table, nor any police car spotted in the area.

Apart from the social workers who brought Jim home when he ran away, and a photographer who once took a photo of Agnes and her brothers, Monsignor Harrington had been the only other person she could ever remember sitting in the living room. Seated on the worn beige two-seater lounge chair, he had gazed at the giant picture of the three, hyper-tense wild horses, their nostrils enlarged, necks straining, manes flowing, as they galloped across an open plain. A thunderclap is evident in their terrified eyes and a jagged flash of lightning has just severed the bruised clouds above them, threatening an imminent deluge. Two pale green patterned ceramic vases, encircled by a ring of thin glass teardrops, sit either side of the fireplace shelf, as if weeping for the plight of the horses above. Apart from the guardian angel hovering over Agnes's bed, the horses and the teardrop vases are the only ornamentation in the house.

As they waited for her mother to join them, Agnes had chosen to comment on the picture:

It might be a scene from the Last Judgement, Father.

It is certainly a powerful image, Agnes, yes.

Are you interested in painting, Father?

Oh, yes. I've been to Rome and seen Michelangelo's work in the Sistine Chapel.

At this, Agnes had rushed up the hall to retrieve The Art Book. She meant to open it at the Sistine Chapel ceiling but had stumbled nervously. Instead, it fell open in the priest's lap at Goya's 'The Third of May 1808'. This page was dog-eared because Agnes was so fascinated by it. The priest had gazed down at the ragged queue of terrified men behind the central figure in white who, waiting to be shot, had his arms flung open wide like Jesus on the cross. And there, of course, was the stained earth below, drenched in blood from those executed. This prompted Agnes to state authoritatively:

Did you know, Father, that Goya watched Napoleon's soldiers execute the Spaniards who fought back against his invasion of Madrid?

She had tried hard to sound knowledgeable, but Monsignor Harrington was handing her back the book in silence. Keen to maintain his interest, and delay her predicament, she had flipped over the page and showed him 'Saturn Devouring his Son' by the same artist. The priest had glanced down at the huge, demented figure, its eyes like cooked egg yolks, its teeth buried in the half-eaten head of a child:

What do you think of that, Father? A monster eating his own child!

Horrible, my child! Horrible! It's his black period. Goya was out of his mind. You'll upset yourself looking at images like that!

And, with that, he had clamped the book shut and, frowning, handed it back. Agnes had regretted her choice, worrying that he might think her morbid. She had wanted to show him, 'The Fall of Icarus' by Pieter Bruegel – a masterpiece she returned to in the book again and again, but the moment had passed.

When Madge had finally joined them, she was wearing what, at first glance, looked like a First Communion dress. She was more than gracious to the priest:

Thank you for coming, Father. This is indeed an honour.

Excuse my neglect, Mrs Keen, in not calling on the mother of one of our dearest parishioners sooner.

Hearing this hopeful start, Agnes had left the room to make the tea. As she boiled the water, she thought of the early slaughtered Christians piled up in the catacombs in Rome.

As there was no door to the lounge room, she had coughed to alert them she was returning with the tray. Then she had laid out the best willow-patterned cups and saucers, silver sugar pot and milk jug alongside the pot of tea, along with the basket of little cakes she had bought at the bakery for the occasion. The tray placed on the coffee table, she had politely turned to leave the room, leaving her mother to do the honours. But, emboldened by the priest's support, she then changed her mind and retraced her steps, saying:

Father? Do you think you could bless our house?

The priest had replied with a saintly smile:

Yes, of course, Agnes my child!

Madge had scowled at her daughter and said:

Why don't we wait and ask Father to come and do the blessing after the cleaner's been?

Quite so, Mrs Keen, although Almighty God doesn't mind a bit of dirt!
Well, *he* mightn't, but *I* do!

Agnes had hoped the ceremony of sprinkling holy water and reciting special prayers with a raised cross would purify the atmosphere in this ugly house. The remark about the imaginary cleaner was a bad sign. There *was* no cleaner except Agnes. Her mother told so many lies, she despaired of her path to redemption.

Madge's wrath, once the Monsignor had departed, was predictably terrible:

Not a word to *anyone* – even the *Pope* – about what goes on inside these walls! Do you *hear* me?! No dirty linen aired in public! You're a nasty, troublemaking tittle-tat! I'll have no social workers or teachers with new-fangled ideas coming here or summoning me *anywhere*! And you'll invite that priest back here over my *dead body*! Have you got that through your *thick skull*!?

The only novelty about this tirade had been that Madge Keen had stopped threatening Agnes with a beating from her father and had given her a clout round the ear herself.

A few days later, when Monsignor Harrington had asked in the confessional about life at home, Agnes was beyond telling the truth. She had replied, with an aching heart, that things had improved since his visit:

Good. When would you like me to come back and bless the house, Agnes?

Not at the moment, Father, as we're having work done. It would be lovely, though, if you come as a celebration when it's finished.

She had used this worn old building works lie for fear of him turning up unexpectedly.

After the failure of Monsignor Harrington's visit, Agnes had felt like a rudderless boat in rough seas. She had also developed an aversion to the smell of alcohol, her stomach turning over at the very first whiff. Obligingly, God then sent a priest with a lilting Irish accent, Father O'Leary, into her life. The new headmistress, Mother Angela, had recently introduced him to the pupils in the chapel after rosary. With her beautiful cornflower-blue eyes, Mother Angela was the prettiest nun Agnes had ever seen. In fact, she and Father O'Leary made such a handsome couple that all the girls speculated about a romance between them.

Mother Angela and the priest jointly promoted the Pioneer Abstinence

Association of the Sacred Heart. While Agnes's companions signed up to abstain from alcohol for a few years, Agnes joined the priest and Mother Angela in taking the pledge for life. She had worn a red pioneer pin, with the image of the sacred heart, on her school blazer. Her pledge earned her a certificate signed by the Archbishop of Sydney. At that stage, desperate for some kind of recognition, Agnes had been prepared to promise anything. It was hardly a sacrifice in any case, as ever since the champagne evening at the St Pauls' house, she hadn't tasted a drop of alcohol. And, given her revulsion at the mere smell of it, was unlikely to ever be tempted.

Mother Angela's kindness and understanding had infused the school with a new harmony but, sadly, this highly welcome enlightenment will arrive in Agnes's final year of attendance.

* * *

Agnes has put her age up by a year and, in the run-up to Christmas, and lands a job in the children's department of Mark Foy's Department Store. Catching the train each morning to the store in the city is proving to be heaven. She is really loving the job and pleases the manager so much that he gives her a bonus on top of her wage. She has decided to use this extra money to give her parents breakfast in bed 'Hollywood style' on Christmas morning. Her brothers will prepare their parents for this surprise while Agnes makes the breakfast, using her new purchases for the purpose.

This morning, she is arranging two narrow-necked white vases, containing long-stemmed red roses cut from the garden, and placed on two white fold-out trays with linen mats. With their mother and father anchored in bed, Agnes and her brothers are enjoying the freedom of having the kitchen to themselves. The salt and pepper sets, from Woolworths, sit next to the roses, along with curled butter in white bowls beside tiny jars of imported English marmalade. She has polished the good silver cutlery with the crest so well that the contents of the tray are reflected in the blades of the knives. Tumblers of fresh orange juice and half grapefruits – with the flesh severed from the skin – are sent up the hall with Agnes's brothers. They are smirking their heads off as they pose as straight-backed formal waiters. A second course of fried tomato, mushrooms, ham and eggs will follow, to be rounded off with hot crustless toast displayed in little toast racks – also from Woolworths. She has wrapped the racks in a tea towel to keep the toast warm, and there is copious hot tea to wash it all down, just the way her parents like it.

Yet, apart from the pleasure of watching the parental jaws in action, the grand breakfast evokes none of the 'oohs' or 'ahs' of delight Agnes has anticipated. After gulping down the last of the tea, the indulged pair stare with bemused disinterest at the three expectant faces of their offspring, who are seated on the bedroom floor patiently awaiting a word of praise or thanks. Still, Agnes, ever the optimist, congratulates herself on the seemingly peaceful outcome of the Christmas breakfast project.

Given the blank atmosphere at home, Agnes is easily drawn into the warmth of the Armenian house across the road. Natasha's mother, Petra, usually invites her over whenever they meet in the street. Sprawled on a Persian rug immersed amongst layers of soft cushions on the living room floor, Natasha and Agnes are treated to mugs of mint tea accompanied by *baklava* drenched in honey and chunks of melt-in-the-mouth Turkish delight. Agnes imbibes the exotic offerings like a visiting ambassador while Petra targets her with the task of luring her beautiful daughter – who spends the holidays avidly reading everything from true romance to the classics – from her luscious rosy bedroom and out into the fresh air for exercise:

She in there *all day*. She get fat and silly. You, Agnes, make her run... jump... yes?

In anticipation of Natasha's transformation, Mrs Arziani has had two posts cemented into the ground on the flat strip of land at the side of her house, between which she has hung up a badminton net. She hands Agnes two rackets and a shuttlecock. Agnes believes she is probably the only neighbourhood child who has yielded to the immigrant's entreaties to prise Natasha out of her room. It seems that Petra's gold front tooth, coupled with housing the 'yellow peril', puts most people off associating with her.

It proves to be a tug of war to get Natasha into the open air and Agnes is, admittedly, more drawn to dally with her in the melting wonder of Rhett Butler and Scarlet O'Hara's tempestuous relationship in *Gone with the Wind* than to drag her outside. In truth, Agnes would like to hide in her friend's cosy and rosy room forever.

When Rita Ryder introduced her to the ballet, Agnes had claimed it as her own. Now floundering with the written word, she can only experience Margaret Mitchell's masterpiece through Natasha. It isn't just the inability to read that has stalled her, but devoid of any concrete prospects for the future of her own, she is drawn to tagging on to the lives of others – her reaction to any stimulus, a pastiche of their reactions. She is turning into a second-hand person as the residue of her former self slips away.

Agnes has turned fifteen. Standing alongside her curvaceous friend, she looks like a stick of celery. Natasha is two years older and, within the space of what seems like the blink of an eye, has shed her puppy fat, much to Petra's delight, and emerged like a butterfly out of a chrysalis, transforming into a great beauty. No expense is spared on the party for Natasha's seventeenth birthday. Arranged on trestle tables, and to be enjoyed after badminton, is a sumptuous spread of chicken in hazelnut sauce, plates of vegetables and walnut salad, followed by exotic cakes. Agnes is the only home-grown guest. Everyone else is an immigrant. She is a novelty – surrounded by the Chinese and the Armenians.

Agnes's own immigrant roots stem from Ireland a few generations back and so she feels fully Australian in this company. To her surprise, they all embrace the favourite local party games. There is pin the tail on the donkey, sit down when the music stops, and pass the parcel. A favourite game with the Chinese boys seems to be the feeding of popcorn to blindfolded girls – especially Agnes and Natasha. Much of the popcorn is deliberately misplaced and, as a result, a sudden growth spurt of rogue popcorn enlarges the small protrusions in Agnes's bodice, while the front of Natasha's low-cut gold dress looks like she is housing two fully grown chickens. Blindfolds removed, both girls snigger as they gaze down at their fronts, simultaneously appalled and delighted. Natasha knows exactly what happened in the bedroom after Rhett Butler carried Scarlet O'Hara up the stairs, whereas Agnes still doesn't have a clue. She wants to ask Natasha about sex but doesn't know how. Gradually, she stops struggling to understand, accepting that she is not meant to know things like other people.

The National Bank of Armenia must have stored its gold reserves in the mouths of the nation. Before today, Agnes has only seen one gold tooth – belonging to Petra. This afternoon, as the guests scatter across the lawn, the wide grins of the Armenians are reflecting the sun's amber rays like a series of human radar stations. And there is Natasha, her own beautiful, white-toothed Australian smile captivating the company as she reigns benevolently over them all like a princess. She will waft out of Agnes's life forever after the holidays, when she commences studying medicine at university.

After Natasha leaves the district, a lonesome Petra will attempt to describe to Agnes the massacre of Christians by Muslim Turks in Armenia – an event too early for Agnes's mother's knitting bag:

Natasha Australian girl. She never see killing. Me and sister… children… see terrible things Agnes… no forget.

Agnes finds these horrors hard to believe. Armenia is an unknown quantity – on the other side of the world. Yet she knows that Petra still feels wary of being spirited back. She watches her as she fervently kisses an icon of the Virgin Mary to ward off danger. The icon, illuminated with tiny candles, resides in a small room, like a miniature chapel, off the living room. And the danger, it seems, is not imaginary, for Natasha once confided to Agnes that her father, the pen-shaped silent man with a face like a whippet – and rarely seen – was still wanted in the old country for some kind of sabotage.

Agnes allows herself to be inaugurated into the ritual of the icon. She hopes it is not blasphemous to kiss it, but she can't refuse and risk offending a neighbour who helped save her life and has made her feel so special ever since. So, she presses her lips unashamedly to the image for she needs all the celestial help she can get.

15

THE KELLYS

gnes's memory fragments. She struggles for chronological order. Tiny snippets remain of accompanying her parents to a polo tournament after her recent fifteenth birthday. She doesn't know how she got there, nor does she recall the matches, spectators, players, or gracious Janie in her sixth-floor finery, nor the fabulous Federation House and Museum with its antique buggies and carriages. Madge tells her how lucky she is to be received at Springfield, as if she's going to be presented at Buckingham Palace itself, but Agnes has no memory of Janie Marble Flood's ballroom – or anything else.

All that remains in her brain is the sense of running from a man late at night. She sometimes wonders if this man was her father but, when she struggles for clarity, the face retreats like a tortoise into a shell and stays hidden. Sometimes a blur of features, the mouth set in an ugly grimace, comes back, but she doesn't know why she had to escape. On the sports field at school, under the Moreton Bay fig trees, with the wind whistling through the rigging of the sailing boats, she could run so fast she would invariably win the school race, confident that few could catch her.

Decades later, more details will emerge and solidify, and Agnes will be able to grasp this vague sensibility of an event:

I jump into an empty wooden crate behind a stable block and clamp my hand over my mouth to dampen the sound of heavy breathing that might alert my pursuer. I hear his loud footsteps pass back and forth, inches from where I am hiding – and then disappear. I wait until all is silent, except for the shuffling and snorting of the horses in their stalls. When I venture out nervously from my hiding place, I will notice the moon appear over a distant mountain, just like it did the night I buried the jewellery in the rose garden. I will scramble up a rough set of stairs on the side wall of the stable block, crawl through a hatch into the loft, and burrow under a horse blanket on a pile of straw. I will be freezing cold this night, for Goulburn is cold even in summer. But I will be comforted by the muffled sounds of the horses: the whinnying, tail-swishing, snorting, munching, and sucking up of water from the trough. Welcome, too, will be the normally abhorrent scent of manure. I have never been with horses so late at night and am comforted that they do not mind me being there.

When my eyes adjust to the light, I will slide out of my resting place and drag a pile of saddle cloths from the end of the loft, placing them under the horse blanket. Then I will hoist up an old saddle and position it on top of the blanket, thinking it will protect me from the rats or possums I can hear scurrying around the roof. I will put a weatherproof cloth on the very top of the pile and will wriggle into the little cubby house I have created and fall asleep. I will wake, snug and warm, with the early light. Soon, the grooms will arrive. Discovery would be an embarrassment for my parents. How could I explain being there to anyone when I can't explain it to myself? A white sky will hang low. The vicious wind outside will cut to the bone. My feet will turn to ice and my teeth will chatter. I will follow a set of car tracks along the side of a fence. I will still be wearing the blue wool dress – specially chosen by my mother for the big party at Springfield. Brown marks from the saddle cloths will have stained the skirt. My patent-leather court shoes will squelch with water. Frost will cover the ground and I will remember thinking how the sheep seem like pencil-drawn outlines on a huge white eiderdown. What happens after that will be lost to me for years, and I will never see the dress or the shoes again.

Agnes now locks herself in the den so her mother can't force her to go to the polo practices at the farm on Sundays, especially as Madge insists her daughter now wear high-heel shoes and stockings like her. But Agnes has to be alone. She has nothing to say to anyone. She doesn't unlock the door of the den until she sees her mother and father drive off, after which she wanders listlessly around the house.

The heavy mahogany table with the clumsy pineapple feet and the sideboard opposite have seen it all. Here she dreamed of being a ballerina. Why had the Ryders abandoned her when she loved them so much? She had been prepared to go on dancing until her toes bled – no sacrifice would have been too great. Her dreams are dead. Death and endings increasingly occupy her thoughts. She imagines herself at the funeral of her parents. Once, when girls and teachers at school consoled a student over her mother's recent death, Agnes found herself secretly wishing it had been Madge.

In the weeks following the polo tournament, she finds it hard to breathe. Clouds clog her mind. She continues the dizzy, disconcerting levitating when lying awake in bed but tries to ignore it. She is a tiny ship tossed in rough seas, but a safe harbour will soon appear in the form of a home of a school friend.

Only one train stop further up the North Shore line, yet the crossing into Roseville via Boundary Road at the top of Archer Street is dramatic. Small houses on cramped blocks give way to dwellings with massive gardens, tennis courts and swimming pools. White-painted windows and a double-sloping roof soften the solid vertical lines of the chocolate-coloured brick bungalow belonging to the Kellys. The family who live there get on with their lives without explaining themselves: they are the Kellys and that is good enough.

Mr Kelly seems as wide and tall as the house, lumbering around like a parody of a military sergeant, giving orders that nobody takes any notice of. He is a self-made man – a successful importer of textiles into Australia from America and Japan. He doesn't *kowtow* to a Rosemont power base as Agnes's parents do, nor does he bother about scoring points for heaven or the state of his immortal soul. He lives in the moment, works hard, and keeps getting richer.

The days float by at the Kelly house, like the melody of a familiar song. In a quiet street with no through traffic, their property is set back in the block. A stone path traverses a manicured lawn to a set of steps, guarded on either side by bird-of-paradise bushes. The path leads up to a front door under a covered veranda. A raised drive on the upper side of the garden ends in a double garage stuffed with bikes and cars. It is a bungalow dwelling, containing five bedrooms, three bathrooms and includes a separate toilet and hand basin in the laundry at the rear of the garage. The recent installation of an indoor toilet, after her barefooted father broke his toe on the way to the lean-to, has not dampened Agnes's delight in discovering new bathrooms.

For Agnes, the underprivileged child, visiting the Kelly home is like moving from the servant's quarters to the main house. But her desire to belong can never be more than a pipe dream. In truth, she slides into the household as a charitable replacement for Maria Kelly's former best friend, who has decided that being bullied is too high a price to pay for lavish Kelly family holidays.

Agnes doesn't deem Maria a bully exactly, but the girl is very direct. Agnes is bewildered when she asks her *why* the nuns pick on her, *why* she stutters when she reads, *why* her parents don't renovate their house, and *why* they don't care where she goes. Agnes wonders all the same things, so has no answers.

It is like asking someone with a crippled leg why they don't walk straight. Admittedly, Maria has started standing up for her at school, but Agnes intuits that her new friend's indignation smacks more of affectation than conviction. It never occurs to her that if she had a supportive family and a rich father, like Maria, her life might be better. She has increasingly come to accept that she just isn't worth much.

Maria and Agnes ride their bikes together over the autumn holidays. Agnes doesn't have a bike, so borrows one of the many spares in the Kelly's overstuffed garage. Now begin some wonderful excursions all over the North Shore, but also the first of many future shabby relationships with domineering friends Agnes fears. But the bike riding will end when Maria is cast in the lead role of a lavish end-of-year school musical and her spare time is taken up with extra singing and acting lessons.

On Maria's 'Big Night', Agnes sits on stage, like a prop, in a formless green satin dress and watches her friend's vocal cords vibrate in her neck. She is fascinated, too, by the minute bell-like bulge of skin between the gap in her front teeth, which somersaults like a punching bag. She will have no idea what the musical is all about, her objective simply being to avoid arousing anger, as any kind of human aggression now makes her tremble like a violin string. In a semi-daze, she will accept her position as an extra in Maria's life. She misses kissing the icon, and the gastronomical delights enjoyed while lounging on the Persian carpet with the Armenians, but since Natasha went to live in a university college, that friendship has become redundant.

Observing Mrs Kelly's passivity is like being bathed in velvet. She sits, still as a sphinx, in a grey wing back chair opposite the front door, waiting for someone to come in. Her abnormally small head, thick wrestler neck and straight, curve-less body, make Agnes think of the Henry Moore stone lady in The Art Book. Because Mrs Kelly has a cleaner who cooks, and three sons in boarding school, she is never pressed for time. Agnes worries with her over how to manage the fine baby hair she inherited from her mother. She adds extra volume by exhibiting a tight perm that doesn't suit her, and wears hairnets in a host of different colours and textures. She favours one embedded with glass beads that twinkles like tiny stars in the sunlight but, indoors, looks to Agnes like a milk-jug cover against flies.

The carpet in Mrs Kelly's vast living room is a strange merge of dark purple, green, and yellow flowers. On a hot day, in the cool, semi-dark space, Mrs Kelly, seated in her wingback next to the piano, looks like a figure floating in a swamp. The top of the piano is covered in silver-framed photos of Maria at different ages. Agnes likes to get them down one by one and listen to Mrs Kelly reminisce about the time each image was captured. Agnes's three favourites are Maria in black ballet gear clashing tambourines, Maria in a red check frock holding a python on the great Barrier Reef, and Maria in a pink swimming costume buried in a cloud of foaming surf on the beach.

The gentle quality of Mrs Kelly's speaking voice makes Agnes tingle, as when the hairdresser cuts her hair. Over time, she gets to know all the anecdotes attached to the photos of Maria but encourages continual reshowings as an excuse to stay close to this calm woman. But she does feel awkward when Mrs Kelly quizzes her for information about Maria and sometimes wonders if Mrs Kelly is only nice to her so that she can find things out about her taciturn daughter. For, of all Mrs Kelly's four children, Maria, the only daughter, is her favourite.

When a pretty girl with a blonde ponytail and curly wisps around her ears arrives at school halfway through term, Agnes holds her breath a little. Jacqueline is from the New Hebrides and is fluent in French as well as English. When Maria captures Jacqueline as a proper best friend, Agnes finds herself turned into a tag-along. Mrs Kelly seems just as smitten with this new friend as her daughter. As Agnes herself was unexpectedly consigned a position in the Kelly household, and is still grateful, she listens without envy to Mrs Kelly's praise of Jacqueline, and her arrival, as if she has parachuted into their lives from heaven. What she could not bear to lose is Mrs Kelly's soothing presence. But Jacqueline will soon meet a boy and turn her back on Maria, and so Agnes's status will be elevated once more.

Desperately shy, Agnes is intimidated by Mr Kelly, making herself scarce when she hears his booming voice. He has a bulbous, open-pored nose like a pincushion and sees the world through a pair of thick horn-rimmed glasses. He spends much of his time overseas. Mrs. Kelly says he is accident-prone.

When Maria's brothers are home on holidays, they enjoy laughing around the dinner table about their father's notorious gaffes – tales that gather mileage in the retelling. Agnes loves these stories and wraps them around her, rather like the anecdotes she has heard about her Grandma. One of her favourites is about Mr Kelly's Alsatian dog, Prince, whom he taught to shake hands in anticipation of impressing an American associate when he next flew into Sydney. After mixing his guest a cocktail in the Hawaiian bamboo bar he imported from Honolulu, he had called the dog over to do its party trick. Prince had obligingly rushed in from the garden and taken such a shine to the Californian that, instead of a handshake, he had hooked both paws onto the astonished man's leg and proceeded to hump it in a frenzy. The vision of Big John Kelly frantically pulling at the animal's tail and yelling 'Get *off* him, you stupid brute!' always sends the entire family – even his placid straight-faced wife – into uncontrollable spasms of laughter.

Agnes notices that Big John's family talk more about him than to him, and although he often provokes riotous laughter and is genuinely much loved, the house is always more peaceful in his long absences. Homecomings from his travels abroad are made all the more spectacular as he always returns laden with gifts. Maria's classmates are in awe of her imported dresses from America and more than a few of them have confessed to Agnes that they feel like tripping her up out of pique.

When he is home, Big John enjoys sailing his boat. Because Mrs Kelly prefers her shadowy wingback chair to sitting on deck with her husband in the full sea glare, Maria and Agnes become Big John's mariners. With his Captain's hat pulled over his ears, he extends loud nautical greetings to other weekend sailors as they traverse the network of inland waters from the mooring at Bobbin Head. At Rosemont, they have a word to describe people like Mr Kelly, dressed like an English Admiral as he strides the deck of his shiny new launch – 'common'. Aunt Sill, in her new-out-of-the-box shoes, refers to the Mr Kellys of the world as 'nouveau riche'. As Australia is only two centuries old, Agnes wonders how long it takes to sanitise financial success.

Agnes longs to belong. To be fully part of the light-hearted Kelly banter. But she will never be more than an observer – a stray cat drinking a bowl of milk at the back door.

* * *

Maria's parents have decided to host the very first mixed evening party for their daughter. It will be the first such party Agnes has ever attended. The long, wide wooden-floored back veranda with its aspect over a vast back garden will make, in Agnes's estimation, a perfect dance floor. Agnes's parents have been invited but have sent their excuses. Parents who do attend will watch their daughters cross the floor to dance with boys – often for the first time.

On the evening of the party, the wooden planks of the veranda pulse as girls in full skirts, bolstered with layers of petticoats, spin like Ferris wheels as they jive to the beat of Chuck Berry and Bill Haley and the Comets. Later, when the lights are turned low, couples shuffle around to the slow rhythm of Frank Sinatra's 'Songs for Swinging Lovers'. Most of the girls have teamed up with boys from the two Jesuit schools – St Aloysius and Riverview – where many of their brothers are pupils. Agnes assumes they will probably go on to marry them, thus avoiding the pitfalls of marrying outside the church.

Agnes's Aloysius boy is called Don. She is entranced by his soulful doe eyes and wistful smile and admires how his pithy remarks cut through the usual soppy sentiment and mindless chatter. Don says what she herself thinks but doesn't dare to say. His intensity manifests a lack of ease that matches her own. No one has introduced them. She had just found herself sitting next to him on a bench at the party, as if it was preordained. Normally she would avoid eye contact, her gaze stuck no higher than anyone's neck – so it is thrilling, this evening, to stare candidly, like an equal, into Don's eyes. Lost in his gaze, the laughter and chatter on the veranda disappear entirely until there are just the two of them in the world. She likes the clumsy way he holds her when they dance together awkwardly at the end of the evening. Don will drive her home in his car and invite her to be his partner at the Cadet Ball. They will share what will become an impossibly short first love.

What is very strange to Agnes is how her father behaved when Don came to pick her up to take her to the Ball. She was wearing an off-the-shoulder dress, its pale green satin underskirt shining through the white, slightly transparent, overskirt. She clutched a white, silver-threaded mohair stole, tastefully draped around her shoulders. Agnes's mother had answered the door, directing Don to wait in the lounge room in front of the storm-crazed horses. As Agnes had rushed out of the bathroom, she collided with her father as he entered the back door. He had, yet again, been in an inebriated state. Used to being ignored, she had been shocked when he stopped and spoke:

Where do you think *you're* going dressed like that?

Before she could answer, Don, who had heard her father's voice, walked out into the hall. He was looking so handsome in his army cadet uniform that Agnes had held her breath. She had never introduced her father to anyone, so initially stumbled for words:

I'd like you to meet my father, Eric Keen. Daddy, this is Don Burns.

Don had greeted Eric Keen confidently, stepping forward to shake his hand:

Good to meet you, sir.

To the young couple's utter surprise, Eric had brushed Don's hand roughly aside and pushed past him, still holding his briefcase. Agnes and Don had no choice but to retreat to the dining room, where they silently listened to his raised voice as he spoke to his wife in the front bedroom:

Where does she think she's going dressed like *that*?!

Your daughter and Don are off to the Cadet Ball, Eric.

Why wasn't I consulted? She's too young to go out with boys – wearing dresses that fall off her shoulders!

Now, Eric, you've lost track. She's turning sixteen next March and most of her classmates will be there.

Don had looked awkward, and Agnes had been beyond embarrassed. Not knowing what on earth to do, she had felt frozen to the spot. The door was suddenly flung open and her father was standing in front of them, swaying drunkenly:

Tell that boy I never want him in this house again!

He had not looked at anyone in particular – in the way he did whenever he opened the 'David Jones' bill – but Madge was quickly by his side. Turning her husband around lightly, she had waved Agnes and Don away with a brief nod.

A few weeks prior, Agnes had heard her mother boast proudly to Marnie, by phone, of the upcoming Cadet Ball with 'the Aloysius boy' and it had made her wonder whether, because of the way her mother saw the world, she was no longer deemed a dangerous single woman simply because a man had invited her out. Hand in hand, Agnes and her beau had run out of the back door to Don's car. How different her life might have been if she had gone on running and never come back.

Agnes has spent her life worrying about what people think of her dilapidated house but, with Don, she feels no compulsion to apologise. Somehow, she knows he does not care what kind of a house she lives in. Not having to pretend is liberating. And, to his great credit, Don makes no comment about her father's churlish behaviour and drunken outburst. To Agnes, it is as if she and Don have jumped into a safe cocoon and can now float over any storm by simply not acknowledging it exists. But Don will never enter the Keen house again. The remainder of their relationship will be conducted outside those problematic walls.

Agnes soon discovers that Don has his own family sorrow, for he is mourning the recent death of his mother and a subsequent estrangement from his father. An only child, he isn't unwanted like Agnes, but shares an incomprehension comparable to that of Shakespeare's Hamlet over his father's too-hasty relationship with another woman.

Father and son live in a hilly backstreet in Lindfield. Only one stop further up the line from the Kelly's place, their two-storey house is so overgrown with trees and shrubs that only flashes of red brick peek through the smothering jungle. Agnes never goes inside, but happily keeps Don company like a fellow surveillance officer, observing the house from his parked car. Don has a pair of binoculars which he trains on the house whenever he knows 'the girlfriend' is there. Out of respect for his mother's memory, he has vowed never to be at home when she is visiting his father.

Once the scarlet woman's car leaves, Don drives Agnes home, pleased to have staved off any unwanted contact with the interloper. In the sanctuary of Don's car, they kiss and cuddle, pulling apart when passion overtakes them – at which point they listen to the car radio. It is as if they are living out a story from the pictures. To avoid her father, Don drops Agnes in Archer Street. Like Romeo and Juliet, the young couple live a clandestine adventure between two contaminated houses.

Membership of the school debating team has helped Don to see both sides of an argument and articulate his thoughts and Agnes longs to emulate his erudition. She talks with him every day by phone in secret, from the handset in the den, and from public phone boxes, and soon realises that bereavement has made him mature for his years. He loves jazz and, when there is no sign of the scarlet woman invading his home, introduces Agnes to Dave Brubeck, Shelly Mann, Gerry Mulligan, John Coltrane and Miles Davis. She loves the way he loses himself in the music, watching avidly as he mimes playing individual instruments. Decades hence, memories of Don will remain embedded for Agnes in the melancholic sound of 'Around Midnight.'

As the light fades down on her own personal interests, Agnes will come to envy her boyfriend's freedom to embrace a full life. Don has such a ready understanding of what he learns and will, one day, return to teach at his old school. With the date for the leaving certificate exams drawing near, Agnes will plead for his help, and he will agree to meet her in the early mornings at 6am, bringing with him a pile of past exam papers. She will marvel at his confidence about his studies. He will park his Holden at the end of Rose Street, near the park, where Agnes will jump into the passenger side with her books. Don will then patiently trawl through various past papers and write out answers to the questions so she can familiarise herself with the kind of thing to expect.

Don will never tell her she is stupid, as others have done. At this time in her life, he will be the only person she can be frank with about her prevailing state of mind. Yet, although she trusts him as if he is part of her, she will never – *can* never – value him properly because she doesn't value herself. Still haunted by nightly levitations, she will lose the ability to recall even elementary arithmetic. She will fall asleep over her books and will not recall how to spell simple words – formerly known well. She will be like an old lady with dementia, her mind seemingly programmed into forgetting. In lucid moments, she will realise she has to fight for a future and, at other times, will wonder if she is actually losing her mind.

She will pray before entering the exam room in Willoughby but, despite a seismic struggle, concentration will evade her. Her head will turn into a radio stuck between stations. She will write a great deal, and then lose track of the question. Sweat will pour off her. The clock will be ticking. She will wrestle courageously but will know she has lost the battle.

After the exams, Agnes will feel estranged from Don as she can manifest no ambition. Her lack of fluency will inevitably hamper future secretarial work and she will be barred from any jobs requiring good reading and writing ability. She will try to put a brave face on a chronic disability.

The tension at home will become explosive and neither her prayers, nor the pledge of total abstinence, will have any effect on her father's heavy drinking.

On leaving her school, her final act of rebellion will be to wire a Real Estate 'For Sale' sign she has found onto the academic establishment's imposing front gates.

* * *

During the run-up to Christmas, Agnes is rescued once again when Mr Lawson recommends her for a holiday job in a little jewellery shop in Victoria Street, situated near his sports shop. Getting up early and walking down Archer Street to go to work feels like a salvation. As she nods and smiles at all the people she recognises who work in different establishments along the way she feels, for a few precious moments, part of a warm and friendly club.

Agnes's boss, Rebecca Sharma, is a thinker. She knows all about philosophy. According to Aristotle's *Ethics*, she explains to Agnes, everyone should activate their potential as fully as possible. As her own path to learning is firmly closed, Agnes tries to present herself at the shop to the best of her ability. She keeps her hair washed and wears it in a neat ponytail. She makes sure her clothes are spotless. She buys a lipstick and attempts to cover her freckles with a light powder.

Rebecca Sharma's small jewellery shop is exquisitely decorated, and Agnes loves to watch her as she constantly, carefully, positions items in the window, deliberately leaving lots of space between them. Necklaces, rings, and bracelets are displayed at staggered heights atop glass cubes. Rebecca has installed a lovely blue and white striped canvas blind to hang over the window and Agnes loves to see the late sun sneak underneath it, the rays refracted by the cut-glass jewellery supports that send vivid rainbows to kaleidoscope around the shop walls.

Rebecca has survived a Nazi concentration camp. Agnes finds it impossible to imagine her as part of the horrible images on the newsreels she once saw. Rebecca never mentions the past, but it is there in the row of numbers tattooed on her arm. Normally, Rebecca will wear long sleeves, but on a hot day she will forget and roll them up:

Life is so short.

Agnes will hear Rebecca state this truism aloud frequently and will try and tear her eyes away from the hideous numbers.

Agnes loves gift wrapping. She uses red and gold striped paper and ties the small parcels neatly with gold ribbon. If she suspects a shy husband is buying a gift for his wife, she engages him in conversation so she can suggest gift-wrapping the purchase. She enjoys working with Rebecca. In fact, she never wants to leave the little shop.

Because of her boss's brisk manner, Agnes will not realise until her very last day how much she has been valued, for Rebecca will give her not only a generous pay packet but a bonus, and a lucky charm bracelet too. When Agnes leaves the shop for the last time, Rebecca Sharma will scoop her into her arms and, eyes brimming with tears, will hug her so tightly she will hardly be able to breathe:

Guard this money for an emergency. Good luck to you, dear girl. Promise you'll come back and see me.

But Agnes never does go back. Rebecca Sharma's emotional farewell is her last memory of living in the area. After that, everything goes blank.

16

THE INQUISITION AT ROSEMONT

gnes has no memory of the months that follow, yet undefined fragments remain, rather like the sight of a familiar dress in a crowd with no inkling of why it strikes a chord. Time disappears from her as it has done with the Goulburn polo tournament. She has no memory, either, of leaving the house on the corner of Rose and Edmond Street. Nor of leaving her white chest of drawers with the ceramic roses. Nor leaving her picture of the guardian angel, The Art Book, the ballet books, the ballet shoes, and all the other lost dreams hidden away in shoeboxes. In the summer of her sixteenth year, everything is swept away, and with it, Agnes loses contact with what defines her.

She hears from someone that she has failed her exams. Her parents' hostility is palpable. She is standing outside a familiar red-brick building with them so it must be serious, as she never accompanies them on an outing for pleasure. They are mounting the steps at Rosemont. The familiar amber letters above the entrance swirl before her eyes. This is her first reference point in months. She doesn't know where she lives. She has so many questions whirling in her head but stays silent.

However, the wonder of the mahogany-panelled entrance to Rosemont remains, along with the line of letter boxes into which she imagines the postman slipping letters addressed to educated inhabitants who read classics like *Middlemarch* and *War and Peace*. It is a summer afternoon in early January 1959 and the red carpet in the foyer is spotless.

Aunt Sill opens the door abruptly and scowls at Madge and Agnes. Primped, ironed and coiffured, she reserves her smile for Eric. Her perfect, just-out-of-the-tissue-paper medium-heeled navy shoes sink into the carpet as she strides ahead like an office receptionist – leading the way to the supreme command.

Grandma is seated on a low tapestry chair in the small antechamber at the end of the living room. When Grandma nods at her, Agnes imagines her thinking: 'Pity she's not very bright.'

Grandma smiles when Eric goes down on one knee and kisses her hand. Bring the sick bucket someone! What a crawler! For all her confusion, Agnes can still see straight through her father. He accepts the offer of whisky and Agnes and Madge agree to take tea.

Aware of his princely status, Eric wanders into the living room and pours himself a generous slug of Johnny Walker into a cut-glass tumbler, adding ice cubes with tongs from a thermos. He swirls the amber liquid around approvingly, before taking a serious gulp. The Grand Matriarch is keen to hear his news, for he is one of the last two of the dynasty managing to keep her beloved game of polo alive. She enquires brightly:

Hope all's well between you and Ben?

Madge scowls at the sound of her brother's name.

Oh, yes, all goes well.

Eric has replied without a second's pause. He is seated on a low chair next to his 'boss' and is jiggling the ice cubes in his glass. Agnes notices that Grandma is wearing her favourite red hat. In fact, she reckons even more feathers might have been added to the adornment on top. The hat sits on Grandma's head at a jaunty angle as if asking for a compliment. Eric obliges:

You're looking wonderful today, Ellen. Red is definitely your colour.

Oh, thank you, kind sir!

Grandma is smiling foolishly, like an aging coquette. Agnes spots that she has lipstick on her teeth. She wants to tell her but expects such an intervention would be deemed impertinent. Eric extends his arm around the back of his boss's chair and makes a corny joke that isn't funny but the three ladies chuckle in unison, in compliance with the rule that all male contributions, no matter how inept, must be responded to favourably.

Sill has spotted the teeth problem too, placing a warning finger against her own lips, and handing her mother a tissue. Grandma takes the hint and rubs them with the vigour of cleaning a window. Task completed, she smiles at her daughter, who confirms the 'all clear' with a nod. Grandma continues the interrogation:

So how are you enjoying living at the farm, Eric?

Thank you, Mother, it's wonderful.

Madge has answered for him.

And how do you find the drive, Eric?

Eric Keen answers this for himself:

No problem. I'm up early with the light to attend the jobs around the stables before I leave for the factory. There's less work as the horses are out in the paddock. I'm on the road before peak hour, so manage to avoid the traffic.

Grandma sits back in her chair. A pronouncement is obviously forthcoming:

Now you're living there, this might be the moment to put the farm into your names. My solicitor can transfer the property into all four names as tenants in common. But he'll include a clause giving you both sole rights over the cottage, which means you'll be able to live there and make improvements without consulting Ben and Beth.

Grandma concludes this news with a benevolent smile, then adds a little stinger:

But there's still time, mind you. I'm not planning on leaving the world just yet.

Sill appears again. She is wearing a white apron over her navy-blue shantung pleated dress and is obviously headed to the kitchen to make tea. Responding to her mother's prod, Agnes offers to help. In the spotless kitchen, she puts four rose-printed china cups and saucers, a matching milk jug, a silver sugar bowl with tongs and teaspoons on a tray, all the while struggling to stop her hands from shaking.

Sill lifts down a box of cakes from a shelf, opens the lid and holds the contents up for Agnes to admire:

I bought these at a new bakery in Double Bay. Aren't they divine! I've cut these round paper doilies so we can put one on each of the three tiers of the cake tray. Now! How will we arrange them?

Agnes knows this is a rhetorical question, as Sill never delegates arrangement to anyone.

She watches her aunt as she fills the silver teapot with hot water and proceeds to carry in the tray. Agnes trails behind her, feeling awkward, with the cake plate. Something is amiss in the room. Things have been said about her in her absence. Agnes closes her ears to avoid listening and stares out of the window at the earthenware pots full of red geraniums. She has always admired the way they adorn the flat roof of the building opposite. The sun on the horizon is still so fierce it looks as if it might melt the boats on the harbour. The sea is drained of colour. The sound of her name draws her back:

Agnes, I've arranged for you to start school at Rose Bay Convent at the end of next month. You will board, so we need to get you fitted with uniforms.

Grandma has dropped this bombshell in a matter-of-fact tone. Agnes is shocked to the core. It is too late for this! Four years ago, she would have been more than glad to get away from her mother, but the horror of more Mother Miriams, more Angels of Death, and still further humiliation over her poor reading abilities, now hit her like a brick in the head. She believes Grandma is sincere in her belief and convictions, but she is no Henry Fonda in *Twelve Angry Men*. She will have no reservations in pronouncing Agnes 'GUILTY' along with the rest.

Madge speaks for her daughter, as usual:

Thank you, Mother. This is *just* what needs to happen. Agnes thinks she can run her own life. She's too self-willed for her own good.

Grandma, thank you, but I can't possibly go!

She has found the words and she has said them.

What do you mean you can't go? What is stopping you?!

I can't concentrate in class. I try, but a terrible tiredness prevents me. I can't control it, Grandma! I'm physically there but lessons come and go, and I don't understand *anything*. Something has happened to me. I stammer and shake when I have to read. They say I'm a bad influence, a troublemaker, not very bright, but it's just that I can't remember things. I try but *nothing* works! I'm giving, and helping, and praying, but it all goes *wrong*!

My dear Agnes, the nuns at Rose Bay will change all this by showing you how to manage a study routine. What you are saying is wild, fanciful talk.

No one can help me, Grandma! Especially not a convent of *nuns*! How can women hiding from the world teach children how to manage it? I *can't* be stuck in another classroom with prissy, gloating, pious girls. The lady in the jewellery shop will give me a job. She likes me. I sold stacks of stuff when I worked there for a while. I learnt things just standing next to her. She knows about Aristotle's *Ethics*. She taught me about European history and all *sorts* of things!

Now you can see, Mother, what incessant rubbish she talks and what Eric and I have to put up with! She doesn't come home when she's told. She spends her time running up and down Victoria Street shopping centre befriending peculiar people. That woman in the jewellery shop is *Jewish*!

Agnes sees red in front of her eyes. It is as red as the outdoor geraniums. She cannot hold back:

Don't you start bad-mouthing me and telling lies when I spend my *life* slaving for you! You've got the *devil* inside you! Monsignor Harrington told me you're going to *hell* unless you come back to God!

Agnes has clenched her fists. She has never felt more like punching her mother. Madge's eyes are gleaming. The fight is on:

You see, Mother, she's got this boyfriend. *That's* why she failed her exams. *All* she can think of is how to see him. She spends all her time in his car, instead of studying for her exams. Imagine, bold as brass, parked near our house! *God* knows what they get up to! Her father and I can't discipline her. She takes *no* notice of us. She's a *delinquent*!

That's not *true*! Don came because I asked him to help me prepare for the exams! He's kind to me and did what he could, but I could hardly see the exam paper for nerves!

Agnes feels torn apart with frustration. She is outnumbered. She can't express herself in the way she would wish to win this losing battle. Grandma is looking confused, and Aunt Sill is glaring at her as if she is a substance capable of polluting the furniture.

Grandma uses her most level tone:

Agnes, you don't know what's good for you. Nobody will employ you without the leaving certificate. It's time to come down to earth and capitulate. Your parents can't cope with you. You'll make new friends at Rose Bay and in six months will forget all this.

Agnes is biting her lip trying not to cry. Nobody ever takes any notice of what she says. Grandma takes off her hat. She is looking irritable. She has some problematic children and now they are producing grandchildren with issues. She has no tolerance for individual differences. She is a black and white thinker. A child is either good or bad and Agnes is clearly the latter.

Eric Keen has remained silent during all this. Agnes is vaguely aware of him wandering backwards and forwards between the closed balcony and the whisky bottle. But she has no doubt that he will be annoyed at her rebellion, for Grandma is offering to take his vexatious daughter off his hands and, what's more, pay the bill. Agnes tries one final time to be heard:

I'd rather *die* than go to that school, Grandma! I can't *bear* it. You can't *make* me. *I won't do it!*

As month upon month of stored rage and frustration well up inside her, she grabs a vase from the shelf above the fireplace and throws it against the wall, where it smashes into pieces. Sill gasps in horror and exclaims:

My Sèvres vase! It's *irreplaceable!*

Blinded with tears, Agnes runs out of the front door and slams it hard behind her. She jumps down the stairs two at a time and then dashes through the swinging door onto Rosemont Avenue. It crosses her mind briefly to run out in the road straight in front of a car, but she keeps going along the pavement. At the end of Edgecliff Road, opposite the Post Office, it occurs to her she is close to Aunt Beth and Uncle Ben's flat. Beth has always been kind. She runs up the stairs to their door and knocks frantically.

When Beth opens the door, Agnes flies into her arms, howling like a baby. She gasps with emotion as she tells her about boarding school and why she can't go. She searches Beth's pretty, distressed face for a solution, knowing in her heart that this poor mild-mannered woman is incapable of anything more than laughing at her husband's bad jokes and writing polite thank-you letters.

On this terrible day, one thing is crystal clear to Agnes. She is crippled inside. She is also aware, although a desperate need to belong blinds her to the truth, that none of the people to whom she is related can possibly help her. Sweet, ineffectual Beth can only dry her tears, offer tender words, and send her on her way.

Predictably, Beth rings Rosemont. Within half an hour her parents pick Agnes up on the corner of Ocean Avenue. They drive in silence through Centennial Park, turning at the showground, then on past the cotton factory, before moving into the setting sun. They are on their way to the new home at the farm. Agnes leans on the front seat between her parents, her head in her arms, desperate for some human warmth.

The shade is down over the windscreen to block out the blinding rays of the western sun. Her father simmers with annoyance. He has forgotten his sunglasses. From her between-the-seats vantage point, Agnes stares at him. Liberated from the glare at the Liverpool turn-off, he has finally stopped frowning. His bloodshot eyes look like two crushed bluebottles. A noble nose dominates a fine broad face, its high cheekbones tapering to a well-shaped rounded chin. It strikes her that he looks Scandinavian, but of course his red hair points firmly to his Irish ancestry. Of course, he might be a throwback to the Viking invasion. But the application of copious amounts of hair oil has turned his coppery mane boot-polish brown. There is something comical, ridiculous even, about the greasy strands that, like the lines of a child's train set, are now plastered to his forehead. Self-absorbed as usual, he doesn't notice his daughter's sharp eyes on him.

Agnes is relieved that, as they approach the farm, neither parent has mentioned during the entire journey what has just happened. Perhaps, like the late-night pillow talk, the drama at Rosemont has been consigned to the void. Forgotten it might be, but she knows all too well that nothing is ever forgiven.

The car radio has been blaring out the latest music hits, interspersed with news of a crisis in Cuba and Buddy Holly's death. Her father changes the station to catch the racing results.

This decisive action seems to bring Madge back from Mars. As if she is reading her daughter's mind, her mother breaks the long silence:

Don't think your father and I are going to maintain you after you snubbed your nose at your grandmother. Free schooling and expenses rejected by Miss High and Mighty who knows *nothing*. And Sill will *never* forgive you for breaking her vase. A French antique from the time of Madame de Pompadour!

But Agnes is determined not to be further crushed:

Well, I'll get a job and save up and buy her a new one.

And what kind of job do you think you can get with no qualifications or training?

I'll find something. Mrs Sharma told me I could come back. And they were pleased with me at 'Mark Foy's'.

This latter remark wasn't actually true, but she had to keep her spirits up.

So, you're going to be a lowly shop girl, are you?

Well it's better than a debt-ridden, immoral wife! I'd be proud to make my own living any way I could!

Will you *shut up*! I'm trying to listen to the radio! I don't want to hear anything more about *her*. She's *finished* as far as I'm concerned!

This was the closest to a direct address she had experienced from her father in a long time.

She senses a conspiracy between these people – her parents – as if she has been set up. The firestorm inside her rekindles. Her guts are swirling like a wild river. She connects with her father's chlorinated swimming pool eyes in the driving mirror:

You're weak and vain! I *hate* the way you suck up to Grandma. You care for no one but yourself. You ignore me and *never* defend me. You blame Uncle Ben for lying, but you lie *all* the time! You're a horrible, sly, whinging, two-faced man with no compassion or pity!

The mask cracks and the monster appears. He whips around and slaps her in the mouth with full force. She tastes blood as she lands on the back seat. The car spins as the monster shrieks:

I'll kill her! I'll damn well *kill* her! *Keep her away from me*!

Reacting to Madge's piercing scream, he grabs the wheel and swerves just in time to avoid a car coming from the other direction at full speed, blowing its horn:

Christ! Look what she made me do! We nearly hit that ute!

Calm down, Eric! Keep your eyes on the road!

Agnes's tooth has cut her lip, but instead of showing a vestige of concern for her daughter, Madge slides along the seat to fill the gap she has vacated and puts her arm around her husband's shoulders. Agnes watches as her mother caresses the back of his neck with her coral-pink fingernailed hand. Agnes knows she is simply a pawn in a diabolical game. They have stolen her life. Their backs unite to block her out.

Her next gut reaction feels instantaneous. Reflexive. She opens the door of the moving station wagon and flings herself out. She rolls over until she drops into a ditch at the side of the road. Her forehead hits the edge of a rock. Blood trickles down her face. Her father drives on. Neither parent appears to look back. Then she hears their car stop suddenly. Agnes can see them arguing through the rear window. The car is only a short distance from the gate of the farm. Agnes's hip hurts, but her legs are still working because she can wiggle her toes. Shafts of sunlight cut through the avenue of gums on the opposite side of the road. Cloud puffs high in the sky look like ducklings following their mother in a line to a pond. She has landed at the foot of the hamlet that includes the general store. If she tilts her head back, she can see the top of the little Anglican Church of the Innocents up on the hill.

Her mother will spread a towel on the back seat of the car to protect the upholstery from bloodstains. Her father's face will have turned to stone.

In less than an hour, he will pull the car up behind an ambulance at the entrance to the casualty department of Liverpool Hospital and, in ten years' time, Madge will drive to that same spot with her dead husband in the back of a car, cradled in the arms of her youngest son, Jim.

* * *

The rosy-cheeked girl at the hospital entrance desk has a miniature nurse's cap perched on top of a tall chestnut bouffant, like the summit marker on a mountain. Overwhelmed with shame, bloody, barefooted, Agnes has hidden her face, like someone avoiding the press, under the blue towel retrieved from the car. Her dress is filthy, and she has left her sandals in the ditch. The beehive nurse shuffles her large body around the desk and gingerly lifts a corner of Agnes's towel:

Hang on, sweetie – we're here to help. I know you're poorly, darling, but we need a few details.

She rubs the back of Agnes's hand as she writes with the other one, beaming intermittently, her pleasant mouth full of metal teeth braces.

No physical wound can touch the gut-wrenching shame Agnes experiences, knowing she is unwanted. No stranger must know this sad fact either. She mumbles her name, followed by the address at Chatswood as she doesn't know the new one at the farm. She wishes Uncle Parry was with her. But no silly songs or jokes to comfort her this time. She is on her own. She thinks of ringing Don Burns. It never occurs to her she might have been killed. She remains obsessed with the sight of her mother invading the space she vacated just after her father hit her in the mouth. Neither of them has ever cared about her education and she has now gifted them the justification to abandon her, once and for all.

Still drowsy from a sedative, Agnes awakes on a narrow bed in a small, curtained cubicle. Everything appears elongated and distorted, including her mother, who has not just one, but three, ugly faces. Before Madge can lay into her, a young doctor with enormous dark eyebrows on his several faces pulls back the curtain and asks how she feels. Madge responds:

She's feeling better now, Doctor, so perhaps we could go as my husband's waiting in the car outside. He's in shock.

But the doctor ignores her. He gently grips Agnes's shoulder as her eyes start to focus and addresses her directly:

I've put four stitches at the side of your head, along with a couple in your lip. Your mother has said you won't be coming back here, so any medical centre in Sydney can take them out.

Agnes counts her stitches on her fingers:

That means I've had sixteen stitches in the sixteen years I've been alive – six in one knee, four in the other knee and now four in my head and two in my lip. There're others too that I don't remember.

She is showing the doctor the scars on her knees as she wants to delay being alone with her mother. Why did Madge tell him she wouldn't be coming back to the hospital? The doctor chastises her cheerfully:

No more falling out of cars, young lady! I hear the door of the car wasn't properly closed, so when you lent on it, out you went. You've all had a terrible shock. Go home and relax and, in a few days, it will be behind you. I told your mother not to blame herself. Accidents happen.

He concludes this advice by winking at Agnes and squeezing her ankle reassuringly. If she couldn't live with the kindly nurse with the bouffant beehive, this jolly doctor would do fine, she thinks with longing. She thanks him but is unable to smile due to the revulsion she feels of being party to yet another of her mother's devious lies.

As she and her mother walk out of the hospital, Madge announces on the way to the car:

Your father wants *nothing* more to do with you. What you said will *never* be forgiven.

Arriving at the farm, Agnes flings the car door open, hobbles barefoot to the bathroom and locks the door. She showers and washes her hair, taking care to keep the water away from the stitches. She eases the last gobs of roadside tar off the side of her leg with her father's hair oil and dabs the thick layers of iodine painted on her legs at the hospital with cotton wool. Leaving the dirty spotted green dress and stained towel on the floor, she wraps herself in a fresh towel and limps her way to a small, dimly familiar bedroom, clutching the little bottle of disinfectant and cotton swabs they gave her at the hospital. She locks the door, towels her hair and brushes it into a ponytail. She puts on clean underwear, a blue cotton dress, clean socks, and an old pair of sandshoes she finds in an unfamiliar wardrobe. The dress is long enough to cover the bruise on her thigh. She still feels wobbly but forces herself to prepare to leave.

She packs a few clothes into a small suitcase, together with her old white plastic handbag, which contains the jewellery shop pay packet she has hidden in there, and a large torch from the back of the wardrobe. It occurs to her that she has no memory of the Christmas or New Year just passed.

Although she does not recall seeing either of her parents again, she remains conscious of their eyes burning into her as she opens the front door and leaves. Harbouring the vain hope that one or other of them will run after her, she saunters at a snail's pace down the path between the rose bushes and out the front gate, but neither mother nor father have followed her.

As the house disappears behind the hill, she is infused with a sudden miraculous flood of energy and quickens her pace along the dirt road. She passes the dam, where Paddy the pony once refused to carry her on his back into the muddy water. The poplars standing sentry along the dairy farm fence shake their heads in a sudden breezy farewell as she crosses the cattle grid onto the Bringelly Road.

Glorious gold, purple and pink lines merge into a sunset sky. She isn't wearing a watch but imagines it could be seven or eight o'clock. She crosses the road out of the shade to where the light is brighter and sets out for Liverpool. As darkness falls, she remembers the torch and lifts it out of the suitcase. Its powerful beam picks up something glittering below the trampled weeds. It is the charm bracelet Rebecca Sharma gave her. She has arrived at the exact spot where she landed earlier, at the side of the road. Lying close by the bracelet is her small blue purse, containing a few pounds. It must have fallen out of the pocket of her dress, and there, too, is a pair of broken white sandals that must have come off in the accident.

Time to take stock. As well as the ten single pounds from the pay packet she already has, there is Mrs Sharma's £10 bonus, untouched too. Whatever she has been doing, she hasn't been spending money. She is rich.

Grandma always said God moves in strange ways. She sits down on a patch of soft grass and prays aloud: Hail Mary full of Grace, the Lord is with thee, blessed art thou in heaven. Thank you for sending me back to this spot.

Shaken by her sudden change of fortune, the floodgates burst. She sobs and sobs. Waves of emotion flood over her until, feeling empty, she hauls herself up and moves on.

The road looks different on foot. Until now, she has always travelled along it by car or on horseback. The Rossmore store is closed. There is a light in a window at the back. She resists a temptation to knock, as leaving home in her present state would be impossible to explain. She regrets her outburst in the car. What came over her? She really didn't intend to hurt her father. The words leapt out of her mouth without even thinking. So little traffic on the road, she could be walking on the moon. But no. She is not wanted. She must accept it. She must plan ahead now. Once in Liverpool, she will catch a train to Sydney.

Agnes enters a stretch of road flanked on both sides by a thick forest. There is no moon. The air is black as soot. She could be walking along a subterranean tunnel. But God has directed her back to the site of the accident so he can't possibly forsake her now. She marches forward like a solder on parade. With a firm grip on the suitcase containing the money for her future life, she tries not to think of the strange restless ghosts blowing their icy breath in her face.

A dull light appears in the distance and she runs towards it, her heart racing. Heaving for breath, she has arrived at the turn-off to the old polo field where the team would practise before Grandma bought the farm. Feeling safe in the well-lit street, she relaxes her pace. The road surface is damp, but the sky is clear and full of stars. The underarms of her blue dress are soaked with her efforts.

Eventually, she comes to Uncle Mack's abandoned cotton factory. She will rest again here briefly, and then walk on, but coherent thoughts from this point in her life will be as scattered as dry winter petals. They will not blossom back into memory until many years later:

By the side of a narrow crossroads, I sit on a bench, put my head on my suitcase, and fall asleep. I do not know how long I have been out until a set of headlights, shining in my face, wake me up. The car is moving slowly towards me along the side street. It stops beside me.

A woman with a wrinkled face like an old road map calls out from the driver's window.

Leaving home, girlie? she shouts. She is taking deep drags on a cigarette. I think of making a run for it, but my fear is obliterated by a heavenly whisper that help might be at hand. I reply in a jokey voice to match hers: Yes! That's right! My parents don't love me anymore! The woman smiles: I'm going to Liverpool, girlie, if you want a lift? Her words all run together in a drawl. I hear myself say: Oh, how perfect. I want to go to the station to catch a train to Sydney. Well, she says, just you bundle your cheeky self in the car and let's get going! I am so relieved I could hug her. I jump into the passenger side and sink my bottom deep into the broken seat, my suitcase tightly clasped on my lap. The car looks as if it has come from the dump and sounds like a lawnmower. It kangaroo-hops along the main road. The back is full of old and broken stuff – shoes, clothes, tennis rackets with holes and golf clubs in split bags. I must have fallen asleep again as I come to with a shock to hear: Next stop Liverpool Station! The woman has called out in a high pitch like a train conductor.

What have you been taking, girlie? You went out like a light! Her voice crackles, and she covers me in a blast of cigarette smoke that makes me cough. Thank you, thank you, thank you, I splutter. Now that's enough of that. I've got you here, and that's my good deed for the year! She is laughing, and I hear the exhaust pipe farting as she chugs away.

I buy a ticket, step straight onto the last train to Sydney, and find a half bottle of abandoned water on a seat that I gulp straight down. There are a few inebriated workmen swaying through the carriage, but they ignore me and I ride safely. The hands on the big clock at Central Station are pointing at midnight when I arrive. I head down the slope towards George Street. The path submerges into a dark, deserted underpass. I emerge in the dull light at a junction of Cross Street and lose my bearings. Unsure, I turn in circles. When I hear footsteps advancing quickly behind, I run straight ahead and find myself in George Street. To my right, in the direction of Town Hall, I see an illuminated neon sign advertising 'Rooms to Let' peeping out of a side street. A woman with thick glasses, seated at a desk inside, is absorbed in an old picture on a small TV. She looks annoyed when I bound up the stairs. Sorry for interrupting you, I say. My parents are arriving tomorrow from Melbourne and I want to surprise them at the station. The woman pauses for a second, then: That's all right, love. If ya got a quid there's one left on the first floor, bathroom down the hall, check out by midday. She doesn't look at me again, keeping her eyes on the TV screen. I fumble through the contents of my suitcase and hand her £1 from the jewellery shop pay packet in the white purse. Hardly looking up, she slides a key over the desk. I scramble up squeaky stairs to the floor above, locate the room number, insert the key and double lock myself inside. I feel a sense of huge relief. There is a sink in the room, so I can pee into it and flush it away with the tap. I take off my shoes and socks and slide between musty sheets.

I must have slept. I can't remember. But I am looking up now at Central Station clock. I am catching a train to Wynyard. I believe I will feel more relaxed back in an area I know well. A new-fangled machine in a shop window in George Street catches my eye. There is a circular assembly line of metal moulds which move into a vat of hot oil, before tumbling down a miniature slippery dip into a sandpit of sugar. The machine is creating doughnuts. Neat holes in their middles, they're like tiny, abandoned life jackets on a shoreline. I buy a bag, sinking my teeth into one after another. I know I have had nothing to eat since a cake at Rosemont the day before. After three or four doughnuts in quick succession, I start to feel sick. The sugar is stinging my lips. I give the rest of the bag to a beggar on the pavement outside a bank who eyes the contents with disinterest and tips the lot in front of his Alsatian dog, who wolfs them down.

I turn up Martin Place, just past the Cenotaph, where a scattering of office workers perch on the steps of the General Post Office. There must be an American ship in the harbour, as sailors with their telltale white caps are milling around as they chat up the girls on lunch break. This is where my mother might have met her Yank, years ago, if she hadn't had me.

Entering the ground floor of 'David Jones' is like floating into an embrace. The pianist in black plays 'Moonlight Sonata' on the raised platform. I watch her fingers float over the keys, happy to recognise the piece Madeleine St Paul played on the night of her father's birthday in Castlereagh. I ride the escalator and check my suitcase into a locker in the Ladies Room on the first floor. After using the toilet, I luxuriate in washing my hands with a piece of scented soap and drying them on a clean white hand towel provided by an assistant. Gazing at myself in the well-lit mirror, I look like I've staggered out of a field hospital in a war zone. There is a chocolate milk stain on the front of my crushed dress from a bottle I gulped down at Central. It adds to my overall dissipated appearance.

Summer frocks on the first floor are draped in red sale labels. As if preordained, a shop assistant, dressed in black, has draped several over my right arm and is whispering in my ear in a way that reminds me of Valerie enticing my mother on the sixth floor: Try these, she says, I'm sure they're your size. In the dressing room, I slip my arms into a green shirtwaister with white buttons and a belt that fits perfectly. I daren't try on anything else. The money has to last. With each twirl in front of a full-length mirror, I feel better: Gorgeous! Perfect colour with your red hair! I hear the assistant exclaim. I ask her if I can wear it now and she tells me no problem: cash or account? Account, I reply, holding my breath, and I give my father's full name like I have watched my mother do a hundred times. A quick call to the Accounts Department and

I am signing a docket in vague disbelief. Emboldened, I sign for some make-up to cover my black eye, a wash bag, toothbrush, toothpaste, new sandals and a white leather handbag. Back in the Ladies Room, I complete the transformation by slipping into the new sandals, transferring my things into the new bag and throwing all the discarded stuff into my suitcase.

At closing time, suitcase in hand, I saunter across Hyde Park to St Mary's Cathedral where I unburden my heart to a statue of the Virgin Mary. Devoid of simple choices, I'm without a wish to go with the candle that I light in the brass stand beneath her. I stroll across the park trying to keep my head clear. The cinema, as so often before, comes to my rescue. I travel back two thousand years to Jerusalem with Charlton Heston in Ben Hur, and leave the cinema exhilarated by the spectacular chariot race at the end. At Town Hall station, I buy a ticket to Roseville, but get off out of habit when the train stops at Chatswood. Now I can see myself walking slowly down Victoria Street past all the closed shops as if in a dream. I pause outside the Town Hall where I danced Cinderella. Now I am hiding in and out of doorways, fearful of meeting anyone I know. But I do linger for a while on the pavement outside the Ryders' house. It is still barricaded against me. If I could only find the courage to knock on Mr Lawson's door. But I don't. Now I see myself dragging my feet up Edmund Street to the home I have no memory of leaving.

The builder has finally arrived. The side path is full of rubble. My depleted memory retains a picture of the architect's plans. I keep walking around the block. Round and round my old home. It is already night. A pile of junk is stacked in the garden ready for a bonfire. I recognise the leg of one of the dining chairs broken in the Mack fight. It lies at the top of the pile like a bygone flagpole. I imagine the future day when the pile is lit and then the bonfire takes hold. I can see in my mind's eye the top drawer of my white chest with the ceramic roses. The bonfire vision continues. Dangling over the edge are the pink ribbons from my toe shoes curling up and scorching in the heat. It is too late to run and save them. Christmas door decorations are swallowed up in seconds. In my mind, I move closer, searching for the books I love. Surely my mother must have put The Art Book and my precious ballet books away safely in a cupboard at the farm? The rabble of Carey children have broken into the garden and now join the new owner's children. They are circling around the flames and waving lighted sparklers in the bright light of the all-consuming blaze.

I turn my back on the house and walk away.

The bird of paradise bushes either side of the steps leading to the Kellys' home have never looked so welcoming. The house behind is dark. I creep along the overgrown side path, shielding myself from thorns with the suitcase, and mount the back steps. God must be with me as I find the door to the veranda open, and Prince doesn't bark. I dart into the spare bedroom, where I often used to sleep. I take off my new dress and sandals and, knowing I'm safe, slip between the sheets. The bonfire in my mind is quenched.

17

MAROUBRA

Mrs Kelly will have tears in her eyes as she looks down at Agnes in bed the following morning:

What a fright you gave me, my poor, darling girl! What has happened to you?!

I fell out of my father's car because the door wasn't properly shut.

Agnes has lied in line with her mother's story. She will be suddenly convulsed with sobs, and Mrs Kelly will gently rock her back and forwards in her arms. But this respite with the Kelly family is fated not to last long, for prescient Aunt Sill will phone Mrs Kelly a few days after Agnes's escape from the farm. As Mrs Kelly takes the call, Agnes will dread to think of the latest pack of lies circulating the Rosemont grapevine.

Mrs Kelly will make a face for Agnes to listen in on the extension as Sill states coolly:

Agnes's Uncle Parry will be coming to pick her up tomorrow at 4pm.

Mrs Kelly will nod at Agnes and say:

She's very welcome to stay with us while she decides what she wants to do…

Agnes will hear the curt woodpecker repeat the statement:

Her uncle will be at your house tomorrow. At 4pm.

Mrs Kelly will persist:

Really, it's no trouble. Agnes wants to stay here. She's spent a lot of time with us, you know. She's like one of the family:

That would be impossible. I must warn you not to be fooled by her, Mrs Kelly. Agnes has a violent temper that can erupt unexpectedly at any minute.

To her great credit, Mrs Kelly will defend Agnes valiantly:

Oh, I've never heard such nonsense! You're talking about someone I don't recognise! The poor child is in need of love and care, not further punishment to make her feel any worse about herself than she already does. She's a victim of neglect!

My brother Parry will be at your house at 4pm sharp tomorrow to collect her. Ensure she is there!

The order will be repeated a third time, then Sill will hang up in Mrs Kelly's ear.

Agnes will be heartened to hear the sting in Mrs Kelly's voice but knows Rosemont's judgement is final. Her grandmother, seriously short of empathy, controls what goes on in her family and Sill is her lieutenant. Mrs Kelly is an outsider.

Agnes will reflect on her untenable position. Uncle Parry is kind enough, but she doesn't want to be cut off from everyone she knows, living miles away with Parry and Marnie in an unfamiliar place. The North Shore is her lifeline.

She will phone Don Burns, and he will come to collect her. Her injuries will shock him. Don will hold her close as she sobs gently in his arms. Now ashamed of her outburst to her father, she will reel off her mother's fabrication about accidentally falling out the car door and babble to Don about parental rejection being the reason for failing the exams. He will be sympathetic but find it hard to understand. About to study history at university and having finally accepted his father's relationship with the new girlfriend, when he drops Agnes back at the Kelly house he will put some money in her hand, kiss her on the forehead and wish her luck. Once she has a job, Agnes promises, she'll pay him back.

In the months ahead, Don will never fail to respond to her plea for financial help and, years later, Agnes will repay him in full.

Agnes's triumphant escape from the farm will no longer have any meaning. She will be ashamed of the way Uncle Parry treats Mrs Kelly when he arrives. Rejecting her offer of tea and leaving the cake she has made for the occasion abandoned untouched, he will indirectly accuse Mrs Kelly of brainwashing Agnes against the family. His attitude towards Agnes will be like a policeman returning an escaped prisoner to jail and, when she still insists on staying at the Kelly house, her mother's poison will slide off Parry's tongue:

The problem with *you*, Young Lady, is that you don't know what's good for you.

None of it will make any sense to Agnes as, when she lived with her parents, she had so little to do with them. Instead of the victim of a violent physical attack herself, she has apparently become the abuser. Parry will declaim like a legal decree:

You're not to go back to the farm. Your father is deeply injured by your behaviour and wants nothing more to do with you.

So what's new!

Agnes will deliberately answer him back to keep her spirits up, desperate to seem independent. But, instead, she will feel a brand-new emptiness welling up inside.

* * *

Parry and Marnie live on the corner of a row of identical two-storey red-brick houses, in Maroubra. The properties are built on narrow blocks and enclosed with grey paling wood fences. The plastic pegs on the rotary clothes line are the only visible spots of colour.

From the fence on the corner, Marnie can be seen every morning through the glass windows of the living room, dressing her three little daughters on a green carpeted floor in front of the TV. It is here, in a space that runs the width of the house and spills into an L-shaped kitchen, that family life revolves.

Today, Parry is bumping the car over a set of tramlines in order to park down a slope on a sandy mound in front of the house. It is like the rough of a golf course. His house looks up, as if in adoration, to a lone tram shed on the crest of the hill above where, in deep despair, Agnes will shortly find herself joining passengers for the long slow journey into the city.

Devoid of tree cover, the row of red-brick houses bakes in oppressive summer heat, giving off a haze like the steam from an old train, in which eerie shapes form and dissolve above their rooftops. Agnes has been dragged to this place in the middle of a heatwave.

In the morning newspaper, dated today, February 1959, there is a photo of a couple frying bacon and eggs on the pavement in Martin Place. In an effort to be friendly, Agnes has handed this newspaper to her Aunt Marnie upon arrival, and can hear herself reciting in an awkward high-pitched voice:

Hello Aunty Marnie. What a relief to enter a cool room with so many fans! Look at the newspaper – it's nearly a hundred degrees and people are cooking on the pavement!

But her aunt, seated on the green carpet floor, goes on folding clothes into a cane basket. She neither greets Agnes nor makes any attempt to take the newspaper, and lets it fall. Parry picks it up, giving his wife a disapproving look. Catching his eye, Marnie changes her attitude:

Excuse me, but I'm halfway through folding the clean clothes from the line.

Parry forces his wife to her feet by lifting the basket and placing it on a chair with the newspaper on top. Marnie, tight-lipped, continues:

How are you, Agnes? I see you've been in the wars. How did you get that ripe bruiser?

But, before Agnes has a chance to parrot her mother's story, her aunt continues gleefully:

I hear you've been giving the O'Connor clan a run for their money. Even managed to unleash the vocal cords of Miss Sill O'Connor, which takes some doing. As you can see, we don't have any valuable antiques here to throw around!

Before Agnes can decide if her aunt's sarcasm is intended to be for or against her, Parry diverts the subject away and onto the children:

Except for *this* precious baby doll!

He is laughing and making honking noises as he scoops up his two-year-old daughter and blows raspberries on her fat tummy. The child squeals and laughs, begging for more and wriggling with delight as her father lifts her up and catches her in the air.

The eldest girl, Mandy, has gently taken Agnes's hand and is looking up at her with a shy smile. Agnes is dangerously close to weeping. Alongside his wife, who is now seated back on the floor with the clothes basket, Parry is now holding the middle child, Penny, on his lap, and is kissing the back of her neck:

Aw, you scratchy, Daddy!

Careful, Parry! You're making her red with your unshaved chin!

Sorry, my little sweet pea!

He kisses the top of the child's head:

What do you think of my lovely girls, Agnes? God has blessed me with a beautiful wife and three *gorgeous* daughters!

As he says this, he puts his arm around his wife's shoulders and kisses her playfully on the forehead:

Get off with you, Parry, you, silly idiot. And don't get the children excited before bedtime!

Parry is wearing a more serious expression for the children's benefit:

Now, children. This is Agnes. She has come to stay and help Mummy look after you.

Agnes, unsure how to act, makes a silly face and waves her free hand like someone slightly demented. Mandy squeezes Agnes's hand tighter. The thumb of her other hand is in her mouth. Agnes wonders if the child is claiming her because she gets the least attention.

Making the best she can of a problematic situation, Agnes initially finds being part of the little tribe on the green carpet comforting: changing nappies, putting on shoes, combing hair and being Mandy's favourite. But she can't put her finger on Aunt Marnie's demeanour. An undercurrent of hostility has continued to emanate from her since Agnes first stepped through the door, and her confusion only increases when she overhears Marnie talking about her on the phone:

She's off with the fairies… daft as a brush… what my friend, Beatrice, calls a few sandwiches short of a picnic. Yet Parry's infatuated with her.

Agnes is unsure what infatuated means. All she knows is she is suffering the same disorientation with her aunt as she did with her mother. As she doesn't know what else to do, she can only try to be as helpful to Marnie as possible. But even this gambit fails when Marnie makes it clear that she doesn't want her help, and so Agnes will spend many mornings looking longingly at the little family group of mother and children behind the sliding bubble glass doors – now firmly closed against her.

She senses she is a pawn in the playing out of some strange kind of 'couple game'. One similar to the type played by her parents. Though this time it's different. Reversed. Her father would ignore her, and her mother would not want her there when he was around. Now it is Marnie who ignores her and Parry who wants her with him all the time.

Practically every morning since she first arrived, she has accompanied her Uncle Parry as they drive the short distance in his car to the beach. Holding hands like two children, they run into the frothy water and frolic in the surf. Agnes reverts into a small girl, inventing silly names for him and falling over laughing. She settles on Horatio Henry and can hardly say the words for giggling. He is lifting her in his arms and swimming out with her into the waves on his back. She is falling into his every caress. He is a strong swimmer and has taught her how to identify the shape and curl of a wave so she can body-surf into the shore. She has mastered the technique and finds the sensation fabulous. It is like riding a magic carpet. Sometimes she picks the wrong wave and ends up in a centrifuge of foam, before being dumped with a mouth full of sand on the shore. But that doesn't matter. It is a form of freedom.

They are barefoot this morning, towels around their shoulders, and are eating hot fish and chips at an outdoor table of a café in the main street overlooking the beach. She watches his pleasant face and remembers overhearing him at breakfast, shouting angrily at her aunt:

Can't you see she's disturbed?! You've got to get over it and be *kind*, Marnie! I'm trying to *help* her!

Instead of replying, Marnie had slammed the door in his face.

Agnes watches Parry scoff down his food. He is quiet for once. He usually isn't, and keeps telling her to 'plug in':

Plug in, Agnes! Plug in!

He repeats this like a cracked record. Agnes usually giggles at this admonition, as she has no idea what he means by it. He has now started to take her everywhere with him. At this café table, as she observes him eating, she realises she now lives to hear him call out for her. She will wait outside the front door and jump in the car beside him, as eager as a pet dog.

Parry never walks anywhere if he can help it. Only yesterday she had ridden with him in the car through deserted streets to the White Horse Hotel. It is his mother-in-law's pub and is in an ugly part of King's Street, Newtown. Jammed between two closed shopfronts with rubbish-stuffed entrances and crumbling yellow-painted cement frontages, the burgundy brick building looks like a palace. The first time he had taken her there, Agnes had counted six front windows facing the street. The middle one, she figured, must have lit the stairs.

She will never see the bedrooms, where she will wonder if guests stay. Whenever she has asked Parry questions about the place, especially the bedrooms, he looks at her in a funny way and puts his arm around her shoulders without answering.

Usually, at the pub, a few old men in singlets would be perched at high bar tables on ugly purple stools, sipping pints of beer and smoking roll-your-owns with nicotine-stained fingers. On their first visit, Parry had told Agnes, as if it was a secret, that the only women allowed in the bar were barmaids. But the gender embargo never prevents him taking her behind the bar to access the huge basement below, where the pub stores supplies. Parry would regularly lift the trap door and take her down the basement steps during the heatwave in order to cool off. She would stare up at muscular men in blue singlets who rolled beer barrels on wooden planks down from an opening in the pavement. The temperature change felt good, but Agnes always finds the big dark space scary as the only natural light trickles through a small, barred window in the rear wall. The lines of these bars casting shadows on the cement floor give the impression of a prison. She has been told that the caretaker apparently sleeps on an old bed in the corner of the basement late at night. Parry likes to stretch out on this bed, too, to soak up the coolness.

In contrast to the basement gloom, the room at the end of the dark corridor, just beyond the bar, leads to the most beautiful light-filled room Agnes has ever seen. The cream carpet on the floor is tasteful and modern and there is a comfortable beige sofa covered in brightly coloured cushions. A shiny grand piano dominates the centre. A cut crystal vase full of long-stemmed fresh flowers elevates the large room – in Agnes's imagination anyway – to the grandeur of a church or concert hall. This is where the owner of the pub, Parry's mother-in-law, lives. A striking gold-framed portrait, in which she looks like a duchess, hangs on the wall behind the piano. A colourful scarf scooping up her loose greying curls, Mrs Beater never looks lovelier than when she plays the piano. Whenever she watches her, Agnes would always think of the handsome women who ran hotels in cinema Westerns: women like the kind-hearted Belle, Rhett Butler's loyal friend and business partner in *Gone with the Wind*.

Yesterday, Agnes had waited, as usual, on a stool outside the door while Parry and his mother-in-law discussed business, after which she had sat on the plush sofa and listened to Mrs Beater play the piano while Parry had conversed with her partner, Harry, in the public bar. Agnes was always glad Mrs Beater never asked her any questions, but simply smiled at her reassuringly, glancing up at her occasionally over the keys. Listening to Mrs Beater play the piano is a brief respite from the deadening confusion of Agnes's daily existence. Compared to this quiet and dignified woman, her fork-tongued daughter, Marnie, seems like an interrogation officer in a repressive regime. According to Agnes's mother, Mrs Beater had got rid of a bad husband and brought up Marnie alone. At some point, she had found a compatible partner to help her run the pub, fluffing off the gossip generated by living with a man she wasn't married to.

As Agnes and Parry finish their customary fish and chips today, Agnes feels a sudden sadness. She is thinking about the coming weekend and is gloomy about not being allowed to be with Mrs Beater. The family make regular weekend visits to Mrs Beater's holiday house on the side of a hill overlooking Pittwater Bay, but this privilege, for some reason, is denied Agnes. After just a brief glimpse of the boats and ferries bobbing on the sea below the lovely tropical garden in front of the house, Parry will always drive Agnes to Palm Beach, where she will spend the day alone. Puzzled by this arbitrary isolation, Agnes has protected herself by entering a fantasy world. She swims and sunbathes – imagining herself on the Riviera as a character in a Françoise Sagan novel. These were books she would love to read, when reading was once a pleasure, long ago.

The loveliest of the Northern Beaches, Agnes likes the way the Palm Beach headland folds around in a protective embrace, for she doesn't speak to anyone all day and the landscape seems to cradle her in compensation for her solitude. Sometimes she wonders if Parry has forgotten her, as he doesn't pick her up until it's nearly dark. If she questions him about enforcing this strange isolation upon her, he will not answer her.

And so, this morning, as they rise from the café table, Agnes sinks, yet again, into a silent and puzzling hopelessness from which it will be increasingly hard to emerge.

* * *

The summer is over, and my uncle abandons me – just like his wife has done. I think it happens after a visit to the White Horse Hotel and a trip under the trapdoor into the dark basement under the bar. But I'm not sure. From one day to the next he treats me like I'm not there. He stops taking me with him in the car. I wait for hours for him at the front door. When I bang frantically on the car window, he waves me away and, one day, he kicks me aside when I grab him. Get away from me, you... you... you! He is yelling without finishing the sentence.

It feels like I'm back with my parents in the car on the way to the farm after the inquisition at Rosemont. I think Parry and Marnie are angry with me because I started a fire in their kitchen. I am not clear on much that happens to me at this time, but I can still see this fire surging up in front of my eyes. Flames rise and lick the walls. Great red tongues eat at the kitchen cupboards and blacken the ceiling. The fire goes on forever, burns forever, in my mind. When I question Parry about the fire, he gets angry and shouts: There was no bloody fire! It's all in your bloody head like everything else! So, I can't be sure, after all, if the fire was real. Or if the strange creatures and eerie sounds that swirl around the hot summer rooftops are real. And because I don't know what is real and what is not, I decide to kill myself. I buy a jar of aspirin at the chemist.

I wander around the beach looking for a place to swallow them down and die. It's too cold for swimming, but there are enough sunbathers at lunchtime for me not to stand out. I will die with my face under a straw hat and my sunglasses on. I have brought some beads to say a rosary while I wait for the end. But it seems I am too stupid even to go ahead and kill myself. Either there are too many people on the beach, or I forget to bring water to help me swallow the tablets. Then I start worrying about leaving my dead body behind, like a bit of garbage, on the sand.

The summer must be over, as now the winter months dissolve into images like the frames in an old silent picture-show: long rides on an ancient tram that shudders along Anzac Parade to Elizabeth Street. Buying The Sydney Morning Herald. *Reading it in The General Post Office building. Answering ads for work and receiving interminable rejections.*

Crippling despair drives me to another suicide attempt, but a couple step in front of me just as I'm about to jump under a train at Wynyard. And I'm thwarted another time when I decide to jump off the harbour bridge as I can't get access to the ledge. I'm not capable of killing myself, yet I die a hundred humiliating deaths when a store detective with a hard face is called to a counter because I am freezing cold and have tried to charge a winter coat to the 'David Jones' account: 'Your signature has been cancelled and if you try and use the account again, you will be expelled from the store'.

I decide to lie in front of Parry's car as he is about to drive off. He gets out of the driver's seat and wrenches me up by the arm: You're mad! Stark staring mad! He is screaming in my face. Even my mother hangs up when I ring her and ask her for money. I am dead to her too. It is only to be expected.

18

COOGEE

oogee is the aboriginal word for 'big smell', at least that's what the fish and chip shop proprietor is telling Agnes, then elaborates:

It's cos the beach is prone to a build-up of seaweed. You should visit the local aquarium. There's a shark there they captured near shore who vomited up a human arm. They identified the owner through a tattoo on it! Hard to believe, ain't it, love? The cops still don't know if the guy was murdered and chucked in or attacked and eaten. But I reckon it was *murder*.

Agnes has walked, out of habit, to the fish and chip shop from the boarding house, situated above the beach in Coogee, and has been waiting in a queue to be served. The boarding house sits on a windy northern headland overlooking the Pacific Ocean and is full of old people. Is it a place for people not right in the head? No chains or straitjackets are in evidence. Agnes has been too afraid to approach anyone and ask. But the question of madness buzzes like a pestering insect around her thoughts. One morning, she had woken up in a room here with no idea how she got there. *Is* she mad? She *must* be because Uncle Parry said so. Now, in her tortured state, mad goes with bad, not very bright, and off with the fairies.

She blurts this observation on madness out loud to a tall lady – a stranger – with alert, grey eyes who is wearing a flowered scarf around her head. She is ahead of Agnes in the queue at the fish and chip shop. The woman laughs and says:

Some are born mad, some achieve madness, and some have madness thrust upon them. But I'm teasing. The real Shakespeare quote is 'some are born great, some achieve greatness, and some have greatness thrust upon them.' He knew a thing or two.

Agnes must look as bemused as she feels, for the woman clasps her by the wrist and looks into her troubled eyes:

Seriously, love, I don't mean to joke. You mustn't worry. People who are mad don't know they're mad. They're taken over by it. Unlike you, they'd never ask the question. Here – let me buy your fish and chips.

The woman's assessment on madness gives Agnes some reassurance, and having little money, she is particularly grateful for the free fish and chips. When she last rang Don Burns, he had said he was sorry, but he had no money left to give her. He had already donated all his savings. In fact, Don has been supporting her since the day Parry dragged her away from Mrs Kelly's house. Whenever she rang him for help, he would meet her in an appointed place and give her some cash. In future, when Agnes can think straight once more, she will realise that Don saved her life.

The lady in the scarf hands her the fish and chips. They are wrapped in newspaper. Fat bruises are starting to stain well-known front-page faces:

Enjoy your meal, my dear girl, and don't you worry yourself about being mad – because you're *not*!

She laughs merrily, jamming the coins from her change in a collection tin for crippled children, before rushing out of the shop.

A couple of minutes later, much to Agnes's amazement, the same woman taps her on the shoulder out on the street and shoves a few pound notes into the open white handbag looped on her shoulder, before quickly running off.

Agnes sits on the beach and devours the hot meal. She hasn't eaten properly for days and is ravenous. She watches the sea being dragged out, as if against its will, and wonders whether she has had madness thrust upon her.

A few days later, after showing Agnes her double-jointed fingers, Jeanette Gibson drags Agnes in to sit with her in the dining room for breakfast. This is how Agnes learns that breakfast is included with her board and lodging. She's grateful, as she has spent all the scarf lady's money on daily fish and chips. Broke again, and desperately hungry, she has even entertained thoughts of stealing buns from the bakery next door, until this welcome revelation.

After the meagre morning meal, Jeanette takes her by the arm and leads her into her room to see a silver-framed photo of a young man with calf eyes and wavy hair. He is wearing an army uniform, cap in hand over his heart, and dominates a small table venerated with flowers and candles. Agnes obediently kneels beside Jeanette on the cushions placed in front of the altar where Jeanette proceeds to call to God to bring George back to her. The strange ritual is completed with Jeanette's full-throated rendition of 'Danny Boy'.

She has a lovely voice which, Agnes will notice, will improve as the days go on. Or perhaps she will become a better listener as she relaxes into a regular morning attendance at the tribute to Jeanette's dead husband.

Mrs Ivy Forsythe, the manager of the boarding house, enthusiastically informs Agnes that Jeanette's world stopped when she received the news of George's death:

Killed by a Jap guard on the Death Trap. That's the name of the Burma railway, love. Built by prisoners of war in brutal conditions. For every railway sleeper laid, a man died, and George was one of them. Cruel bastards those Japs. But *I* think our Jeanette was a bit soft in the head even *before* she lost George. She's my Ron's sister, but she's such a handful. We don't know how much longer we can keep her here. With no grave or dog tags and only one man's testimony, she's decided poor George is still out there somewhere. So, she goes on waiting for him to come back. Like two lovebirds in a cage, those two, by all accounts. Eyes only for each other. Inseparable since teenagers. The shock sent her over the wall, and she hasn't been able to climb back. A real Humpty Dumpty. But she's a harmless soul, mumbling away to herself as she combs the streets looking for him. Only last week she got lost and the police brought her back. She told the cop she had found George outside the bottle shop. She's a hoarder. It's a sickness she can't be cured of. Once a week, my Ron and I sneak in and remove the junk she's forgotten, otherwise you wouldn't get in the door. It's a bit of a lark really, Jeanette brings it in, and we pack it in bags and take it out. Better not get too matey, love, or you'll never have a moment to ya self.

Given this life story, Agnes wonders if someone at Rosemont, or whoever it was who organised the boarding house, has said anything to Mrs Forsythe about her. She searches the woman's heavily made-up pudding face for clues but can't detect any. Just in case, she mostly tries to avoid her. She avoids, also, talking to the elderly residents, scared as she is that they might ask what she's doing there. And the truth is, she doesn't know. So, she finds herself embracing Jeanette's crazy world as a welcome hiding place.

The fall off the wall had not daunted Jeanette's determination and Agnes admires that. Though she is half Jeanette's age, Agnes knows in her heart that they are both destined to be lost souls. Jeanette's long, droopy, imploring face resembles a cocker spaniel waiting to be taken for a walk and so, when requested, Agnes readily agrees to join her for beach explorations. The two of them write silly stuff in the sand with sticks and measure the size of their footprints before the tide sweeps them out to sea. Jeanette has long and prominent big toes. Agnes has read somewhere that this has a connection with a person's mental state and is relieved to see her own toes sloping neatly in a line. As she sits on the beach with Jeanette for hours on end, she constantly jumps on invasive wild ideas around the theme of sanity as, despite the scarf lady's reassurance, she remains haunted by her Uncle Parry's accusation.

Since meeting Agnes, Jeanette has started taking an interest in her appearance. She attempts to tame her wild frizzy grey hair in plastic rollers that she even wears to bed and has started applying make-up. It crosses Agnes's mind that her arrival, and friendship, has resurrected Jeanette's hope of a reunion with George. Most guests in the boarding house avoid Jeanette, but Agnes finds it a soothing relief to listen to her idle chatter as she sits back on a comfortable floral lounger in Jeanette's room, and watches Bluebell, Jeanette's canary, perform his acrobatics in a tiny cage as he gulps down seeds and makes tiny sprays in a little water trough. The rubbish in Jeanette's room is piled high: boxes, newspapers, books, clothes, shoes, bits of furniture, fishing baskets and lines – the clutter of objects precariously stacked to the ceiling. Agnes has started to notice that Jeanette stutters over words, and often loses track of her thoughts. In mid-sentence she will forget what she wants to say and appears as surprised by the phenomenon as Agnes does herself.

Barred from the 'David Jones' account and the cold now really setting in, Agnes finds herself shivering on the street without a coat and has no money to buy one. But Jeanette comes to her rescue. On a particularly chilly day, Jeanette marches up to her and hands her a good-quality green wool coat with a brown velvet collar that she says she found at a bus stop. It is a little big on Agnes – she has lost so much weight – but it looks good on her. She suspects Jeanette may have stolen it, as it is hard to imagine anyone abandoning such a lovely garment at a bus stop. But at least she is warm now, and secretly hopes the coat won't be spotted in the street and reclaimed off her back.

As for Jeanette's own clothes, nothing the woman wears matches. Mostly, around the house, she tends to favour a pink chenille dressing gown, adorned on either side with a red cloth carnation held on with enormous safety pins.

Mrs Forsythe has revealed to Agnes that her husband, Ron, handles the pensions paid to his sister by the Australian government. As Jeanette never has any money, it occurs to Agnes he might be putting it straight in his own pocket.

This wintry morning, with a chill wind rattling at the boarding house windows, Mrs Forsythe has just handed Agnes an envelope. Tucked inside is a map of the area with a tram stop circled in red biro. The map nestles next to a small pile of pound notes. Agnes unfolds a typewritten note which bears the cotton factory's letterhead:

Be careful of this money as there is no more. GET A JOB.

The author of the unsigned note goes on to include instructions on how to find this elusive employment:

BUY A *SYDNEY MORNING HERALD*. GO TO THE GENERAL POST OFFICE. SEARCH THROUGH POSITIONS VACANT AND APPLY FOR WHATEVER!

This is the first time she has been given money since she escaped the farm. Agnes wonders if this missive has come from her father, or Rosemont, but it really doesn't matter as she deems all her family to be simply one giant antagonistic conglomerate. It isn't a huge sum, but it is something. Presumably, paying one's boarding house accommodation fees is considered adequate help for such a delinquent. How did this family of hers think she has managed without any spending money all these months? The bullying, unsigned letter plunges her into a dark state.

There is a rocky shelf, called Wedding Cake Island, which protects Coogee beach against turbulent seas in rough storms. Perched high on the cliff above the beach, the boarding house receives the full brunt of spray from the huge waves crashing against the escarpment opposite. Such a storm strikes soon after Agnes receives the loveless letter. Lashing rain, driven by fierce winds, pounds at her bedroom window and shakes the timber structure of the house, which shudders and creaks like an old boat. The noise is deafening. Isolated indoors, she can sense herself sinking deeper and deeper into despair and, when the vicious wind abates, she exits the building and walks slowly towards the cliff edge, feeling increasingly drawn to jump into the raging foam below.

A part of her mind is seeing herself like Maxim de Winter in *Rebecca* as he stands on the edge of a precipice somewhere on the French Riviera. She recalls how, when he notices the young woman who will become his wife watching him, he draws back. Then, just like in the film, she thinks she sees Jeanette. It *is* Jeanette!

The sight of Jeanette silently observing her makes Agnes pull back from the cliff edge. She is trembling when she runs to her friend. Instead of the usual pat on the head, Jeanette puts her arms around her like a proper sane person and holds her tight. Agnes enjoys the physical human contact for as long as she dares, then runs down onto the beach, feeling the exhilaration of the wind in her hair. She is telling herself in her head: You don't need permission from *anyone* to go on living. So go on living. Go on *living*!

The following day, when Agnes returns from the city, where she is dutifully seeking employment, Mrs Forsythe informs her:

She forgot to blow the candles out after the usual morning nonsense. Flames took off after igniting a pile of papers she'd got out of the garbage the night before and left on a chair next to the altar. Ya saw the room, Agnes, so ya know better than anyone – a disaster waiting to happen. Ron said the council owe us for burning all the municipal rubbish for them! The room is gutted! Mind, the fireman's hoses have caused as much damage as the flames. My Ron was on the desk when he sees the smoke waft by and he's out of the chair in a flash. As soon as he opens Jeannette's door the flames take off like they've been hit with petrol. Our Jeannette caught alight when she ran to save her precious picture of George and her bird. Ron wrapped her in a blanket, but she fainted with the smoke. Reckon she's developed a weak chest roaming outside in the cold at all hours. If Ron hadn't been there, she would have died. It's a miracle Ron contained the blaze before it spread to the rest of the house. By the time I got back from the butcher's, the firemen had the room soaked. They managed to save her wedding dress – stored under the bed in a metal box – but she doesn't want it. Ron told her the fire wasn't her fault. She told Ron he'd always hated her and she's leaving before he poisons her. How's *that* for gratitude to a loving brother who's cared for her all these years? Agnes doesn't believe Mrs Forsythe when she says it was

Jeanette's idea to leave, for she is fully aware of the woman's desire to get rid of her vexing sister-in-law. She is proved right when Tom – an old man with hooded eyes and a flat nose like an owl who also resides in the house – tells Agnes that the Forsythes are shipping Jeanette out to a 'mental home'. He also reveals that Jeannette owns half the place as the parents had left it jointly to both siblings. Seated with Tom in the empty dining room, Agnes discovers that for want of asking a simple question, she has, all this time, forgone the evening meal which is included with her lodging fees. Jeanette always ate with her brother and sister-in-law and so the elderly residents in the boarding house had assumed Agnes had joined them. She simply can't believe that she could have enjoyed a solid cooked meal each evening and not gone to bed hungry all this time. She wonders why Mrs Forsythe didn't notice her absence from the dining room or ever mention it.

As Jeanette waits for a place to come up in a psychiatric centre, the destruction of her room and her precious belongings will take its toll on her. She will be mad because she looks mad. Most notable to Agnes will be the loss of interest in her appearance. Hilda, old Tom's wife, will make efforts with a hairdryer but fail to tame Jeanette's wild hair after she helps her wash it. It will stand out in a giant fuzz, a resemblance not improved by the rouge Hilda applies to Jeanette's sunken cheeks and the smear of lipstick to her cracked lips.

In a kind attempt to make her friend feel better, Agnes will quickly scribble a few lines in memory of their beach walks beneath the moon:

When our hearts are full of sadness
We've got the moon
When we're all choked up with loathing
We've got the moon
And when those we love betray us
The moon never will

She knocks on the car window to get Jeanette's attention after they help the subdued and silent woman into the back seat, but Jeanette hangs her head and doesn't look up. Her poor burnt arm is still in a sling, so Agnes slips the paper with the verse through a crack in the top of the window and watches it fall to the floor as the car drives off.

Mere minutes after Jeanette's departure, a rubbish truck will arrive to clear the last of the charred debris from her room so it can be decorated and rented out.

* * *

Agnes is up early the next morning. After Jeanette's departure she feels a fresh determination to regain her own sanity and track down that elusive job. Once again, she washes her long hair – which hasn't been near a hairdresser in years – scoops it into a neat ponytail and covers the elastic band with a length of green ribbon Jeanette gave her. A clumsy woman on the city tram having snagged her last pair of nylons with an umbrella, she decides to wear them with the ladder on the inside of the leg. She stains the bald patches on the fronts of her patent leather court shoes with boot polish but finds to her dismay that no amount of rubbing alters the textual contrast. While brushing down a caramel tartan kilt Jeanette has also given her, she discovers moth holes inside the pleats. She dismisses this concern as she reckons the holes won't be visible whilst sitting still at an interview. She rolls the long skirt over at the waist, pulls a nutmeg-shaded lambswool jumper over her head, fixes a white detachable lace collar inside the neck and decides that is the best she can do. There is no denying she looks shabby, but with the smart bus-stop winter coat over her arm, hiding skirt and stockings, she reckons she might manage.

She catches the new 7.30am bus service in the main street, which cuts the time of the tram journey to the city in half. She is deeply grateful this route exists, as to experience further creaks, screeches and bumps on a shuddering tram is to be sent back into the torturous atmosphere of Parry's baking red-brick house situated below the lone tram shed. She does not know it now, but the memory of those long, bleak rides in the darkness, returning cold and hungry from the city to relentless hostility after her aunt and uncle's inexplicable rejection, will haunt her for years.

On the bus, the mildew smell from the coat of the stout man beside her dampens the pleasant aroma of the new upholstered seats but, as the bus pulls away from the kerb, the smooth motion of the wheels on the newly tarmacked road starts to fill Agnes with hope. She is still digesting the delicious cottage pie from the very welcome evening meal last night, so deliberately hasn't bothered with breakfast to avoid any distraction to her renewed determination.

The General Post Office looks sombre, its stonework dark from an earlier downpour. But nothing diminishes the wonder of the colonnade along Martin Place, and resolute Queen Victoria gravely presiding over the main entrance, flanked by allegorical figures bearing the British coat of arms. Having bought a copy of the *Sydney Herald* as usual, Agnes's arrival in the city centre is so early that she decides to splurge on raisin toast and coffee in Angel Place. It's the first time she has felt courageous enough to sit in a coffee shop like a proper grown-up – all on her own.

She is utterly amazed when her first phone call from the Post Office, on the dot of nine, and in response to an advertisement for a receptionist/tea lady at an import/export company, goes straight through to the Personnel Manager:

Timing is everything.

So says the smooth male voice on the other end of the phone, then follows up with:

If you're at the GPO, why not come straight to the top of York Street for an interview?

As Agnes rushes down George Street, she recalls what old Tom, over the evening's meal at the boarding house, said she should do if she got nervous:

Imagine your interviewer on the toilet. In the good old days, I had them on and off the 'john' in boardrooms all over Sydney and Melbourne – faces straining with constipation. Works *every* time.

The atmosphere on the street is electric. Office workers are dashing to be at their desks by nine and the exit from Wynyard station is so congested that Agnes moves onto the road to avoid a bottleneck. The early rain intensifies the sound of screeching brakes and horns as traffic crawls bumper to bumper. Agnes feels elated to be part of the energy powering the city. She really is starting to feel alive again as she spots the building where Mr Watson is, apparently, waiting for her arrival.

Mr Watson will not be the rugged Heathcliff, seething with passion, promised by the velvet voice on the phone. His short legs only just reaching the floor under the desk, and with visible chest bumps straining under his shirt, obesity will make him look older, while plump cheeks affirm youth. But the laugh lines around his eyes will put her at ease and she will move forward in such a hurry to greet him that she knocks over the umbrella stand:

Gosh, I'm so sorry!

She will return the stand back in place, hoping he hasn't got a glimpse of her laddered stockings or bald shoes, and will still be gasping for breath, having taken the stairs two at a time up to the second floor. He will not seem to be staring at her legs. So far, so good:

Well, you can see *I* don't do much running. A bit of a tum-tum to go with the double chin!

He will chuckle at his own remark and rub the protruding bulge under his shirt with his small pudgy hand. Aware it would be inappropriate to agree, Agnes will shrug and smile and feel another rush of energy surge through her body. She will stand up straight in front of his desk and speak firmly, giving her age and name, and employing the tone and inflections cultivated at her school elocution lessons. As she will tell Tom later, there wasn't time to put Mr John Watson on the toilet, for he decided to give her the job there and then: a) to avoid further interviews, and b) because he was dying for a cup of tea.

She will shortly get to know that John Watson is the boss's lazy son – humoured by the staff, but ridiculed behind his back:

Well, my girl, you went to a good school all right, same as my sister, but you don't have to be Einstein to make the tea and take it around the office. We'll require you to do errands and learn to use the switchboard, so you can fill in when the operators go to lunch. Do you think you can do that?

I *know* I can, Mr Watson. You won't be disappointed!

Clasping the bus-stop coat in front of the damaged nylons, she will follow him to the switchboard on the other side of the aisle with its red lights already flashing above rows of black holes. Agnes will recognise this from office scenes she has watched at the cinema.

Mr Watson will tell her that his phone extension is 'three' and his father's extension is 'one' and that she will quickly learn "where we all are".

As Agnes leans forward for a closer look, she will drop her coat and immediately cross her ankles for fear of exposing the laddered stockings. Mr Watson will look at her oddly and ask her if she "wants to use the little girls' room" which she will decline, telling him that she is just trying to cover the ladder in her stocking – uttering this with a candour that surprises even her. He will say:

Ah-hah! I see before me a stairway to paradise…

He will be chuckling as he bends down to observe the point where the ladder disappears under her skirt, and Agnes will step back with a combination of surprise and disapproval. She will learn to keep clear of his wandering hands over the next few months.

He will say:

Can you start straight away?

She must have got the job! He *seems* to be sincere. Sudden waterworks will threaten to trip her up simply because a pudgy man with short legs offers her a lifeline. After so much deprivation, the least kindness has the power to reduce her to a weeping wreck. She will pinch her thigh through the skirt to regain her composure. He will scribble a note, sign it, and leave it on someone's desk. Agnes will just about make it out: 'We have a new tea lady called Agnes Keen. Record her details, show her how to use the switchboard, petty cash, and be kind.' Agnes will be somewhat disconcerted by 'be kind' and will wonder if it may also be a request on his own behalf. He will smile at her and declare:

Well now, Agnes! Welcome to Shipwrecks and Pirates, Import Export Agents. Cable and Watson to you!

She will smile at him politely. Months of rejection over at the mere passing whim of a small fat man.

19

THE ENSEMBLE THEATRE AND NURSING

I t is Saturday morning and Agnes has spent one week at Cable and Watson. She throws a few things in a bag and catches the bus from Coogee to the city, wearing a new pair of nylon stockings and a pair of red court shoes she has bought with Friday's pay packet. Next week she will buy a new skirt. The green bus-stop coat reminds her of Jeanette who had died from a heart attack shortly after arrival at the psychiatric centre. Agnes goes on talking to Jeanette in her head as if she's still alive. She likes to imagine her wearing her wedding dress, seated on a cloud in heaven, holding hands with her beloved George.

Agnes strides up Martin Place with her head high and shoulders back, adopting the posture Rita Ryder taught her for the fifth ballet position. The warm sun on her back fills her with optimism. Spring has finally arrived, the days are long, and the flowers are out. She waves to Queen Victoria over the entrance of the General Post Office. Details on façades of buildings, the specific garments people are wearing, all jump out at her as her eyes focus sharply on the world around her. Earlier that morning she had rung Maria Kelly and is now on her way to see her.

As the train speeds over the harbour bridge, she feels the way a prisoner must feel after release from jail. Her lighter heart leaps at the sight of railway stations she knows well. She is to stay at the Kelly house at weekends and join Maria at her Saturday morning acting classes at the Ensemble Theatre.

Maria is waiting impatiently when she arrives, worried that they will be late for the class. She is briskly informed by Maria that they have an hour to get to the 11am session. So, within minutes of dropping her bag in the spare room off the veranda, she is in the back seat of Mrs Kelly's Mercedes speeding down the Pacific Highway to Kirribilli as Maria gushes from the front seat:

It's called method acting Agnes and it's *fantastic*! You know, Marlon Brando and James Dean are both method actors? And wait till you see Hayes Gordon. He's like no one you've ever met. He's been in *stacks* of Broadway musicals. They blacklisted him in America for being a Communist sympathiser during the McCarthy era and he got *no* work after refusing to sign the oath of loyalty, so he upped sticks and came to Sydney. He says he's not a Communist but a man of principles. In the class we focus on not just making faces but *feeling* our way into the part. You don't pretend but actually *become* the character. You'll *love* it, Agnes! It's just so exciting and different!

As they leave the sunlight behind and tiptoe down a ramp into the hallowed atmosphere, Maria explains that the theatre auditorium is 'in the round' like a Greek or Roman amphitheatre.

The class already underway, they slide into the first two seats – just inside the far entrance:

Don't sit there! Come closer, so you can hear what's going on!

For a moment, Agnes has not grasped that the man on the far side with the deep American accent is addressing them:

Come, Marline! Bring your friend and sit here!

Puzzled, Agnes follows Maria across the stage to some front row seats directly across from a black-bearded man with a large face. His eyes are hidden behind tortoiseshell glasses and overhung by a shelf of bushy brows. Maria whispers to Agnes covertly:

Marline is my stage name.

Agnes has noticed that, compared to fellow students who are wearing leather jackets, boots, velvet caps and slouching willy-nilly amidst tangles of coloured scarves in the rows around them, Maria née Marline and herself, both clad in skirts and twinsets, could not look more out of place.

Hayes Gordon first sounds to Agnes as if he could run the world. His presence both mesmerises and intimidates her. A lone spotlight from above encircling him like a halo, when he looks at her, she feels as if he is boring a hole in her skull. She would quickly discover that most of the group were already devotees of The Method.

Names like Stanislavski, Lee Strasberg, Stella Adler and Elia Kazan are constantly referred to by Hayes and are seemingly familiar to all present at the lesson. To Agnes, this 'method' of acting sounds equally fascinating and bewildering.

In the second hour of her first session, their instructor calls upon the group to team up with partners to play 'actions'. Ten minutes are allotted to integrate a specific action into a story backstage, then to be ad-libbed on stage for the benefit of the group. The audience's task is to identify the action, the motivation, and assess what each performer is trying to achieve.

A young guy called Brian, wearing a James Dean leather jacket, approaches Agnes to be his partner. Fearful of something beyond her comprehension, she suggests they weave their story around buying and selling, as what could be more straightforward than that? Brian takes the initiative and plays a clothes vendor in a street market rushing to finish the day's trading so he can get home to give his diabetic mother an insulin injection. One more sale will top up the rent due on the house he shares with her. In her head, Agnes returns to the cold winter when, without a coat, she used to warm her freezing hands and arms under hot water taps in the 'David Jones' Ladies Room. The ad-libbing simply flows between them as Brian proffers his leather coat as a prop and says:

Here – try it on.

Oh, my God, it fits perfectly and it's *warm*!

Brian does up the buttons:

There you are – snug as a bug in a rug.

I'm *never* going to take it off!

Agnes laughs as she twirls around while savouring the new comfort:

How much is it?

£9 will be fine. It's a bargain.

But I've only got £5. It's all the money I've got in the world!

Perhaps you can find a bit more in your bag?

Agnes tips the contents of her bag onto the table on the stage but finds nothing. She holds up an imaginary five-pound note and pleads with him, but Brian insists on the full amount.

How can you be so *mean*?!

Agnes hears herself shouting, her throat all choked up, as if this 'Brian', this new acquaintance of only an hour, is alone responsible for her life of suffering. Her voice reaches a crescendo of pain:

I'm going to run off with it and not pay you a penny *unless you agree*!!

Brian jumps over the stall counter, grabs her arm and starts to unbutton the coat, but stops suddenly when he sees her eyes full of tears. He puts his arms around her and hands her a handkerchief out of his pocket:

Here. Give me the £5 and that's the end to it. I'll rob a bank on the way home for the rest.

Agnes hands over the money, kisses Brian on the cheek, and walks off the stage to a considerable ripple of applause. The discussion that follows their exercise is brief, as the 'action' is abundantly clear to all.

At the end of all the performances and discussions, the group individually approach Hayes to pay him for the class. When it is Agnes's turn, she is thunderstruck when he pulls her aside:

You have the talent and the looks to go with it. If you want the stage, it could be yours for the taking. It's you, Agnes, who must make the commitment to work on yourself. As Stanislavski says: 'The body is just the instrument.' See you next week.

Agnes and Maria join some of the group for coffee afterwards:

Well! I'll be able to say in twenty years' time when you're famous, that I was there the day the prediction was made!

This somewhat snide comment has come from a wide-eyed girl in the group, who had overheard what Hayes said to Agnes. A little annoyed to have her special moment quashed, Agnes manages to stammer a polite riposte:

I'm sure he says that to all the new arrivals to keep them coming back.

But she is suitably cowed nonetheless and wishes she could evaporate. Maria rushes to Hayes's defence, describing him as 'a man of principle' who means everything he says, and Agnes tries hard to dismiss any lingering doubts of his sincerity from her mind.

In the classes during the weeks that follow, Agnes will shine during one session, and the next will feel out of her depth and fall into despair. The truth is that she has been conditioned to feel comfortable in the shadows, yet she will still manage to reconnect with her ability to amuse, drawing on the comic techniques she once used to entertain her classmates at school. However, during one session she will experience a minor nervous breakdown as she attempts an exercise which Hayes calls 'Emotion Memory'. It is a technique exploring the theory that any emotions necessary for a part cannot be called up to order but will emerge naturally by recalling the setting in which the event that prompted that emotion took place. Agnes will conjure up her little bedroom in Chatswood: the light, the smells and scents, the atmospheric temperature, the familiar sounds. Strongly reliving, too, the precious objects in the room she once treasured, she will end up shattered – an emotional wreck – on the floor. She will be acutely aware that in the course of the exercise she was momentarily devoid of her normal compulsion to cover up and invent. She will feel exhausted.

A tall, thin young man with small round glasses and curly hair will approach her afterwards in the foyer and observe:

That was quite a reaction.

I know. I feel really ashamed. I have big memory gaps in my past. I know that I've lived that passage of time, or I wouldn't still be here. But it's all a blank. It's like I'm followed by what's hidden. I can't really put it into words. The truth is, you see, I lived in a very unhappy house. Just now, during that exercise, was the first time I have ever spoken honestly about it.

The young man will look at her intently and say:

I'm presently studying psychiatry and one major thing I learned from Freud is that nothing is ever lost. It is all inside you. One day, when you feel strong enough, if you wish, you can find what you believe *you* have lost.

Agnes will absorb the remark and then feel compelled to ask him whether, in order to be a method actor, a person inevitably had to be screwed up.

He will smile at her sympathetically and tell her that every development of the person and the personality is fraught with misunderstanding and suffering. He will tell her that the plays they put on reflect life. And that life is unavoidable.

* * *

After three months, Agnes is feeling comfortable in the job at Cable and Watson. She enjoys working the switchboard and, after a few initial minor mishaps, knows exactly what plug goes where. What she has absorbed of switchboard lingo from films has been enhanced by listening to Doreen and Brenda – the two straight-talking, unsentimental girls who alternate as the voice of Cable and Watson and who are always up for a laugh.

Doreen explains the golden response rule, winking at Agnes as she rolls her tongue around the company name:

You've got to learn how to put on the dog. Repeat after me: *Good* afternoon, Cable and Watson. Can I *help* you?

Agnes has been waiting for the unkindness Mr Watson alluded to in his note on her first morning to manifest, but none occurs. Any antagonism from the two operators, if you could call it that, is clearly aimed at him. His light would ignite on the switchboard and one operator would say to the other: It's that old poofter again! as she squeezed her nose with her fingers in imitation of his rather effeminate lilt. But whilst making fun of him, at the same time the two young women protect him from being caught snoozing, or with his head in a girlie magazine.

Both good-natured, bosomy, curly-haired brunettes, they have been working together for so long that they've taken on similar mannerisms. Agnes now finds it hard to imagine one without the other and looks forward to their sassy remarks to some of the callers:

No, sorry Madam – this is Cable and Watson Import/Export. We don't sell oysters. CLICK.

Apologies but we are *strictly* import/export. CLICK. The silly old cow is back *again*, Brenda! No, madam, no flat-head, or prawns either. If I'm not incorrect, madam, I think you need the sea, or, at best, a fish shop.

At such moments they will both explode with laughter. Their humour is so infectious, Agnes often spends the entire day struggling to keep a straight face. On the other hand, their professionalism, when implemented to the full, is so slick that Agnes believes Doreen and Brenda could run the company.

What will change everything at this happier time in Agnes's life is a call from Grandma. As Agnes has never spoken to her grandmother, or to anybody for that matter, on the boarding house phone, she had not recognised her voice:

How are you, dear?

Oh Grandma, it's you! I'm fine thank you. I got myself a job on the switchboard with Cable and Watson. They're… they're a famous import/export company in York Street.

She has deliberately left out her start as a tea-lady. That would seem far too common. Agnes has started to stumble over her words. As she hears her grandmother's steady breathing on the line, she feels like a small, insignificant child. Grandma intones:

I hope you are going to Mass on Sundays.

Oh… yes, Grandma… *of course*, Grandma!

She has lied clumsily, having lost sight of her religion months ago. Grandma continues:

Well, I just want to let you know – you have been offered a place to train to be a nurse at St Vincent's Hospital. Your Aunt Sill trained there if you recall. You'll be receiving a letter with detailed instructions in the next few days. Goodbye for now, dear, and make sure you adhere to the sacraments.

Grandma's voice had been as neutral as a cloudy day – so lacking in highs and lows, it might have been a recorded message. She still ran everyone and everything. Certainly, such interventions had been synonymous with punctuating cataclysmic change throughout Agnes's life. Now she racks her brains in a panic.

Wildly enthusiastic about Hayes Gordon and his method acting classes, she had blurted out her new passion for the stage to all and sundry, including Mrs Forsythe, which was probably how it had all got back to Rosemont. There, in those hallowed halls of rigid Catholicism, the mere word 'theatre' would have alerted The Matriarch that one of her 'souls for heaven' was in mortal danger.

It also occurs to Agnes that having her reside in the nursing home would save on the boarding house fees that Grandma was doubtless providing. Although, since she landed the job, she herself had been paying Mrs Forsythe for her room and board direct. Probably the same brotherly scoundrel who had dispatched Jeanette was collecting money at both ends. Yet, as much as life had altered for the better, as much as her self-confidence had increased, it was still beyond Agnes to challenge her grandmother.

Decades later, Agnes will know that, could she live her early life again, this would have been the point when she might turn her back on the lot of them – grandmother, parents, aunts, uncles – and go her own way. But, broken inside, unaware of alternatives, the drive to redeem herself in their eyes had outweighed everything else.

A further pull towards her serious consideration of a nursing career has been that Maria Kelly is on the point of departing, with her aunt, on an ocean liner. A world trip apparently. Agnes has shared her friend's burning ambition to be an actress but felt she could only achieve it with Maria's support. With Maria's friendship fading away on the beckoning horizon, she has convinced herself that the rawness of the emotional memory experience at the theatre has left her so deeply unsettled that she cannot risk repeating it. By tending the sick, she reasons, she would be doing God's work. And taking this path would relieve her of all other supplementary acts of charity to stay alive.

Strangely, to be selected to train at St Vincent's has planted an intriguing seed. It is causing Agnes to feel as if she belongs. She, too, could finally become a secure and trustworthy part of the family dynasty – dynasty of polo, of educating boys at St Joseph's and girls at Rose Bay, of expensive brand labels, of Royal Doulton tableware, of crested silver-plated cutlery and sedate Regency-striped dining room chairs.

And what is more, she really likes the look of the white starched belt of the uniform with its one blue stripe pinching in her slender twenty-two-inch waist.

* * *

Although part of the New South Wales state public health system, St Vincent's has remained under the auspices of the Catholic Church since its founding by five Irish Sisters of Charity in 1857. Its mission? To give quality care to the poor. Today, one hundred years later, the spirit of compassion and dedication is still alive in the Women's Accident Ward on the second floor where Agnes has been posted after her initial three months' training.

Marcia Weldon's bed is directly opposite the door of the first of the four bright second-floor rooms that make up the ward – two at the front of the building and two behind, and which overlook the hospital courtyard. Both of Marcia's legs are locked into a series of complicated traction of weights and pulleys. Agnes has found herself instantly mesmerised by the golden flecks, like trapped stars, in Marcia's violet eyes which, combined with her fine features and thick black curls, make her beauty endlessly fascinating. Speculation runs high on the ward about what drove Marcia to jump off The Gap – an infamous suicide spot on the south-facing sandstone gateway to Sydney Harbour.

Agnes feels excited at the prospect of conversing with the glamorous Marcia before coming on duty each day, for Marcia's rescue and survival is nothing short of miraculous. Married to a well-known Sydney businessman, news of her attempted suicide is reported in the newspapers. Agnes has read snippets of an article in the nurses' station which quote a male 'colleague' of Marcia's – who worked with her in the same advertising agency. The colleague states in the article that, upon parting with her after work, he had chanced to look back to see her change direction and board a tram to Watson's Bay. What's she doing, he had asked himself? Her car was still in the car park! Turning tail, he had run down the track, managing to leap onto the last carriage of the same tram. After floods of passengers alighted at Double Bay, he had struggled to locate her within the tram. Did he miss seeing her get off? It isn't until passengers thin out after the Rose Bay stop that he spotted her near the front. Not wishing to be seen following her, he had buried his head in a newspaper in the last carriage, keeping her in view. When the tram had pulled its weight up the hill to the very last stop at Watson's Bay, Marcia apparently didn't pause to contemplate matters, but had dashed straight up the hill to the cliff edge – and jumped.

What her 'colleague' saw when he looked down was Marcia's slightly built figure limply suspended in the air, her full red skirt billowing on either side of her like the wings of a flamingo. Her survival, it seemed, was dependent upon a piece of handwoven cloth breaking her fall. Describing his heart being in his mouth as he watched a fireman being winched down to rescue the unconscious woman, it seems that Jock Grace's lovelorn instinct to follow his secret *amorata*, Marcia, facilitated a rescue that saved her life.

Having regained consciousness after several days in intensive care, Marcia is now recovering in Women's Accident Ward. Both legs in plaster, she has occupied the bed for over a month prior to Agnes's arrival. Agnes has found her to be a kind and gentle soul and at this very moment, Marcia is trying to soothe Agnes because an old lady has just died as Agnes stood at her bedside. Agnes has never seen anyone pass away, nonetheless it had been instantly clear to her that death had occurred: fluid from a drip in her nose had bubbled out of her mouth and her chest had rattled like an old exhaust pipe. The poor old lady wasn't an accident patient but had been brought to the Accident ward for lack of space elsewhere.

Agnes has now rallied sufficiently to call Sister Teresa, who swiftly pulls a curtain around the bed, closes the patient's eyes and disconnects the drip. Then a senior nurse arrives to lay out the body. To her horror, Agnes is instructed to assist in this task while the nun in charge goes to phone the patient's relatives. Then, to add to her turmoil, she finds herself landed with the job of taking the corpse to the mortuary. Sister Teresa pinches Agnes's cheek:

It's the living you've got to worry about, not the dead. Sorry to send you down on your own, but we can't leave her here a minute longer and I have to attend an emergency. Don't look like a stunned mullet! Just go!

A body completely covered by a sheet on a trolley was a scene straight out of the cinema and it hasn't occurred to Agnes it would be a frequent occurrence in a big hospital. She has difficulty manoeuvring the castor wheels of the heavy trolley out of the ward door. They wanted to go every other way but straight ahead. She has looked around just in time to see Marcia Weldon smiling at her sweetly, raising one arm with her fingers crossed, to wish her luck.

Within seconds of knocking on the mortuary doors both sides are flung wide open and a short, stout man in a dustcoat scurries sideways across the white lino floor, exactly like a giant crab:

Hello. I'm Mortuary Mick. You've come to the right place. I don't need to ask what's under the sheet!

He helps her guide the trolley to the front of a stainless-steel fridge with many doors, flings open one door. Agnes gasps out loud. Through the gap, she can see naked bodies. Mick snorts:

What did you expect? Frozen peas? Nothing exclusive here, Blue Eyes! All stiffs together in the same cooler. Lawyers, politicians, dunny-men, street sweepers. Death is real democracy. We don't ask if they like the company. This is where all divisions stop. No protests for equal rights and no changing fridges. Our inmates don't need sheets or blankets because their winters and summers are over. Now what's the name?

I… I don't know…

Mick winks at her:

Name will be on the tag around the foot or the right big toe. And what's more, there's no need to whisper. This ain't a church.

He writes the dead woman's name in a book beside a number and then slips a card with the same number into a plastic slot on the front of the fridge tray. Agnes notices a swarthy young man with a five o'clock shadow sitting at a desk nearby and watching a football match on TV. Mick says:

Okay, gorgeous. Now we got her registered, just slide her down onto the slab.

She is horrified at this lack of reverence and that she is obviously expected to tip the body onto the slab herself. There is a huge cheer from the football crowd on the TV.

Mick yells:

Christ, was that a goal, Louie?

Louie keeps staring at the screen:

You said it, Mick! Our boys are doing serious damage. With five minutes to go, it's all over bar the shouting!

Mick sidles up to her:

She hasn't been down here before, Louie, so we'll give her a demo, shall we? Okay Blue Eyes – here comes the slide…

Agnes watches in amazement as Mick lifts the sheet to reveal the naked form – already unrecognisable as its former self. With a flip action of the trolley, the body sails through the air, landing on the slab outside the fridge like a small plane making a smooth landing. The body is then shunted unceremoniously into the chilly depths.

Having seen enough, Agnes flees the mortuary and dashes up three flights of stairs to the ward as if the devil is after her. Here she finds the lovely Marcia waiting for Jock Grace's visit. The 'colleague'. She has come to realise that Jock is deeply in love with Marcia, for he visits almost every day, bringing flowers, perfume, and delicious nibbles from the gourmet delicatessen. Surrounded by so many opulent blooms in vases, Marcia looks like a film star. Her locker is a veritable fragrance counter, and all the nurses get a squirt, including Sister Teresa who, Agnes notices, is never shy in coming forward for a refresher. The other nurses often gossip about how much younger Jock is than his paramour. Practically a twenty-year difference, they reckon.

A tall nurse with big shoulders, who is planning on working with the flying doctor service, is particularly scathing:

She's a well-known baby snatcher – *that's* why the husband left her. One young man in the bed too many, as *I* heard it.

The same nurse would tease the besotted Agnes and tell her to shine up her rose-coloured specs.

It will be on Agnes's days off that Marcia is due to take her first steps. But, sadly, the fairy-tale months in 'Women's Accident' will end when Marcia steps forwards out of the ward on handsome Jock's arm. The blood clot that blocked a perforation in her spleen will dislodge and create a massive internal haemorrhage. They will rush her to the operating theatre, but it will be too late. She will die on the operating table. Agnes will be devastated. So much so that she will not know where to put her sorrow. She will hate to think of Marcia's beautiful mortal remains being see-sawed into that awful fridge in the mortuary.

But there will be little time for further contemplation as, within days of Marcia's death, Agnes will find herself posted to the ground-floor section of the private hospital, which is situated in another building at the far end of the hospital garden.

Here, her life will falter once again.

* * *

Face down is how Agnes has landed in St Vincent's 'Ground Floor Private' on her first morning, having tripped on the last step at the main entrance. Her fate is sealed when she feels the iron grip of a strong hand hauling her to her feet by the collar and a snarling voice close to her ear:

Don't you know junior trainees should use the *side* entrance? What do you mean crashing in here and making such a spectacle? What's your *name*, nurse?

Agnes Keen.

The owner of the voice sizes her up:

Ah. You're the *new* one. The last one was hopeless and now they've sent an even sillier version. And why are you covered in make-up like a common tart? This is a hospital, not a stage set. And loosen that belt before you die of asphyxiation.

There is no time to reply as Sister Scruggs, who is wearing a double-sized veil which is splayed out like huge white batwings, takes off at speed, whilst ordering Agnes to follow. Agnes dutifully traipses after her over plush red carpet – more indicative of an upmarket hotel than a hospital. Abruptly, they turn off into a narrow, brightly lit, white-walled passageway which opens into the working area of the hospital. In the bright light of the sterilising room, Agnes observes that the Head Sister's double-sized veil is matched by a shelf of a bosom large enough for a cat to curl up on comfortably, and with room to spare. The tightly fixed veil around her hairline is stretching the skin on her forehead and causing the bulging king prawn eyes she is now focusing on Agnes to slant with malice. She says:

You will have learned in your initial training about Joseph Lister – pioneer of antiseptics. So, you understand why we sterilise. Here, we strive for exceptionally high standards – from the smallest to the most complicated procedures. *Do* you understand?

Yes, absolutely.

Agnes has replied politely but finds herself struggling to control an urge to mimic her superior's owlish blink. The nun continues:

Very well, close your mouth and try and look intelligent. Your job this morning will be to kill off microorganisms by putting everything you see on the left of the sink through the steriliser. By which I mean *all* these stainless-steel bedpans, bottles, jugs, kidney dishes and sundry objects. The machine is programmed to maintain boiling temperature for half an hour. Twenty minutes is sufficient, but we give it that bit extra to be sure. Any questions?

No, I understand the procedure. I've done it stacks of times in the main hospital.

After this slightly flip remark, Agnes braces for the inevitable backlash:

The public hospital is *not* the private hospital, nurse. We expect the very *best* here and will *not* tolerate the shoddy attitudes so many of you young girls bring here.

Sister Scruggs stands up from her chair, and the bosomy shelf rises to point at Agnes accusingly:

Find me when you finish, so I can inspect the job.

She turns swiftly and marches off briskly like a military officer after a drill.

It takes Agnes an hour to complete the task. Unable, after an extensive search, to find her superior as ordered, she returns to the sterilising room feeling dejected.

Her back to the door, Sister Scruggs's unexpected lightning entrance makes her jump. After a cursory glance at the pile of steaming hot sterilised objects, the sister shouts: DO THEM AGAIN!

Agnes presumes she is being punished for not reporting back as ordered, and so tries to explain herself. But her efforts fall on deaf ears:

You will *always* locate me via the staffroom just inside the main entrance. Now do what I've *told* you to do and REPEAT THE JOB.

Apologies, Sister, but I thought I wasn't allowed in the staffroom.

The head nursing sister glares at her:

You *supremely* silly girl! Yes, you're not allowed use the facilities there, but you've got a hand to knock and a mouth to *ask*, have you not?!

After the command to resterilise is issued for the third time, Agnes knows she is being tortured by a sadist. It's February. The temperature outside is warm, but it must be a hundred degrees in the sterilising room, and she is soaked through with steam and perspiration. Too scared to ask to leave for lunch, she goes without. When Sister Scruggs finally dismisses her after she completes an order to clean the staff kitchen, Agnes is on the point of physical collapse. Slinking out of the side entrance, she hears her name:

Nurse Keen! I'll expect you tomorrow at 8am! And *don't* come looking like a sideshow!

Since being made up by an attendant at a cosmetic counter in 'David Jones' Agnes has continued to cover her freckles with a light coat of pancake foundation. She also slightly darkens her fair eyelashes with a touch of mascara. As she stares into her morning mirror, she is starting to see a person she likes, and now feels naked without the usual added extras.

This morning, as she debates whether to put on make-up or not, she feels the beginnings of a cold dread. She does not want to go back to the private hospital – isolated from the good-natured public wards, the cheering morning sunlight, the sound of patients' radios, the antics, the stories, the laughter, the camaraderie between the nursing staff. The private hospital, by comparison, is a tomb. But, at eight sharp, she duly returns. Down on her knees, scrubbing the floor of the staff bathroom, she manages to hold her tongue, but with each unreasonable task, she is beginning to nurture a deep hatred of Sister Midge Scruggs, fervently wishing the obnoxious woman would disappear off the face of the earth.

Her wish will be answered when, after a week of persecution, the Head Sister leaves to attend a nursing conference in Brisbane and is replaced by a temporary sister. This woman will be as easy-going and jovial as Scruggs is strict and unyielding and Agnes will happily accompany the pleasant Sonia Williams on her rounds to take the patients' temperatures and blood pressure.

All the private rooms have en suite bathrooms – the most luxurious enjoying the added benefit of a balcony overlooking the courtyard garden – and Sonia will put Agnes in charge of changing the water in the copious vases of flowers in the patients' rooms. Agnes will love arranging the beautiful blooms in fresh water and will make great efforts to vary the display in the vases each day. She will even receive several compliments on her artistic creations from visiting friends and relatives.

One patient, the recipient of particularly extravagant floral displays, is a wealthy brewer called Mr Green. He, according to rumour, has a sizable bequest in his will in favour of the hospital. Although never openly alluded to, the permanent staff are conscious of humouring the old man and his visitors.

Mr Green's faded brown eyes become particularly bright whenever Agnes brings an elaborately wrapped new bunch of flowers to his bedside for his inspection. Sniffing the perfume of the lovely roses and carnations sends him into an ecstasy of delight and he claps his hands like a child when she walks in, and squeals – Hurrah! Hurrah!

But, one day, any trace of Mr Green's supposed senility will disappear when she offers to help Sonia, the temporary sister, wash him, then dress him in a fresh pair of smart paisley-patterned silk pyjamas. Treating him like a baby, smiling and exclaiming how good he looks when she finishes combing his wiry grey hair, Sonia will not realise what a Pandora's Box she has opened as she and Agnes minister to him at either side of his bed. For, when Agnes leans over him from her side, he will shoot his hand up under her pinafore and start squeezing her breasts. It isn't until Sonia gives his hand a gentle tap and tells him playfully that he's 'a naughty boy' that he will retract his fingers with a cheeky smirk. Inexperienced Agnes will be shaken, but Sonia will make light of it as she explains gently that these 'old boys' sometimes do naughty things of which they are hardly aware.

After the Brisbane conference, having spent a long weekend at Surfers Paradise with the other nursing sisters on the trip, Midge Scruggs will return with the golden glow of a slight suntan and the dark circles expunged from under her eyes. In fact, she will look to Agnes as if she has finally joined the human race. Because of these outward signs, Agnes will hope the holiday has transformed her persecutor's mood and will be further encouraged when she catches sight of Sister Scruggs fawning over several grateful, elderly patients on the red carpet at the hospital entrance. She will be relieved, too, to hear that Sonia is staying a further week while Scruggs writes up her conference report.

In the absence of her nemesis, Agnes has been applying a tiny dab of pancake, and painting her lips with the palest possible lipstick. As Sonia hasn't objected to this hardly noticeable facial improvement, Agnes has felt vindicated. But a catastrophe worse than a make-up transgression will happen. And it will happen unexpectedly.

Mr Green, unusually frisky, will be singing and clapping his hands like a young boy as she and Sonia go about the usual routine of washing him and changing his pyjamas. He will have his head down and will pretend not to see Agnes when, a little later, she returns with a lovely bunch of long-stemmed red roses that have arrived for him at the front office. As she presents them to him, he will suddenly grab one of her arms in a surprisingly tight grip and, with the other, tear the buttons off the front of her uniform, grab one of her breasts and start squeezing it like a pump. She will be so shocked she will freeze like an animal in a bright light. He will jump up from his bed and force his tongue in her mouth, his body gyrating frantically up and down.

When Agnes eventually manages to push him away, he will become enraged and scream: You whore, you bitch, you *fucking cunt*!

Stunned by his strength and vile language, she will be even more horrified by her inability to scream and defend herself. It will be beyond unfortunate that it is Sister Scruggs and not Sonia who rushes into the room. Had it been Sonia, Agnes's whole future would have unfurled differently.

She will find herself staring down at the bed – now a tangled mess of cellophane and rose petals. And she will notice, with horror, her pink lipstick smeared on his lips. She will struggle to smooth down her hair, for not only did he tear off her cap, but has yanked her tresses loose, free now to fall wildly over her face.

Incensed, Sister Scruggs will say:

Look what you've done to this *sweet* old man, you common hussy! Calm down, Mr Green, calm down now. Everything is all right… you've just had a fright… there… there…

As Sister Scruggs gently strokes his brow, Mr Green will shoot a brief glance at the bosomy shelf right under his nose but decide against it. Defeated, he will sink back on his pillows, still sobbing angrily. Scruggs will push the buzzer to summon Sonia and hiss:

Nurse Keen has provoked a disturbance. Bring a sedative for Mr Green and get someone in to clean up this mess. No, don't pick the roses up. Throw them out. Better he doesn't remember them.

Then Agnes will feel the steel fingers close around her arm as Scruggs pulls her away as if she is a thief she has just apprehended. She will be dragged into the sterilising room and lambasted:

Straighten yourself, you foxy minx! What do you mean by provoking that poor old man?!

But I *didn't* provoke him! You're blowing the whole incident out of proportion. It is Mr Green who assaulted *me*!

How *dare* you talk to me like that you insolent, insignificant girl! That man has your lipstick on his mouth! Didn't I tell you *not* to wear make-up! You were flirting! You provoked him!

Aggrieved at the injustice, Agnes will strike back in her own defence:

You are the meanest, nastiest person I've ever had the misfortune to meet. Everything was *perfect* last week when you were away. Ask the temporary sister! *She'll* tell you what a good job I did!

But Scruggs is not to be swayed:

And it is *my* job to sort the wheat from the chaff. And *you* in my opinion are chaff of the *worst* kind! You are DISMISSED and don't you dare to come back here! Get out of my SIGHT!

Within minutes, news of Agnes's dismissal will reverberate around the floor and cross the garden to the public hospital. She will tuck her hair inside her nurse's cap, straighten her uniform as best she can and slink back to the nurses' home. Her companions will be sympathetic and will recount infamous stories of other junior nurses who reached an abrupt end to their careers after a run-in with the draconian Scruggs. Then a secretary will find her at lunch with friends in the canteen and will tell her to go to the matron's office at 4pm. Everyone will know what this means.

At the interview with the matron, Agnes will be asked if she has a vocation for nursing. As she has never asked herself if she wanted to be a nurse she will stare back in silent amazement. They will both sit quietly, with the unanswered question hanging in the air for what seems like an eternity, then:

Well, child, your reticence indicates nursing isn't for you. A girl chosen by God to nurse the sick wouldn't hesitate to affirm her devotion. I have read Sister Scruggs's report. She considers further training to be neither beneficial to you, nor to the hospital. Would you like to read what she has said?

Agnes will decline. Desperate to get out of the place as quickly as possible, she wants to run a mile from this condescending woman who, nevertheless, provides the coup de grâce:

I will contact your grandmother personally and let her know of Sister Scruggs's conclusion. For now, I would like to thank you for your work with us. Here is the pay that is due to you, plus an extra week in compensation for the abrupt departure. Sign this form and you can leave tomorrow. I wish you every success in finding a suitable future career.

Barely glancing at the form, Agnes will sign where indicated and, when she returns to Ground Floor Private to collect her bag from the sterilising room, she will overhear one of the senior nurses – someone she has never known or met – describe her as provocative and flirtatious. Although this is a description she doesn't recognise or understand, she will be instantly plagued with the old shame.

When she eventually summons up the courage to ring Grandma in an attempt to explain her side of the story, she will be tersely told by lieutenant Aunt Sill that they have already heard from the hospital and that her grandmother has nothing further to say to her.

Agnes has failed to fit in again.

20
ROSARY VILLA

Seeking sanctuary, Agnes dashes past the bird of paradise bushes, up the stairs and is delighted to see Mrs Kelly through the wire door. There is the familiar floral carpet and there is Mrs Kelly, seated in the wingback chair next to the piano. Hugging and kissing Agnes, Mrs Kelly displays the usual pleasure in seeing her, but is seemingly so concerned about Maria's current boyfriend that her first utterance is mystifying:

What's wrong with the boys from Riverview and St Aloysius she grew up with, Agnes? She sails back into The Heads and takes up straight away with a short, oily-haired Portuguese who plays the guitar in a Sydney nightclub! Imagine! She's even besotted with his foreign accent. Take your bag to your room and I'll make us a cup of tea.

As soon as they sit down at the kitchen table, a car horn sounds outside the window and Agnes looks eagerly through the glass. She's back. It's Maria in the white Austin Healey with caramel leather seats which, Mrs Kelly tells her, Big John bought his only daughter for her birthday. Maria looks very glamorous behind the wheel and is sporting a pair of sunglasses and a red scarf like Audrey Hepburn in *Breakfast at Tiffany's*. Agnes notices the boyfriend's hand is resting on her thigh. The dark shades he is wearing, combined with the pencil-thin moustache, make him resemble a gangster in *The Untouchables*. Perhaps, Agnes thinks, she has become jealous of her old school friend, or is it that the gulf between them has grown too great? As she watches Maria, she realises they inhabit polar-opposite extremes. Maria is now the mythical figure on the prow of the ship as it tacks across the ever-changing face of the sea, while all Agnes wants to do is drown herself in it.

She is still shaken by the hospital attack. The bruise on her breast is still visible, and the vile taste of the old man's tongue in her mouth seems constant, despite her endless toothbrushing.

The boyfriend – Diego – has just kissed Agnes's hand like a courtier. He is half a head shorter than Maria, which makes his strutting, debonair posture even more comic. Maria gushes:

Oh, I've got *such* a lot to tell you, Agnes!

This is a time-worn cliché. Maria always uses it as a preamble, but then never tells her friend anything of value. Furthermore, she seems bored when Agnes tries to share what little news she herself has to impart. It has always been like this between them. Agnes realises she has never felt more like a shabby object of charity than she does today. She has always tried to be like Maria but now, in this all-too-familiar room, she knows in her heart of hearts this will never happen. Nor does she want it to. Not any longer.

As Maria rambles on and on, Agnes is starting to feel claustrophobic. There is an unsettling crudeness about her old friend that she has never noticed before. And the new open-mouthed, head-thrown-back laugh only emphasises the odd little gap between her front teeth.

Diego and Maria are staring at each other in such a lustful way that it feels improper to look at them. As well as the new false laugh, Maria has developed a stagey speech pattern to go with her name change. She now calls herself 'Madeleine de Killarney'. Killarney is the Irish county the Kelly ancestors apparently hailed from. It's clear to Agnes that Mrs Kelly, devoid of commercial awareness, is obviously hurt that her daughter intends to throw away her grandmother's name for the sake of marketing her spurious theatrical career:

Do you think you'd have ever heard of Marilyn Monroe if she'd remained Norma Jean Mortenson, Mother?!

When Diego makes his excuses and goes out to the car for cigarettes, Maria follows. Within minutes, an argument erupts. Agnes and Mrs Kelly watch from the kitchen window as Maria gesticulates wildly:

After *that*, Diego, I'm *never* going to speak to you *again*! I'm *not* going to give in to you!

Maria is now running down the back garden with Diego in pursuit. Suddenly, they both disappear behind the garden shed. Mrs Kelly shrugs her shoulders:

It's been like this every weekend. So many mood swings in a day, I've lost count. She screams at him and slams the phone down. Then the next minute she's backing out of the drive in the new car to go and see him. I'm mystified! She didn't even *visit* Portugal on her world trip!

Now it is Diego's turn to flee. He dashes up the garden with Maria in hot pursuit. She grabs the hose as she passes and turns the nozzle to a full jet. Diego zigzags from side to side to dodge the stream, but Maria hits him full on. Then Agnes hears the whizzing engine of a Vespa speed out of the drive as Maria screams:

And don't you *dare* come back here! If you do, no one will let you in!

Agnes is glad she isn't Diego. Maria's tantrums have always frightened her. Her friend bursts into the house in a rage, banging the side wire door behind her:

That *bastard*! I'll get him! *Nobody* speaks to me like that!

Maria dashes into her bedroom, where Agnes can hear her throwing things around. Mrs Kelly shrugs:

It's like this all the time. They blow hot and cold, as if winter and summer are colliding. A kindergarten pantomime, that's what I call it.

Maria may have seen many wonders on her travels: the Eiffel Tower, St Peter's in Rome, Buckingham Palace, the Tower of London, Trafalgar Square, but has made no interesting observations whatsoever except to eulogise about how much she likes to hear Diego speak to her in Portuguese, even though she doesn't understand a word. Also, Agnes is painfully aware that neither Mrs Kelly nor Maria have asked her anything about herself. She has made a mistake rushing to see them straight after her dismissal. The penny dropping, she asks Mrs Kelly if she may use the phone to ring Pamela Thomson. This is the sister of a hospital acquaintance who has kindly agreed to enquire about accommodation for Agnes in the same hostel she occupies.

Thanking Mrs Kelly for the tea, shouting farewells through the closed bedroom door to a fuming Maria, Agnes grabs her bag and sets off back to the station. By the time she arrives at Darling Point, kindly Pamela Thomson has already arranged a room for her in Rosary Villa hostel.

They sit together on a bench in the garden:

So, sorry, Agnes, to hear what happened. My sister Janet was sick for weeks after being tortured by Scruggs. She could have strangled her. Nobody understands why the hospital puts up with that two-faced bitch. She's got to have the dirt on someone important, they reckon. After she dismissed Janet, my father, who's a doctor in Armadale, went to the hospital and protested. Janet was reinstated with a guarantee that she'd never be sent over to the private hospital again. So, you see, we know what you've been through.

At the unexpected sympathy, Agnes feels the waterworks mobilising and pinches her leg to divert the flood. She tries to ignore the growing telltale golf ball in her throat. Pam says softly:

You don't need to take this lying down, Agnes. You can protest the dismissal, like my father did.

Agnes tells her that it's no use. That she rang her grandmother, but she wouldn't speak to her. That Aunt Sill made it clear Grandma wanted nothing more to do with her. That becoming a nurse was always Grandma's idea, not her own. That she did it to win a place in her heart, but now doubted she had one. An institutional life wasn't for her.

When Pam leans forward and asks if Agnes has any ideas what she would like to do, Agnes replies with a new assertiveness:

Any job away from authoritarian oppression. With the money I've saved, plus the hospital wage, I'll have enough for a few weeks to pull myself together:

Pam nods, then says:

No hurry. Room and board here couldn't be more reasonable. Sister Benedict told me you can have the rest of the week for nothing. Go to the office on Friday and give her a week's rent in advance and you can stay for as long as you like. Oh, and they require a week's notice if you wish to leave.

Agnes reaches for Pam's hand:

Thank you *so* much!

My pleasure. I'm off home to Armadale for the weekend. Give yourself a few days to recover and, when I return, I'll help you find work. Now then – it's high time I showed you around!

* * *

Agnes has been allotted a small room on the second floor of Rosary Villa. Her bed is under a large window looking out over the front entrance. Not only has Pam made up her bed with her own sheets, lent her a blanket and a towel (inmates must provide their own linen) but she has left her a bowl of fresh fruit. There is even a little bag of lavender tucked under her pillow. The Almighty has intervened to show she truly *is* valuable. Agnes feels her energy returning. Regardless of what they think at Rosemont, or at St Vincent's Private Hospital, she is newly determined to survive.

Rosary Villa is run by the nuns of the St Joseph religious order of California and can accommodate up to eighty girls. The high ornate plaster ceilings, oak-panelled entrance hall and monumentally grand staircase hark back to its origins as a palatial home – once known as Hopewell House. The spacious library on the ground floor celebrates an incarnation as an exclusive finishing school, but no visible evidence remains of its role as a service headquarters during the Second World War, nor as a private hospital after the declaration of peace. Positioned like a palace on the shore of the Eastern Harbour, ferries, yachts, and flurries of boats can be seen from every corner of the sweeping grounds. Indeed, the winding, overgrown drive to the grand entrance reminds Agnes of the opening descriptions of Mandalay in *Rebecca*. High stone pillars either side of the entrance support wrought-iron gates in decorative panels. The imposing gates are rusted at the edges and have been open for so long, they look as if they will never close again.

Agnes stares upwards to see branches of tall trees join arms in an arch high above the drive, while low-lying shrubs encroach like a miniature green army, substantially reducing the width for traffic on the road. Clumps of hardy weeds in the centre have taken advantage of the washed-away gravel, but the driveway ends in an expansive circle, allowing cars to turn and park at the grand set of double oak doors that are closed on the dot of midnight. The team of gardeners that the extensive grounds require to fight nature are seemingly not available.

Instead, the hostel is staffed by a hard-working band of five nuns who struggle to run it alone as a way of keeping their charges low. But low prices do not mean low standards. The enticing aroma of bacon and eggs mingles with that of percolating coffee, permeating the double-height wood-panelled dining room at breakfast time. Here, Agnes finds herself in heaven, piling her plate with what is on offer: sausages, mushrooms, grilled tomatoes, baked beans, toast with marmalade and giant mugs of tea. The slow disappearance of the mouth ulcers with which she has been afflicted since starting work in the private hospital heralds the happy fact that her constitution is improving. Unlike the agonising self-consciousness in the residents' dining room at Coogee, being amongst girls her own age allows her to blend comfortably into the background. And so, each day, she settles contentedly at a small corner table overlooking a mass of tangled branches which push against the glass as if wanting to be let in. All the ambient sounds of the place: the girlish chatter, the radio in the open kitchen, plates being stacked, chairs sliding on a wood floor, hurried steps in high heels, are reassuring, giving Agnes the impression that she has been spirited back to a time before she 'disappeared' from the corner of Rose and Edmond Street.

Breakfast is the only meal on offer at Rosary Villa, and Agnes duly fills up for the day, slipping sausages, bread rolls, biscuits, and fruit into her bag as the other girls do. She eats this secret hoard on a bench in the garden during the long and muddled days ahead. On Friday evenings she watches as the place pulses with shouts and laughter, for girls are lining up to pay their weekly board to a hook-nosed old nun in a back room who barely looks at them. Haunted by her mother's bad debts, Agnes is always scrupulous about paying what she owes.

After a few days spent in the sanctuary of the hostel, Pamela Thomson's return is like a further gift. She is beaming when she spots Agnes at breakfast. The sunshine in the young woman's smile reassures Agnes of a sincerity that will never wane:

Hope you've recovered, Agnes! Did I tell you my sister was so shattered after her ordeal with Scruggs, my father gave her a week's holiday in Hayman Island! By the way, I thought of the *perfect* job for you while I was away! Working as a Registration Clerk!

Agnes pushes for more details. It was the same work as Pam did as a law student. The job seemingly entailed the filing of documents at public offices and was the outside legal work generated by a solicitor's practice. She learns that law students like Pam, articled to solicitors, did the same work as a salaried Registration Clerk but, because they got time off for lectures and seminars, they were paid less. Agnes admits that it did sound appealing and agreed with Pam's shrewd observation that it would alleviate the scrutiny she loathed as she would be mostly out and about – away from prying eyes. Puffing on a cigarette, and between sips of black coffee, Pam continues to map out Agnes's future as if it is the most natural thing in the world:

I'll ask in my office and put the word out on the network. We'll talk tonight. Chin up! Get ready for something new! *Arrivederci, bambino*!

And, with that, she blows Agnes a kiss and whirls out of the door.

Agnes is punch-drunk with astonishment. In a curious way, she has Scruggs's brutality to thank for Pam's empathy. She might become a Registration Clerk in a legal firm! She might yet show that bunch at Rosemont that she is a person of substance!

In a few days, Agnes will arrive in Pitt Street and enter the building above Pellegrino's Catholic supply shop where Grandma once bought her a white missal as a First Communion gift. For reference purposes, Pam will have asked the girl leaving the clerk's post to recommend Agnes for the job, and, as a reward for protecting him from being caught snoozing, or with his head in a pin-up magazine, John Watson will compensate Agnes with a glowing testimonial. Ever the practical joker, he will hand her two: one from Cable and Watson and the other from Shipwrecks and Pirates.

Wandering the Sydney streets like a stray dog for months has meant that Agnes knows her way around the city, but Pam helps her to pinpoint the location of the Law Courts in Macquarie Street, the Probate Office in St James Street, and the Registrar General's offices opposite St Mary's Cathedral. And, after accompanying Agnes on her first morning rounds, her new friend will declare:

Now you can say in all honesty that you are an experienced Registration Clerk!

Agnes is in awe of how Pam simplifies the seemingly complicated, and still manages to look her magnificent self though staying up half the night studying. More importantly, Pam has unwittingly offered Agnes an image of herself she can finally agree with, and so she stops apologising for herself to people.

On her first day at the Pitt Street office, Agnes will be relieved to be allotted an isolated desk in a nook near the strong room, with no one looking over her shoulder and where she can easily hide her poor writing skills by secretly editing reports to the solicitors using a dictionary concealed under the desk. She will start at 9am prompt, sort out the written instructions from the solicitors, and set out to be ahead of the queues at the Public Offices that open at 10am. She will soon be greeting familiar faces on the beat, added to which Pam will introduce her to the few other women studying law. Agnes will greatly enjoy listening in to their lively chat in the Ladies Common Room at the Law School in Elizabeth Street.

Her favourite part of the job – searching for property titles at the Registrar

General's offices – will soon diminish, however, as the Pitt Street firm opts to abandon property conveyancing in favour of divorce litigation. Divorce has been something Agnes is only familiar with from the publicity given to Hollywood film stars, many of whom she is aware remarry multiple times. The very idea of anyone divorcing at Rosemont would be tantamount to everlasting shame, yet it is clearly a lucrative business in the Pitt Street office. She will discover that divorce on the grounds of adultery is the quickest way to untie the knot. Thus, although it might not be the cause of the marriage breakdown, many Pitt Street clients will follow that route to a swift 'decree absolute'.

As well as apprehending incriminating photos of genuine adulterers, the detectives housed in the office next door provide a professional co-respondent for the incriminating photograph. This is how, to Agnes's amazement, Charline, the office receptionist, met her second husband. In fact, the vagaries of the law will open a door in Agnes's mind that will never close. A door to an entirely different world. With a surge of life force, she will resume the Saturday morning acting classes at the Ensemble along with Maria, who will have changed the Portuguese boyfriend for an Italian, and with the same accompanying fireworks. But Mrs Kelly will at least be comforted by the fact that her wayward daughter had been to Italy.

After a while, Agnes will be offered a part in a Victorian melodrama called *The Drunkard*. To allow the fledgling theatre group to build up sufficient capital, rather than being paid, devotees of The Method have agreed to take on minor roles in exchange for future shares in the company. Agnes's few lines will be hardly more than an extension of the scenery but, encouraged by Maria, she will delude herself into believing it is a good beginning.

As it is impossible to finish late in the theatre each night and still be on time for work the next day, Agnes will apply for – and secure – a job in a big solicitors' office where there is a variety of work, lots of interesting young employees, and which, crucially, starts an hour later in the mornings. The young dishevelled junior partner in the firm who will interview Agnes will declare himself a theatre fan and she will suspect that his enthusiasm in having a budding actress on the staff has landed her the job. With her one scripted line in *The Drunkard*, she will feel like a fraud when he seeks her out to talk earnestly about plays, for she lives in such a twilight world that it never occurs to her to inform herself fully about the works of Ibsen or Chekhov. She will nod approvingly and try to look intelligent as he raves on about *Miss Julie* or *The Cherry Orchard*, her ignorance being insignificant compared to the agonising awkwardness she will suffer when she discovers a few love letters in a pocket of the briefcase he lends her in which to carry her work.

She can't possibly give the briefcase back, as he will assume she has read the letters. These missives will, as a result, become a great source of speculation and amusement in the Ladies Common Room at the Law School and will be passed around her new acquaintances. Phrases like: 'we have such fun in the shower, Poppet… I've smelled you on my skin all day… can't wait to taste you tonight' will spin through Agnes's head, making it difficult for her to maintain a dignified demeanour when reporting back to him. Yet she still resists informing herself fully about sex, which is probably why she has found the flashbulb naked bodies of the divorce petitions in Pitt Street so disturbing. That said, the two lovers' sweet written pleasures will often flick through her mind in the future – and she will, one day, compare their tender intimacies to the abuse she herself is fated to endure.

As for the passionate letters, they will eventually be consigned to one of the law student's lockers and forgotten.

The joy of having Pam in her life will be abruptly swept away due to the pressure of her new friend's preparation for exams. This means Pam will no longer be able to seek Agnes out for walks in Centennial Park on Sundays after Mass or to enjoy their regular meal together in the evening in Rushcutters Bay. Agnes will begin to feel left out, and rather envious of Pam and her close friends' dedication to study.

And then, exams complete, and when Agnes looks forward to returning to their old friendship routine, Pam will meet Paul at a university college party and fall in love. Six weeks into the romance, Paul will graduate as a veterinary surgeon and propose – their small, happy, rushed wedding precipitated by the fact that he has accepted a job in a veterinary clinic in Victoria and wants Pam to accompany him:

I always knew you were special, Agnes.

These will be Pam's final words to Agnes as she walks out of her life on Paul's arm. There will be lengthy intervals when the friends do not see each other, but they are destined to remain close until Pam's tragically early death.

The accompanying numbness that follows Pam's newly-wed departure will obliterate Agnes's initial rosy view of her new surroundings. Ten years since its conversion into a hostel in 1950, she will notice that her current residence is badly in need of a face lift – the deterioration evident as autumn turns to winter and the cold wind whistles through the badly fitting windows to swirl, unchallenged, around the corridors. She will notice that the pale blue and white painted rooms and dormitories are marked with dirty scrapes from the constant movement of furniture and suitcases, that buckets sit under the roof on the top floor to catch drips from a leaking roof, and that there are falling plaster patches in the grand ceiling, reminding her of the untethered deterioration of the house where she grew up.

The encroaching dreariness will be further exacerbated when Bridget takes up residence in the other bed in Agnes's room. With a face full of festering pimples, Bridget will be almost permanently slathered in a white cream that makes her look like a performer in Japanese Kabuki theatre. This leaden roommate all but ignores Agnes but does, fortunately, go home to the country on weekends to see her family.

Families abound. Most of the young residents in Rosary Villa have photos of their parents, siblings, or pets on their bedside tables, along with teddy bears and other cuddly toys adorning their pillows. As Agnes has no reminders of the family she would prefer to forget, she will dip into her savings and buy a small record player and a selection of the ballet music she discovered with Rita and Mrs Ryder. At weekends, when Bridget leaves, she will float back to happier times through the music of *Swan Lake*, *The Nutcracker* and *Cinderella* and she will tell Bridget that her parents bought her the record player and had it delivered from 'David Jones'. She will say this so she will not seem like some sad and lonely misfit, but someone who belongs. Belongs to a loving, caring family. But dull, boring Bridget will not care if the gift came from the prime minister himself.

Agnes will remain addicted to the practice of inventing gifts, and making up stories about non-existent relationships, just as she did at school.

21

CHARLES BURGESS

A gnes could have continued juggling the job at the solicitors' office with her small acting part at night if Charles Burgess hadn't crashed into her life. She can't remember how, or where, she met him. Given her childhood conditioning, it seemed he had been shadowing her all her life. But she does recall that there were no flowers, no hand-in-hand strolls along the beach, no running together through soft meadows, no dazzling smiles or stars in the eyes over candlelit dinners. Charles Burgess seemed to spring out of nowhere, like a noxious weed, and cause her to disappear into a labyrinth she could not find her way out of.

She finds much of what he says in his put-on English accent incomprehensible, but never questions its validity. He flaunts a superiority based on some half-cocked English aristocratic pedigree: a family tree that connects him back to a Hampshire Earl on his father's side. Or it might have been Norfolk – or possibly Suffolk. These are names that mean nothing to Agnes. Never has it occurred to her to look at a map of the world, let alone England, to locate countries and places she hears about.

Charles struts along, his nose in the air. He is swinging a black umbrella and is on his way from Wynyard Station to work in a stockbrokers' office in Hunter Street. He is dressed in one of the bespoke suits he buys at Hunts Menswear shop in George Street. He also favours sports jackets and handmade shoes. Nothing adorns his noble person that isn't imported from the land of his ancestors. He concedes the wool might have been shorn off an Australian sheep but says it transcends its lowly origins by being fashioned in the mills of Yorkshire. He complains of being persecuted by crude, uncouth fellow Australians whom he sees as inferior. Just like Agnes.

The overblown 'old country' history is tacked onto a middle-class childhood. Charles has an older brother, Ronald. They both reside in a Tudor revival house in Killara on the North Shore. Ronald has assumed the responsibility of caring for a grieving mother and problematic brother after his father's sudden death.

Not only has Ronald's training in the law allowed him to take over his father's legal practice, but he has been able to defend Charles on a charge of manslaughter after his girlfriend, Sally-Ann, was killed in a car accident. Agnes learns that the British racing-green Morgan sports car Charles had been driving had skidded and hit a tree on a stretch of the Pittwater Road. Ronald had briefed an eminent Sydney QC, who had meticulously stage-managed Charles's defence appearances in court, and successfully got him off.

It is not long after his liberation from a potential jail sentence that Charles appears outside the theatre at the end of the evening's performance and offers to drive Agnes home. Being claimed by someone fills the great emptiness she feels after Pam's departure. Maria, her only other friend, has moved in with her Italian and now sees Agnes rarely.

Agnes has never expected the lift home to become a regular event, but there Charles constantly is, waiting outside the theatre every night, a pair of thick-rimmed tortoiseshell glasses enlarging his restless, hawk-like hazel eyes. Eyes which, for some reason, alarm her. The lifts are convenient, but what she just cannot comprehend is why Charles drives so fast, having initiated an accident that killed his girlfriend.

This evening, she chastises him angrily:

Safe Volvo or not, no car can immunise you against having another accident if you drive so recklessly!

He has just screeched to a halt at the door to Rosary Villa after a terrifying ride at top speed.

They have started kissing in the car whenever he drops her off. Relief, rather than desire, prompts her submission to this intimacy: relief that the car hasn't smashed into a girder on the Harbour Bridge or spun off the Cahill Expressway into the harbour. She sometimes imagines Mortuary Mike telling her estranged family – when they identify the body – that he once knew her. The outburst from the back seat of her father's car that fateful night on the road to the farm would be silenced forever in their minds. Loss would stir the sympathy of the beloved polo friends. Indeed, Agnes's early death might well prove to be the perfect gift.

But she no longer wants to die. And Charles, it would appear, is not about to co-operate with her efforts to remain alive. Her requests to him to slow down only make him drive even faster. She gradually learns to humour him in the way she humoured her father when he got drunk. She already knows intuitively that, like Eric Keen, Charles never forgets a real – or imagined – slight. Behind a seeming silent passivity lurks, she has come to recognise, that same whirlwind of inner rage that never goes off the boil.

She has started rehearsing a speech in her head to get rid of Charles but, when the moment arrives to deliver it, she crumbles. To her self-disgust, she goes on tolerating the fear of mutilation or extinction by road accident for a few more days but, after a particularly hair-raising journey, finally manages to summon up the vestiges of her courage to say:

I don't want you to come and pick me up from the theatre anymore.

He responds with an ugly chuckle:

You think you can just get rid of me like that?

It's not a matter of getting rid of you, Charles. I just don't want to continue this. I'm staying with Maria tonight. So – goodnight. And please don't come here again.

Having delivered this with as much gravitas as she could muster Agnes runs off towards the flat Maria secretly shared nearby with her boyfriend, Mario, and another actress. As she flees, she can hear Charles drive off with the customary screech of tyres and could hug the nearest tree with relief.

After this coup, she gratefully returns to her old routine of stopping off in a coffee shop near Milson's Point with some of the cast after the performance in order to swap anecdotes about that night's audience.

A fortnight passes with no sign of Charles and, feeling confident that he has gone for good, she stops sneaking out of a lower side door and scurrying like a rat up a dark parallel street to the station in case he happens to be parked nearby.

She will still be able to summon up this sense of deep relief years down the line. And she will also be able to recall how briefly it lasted:

I wake in my small bed in Rosary Villa with a premonition I can't identify. There has been a raging storm all night and I have slept little.

299

I'm running late but just manage to catch my usual bus, spending a miserable time standing – no free seats – and shaking raindrops off my sodden coat. The downside of being a Registration Clerk is having to be out on the streets on rainy days whilst the others in the office are safely tucked behind their desks.

The show is over. I'm worn out, but it went well. Then I see him. Waiting at the Stage Door.

At first, I don't recognise him because he is wearing what he describes as a Harris Tweed cap. It is pulled down over his eyes. Standing guard by the open door of his car, he looks more like a chauffeur than the potential heir to a so-called grand estate. The impact of his appearance is further diminished by the fact he is wearing gumboots. No ordinary gumboots, he informs me, but Wellingtons – lined in cashmere wool from Hunts.

Don't worry, he says. I've no intention of picking you up regularly like before. Jump in the car. I've got a surprise for you. He sounds quite breezy for Charles. Even carefree. Something about the way I had woken up that morning makes me hesitate by the open door of the car. I am not sure what to do. I don't want to ride with him, but I am the last one out of the theatre. Come on, he says. Don't be afraid. I'm not going to bite you. He never refers to me by name. I follow suit by never using his. Christian names are too intimate for whatever is between us.

Standing near him again makes my skin crawl. My heart thumps in my chest so hard I think it might come out of my mouth and I consider dashing back into the theatre but then remember the click of the caretaker's key behind me. It is very dark. There is no one around to help me. Lacking a better plan, I take off down the street. The lights on that side of the street are out, which make it impossible to see the pavement. But I am a good runner. A fast runner. Pumped with adrenalin, I know I can outpace him, especially as he is wearing gumboots. But I trip over a raised paving brick and land flat on my face. Charles is suddenly on top of me – pulling me up. I glance down and see I have torn holes in my stockings. The grazed skin on my knees starts to sting in the cold night air. Charles yanks my arm tightly behind my back, picks up my handbag, and frogmarches me back to the car.

I can't speak. He reeks of silent anger. He shoves my head down and pushes me roughly into the passenger seat and, in what seems like the blink of an eye, he's in the driver's seat. I see him press a button on the dashboard that locks the car doors.

He takes his time pulling on a pair of tan driving gloves, turns on the engine and drives off with the customary foot flat to the floor. I want to scream but my mouth is dry and, anyway, nothing would come of it. We speed up the deserted Pacific Highway and, as I dig my fingernails into the upholstery and wait to die, I wonder for a while if he might be taking me to meet his brother. But he drives straight through Killara.

We turn right off the highway at Pymble Shopping Centre and he twists the Volvo down tree-lined streets past winding rows of houses. Then we are on a dirt track in the bush. The high beam of the headlight picks out thick shrubs that scrape the sides of the car.

The windscreen wipers sound like a drumbeat. He pulls up abruptly in the centre of a small clearing. I can glimpse a patch of thick gravel surrounded by low spindly shrubs. When he turns off the headlights for a few minutes it is so dark I can see nothing.

He laboriously removes his gloves, folds them into the Harris Tweed cap and places the cap on the dashboard. The sound of the rain on the roof is deafening. He has not said a word to me since he told me to get in the car. I am more afraid of his silence than of the endless monologues that I have never understood. He reaches down and, with a flick of a lever, my seat tips back. A further flick and he is at the same horizontal level. I am trapped. His perspiring skin has a sweet smell I can't identify. I do get a little excited when he starts kissing me and putting his tongue in my mouth, but soon he wants more and snarls at me like a ferocious dog when I try to move his hand away from under my dress. Then he pushes his finger deep up inside me. My head starts to spin and I feel sick. I don't want this to happen and tell him I am a virgin and ask him would he please stop. He doesn't stop and I wrestle away and shout for him to get off me. But I know he is determined when I feel the elastic of my underwear bruise the side of my hip as he wrenches them off. Then he shoves my skirt into my mouth. I shout no, I beg no, I cry no, but he prises my legs apart and thrusts himself inside me. He moves frantically, hurting me, then cries out like a wounded animal and sinks on top of me. So, this is sex. After what seems like an eternity, he lifts himself up, grazing my shin with the toe of his boot.

He turns on the inside light of the car, checks himself, and says: Where's the blood, you whore? I just slid in like butter! I suppose you put on this virgin act with all the boys! I tell him I didn't want him to do it. That he forced me. That I'd never really seen sex or known how it was done.

I tell him that my mother said girls had to be careful as they can break their hymen riding horses and that this must be what had happened to me. He laughs mirthlessly and says: Well now, if you really did lose your virginity to a horse, you've just lost it to a man. I have made you a woman. It was as if he had given me a gift, instead of stealing what was never on offer.

He drives me home to Rosary Villa in silence. We pull up under the hanging trees on the gravel entrance way in the early hours of the morning. He grabs my wrist tightly as I attempt to slide out. He says: You belong to me. You know that don't you? Never, ever run away from me like that again. And if you tell anyone about what happened tonight – I'll kill you.

That night, Agnes will lie motionless in bed until exhaustion swamps her churning thoughts. Conditioned when attacked to retreat inside herself and to try and expunge it from her mind, Agnes will be unaware that she has just been raped. The accident with the girlfriend had left Charles with deep scars across his forehead and she will wonder if he had left his sanity in the mangled wreck on the Pittwater Road. He could be an escapee from a mental asylum for all she knew. But because she knows nobody he knows, there will be no one to ask.

Charles will now exercise a ruthless hold over her and refuse to answer any of her questions about his past. Instead, he will go on monotonously recounting the fanciful tale of his illustrious British heritage. And increasingly fearful of his violent temper, Agnes will meekly submit to his constant sexual demands in the back seat of the Volvo. As a further indignity, he will leave her, like an unwanted package, in that same car, having parked it outside his house while he goes in to eat with his family.

That first brutal night in the rain will be repeated in other parking sites all over Sydney, and Agnes won't be able to shake the possibility that Charles might have captured poor, dead Sally-Ann and held her as a psychological prisoner before bringing about her demise, and that perhaps he is now doing the same with her.

By the time they are spending 'social' weekends in the house of Charles's middle-aged colleague from the stockbrokers' office, Agnes will have left the Ensemble Theatre and will be on the verge of losing her job for arriving late to work once too often. Devoid of sleep and proper nourishment, she will find it increasingly hard to function. When she announces her departure from the theatre company, Hayes Gordon will rub salt in the wound by reminding her she could potentially have a successful acting career if she would only apply herself, and that he had planned to offer her the role of Laura Wingfield in *The Glass Menagerie*. Agnes will stare at him with helpless regret, for she knows that Laura Wingfield, based on Tennessee Williams' own sister, is as fragile as the tiny glass animals she collects. This, she will think, must be how others see her.

She has lost her way. Charles has perforated her will, and she will gradually forget that she ever had an ambition to be an actress – or anything else.

* * *

The theatre now a fading memory, Charles's serious stalking of Agnes begins. Now he waits outside the solicitors' office after she finishes work, where they acknowledge each other undemonstratively, like one spy passing a message to another. She follows him obediently down the street like a dog on an invisible lead.

Having introduced her to his colleague, The Honourable George Barrington – an Englishman who lives in a single-storey brick house on the crest of a hill in Northbridge – they now weekend there regularly. George's house hides behind a wall high enough to impede the gaze of inquisitive neighbours. Agnes considers it a muddled back-to-front construction, with the living area and kitchen at the back, and the bedrooms at the front. She can see that it is the result of the merger of two semi-detached houses situated in the corner of a large block of land. Squashed up against the neighbour's paling fence on one side, the property looks like a troublesome child in the naughty corner. Wooden gates access a gravel drive that leads to a double brick garage, where Charles parks the Volvo.

On Agnes's first visit, George Barrington trips on the step down into the living room from the hall as he tried to avoid bumping into all the pieces of furniture arranged in a line in the middle of the room. Copious jars and plates are displayed on top of a variety of chests of drawers, narrow tables and sea-chests positioned against the far wall. The large space is stuffed with antique objects, and the walls are covered in paintings. This, she would come to realise, is because it once doubled as a showroom for The Honourable George's antiques dealing.

The gentleman in question quickly draws Agnes's attention to a picture on the wall of a straight-backed elderly gentleman on horseback who is wearing a red military jacket with gold epaulettes and sports a row of gleaming medals pinned to his chest. The Honourable George asks Agnes:

Does this grand gent look like anyone you know?

Well… he looks a bit like you.

She knows this is what he expects her to say, but she doesn't need to pretend as the rangy body, the grey hair, hooded eyes, and long pinched nose of the man in the portrait bear an uncanny resemblance to her host:

Indeed so, my dear! A relative of mine back in the old country!

Agnes develops an instant aversion to The Honourable George. He is pompous and snobbish. But she feigns a continuing interest in him and his possessions as he shows her and Charles to their room – and to the antique oak four-poster bed they will come to regularly occupy.

George proves to be an excellent cook and an attentive host. Agnes feels her usual lethargy lift when he brings the food dishes to the table, for she hasn't eaten a proper meal in months. Out of the habit of using a knife and fork, she initially feels like a street urchin. Everything tastes delicious, and she indulges herself in second helpings of fresh baby carrots, beans, potatoes, onions, pumpkin – all baked to crispy perfection. George keeps carving more meat from the juicy joint and bringing additional hot vegetables from the oven. Agnes is feeling so full she struggles to find a place for the strawberry soufflé which George serves with a smile and a glass of champagne. She has not realised how poorly nourished she has become, living largely on doughnuts and sporadic hamburgers as is her habit.

But she is certain of something – that she now feels fatigued all the time and is finding it increasingly hard to concentrate on her job.

It must be early spring, Agnes thinks, as clumps of hydrangeas and poinsettia bushes are in flower, and it is warm enough to leave the windows open. They are seated on Windsor chairs around a gateleg table and are overlooked by an oak dresser with jugs and mugs hanging from its ornate hooks. Pretty rose-patterned dishes balance on its narrow shelves. It is like being part of a period theatre set.

In future, her delight in the delicious cooking at the Northbridge house at weekends will not quell her impression that there is something decidedly unsavoury about The Honourable George. But she will keep it to herself, as Charles appears to worship him like a god. She will observe how he hangs on George's every word, strolling around the antique-filled house with the same pearl-eyed trance as he adopts when shopping at Hunts. She will note how impressed Charles appears to be with the way the older man speaks, dresses, and conducts himself. She will discover that the two men are working on a company merger together, the details of which she won't understand, but so important is it to them that they will often sit at the gateleg table discussing their precious project late into the night. 'Pukka' is one of the frequently used words she will overhear – one of many words that litter the repartee of upper-class gibberish they exchange. It will all come to sound utterly ridiculous and meaningless to her.

The rich Saturday night meals having become routine, she will start to leave the men to their overblown camaraderie and escape to the four-poster bed where she will sink gratefully into a deep sleep. Saturday night's sex will be transferred to Sunday mornings. And, with the freedom of movement in a bed of their own, Agnes will observe that their coupling has taken an experimental turn – she is directed to be on top and arch her back. Their window wide open to the elements, their gyrations in the four-poster will be visible to the great outdoors, and when Agnes becomes concerned at this, Charles will assure her there is nothing to worry about. Nobody could get into the grounds. Agnes will admit to liking the feel of the sun on her back through the window and will settle in to abandoning herself to their acrobatics.

But, on one particularly warm and tranquil Sunday morning, she will hear a rustling sound that will appear to emanate from a clump of poinsettia. Then several logs will tumble noisily to the ground from the woodpile at the side of the window. Alerted to further movement behind one of the tall clumps of hydrangeas, she will presume it is a possum – or possibly a stray cat. But, turning her head fully to see more clearly, she will spot that the cause is in fact The Honourable George. Her host is so engrossed in focusing on his guests' genitals in action through a pair of binoculars that he has blown his cover.

When, later that day, she will mention this to Charles, he will snigger like a schoolboy:

If Old George gets a bit of fun out of being a peeping Tom, well it doesn't hurt you or me or anyone else, does it?

She will leave their bedroom in disgust, clear in her mind that Charles is complicit in George's spying. It seems she has been the only one unaware she has been performing in a regular weekend sex show for her host's titillation. She will feel nauseous with betrayal.

The following weekend she will use the excuse of a heavy cold not to accompany Charles to Northbridge, though there will be a vestigial regret that she will be missing out on the crab soufflé and cherry trifle George has promised to serve up. To top it all, when she rings in sick to work the following Monday, they will politely tell her not to bother coming back as she has left out an important easement on a search at the Registrar General's Offices. This oversight has severely affected a client's purchase. Fortunately for Agnes, the solicitor concerned was suspicious enough to check the title deed himself before letting his client sign the contract.

Sincerely sorry to leave the firm, Agnes will be deeply ashamed to have let people down who have been good to her. Most of all she will miss the companionable jokes and laughter. Too ashamed to go anywhere near the Ladies Common Room, she will drift around in that all-too-familiar twilight world she has occupied before. But, this time, she will find it increasingly difficult to pull herself together. A chronic tiredness seems to be seeping into her bones like a subtle poison. But, because no one ever asks her how she feels, she rarely reflects on the state of her body.

Yet there will be a glimmer of light. The budding playwright work colleague, who had lent her the infamous briefcase, will give her an undeserved reference. On the strength of his generosity, she will manage to land another job – as a Registration Clerk with a firm of solicitors near Central Railway Station. Happily, the new location – at the other end of town from Charles's office – should make it easier to avoid him. But, after working there for only two weeks, Agnes will collapse on the pavement in Pitt Street and know no more.

When she opens her eyes again, she will find herself in bed at the family farm. The room will be spinning, and she will be completely unable to focus or hold her head up. She will hear:

There is no time to grow a culture. Her condition is critical. I'll be back as quickly as possible with a broad-spectrum antibiotic. It will hopefully kill the infection.

Agnes will hover between life and death in a raging fever. The doctor will come every day and give her an injection, and Uncle Ben and his children will visit her at the weekends and stand at the bedroom door. Their voices will sound like the buzzing of a distant beehive. After two weeks, when she is finally able to sit up, big chunks of white crust, like slithers of hard chalk, will start coming away from her throat. She will discover it was Charles who drove her to her parents, a journey of which she will have no memory. Charles. Shadowing her still.

* * *

During her slow recovery Agnes reflects for hours on end upon the subject of madness. She recalls what the lady in the fish shop at Coogee said. Could Charles's absolute assurance that she will be in his life, *must* be in his life, be a sign of an unhinged mind? She plucks up the courage to mention her fear of him to her mother:

I'm scared he's going to kill me in a road accident, the way he killed his former girlfriend.

The retort from her mother is rapid and vicious:

Well, if he *is* off his rocker, you make a good pair. Expect he'll be coming to pick you up soon.

Agnes is aware that her father's return from a business trip looms when her mother shows these old familiar signs of wanting to get rid of her.

Sure enough, Madge rings Charles behind Agnes's back, waiting till shortly before he is about to arrive to tell her daughter he is on his way. Agnes berates herself for not predicting the deceit. Though grateful for the clean room allocated to her in her parents' house, and for the sustaining meals provided by Madge during her recovery, she cannot relax for nothing has changed.

The day of the expulsion, Madge tries to soften the blow by calling her Darling and Possum and sharing bits of family gossip. She even gives Agnes one of her sixth-floor frocks as compensation for her betrayal. It is pink linen with raised embroidered white flowers bordered in a darker pink with flecks of olive green. It is left on the bed for her when Agnes gets out of the bath. Agnes says:

Thank you, but I don't want it. Pink's your colour, not mine.

Don't talk back to me! The clothes you arrived in were worn out and, given the nature of your illness, I threw them away!

All Agnes will be left with of her own possessions is a handbag and a pair of shoes. As a result, she has no choice but to accept what is on offer from her mother, right down to underwear and stockings. But she does try to assert herself one last time:

Why did you call Charles today? Why don't you want me to see Daddy?!

It's got nothing to do with me. Your father doesn't *want* to see you. He still hasn't got over that episode in the car!

But that was nearly two years ago!

You dug your own hole, Agnes, and now you must lie in it.

The departure hour is imminent. She is hurt and angry, but the truth is that Agnes is not safe at the farm. And never will be. And, although the air is wonderfully fresh and the roses that line the sides of the path to the front door are in full fragrant radiance, all Agnes will think of as she gazes out on the garden is climbing into the beating heart of a giant open rose, travelling down its stem, and burrowing down through the soft earth to find a peaceful place.

The way Agnes's mother flirts with Charles when he arrives to pick her up will shock her, but she will know full well that her mother, in her predictably perverse way, is displaying to her daughter how attractive she is to her own man. It is a competition. It always has been.

PART FOUR

I am not accustomed to telling myself what happens to me, so I find it hard to remember the exact succession of events – and I can't make out what is important.

Nausea by John-Paul Sartre

22

A CHILD FOR GOD

I t has dawned on Agnes that she has missed a period. She never keeps a check, but it seems ages since the last one. After feeling sick all morning, she makes an appointment to see a gynaecologist in Macquarie Street. As soon as she steps out of the lift, she knows she has made a mistake in choosing a lavishly decorated place such as this, frequented as it obviously is by the wealthy and well connected. But, lost in her usual muddle, it was the first port in a storm that sprang to mind.

The gynaecologist confirms her worst fears. She is just over two months pregnant, and the baby is due on 30th September. He tells her that she has a big surprise to impart to her husband that night. Surely the man has seen that she has no wedding ring on her finger. She does not respond. Disoriented, she trips over the chair as she stands up, bracing herself to leave:

Are you all right, Mrs Keen?

Yes… yes… thank you…

He tells her to make an appointment with the nurse to come back in two months when she will be kitted out with a book on how to look after herself. He tells her there is absolutely no reason, at her age, not to expect to have a perfectly normal pregnancy.

With that, the white panel door gently shuts behind her and she is thrust into a new world of confusion. She finds it hard to accept that Charles's perverse enslavement could result in a baby. The idea of marrying him is inconceivable. She could try and arrange an abortion, but she has no money and, after all, having an abortion is a mortal sin. The only person she can think of turning to is a priest in the confessional. And so, she wanders down Martin Place in the general direction of St Patrick's Church. It is where her mother claimed to attend Mass when Agnes sought Monsignor Harrington's help to save her soul. Now she must save her own.

It is just after five and still stifling hot. Red, sweaty-faced office workers are heading for trains and buses to take them home. A man wearing a loose striped shirt bounces in front of her. He is swinging his briefcase and singing a Frank Sinatra song to himself. It is her favourite. She, too, often needs someone to cheer her 'all the way'.

He and the song disappear down the ramp to Wynyard station. She can still find the buzz and expectation of the morning rush hour exciting, but the streets emptying out at the end of the day inevitably fill her with a strange sadness.

After the din of cars accelerating up Grosvenor Street, the silence inside the big doors of the church is bewildering. The click-clacks of her high heels echo sharply as she stumbles down the central aisle and slides into a pew. There is a short queue outside the confessional box. She notices a coffin on a brass stand inside the altar area with a woman's straw hat on top, its brim adorned with colourful dried flowers. Mourners in black are sitting in the pews directly in front of her. She wonders if, when Grandma dies, they will put her red hat with the feathers on top of the coffin.

Suddenly, it is her turn for the sacrament, and she is kneeling inside the confessional box. When the shutter opens, her mouth goes dry and, predictably, she can't find her voice. The priest speaks softly:

Go on, my child, don't be afraid. You are safe in the house of God:

Bless me, Father, it is fourteen months since my last confession.

She has plucked the number of months out of the air as she cannot count back past all the dark parking spots and George's watery eyes squinting through his binoculars. She is astonished by the priest's calm reactions to all the back-seat, out-of-marriage sex, the eating meat on Fridays, the missing of regular Sunday Mass and the persistent suicidal thoughts.

The latter had haunted her as little as fifteen minutes ago, when the possibility of a watery grave in the harbour had, once again, crossed her mind. Murder – and it isn't as if she hasn't contemplated it before – is now the only mortal sin she still has in reserve. Had she died from the recent ugly throat infection, she would have been bound to go straight to hell. She prays she has come back to the Church in the nick of time. The penance the priest hands out – chanting a few rosaries – seems insignificant compensation for the utter relief of unburdening her soul.

After the absolution, the priest invites her to the annexe at the side of the church to discuss the pregnancy. The man she imagines from the voice turns out to look completely different to the man she had pictured in her head. Father O'Donnell's freckled face and red hair makes Agnes feel she is in the safe hands of someone from her own tribe. The apprehension that foreshadowed the unexpected interview vanishes with the compassion shining from the priest's autumnal eyes. When she explains how she would like to go it alone and not tell her parents, or anyone else, he smiles reassuringly and says:

You'll be safe with Sister Wilfred at St Anthony's home. She's helped a girl I know. Your privacy will be absolute.

His final words are a wondrous revelation, and one that she interprets as a sacred prophecy:

This is a new beginning. You will have a child for God. The seed in you is sanctified.

The priest walks her to the door of the sacristy and shakes his hand warmly, apologising for the abbreviated proceedings because he is due shortly to officiate at a funeral service. Agnes looks into the man's kindly eyes and thinks of the Virgin Mary after the annunciation.

She has been born for this moment. A child for God. A child for God. She keeps repeating the phrase to herself, marvelling at how much joy could suddenly enter her life in such a short space of time.

* * *

It is nearly the end of March, but the muggy summer weather persists. Agnes's top priority is to nourish the child inside her. She pays attention to her diet and tries to regain a regular sleep pattern. After work back in the solicitor's office at Central, she visits a delicatessen to buy egg and salad sandwiches, bananas, apples, and yogurt. Then she catches a bus uptown to have a picnic on the grass at the Domain opposite the Sydney Art Gallery. It is all part of her plan to avoid Charles, as he would never think to look for her there.

Charles has no idea about the pregnancy. The drive back from her parents was stiffly polite, neither of them speaking much. She needed time to recuperate, she told him. This might buy her some precious respite from his attentions. She must, at some point, of course, find the strength to rebuff him completely. All her life on standby to serve others, she now feels strange in these attempts to carve out a tiny space for herself. Nonetheless, her all-consuming desire for a little peace is still tempered by a haunting self-consciousness – a mad preoccupation about what others will think of her eating on the grass, there, in solitude.

After these quiet evening picnics, she stays in the city and goes to the public library where she sits in a haze and watches other people read books. Agnes has always loved books and feels desolate that she has been barred from opening their covers. She wonders how the readers know what the index categories stuck on the walls beside the shelves mean. She presumes clever people, like her Aunt Charlotte, somehow just magically ingest such things. She sits, utterly estranged from her surroundings, shrouded in a mist of longing. It never occurs to her that she could ask someone what, for example, 'Fiction' means. Instead, she accepts her ignorance and tries valiantly to hide a vulnerability that, she thinks, must be painfully obvious to all.

* * *

The short time Agnes is told to wait in the white lace-curtained parlour at St Anthony's home is an agony. A picture of the Sacred Heart bears down on her from the wall opposite, as if it is about to crash-land on her head. She doesn't feel she can move to another chair because the brisk nun who answered the door pointed to this specific one – as if it was the approved spot for all girls in her predicament. The scowling woman hadn't been amused when Agnes had brightly announced 'Avon calling!' when she first opened the door. Regret at this earlier stupidity has increased her anxiety, a state further exacerbated by a ticking clock that seems to reverberate right through her.

The door swings open in front of Sister Wilfred's office with the force of a Southerly Buster. A short, dumpy nun, with cheeks like newly polished apples, greets Agnes like an old friend:

Well, well, well, Agnes, *here* you are! Sorry to have kept you. Good to see you!

The nun looks Agnes up and down as if assessing her reproductive potential. She beckons Agnes inside her office and directs her to be seated on the other side of a large untidy desk. Then the woman begins scribbling furiously onto a lined writing pad:

I'm coming to you. Just got… got to finish noting this down before it goes out of my head…

The pale-yellow walls in the office smell of fresh paint and are bare – except for a large photo, in a splendid frame, of a gigantic red bull. The magnificent beast sports a purple ribbon trimmed in gold around its neck, upon which is written 'First Prize':

I see you're looking at Sam – our prize Santa Gertrudos. Isn't he *something*! He looks dangerous with that great head and shoulders but he's as docile as an old tabby. I'm about to reinstate shots of all our other stud favourites now the walls are dry. They're all Gerts. They resist disease, you know – *and* changes of temperature.

Sister Wilfred stops abruptly and rummages in the drawer of her desk, before leaning across the wide space and, with an almost parental pride, spreads six photos of similar equally adorned beasts across the desk:

These are our other winners. Aren't they beautiful? Such smooth, silky coats! Wonderful mothers! They calve easily and have plenty of milk.

The nun pauses and looks directly at Agnes, as if waiting for a comment. Agnes obliges:

Well, Sister, if I'm ever in the market for a handsome beast, I'll know where to come.

The little nun smiles, picking up the intended irony:

Well, *of course* you will. You'll have to excuse me bombarding you with the Gerts. My sister runs a sheep and cattle station. Five thousand acres that touch the Murray River and ribbon back into thousands of acres of dry pasture outside Mildura in Victoria. Years ago, my father went to Texas and bought a small starter herd from the King Ranch. They came up with the breed in the twenties by crossing a Brahman with a shorthorn, you know. Before I became a nun, I worked the station with my sister.

Looking closely at her face, Agnes suspects the deep frown lines across the nun's brow are probably the result of years of working out in the hot sun on the ranch without a hat. Sister Wilfred asks breezily:

So how many months are you, Agnes?

Just over two – I think. Sister, please, I don't want my parents to know, nor be forced to marry the father. He would definitely make my life a misery.

The nun pauses, then:

I see. Well, if you remain healthy, there's no reason why we can't arrange a good cover story while you're here. My sister June, on the Mildura property – you give family and friends *her* address and she'll forward on their mail to us here. You send all *your* letters home to *her*, and she'll post them on to your parents with a Mildura post mark. I'm around if you need any reference material about life on the property. The Gerts should provide a good sentence or two! Oh, and you'll have a false name here to protect your identity.

Agnes can't quite believe it. All this subterfuge willingly laid on for her convenience!

The highly resourceful Sister Wilfred continues:

All the girls go to St Margaret's hospital for the delivery and most have their babies adopted into good Catholic homes. We try to match the adopting parents to the birth mother's own background.

Agnes has always wanted to be someone else, so the prospect of a change of name is thrilling. She considers this for a few seconds, then:

I'll call myself Katherine De Winter, Katherine *Lea* De Winter…

Experiencing huge relief beyond her dreams, she now relishes the fact of becoming a *Rebecca* character. It is the icing on the cake! Also, this Mildura ranch cover story is an absolute godsend. No one need know a thing! She feels a surge of renewed confidence. She has only ever been a conversation piece and now she'll be directing the dialogue:

I know, Sister! I'll tell my mother I got a job in Mildura as a governess! She loves anything to do with country properties!

Sister Wilfred smiles at her kindly, then fills in an admission card. Agnes is expected to arrive back at the St Anthony's home when she starts to show around four or five months. She likes Sister Wilfred – the woman's slow drawl clearly has been nowhere near an elocution lesson. It is such a relief to deal with someone so down to earth. Everything is crystal clear. There is no hidden agenda. She is beginning to feel secure. Agnes might be an outcast from her family, but she knows she belongs to the Catholic Church and is having a child for God.

On the train back to Sydney her mind races with plans for her future. She will have to get an extra job and start saving so she has money for the months spent at St Anthony's till the birth. And then there is the list of required clothes Sister Wilfred has given her. She suddenly remembers a sign she once saw in the Singer sewing machine shop in George Street offering 'Six-week Sewing Courses'. She will enrol and make her own maternity smocks! She keeps pulling out the paper Sister Wilfred gave her with the cover address in Mildura. She is no longer a leaf blowing in the wind. At last, at *long* last, she feels there is a frame around her life that she can fasten things onto.

But the major obstacle, of course, is how to handle Charles. She has managed to avoid him for two weeks, but fears a showdown is looming. She looks down at her wristwatch and sees it is 6.30pm. She normally doesn't go back to Rosary Villa till 8pm, when she knows he is at home having dinner with his family. But everything is going so well today, she decides to take a chance. Also, she is starving. She has bought slices of ham, a few tomatoes, an avocado, a tin of asparagus and some apples and grapes in a shop at Central Railway Station and plans on having her picnic on a bench in the Rosary Villa gardens instead of going to her usual haunt at the Domain.

She realises she has made a terrible mistake when she reaches the rusting entrance gate, for she can see his Volvo parked on the gravel in front of the front door. Perhaps he hasn't seen her in the rear-view mirror. Her first instinct is to slip into the gardens and hide in the thick foliage until his car leaves. But there is no time. He has looked up and already spotted her.

He jumps out of the car and runs to where she stands, frozen like a stunned animal in a bright light. She can see the simmering fury in his cold hawk eyes. It *has* to be now. It *has* to be said:

Go *away*, Charles! I can't see you anymore!

As his face contorts into the familiar ugly grimace, Agnes's fight dissolves into flight and she takes off down Thornton Street and rounds the corner towards the yacht club. Clasping her bag tightly under her arm, she jumps the low fence into Rushcutters Bay Park and speeds across the grass. As she runs, her precious fruit and vegetables fly out of the bag, rolling over the grass in front of her. She turns to see he is gaining ground. Instead of heading towards the yacht club, where there are bound to be other people around, she foolishly aims for the Moreton Bay fig trees at the far end of the park.

She must have slowed down, for he has caught her up. He tackles her around the legs like a rugby player – exactly how her father had done when, as a child, she had attempted to flee the house. She comes down heavily, grazing hands and knees. The tin of asparagus remaining in her bag pushes sharply into her chest. He has his arm around her neck, letting loose his rage just the way her mother used to do, slapping and punching her. It is when he lands a forceful blow to her side that she lets out a piercing shriek, fearful he might injure the baby. This makes him stop. In that moment, she is full of such hatred she could thrust a knife into his heart. Instead, she curls up to protect herself, burying her face in a patch of cut grass and inhaling its sweet aroma. If only she could just stay like this, and he be gone when she lifts her head. *Please* God let him go *away*! But, when she opens her eyes, he is still standing there, looking down at her. She has vowed not to tell him. Never. But, overwhelmed with emotion, afraid for her life – and that of her baby – the story pours out of her:

Well, I hope that punch hasn't injured the baby! I'm *pregnant*, Charles, and I'll be having it adopted! *Please*, I *beg* you, you *must* find it in your heart to leave me alone! I need to do more work to save money and prepare for my confinement!

There is a long pause as he computes this information, then he speaks:

This is all your *own* damn fault! You've made me look like an *idiot* running all over the place after you! *Why* are you avoiding me? What have I done? I took you home to your parents, didn't I, when you were sick? I brought you back too! You're my *girlfriend* and I can't live without you!

His raptor eyes are heavy with fatigue, but he speaks like a quickfire salesman:

Forget adoption. I can marry you and we can have the baby together. I *promise* I'll change. If you give me another chance, *everything* will be different!

She has never heard him talk in this emotional way before. He has sat down beside her on the grass. She stares in disbelief as he rambles on:

It's all gone badly wrong with George. I don't know what's going to happen. We are under investigation for insider trading. George is facing a charge of embezzlement. The merger is suspended. That's why I wanted to see you. To tell you there will be a court case:

Any chance of you both going to prison?

But her pointed sarcasm is lost on him. Her heart sinks to realise he has time on his hands again. She suddenly feels oddly responsible for him. But why *should* she? It makes *no* sense, this crazy tendency of hers to feel sympathy for her attacker over herself! Her head feels as if it is being sawn in two. This, surely, is the real madness she will have to fight all her life.

She musters all her dwindling inner strength:

Charles. *Listen* to me. I will send a note to everyone in your office and *kill* myself if you *don't* leave me *alone*!

She can feel the bruising coming out on her face and her hip is hurting like hell where he felled her to the ground. A gust of wind blows through the park, rattling the papery leaves of the fig trees. It sets the rigging on the sailing boats at the yacht club clanging. As the wind strengthens, it starts to rasp the surface of the sea and a swirl of dust sweeps towards them. She jumps up from the grass and starts jogging up the hill, attempting to shield her eyes as she goes. Inevitably, Charles follows close behind. She can hear him coughing and choking on the miasma as he follows her back to Rosary Villa.

At the gate, he puts a restraining hand out:

Let's not say goodbye like this. Please. Let's drive to the Botanical Gardens where we can walk together and calm down. Just for a bit, all right? You owe me that at least.

Something – she will never know what – will prompt her to make this concession and she will climb, once again, into the Volvo death seat. Charles will drive in the usual reckless fashion along New South Head Road, through King's Cross and down William Street. He will park the car at Lady Macquarie's Chair, and they will walk along the pathway by the edge of the harbour and talk. It will be a civil exchange, with no heightened emotion. She will speak with him calmly as she does not want to ruin one of her favourite places – a place where she usually finds beauty and peace.

It will already be dark when they arrive back at Lady Macquarie's Chair and where Agnes will announce that she is not getting in the car and will be catching a bus. He will look at her sharply:

Don't be silly. Oh, all right then. At least let me drive you to the bus stop.

Again, she will go against her instinct, get back in the car, and will end up in a dark corner under the Harbour Bridge – with Charles on top of her.

In the confessional box the next evening, Father O'Donnell at St Patrick's will advise her to go to the police. He will give what happened to Agnes under the bridge the name it deserves. He will call it 'rape'. It is a police matter. But she is fearful, she tells him, that the police will want to arrest her assailant and will also want to contact her parents. All she wants in the world, she says, is to quietly move on. To have her Child for God.

Father O'Donnell will advise her to avoid Charles completely. To keep to public places. To hold her nerve.

If she only had enough money to move out of Rosary Villa, Agnes will reply, then she could probably manage to do all this. But how?

Shortly after the discussion with the priest, a minor miracle will occur. Ever persistent, she will land an extra job: a post as a cleaner in a language school at Central where she starts at 4am each morning, finishes cleaning at 7am, then returns to a tiny studio flat housed within the school that she has convinced her new boss to rent out to her for three months. Here she will shower and get ready for her other job as a registration clerk with the solicitors nearby. It is hard going, and makes for a very long day, but those three extra early hours will make her good money. She will love having a little kitchen all to herself and will, every morning, cook up hearty egg and bacon breakfasts and be sure to include a large glass of milk for baby. She will start talking to her Child for God and will feel certain she is having a girl.

Three months into the pregnancy she will start throwing up in the morning and will give up the big breakfasts for a few weeks. Then the sickness will pass. Building on what she has learned from Mrs Ryder, and the Singer Sewing School in George Street, she will make two smocks – one out of pale-blue wool and the other from olive-green corduroy. The smocks will be hung up ready to be packed in her bag when the time comes to go to the St Anthony's Home.

She will be catapulted up from simple contentment to seventh heaven when she returns briefly to collect her mail from Rosary Villa and finds a letter from Charles's brother Ronald. It informs her that Charles has been placed in temporary custody with George – pending an appearance in court. Able to breathe deeply again, and all prayers answered, she will no longer have to look over her shoulder – at least for a while. She feels completely justified in not responding to Ronald's letter – jail being precisely the right place for rapists, perverts, abusers, and embezzlers.

As predicted, Agnes's mother will lap up the news of the fictitious governess post at the Victoria ranch with unimaginable delight. Within a few minutes of hanging up the phone, she will ring Agnes back, hungry for yet more details. The inspired fabrication will reinstate Agnes into the family fold, albeit temporarily. Madge may know the names of all the wealthy property owners in New South Wales but, fortunately for Agnes, is unfamiliar with those in Victoria. This means Agnes can now happily provide her own fictitious input, which saves her mother the bother of making it up.

When the time comes to go to St Anthony's, she will terminate her two jobs, pack up her few possessions, and pay the nuns to leave the moving boxes in the storage room at Rosary Villa. Then she will splurge on a taxi and stroll into the main hall of Central Station where, for appearances' sake, she will wait on the platform beside the Melbourne train until it pulls out without her.

Swinging her suitcase, handbag slung over her arm, she will descend the stairs from the main hall to the suburban lines below. As the train passes station after station heading west out of Sydney, Agnes will congratulate herself that another future is beginning – a future for her and her Child for God.

23

ST ANTHONY'S HOME FOR UNWED GIRL MOTHERS

gnes's arrival at St Anthony's is an anticlimax. To start with, there is nowhere to hang her clothes. In a kind of mad protest, she resists moving in. Admittedly, she hasn't had a clear idea of how it would be and, in her imagination, has imagined a comfortable room of her own as compensation for the huge effort she has made in getting there. Instead, she is shown into a narrow, grey-curtained dormitory cubicle with an iron bed and a small bedside table. On the bed she discovers a thin mattress, rough sheets and army blankets submerged beneath a beige chenille bedspread. The accommodation reminds her of a detention centre for young offenders she once saw at the cinema. Adding to the shock, she will shortly find it hard, too, to get used to the snorting, snoring and occasional nightmarish shrieks from the other cubicles along the austere row.

The home comprises three buildings. The unwed girl mothers sleep in a long, narrow two-storey building that borders the back of the block. It is accessed by a road, big enough for a car, that traverses in a straight line from the tall iron gates at the street frontage. The caramel rectangular brick building – The Archbishop Kelly Wing – that lies to the left of the huge iron gates is where the nuns reside and where Agnes first met Sister Wilfred. A small brick chapel nestles opposite the Archbishop Kelly Wing on the other side of the road.

After her initial childish protest about the accommodation, Agnes sits down on the edge of the hard iron bed and makes a list of advantages on a piece of paper:

1. All the beds are occupied except the cubicle next to me.
2. I have an end cubicle next to a wall, thus can access the loo at night without disturbing anyone.
3. I am on the right side of the tower, so I look down on a glorious jacaranda tree and have a spectacular view at night all the way to the city.

She unpacks her suitcase but leaves the fine full-length blue wool dressing gown with its satin piping edges in the bottom of the case – ready to wear to the hospital when the time comes. The dressing gown is a purchase she has splurged out on. It has cut into her savings but, she reasons, a girl needs something special for such an important event. She sees it like a going-away outfit after a wedding for, after all, the ultimate trip to St Margaret's hospital will be the beginning of the end of the story.

She stores her underwear, stockings, jumpers and shirts neatly in the bedside table and hangs the two smocks over the iron railing at the back of the bed, along with the skirt and jacket she arrived in. After lights-out at 9pm, when the world beyond the home is still awake, she slides the grey cubicle curtain open and looks out of the window. She has put the army blanket around her shoulders and is watching the shadowy forms of the nuns who move, like ghostly spirits, between the convent and the chapel. Streetlights cut strange shapes into the dark no-man's land between the nuns and the front gate. The forlorn view to the city by day has turned into a fairyland of tiny lights at night. She feels claustrophobic when she draws the drab grey curtains closed, feeling hemmed in, and so keeps it open. She eventually falls asleep propped up against the cold iron bedhead.

Agnes soon learns that it is the unwed girl inmates who run the home. Everyone works at chores and duties. While the rest of Croydon sleeps, lights go on in the dormitories at 5.30am. Work starts for Agnes in the nursery at 6am – alongside Sister Bernadette. This occupation evokes memories of the sterilising room in Ground Floor Private, although the young nun's sarcasm is a mere irritant compared to the relentless cruelty of the heavy-breasted Scruggs. Yet the same hostility towards her, it seems, has been carried over:

Didn't you go to school? Haven't you got *eyes*? Didn't you listen to what I *said*?

Such acerbic comments hover constantly in the background as Agnes cleans, makes beds, and bathes and dresses the sweet little orphans whom the home also houses. She decides not to let the stiff-necked nursery nun get to her. Whenever she sees an opportunity, she steps in to help. She often asks Sister Bernadette's opinion and dutifully turns the other cheek to her insults until they stop coming.

After a few hours of heavy work, she is always ravenous. She thinks of food all day. Fortunately, in stark contrast with the spartan accommodation, the meals are tasty and plentiful. Breakfast is piping-hot porridge with honey and milk. There is an urn to make tea on a corner table and there is as much sliced bread as you like to make hot toast with butter and marmalade. All the tables have bowls overflowing with fresh fruit, jugs of milk, and jars of iron tablets to make the babies' bones strong. There is bacon and egg for breakfast on Wednesdays, and Agnes's favourite – frankfurter sausages – on Sunday.

Lunch and dinner are just as delicious and plentiful. There is a baked dinner on Saturday night instead of Sunday lunch because most of the girls go out with their families on Sunday. Wednesday is rissoles with thick gravy, mashed potatoes and beans or peas, and Friday, of course, is fish and chips. Agnes can recognise the day of the week by what is on the menu. A matchstick when she first arrived, within a few weeks she has put on weight, and the bump she has so carefully guarded from view pops out in solidarity with her pregnant companions.

The dining room in the Archbishop Kelly Wing doubles as an assembly room and is where Agnes discovers, to her delight, that she is to receive a weekly payment from the Social Security Department. This means that, after the splurge on the blue dressing gown, her savings balance is as before, and is set to increase every week. The social security, she discovers, will also pay for the ambulance to the hospital, and the return ride to the home with baby in a taxi, together with a small amount after the birth to help get started again.

Soon after Agnes's arrival, the nun who runs the kitchen falls off a ladder and breaks her hip. The unwed girls who work beside her, much to Sister Wilfred's surprise, proceed to produce the same high-standard meals without her. Agnes enjoys assisting these girls in the kitchen – chatting with them around the unstable old table, peeling potatoes, shelling peas, top and tailing beans or doing whatever is required. It is here she picks up tips about managing the birth – a dose of castor oil can, apparently, bring on a recalcitrant labour or can be taken when already in labour to hurry it along. It is rumoured that the staff at St Margaret's Hospital treat the unwed mothers as second-class citizens so, the advice is, the less time spent there the better. The trick, apparently, is to arrive at the hospital as close as possible to giving birth. Ideally, the moment to call the ambulance should be when the labour pains are no less than five minutes apart.

Nobody talks about the past, although vivid individual stories of suspect truth circulate the corridors. However, contrary to the norm, everyone knows Annie's story.

The beautiful thirteen-year-old with wild black curly hair and full strawberry-tinted lips is having her father's baby. Annie, like Agnes, never has any visitors. It is rumoured she has been taken into care by a social worker, but no one knows for sure. She rarely speaks and Agnes wonders how aware she is of what has befallen her. She likes to be on the move and comes to life when relaying messages or fetching supplies from the storeroom. But, some days, she will fall into a listless trance and not come to the kitchen, where she usually works alongside Dawn – a warm-hearted and chubby-faced seventeen-year-old.

Concerned for Annie's sanity, Sister Wilfred appoints the child as St Anthony's 'official messenger' and Dawn – and the group in the kitchen – make her a set of pink paper wings that she wears on official duty. Along with the presentation of the wings on her birthday, she is given a copy of *Black Beauty*, which she carries everywhere she goes.

As for Dawn, she laughs her way through the day and loves baking. Visitors to the kitchen, including the nuns, are invariably treated to a coconut slice, jam tart or shortbread biscuit hot out of the oven. Dawn comes from a family of chefs and is given free rein to experiment in the kitchen with beautiful little Annie at her side. Her parents keep her stocked with spices and condiments when they come to take her out on Sundays. These days, Agnes finds herself hanging around the kitchen door like a hungry dog, keen to lick the mixing bowl or whatever else is in the offing. Even Sister Wilfred, not much given to the delights of the senses, readily confirms that Dawn's reign in the kitchen is a gift from above.

After a month of pulling herself out of bed in the dark, Agnes starts dreaming of improving her lot at the home. Work in the office is undoubtedly the top job – the handful of unwed girls who work there enjoy the privilege of starting at the later hour of seven, when they attend morning Mass alongside the nuns, then enjoy a leisurely breakfast, and still have time to return to the dormitory before getting started at nine – like any Sydney office worker. Agnes determines to break into this inner circle, for laundry, kitchen, and cleaning duties smack of her past enslavement.

One evening, before lights out, she will sneak downstairs and boldly confront Sister Wilfred on her way to the chapel. She will be overjoyed with the nun's reaction:

If working with us would interest you, Agnes, I'll keep you in mind. One of our office girls is due any day now so, when she leaves, I'll give you a try.

Even at this desired distance, Agnes's relationship with her mother will traverse the extremes. One minute she will be insulting Madge under her breath for a remembered attack, and the next she will be labouring over heartfelt letters to impress her. There will be flowery missives of events related to her by Sister Wilfred – as arranged between them – winging their way North. Long paragraphs will describe horseback-riding the boundaries of the huge property where Agnes supposedly works as a treasured family governess. She will describe watching a man on a tractor winch one of the giant Santa Gertruda cattle out of a patch of quicksand. She will describe helping the flying doctor – who has just landed on the property in a light aircraft having been guided by the name 'DUNROVEN' emblazoned on the roof of the homestead. Madge will learn how the doctor plans to airlift an injured farm worker to hospital. To add further authenticity to her audacious cover story, Agnes will forward a newspaper article, supplied by Sister Wilfred's sister, which is headlined:

'MILDURA – THE MEDITERRANEAN IN THE OUTBACK'.

She will also enclose a couple of extra photos of the prize bull featured on Sister Wilfred's office wall.

Madge's effusive replies will confirm Agnes's achievement as a temporary member of her polo circle. Thus, Agnes's country life inventions will grow even more elaborate. Many of the activities she invents on the property will not match the seasons but, fully aware she isn't corresponding with an enquiring mind, she will steam ahead regardless.

Life, under the circumstances, couldn't be going better but, exactly like a character in a Greek drama accused of dangerous hubris, Agnes will be struck down. A note will arrive from Sister Wilfred via Annie the messenger to tell Agnes that Charles has been in contact and will be coming to the home on Sunday afternoon to take her out. What?! How on *earth* did he track her down?! The only thing she can think of is that she must have blurted out the name of St Anthony's the evening he assaulted her in Rushcutters Bay Park.

The bottom will drop out of her world. Has he broken out of prison? Did they drop the charges? What is God *thinking*?! The thought of Charles careering around, free as a bird, to collar her out here in Croydon will sicken her to the stomach and she will try, though unsuccessfully, to see Sister Wilfred before the appointed day. Despite the nun's cattle-loving toughness, Agnes fears Sister Wilfred might have been taken in by the blandishments of the opposite sex. Had Charles spoken to her on the phone? Or had he already *been* here, charming her with his bespoke wardrobe and slick North Shore manner? Was she taken in by the same marshmallow sentimentality that dulled her grandmother's perception of the men around her? Didn't Sister Wilfred recall Agnes's aversion to the father of her baby? The agonising countdown of days, hours and minutes till Sunday begins.

Agnes has always associated bad weather with Charles. And, true to premonition, she is woken by a violent storm in the early hours of that dreaded Sunday morning. The wind howls around the building, smashing against the windows like the fist of someone desperate to be let in. Agnes hovers for the rest of the night on the edge of sleep and wakes exhausted. Between morning downpours, she will keep nodding off during Mass. Her stomach will be so churned up she will even forgo Sunday's frankfurter sausages.

She will spot him from the window of her cubicle, parking his car. The wind will have dropped. The branches of the jacaranda tree at the entrance to the dormitory block, which had swirled all night like the tentacles of an enraged octopus, will hang limp. She will smell his irritation as he struggles to navigate the tight parking space. She will flinch inside as he kicks the gate that resists his effort to open it. She will hate intensely his self-assured stride as she watches him carrying what looks like a cellophane-wrapped bunch of white arum lilies mixed with carnations, doubtless intended for Sister Wilfred, to further smooth his way. She had never received flowers, or anything more than dull conversation, forced sex and dangerous driving.

Annie, wearing her pink wings, will keep running between the office and the home – informing various girls that their visitors awaited them in the parlour. Even up to the last minute, Agnes will hope the Lord will intervene and Sister Wilfred will smell a rat and throw the flowers in Charles's face. But the hope will disintegrate when she hears the little winged messenger bound up the steps to impart the bad news to her with her customary smile.

In some sort of feeble defence, Agnes will have deliberately tried to look as unattractive as possible, but her efforts will be wasted as Charles will hardly look at her. He will be self-absorbed, the pupils in his eyes dilated and cold. There will be the usual one undercover spy to another nod. A mild clap of distant thunder will sound like a drum roll as Agnes slides into the dreaded passenger seat. The rain will continue to pour down as he pulls the car away from the curb. The windscreen wipers will labour to clear the glass. He will seem oblivious to her existence and, if anything, annoyed by the noisy intrusion of the rain as he speaks in agitated broken sentences:

You can't imagine. Things are horrible for me. I'm bloody *innocent.* All this shit is George's mess. *He* dragged me in. The man can't lie straight in bed! After the trial here, he'll be extradited to London. He's been charged with insider trading. *And* embezzlement! Losing our jobs isn't enough it seems. *Now* the company is colluding with the enemy to blacken our names.

His voice will sound strange and staccato as if he is only half present. For all Agnes will care, he could drive into the sea and tell it to the fishes. She will grit her teeth, then ask, with more than a hint of disdain in her tone:

So – what was it like in prison?

What do you *think* it was like! Bloody horrible! Ronald paid bail money and got me out. Now. *This* is what we are going to do. My brother thinks it would be a good idea if we got married. Being a newly married man and father will help my case – and my mother is willing to care for the baby. I'm sure your parents will see the sense of our plan.

Agnes will be flabbergasted but will not have lost her spirit, nor her fight:

Well, I'm certainly not getting married to keep *you* out of jail, Charles! I have made my arrangements and am sticking to them. I only agreed to see you today to tell you not to come back:

You little *bitch*! How *dare* you talk to me like that?

She will observe that he is working himself up into a rage, as he usually did when things didn't suit him. Her stomach will somersault when he turns off the Parramatta Road, along which he has been driving at a leisurely pace. He will start speeding and screeching around corners like a police car giving chase and she will grip the sides of the seat so tightly that her fingers will break through the upholstery underneath:

Let me out, Charles!

She will bang her fist on the closed window:

Let me *out*!

He will scorch down a deserted tree-lined track that runs parallel to an empty park. She will spot picnic tables and barbeques and look around frantically for someone to help her, but everyone will have fled the rain. Damp smoke will still be rising from a drenched fire grate. Just beyond the park boundary, he will drive into what looks like an overgrown abandoned building site and she will wonder, yet again, how he knows all these secluded places. He will stop the car suddenly – opposite a clump of tall trees.

He will be instantly on top of her, and horribly rough. She will be in mortal fear for the baby and then astounded by the way he kisses her on the cheek when he drops her back at the home and says – I'll see you next week. As if they have just been out for tea and scones.

Agnes will come down with a virus and not be able to go to work. A nurse will guide her to the Infirmary on the floor below. In a haze, she will tell the doctor she has always been susceptible to bad throat infections. Once again, antibiotic injections will come to her rescue, and she will feel better but, when Sister Wilfred appears a couple of days later, Agnes will be in such distress that she rounds on her:

Why, Sister? *Why* did you let him take me out on Sunday?!

What do you mean, Agnes? What happened?

He raped me! In the car! Father O'Donnell said that if it's against your will, it's *always rape*!

Agnes will hear herself shouting this for everyone to hear, but will not care:

He's talking about marrying me just to help his court case! I'm trapped in a vicious cycle, Sister, and with no way out! It's a pattern I've *always* had to endure!

My God! You, *poor* child! Well, he's certainly not coming here again. I'll make sure of *that*!

And Sister Wilfred will take her into the haven of her office, sit down beside her and gently hold her hand:

You should have spoken out earlier, Agnes. I'm so sorry. Mark my words, it will *never* happen again. I will protect you with my last breath.

The nun will put her arms around Agnes, and she will feel the shape of the metal cross around the woman's neck pressing into her shoulder. Relief will throb through her. After a lifetime of temporary respite before the next attack – and the next – and the next – there is something final and permanent about these moments of love and comfort that will give her fresh hope.

But Agnes will never be so aware of the distortion of time and place that haunts her footsteps as on the following Sunday morning – when she spots Charles's silver Volvo. It will be unusually neatly parked on the street and, for a second or two, she will doubt it belongs to him. But no – *there* he is – striding up to the convent door with the usual pugnacious assurance of being the one in control. The hypocritical bastard will be carrying another bunch of flowers and Agnes will observe Sister Bernadette open the door to him. Charles and his bouquet will be swallowed up inside. What will Sister Wilfred do? Has she told Sister Bernadette the score? *Will* these nuns be able to protect her, as Sister Wilfred had promised? The street and the home deserted, the atmosphere to Agnes will feel like the running of the Melbourne Cup when, on one day in November at precisely 3pm, everyone abandons what they are doing to listen to the horse race. But she will continue to wait. It is all she can do.

What happens next will be beyond analysis or prediction. The front door of the convent will burst open:

Katherine! Katherine! Where are you?! You *belong* to me, Katherine!

For a crazy moment she will think of Heathcliff in *Wuthering Heights* who clawed at the soil of Kathy's windswept grave on the Yorkshire moors. She doesn't associate her adopted St Anthony's alias with herself and is amazed that he is using it to find her. He has never used her given name to her face in all the time she has known him. He must be coming to kill her for betraying him. She can feel his seething fury in her bones.

Crouching down by the open window, she will be astonished to hear Sister Wilfred raise her voice to cattle-herding levels:

I am warning you *again*, Mr Burgess! The police are on their way! Now kindly stop shouting and *behave* yourself!

Agnes will risk a glimpse through the window. She will see Sister Wilfred wielding a five-iron golf club, and Charles now firmly backed up against a wall. Sure enough, she will detect the whine of approaching sirens and, as their noise increases with proximity, and the police car enters the gate, Charles will seem to shrink into nothing. He will never return.

24

REBECCA LEA

After Charles's arrest, Sister Wilfred accompanies Agnes to the Infirmary where they run her a warm, relaxing bath. A short time later, the feisty nun personally serves her a hot mug of tea. As Agnes sips at it, Sister Wilfred addresses her formally:

Now, my dear girl, it's over. I've asked you if you wish to press charges against Mr Burgess and you have declined. But I'll ask you again. Are you sure this man should be allowed to have inflicted such a crime upon you without a reckoning?

I don't want that, Sister. I just want to forget him – and *everything* about him.

So be it. I'll be guided by you. Now then. Tall in the saddle, yes? We've got work to do. I want you to help me in the office.

Yes. Agnes has been promoted. The wiry nun with the five-iron could not eradicate the effects of a lifetime of abuse, but having someone defend her willingly, and respect her wishes, will forever be a pivotal turning point in Agnes's life. Although self-recrimination, regardless of the support, will continue to haunt her, and she will seek out Father Dominic to hear her confession in the chapel. Why, she will ask him, in contrast to the shy, deferential girl she believes herself to be, is she haunted by being a temptress? Does she act in ways she isn't aware of?

The priest's kind and wise assurances of her innocence having propelled her into a new state of religious devotion she is now first in the chapel for morning Mass. She has established her spot at the end of the front pew, as close as possible to the presence in the tabernacle. Her sin-stained soul has been washed clean. She walks up to the altar rails to take Holy Communion freely with the others and vows to herself to prove her worth. A further surprise is the way Sister Wilfred has started to seek her opinion about the running of the home:

You're a sharp observer, Katherine. It's gratifying how much you notice. I'm blessed with your presence!

Because St Anthony's has a policy of never turning anyone away, there is a sudden influx of desperate pregnant girls, abandoned orphans, and – for the first time in its history – a newborn baby has been left – like Moses in the bullrushes – at the gate of the home in a laundry basket.

A shy, lanky-legged girl from Queensland, who wears a look of constant surprise and is afflicted with a nervous cough, moves into the cubicle next to Agnes. The girl's thin body exaggerates a modest bump and her soulful hazel eyes remind Agnes of a saint on a holy card looking to heaven. Her new neighbour hangs a calendar on the metal headboard of her bed and, first thing every morning, ticks off another day – like a prisoner marking off the term of a sentence.

In fact, it feels to Agnes as if all of Sydney's dispossessed are heading to Croydon. The deluge is putting a strain on an institution which is totally self-funded. What had seemed like a sleepy place when she arrived is now heaving at full capacity. There isn't a vacant bed to be had. Suddenly, more money is urgently required to keep the home afloat, and Sister Wilfred makes an appeal to the local Catholic business community at a special meeting in the dining room.

The first to come forward is a regular donor called Mr Reuben F. Scarf. Agnes is amazed to learn that this well-built man in the pinstripe suit is behind the familiar radio slogan 'Scamper down to Camperdown on the Parramatta Road for a Scarf suit!' In Sydney, Ruben F. Scarf is as synonymous with men's suits as Mr Kellogg is with cornflakes. She soon comes to realise that St Anthony's is like a branch office of the Scarf empire, for the famous firm supplies the letterheads and stationery and undertakes special print runs for funding appeals. Mr Scarf's building company even attends to repairs and construction work at the home.

Agnes learns to type. As the letters requesting donations are in a pre-printed format, she doesn't need to worry about bad grammar and not being able to spell – she only has to copy the names and addresses accurately onto the envelopes. Initially, she struggles, and worries she might be demoted, but manages to cope by staying late in order to equal her output to that of the others.

Sister Ambrosia, who manages the office, is Sister Wilfred's antithesis. She is tall, with a soft, rounded figure. Agnes imagines that the billowing pleats of her brown habit must consume a whole roll of fabric. Patient and softly spoken, she glides around the office like an ocean liner in a calm sea. Her milk-white skin is as smooth as silk, and her large watery grey eyes radiate a pious religious fervour that Agnes has learned to mistrust. Sister Ambrosia appears to be particularly fond of Teresa – a green-eyed beauty from Melbourne who works alongside her in the office.

There is a third member of the office team – Nola. With her broad shoulders and big hands, she looks more like a man than a woman. Long hair might have softened her appearance but, as if in defiance of femininity, she wears it cut short like an army soldier. She prefers to walk around in a loose brown dustcoat like a warehouse worker. It is hard to see that Nola is pregnant as her bump is dispersed between her back and sides.

Having all but ignored Agnes during her first days in the office, today Nola has elected to sit with her at breakfast and is focusing fiery nut-brown eyes on her with an unnerving intensity. She asks:

Do you mind if I sit here and talk to you?

No, not at all – go right ahead.

Agnes is surprised by the feminine quality of Nola's voice. She smiles at her encouragingly and the nervy young woman seems to relax a little:

Every day I look at myself and *can't* believe it. I don't even *like* the opposite sex. It's all down to a silly event when I joined some university mates for a night out. We were in a pub by the Swan River. To celebrate my birthday. Big mistake. I stayed too long and drank too much. The dregs of humanity hang out there. They got themselves a good Chinese chef aimed at improving the tone, but it's hardly touched the edges. The place is, and will always be, a sleazy joint. Agricultural Science PhD students. That's us. I'm the only woman but I've always been treated as a bloke, which suits me fine. Our group got loud and boisterous but mild compared to the lousy drunk sailors a few tables away. This creep kept looking at me. Men don't normally look at me, so I stared back – more out of curiosity than interest. I did have a boyfriend once, who I gave up on after no end of grief. In favour of a career, you see.

I *love* my work – fulfilling my ambitions means everything to me. Anyway. I didn't give the bloke at the bar another thought…

Agnes is finding herself fascinated by this story, but is aware of the note of stress that has now entered Nola's voice:

After leaving my mates, I took a shortcut through an abandoned building site. Ugliest place you ever saw – bags of cement gone hard, broken tiles, rusting reinforcing rods, empty bottles, cans, sodden piles of newspapers, weeds growing out of rotting clothes. The sailor who had stared at me had followed me. There was an almighty struggle. I'm pretty strong, but he was built like a gorilla. Would you believe that the bastard put me in a choke hold and raped me!

Agnes knows this is a rhetorical question. She is feeling a little sick. Yes, she wants to reply. Yes, I *would* believe it. Nola continues:

The cops never found him. I don't think they even tried. They made me feel like I'd made it up because who'd bother forcing themselves on *me*! I wish I'd just kept it to myself!

Agnes can't think of anything to say to comfort her. She has never known anyone like Nola, nor heard a story like that before, yet her own tale, apart from its upper-class pretensions, isn't that different. Nola is looking into the middle distance:

I hate being a victim. Paying for that arsehole's sin! And I hate feeling I've been expelled from the land of decent people. I still want to smash his fucking head in! And I'm starting to hate this sanctimonious place. They just ignore the sad facts – it's like we acquired these bellies by divine intervention! I look at little Annie and hate the hypocrisy of the Catholic Church. Giving birth to her father's baby! How barbaric is that?! And doesn't this place seem like a baby factory to you? We're all making a product for someone else! I keep asking myself – is this what I *want*? I regurgitate that question obsessively. I was in complete shock when a priest advised me to come here.

Eventually, Agnes will discover that Nola is the eldest of five children from an Irish Catholic family who eke out a living on a small, freezing farm in the Snowy Mountains. To bring in extra cash, her father, a bad-tempered boozer who beats his wife, works in a local tanning factory. Nola will tell Agnes that there wasn't a day she didn't yearn to leave home. Fortunately, exceptional exam results landed her a scholarship to a good high school in Melbourne, where she stayed with an aunt who worked for the government.

But, after an almighty row with the aunt – over what, Agnes was never sure – Nola moved to Western Australia to do her Master's degree.

Over the next few days, Nola will declare that she belongs to a left-wing group at the university and is interested in the ideas of Marx and Engels, both of whom Agnes will be ashamed to admit she has never heard of:

Crikey, Katherine! *Surely* you've heard of the Russian Revolution!

Agnes will reply apologetically, exposing her limited historical knowledge outside the modern newspaper headlines in her mother's knitting bag. She will wonder if Nola might be a Communist. But what did *that* matter? She will learn about the ten days that shook the world and will be given a copy of the Communist Manifesto as a farewell present.

By choosing Agnes as a confidante, Nola will balance out the sides in the office: Agnes and Nola verses Teresa and Sister Ambrosia. Nola will harbour a particular aversion to the Melbourne Princess – as she calls Teresa – that goes back to a time when, as a student, she worked in the summer holidays for a newspaper owned by Teresa's father. She tells Agnes:

She lives in a mansion, Katherine! In Saint Kilda! And it's *my* belief a sizable donation explains her pampered presence! Note, she's the only one with a room of her own in the convent. Her golden era here will surely end in an eye-watering tip from Daddy. Connections, my dear Katherine, are everything – even in *this* dump.

With her graceful long neck, head of vibrant chestnut curls, smartly dressed in tailored maternity outfits and expensive Italian shoes, emerald-eyed Teresa will look to Agnes like a member of the British Royal Family. She will cast the occasional glance at Teresa's perfectly formed long fingers, which are covered in rings, including a particularly beautiful gold band embedded with tiny diamonds that she twirls absentmindedly around her wedding finger. But Nola will mutter contemptuously:

No, my dear Katherine! It wasn't slipped on at the altar but is an accessory to predicament!

Agnes will continue to be dazzled by her new friend's ability to articulate her thoughts but, more than anything else, she will love Nola's ability to laugh at herself. On Sundays, the two friends will fall into the habit of strolling together to Croydon to have a milkshake with Annie – who will be carrying *Black Beauty* in a cloth bag that Dawn recently made especially for the purpose. With Annie tagging along faithfully, their first stop will be the newsagent's store, where Agnes will buy a sketchbook and the *Woman's*

Weekly, while Nola will be keen to read in a newspaper the latest on the Eichmann Trial in Israel and will declare to all present:

It's phenomenal how they tracked the bastard down in Argentina!

Nola will read aloud selected political excerpts, while Agnes surreptitiously flicks through the social pages in the *Woman's Weekly* to see if any of her mother's polo friends are featured. No peculiarities or differences will be able to dispel how relaxed and happy Agnes feels sauntering along beside her new friend. She will find herself telling Nola of some of the confusing events she has lived through since leaving school and will enjoy sketching her strong and determined face in her new drawing book.

* * *

The first task in the office is opening the mail. Teresa does the honours with an ornate Eastern letter opener with a black handle embellished with a golden dragon – an impressive implement sent to her from Saint Kilda for the purpose. Teresa leans gracefully over Sister Ambrosia's big desk in the centre of the room. The desk is situated under a high opaque glass window from whence the light picks up the adoring expression on the fervent nun's face as she watches Teresa's slender fingers deftly unclip the cheques and pile them into a box to be entered into the bank book. Every action is completed with the intense self-preening of a cat assiduously licking its paws. Teresa also does the bookkeeping although, unbeknown to her, Nola and Sister Wilfred check her work in the back office. It seems Teresa is no arithmetical genius.

Because she knows shorthand, Nola sometimes acts as Sister Wilfred's secretary. She performs her tasks perfunctorily, adhering to the unwritten and unspoken law that nobody must be seen to outshine the resident Princess.

As for Agnes, her star is being elevated by the day. She takes the mail to the Post Office and joins Teresa and Nola on Monday nights at a table in the convent to count the money from the collection tins gathered from shops around Sydney. The tins from the fish and chip shops smell of stale batter, and the coins are covered in salt, but they are always the fullest. Agnes imagines a line of workmen donating the change from their fish and chips orders out of their Friday's pay packet. Sometimes, however, she feels like she is running to catch up with Sister Wilfred's high expectations.

Only yesterday, upon seeing some of the sketches in her new drawing book, the nun had asked her to come up with a new design for the outside of the collection tins. Heart racing, Agnes had managed to finish the unexpected assignment and leave it on Sister Wilfred's desk in good time for the designated deadline.

That evening, Annie accompanies her to the parlour where Sister Wilfred and Mr Scarf are seated side by side, below the picture of the Sacred Heart. Sister Wilfred announces:

I'd like to present Katherine, our resident artist, who made the drawing for the new collection tin.

Mr Scarf stands and shakes Agnes's hand warmly, while Agnes awkwardly tries to hold her bump in and look professional. He says:

Sister has told me about you. Good to meet you at last, Katherine. Lovely design – thanks.

Agnes will recall this rare moment of male praise a few years later when she sees one of her tins on a Sydney shop counter.

But the pinnacle of the honours conferred on her will be laying out the priest's vestments for Mass. This will make her fervently wish she had remained alert to content and detail during the hundreds of Masses she has slumbered through, having reserved her attention exclusively for any bursts of glorious sacred music.

Regardless of these perceived failings, the yoke of Agnes's past disappointment with the church has been lifted by Father Dominic. Not since she appealed to Monsignor Harrington to save her parents' souls will Agnes feel so fully at ease with a priest again – although well-intentioned red-headed Father O'Donnell, who had directed her to the unwed young mothers' home, comes close.

While Father Dominic prepares for Mass, he inspires her with the extraordinary history of the church. He makes her feel she is part of a family, as a brick is part of a building.

On their final Sunday together, Nola and Agnes will walk alone to Croydon, as Annie will have gone to the cinema to see *The Wizard of Oz* with Dawn and her parents. Agnes will be glad to have Nola to herself, as she is keen to ask her opinion on something troubling. Having requested her mother to send a specific photo featuring her standing with her parents, Madge had sent it off to her, but with Agnes cut off the end. The fact that it was the only image in existence of the three of them has only spotlighted the hurt and disappointment. Agnes will make a logical link, confiding to Nola how her mother moved towards her father to fill the space she vacated when she was flung back by his blow, a rejection which caused her to jump out of the car. Nola will stare down at the photograph and say:

From what you've told me, Katherine, your mother's a bitch. The set of the mouth, the tight face and lacquered hairdo say it all. She's an ignorant clothes horse with her head up her own fundament.

Agnes will probe for more enlightenment:

But why, Nola? *Why* would she do that? After all the lovely letters I've sent her? She even reads them out to her polo mates. She calls me Possum and Darling in her replies, and I had forgiven her *everything*! She's been telling me there is always room for me in the new house at the farm. I thought she was finally *proud* of me! That we were reconciled! I don't understand this rebuff, after so much effort to please!

The more Agnes speaks up, the hollower she will feel. And the harder it will be to stop talking. She will feel she is out there in the ether, mouthing words in a vacuum. Aware of her distress, Nola will butt in:

Perhaps you think too much about her and not enough about yourself?

But Agnes will still try to make excuses for her Machiavellian mother. It is second nature to her. She will say:

I wanted to have the photo in my cubicle – as a kind of support while I wait to give birth. Maybe she cut me off because the photo didn't fit the envelope? Do you think that's it? She's always impatient. She would have been annoyed to have to look for a bigger envelope. There could be any number of explanations that have nothing to do with rejection. She's right whenever she blames me for enlarging on small matters. Forget what I said. It's only a dumb photo.

Nola will put her arm round Agnes's shoulder and speak very gently:

My dear Katherine, you don't have to be Einstein to understand the symbolism of being cut out. Listen to me. By brutally abandoning you, neither parent gave you a chance to abandon them. Do you see? When conditions in a country become intolerably unjust – like in France in 1789, and Russia in 1917 – a revolution erupts that topples the old order and creates something new. It's exactly the same with families. One day, the foundation cracks, and no amount of paint or wallpaper can prop up the crumbling edifice. This photo should be the catalyst for personal revolution and change. Banishing a cruel mother from your life is an affirmation of your self-worth. Life is change and change is life. You have great chances ahead of you, Katherine! Reach out beyond your family and embrace your *own* future!

Agnes will trust the genuine warmth in Nola's eyes. She has loved listening to her over the days. She has marvelled at how bravely Nola has stood up for her rights at university. With what fortitude she has overcome the difficulties she has encountered in the man's world of academia. But, in this instance, Nola will be talking about a place Agnes doesn't inhabit. The guidance Nola has just imparted will frighten her. She will feel ashamed of bad-mouthing her parents. She cannot imagine walking away. Because of her grandmother's pervasive influence, she carries the sanctity of the family in her very bones. Yes, Nola might have given eloquent expression to the pain residing deep inside her, but she cannot let the relief she feels settle and take root. It is impossible to accept.

The short-lived friendship with Nola will wobble badly when, after a crisis of conscience, Nola makes a big decision about both her baby and her beliefs, declaring:

Katherine – I'm *so* excited! I've finally made up my mind. I'm going to *keep* my baby, *leave* the Catholic Church, and become a *Protestant*!

Agnes will be aghast:

A Protestant! You must be joking, Nola, I've spent my *life* avoiding them!

Nola will not be deterred in the least:

This is not a sudden decision. I've been contemplating it for weeks. I rang my aunt in Melbourne and told her everything. Would you believe it, she was delighted to hear about the baby and she doesn't blame me for *anything*. She's offered to help me! She'll come to Sydney when the baby's born and we'll return to Melbourne *together* – all *three* of us! I'll stay with her while I get back on my feet. She's agnostic, but respectful of others' beliefs. My being or not being a Catholic is of no importance to her. I'll turn thirty next week and for sure I'll never have another child, so, you see, I'm liberated at *last* from the sin and forgiveness merry-go-round! The church doesn't own me – I own *myself*! That's what the Reformation was all about, Katherine! Supremacy of scripture. The Bible open to individual interpretation. Your spiritual development in your *own* hands. Individuals standing alone with their conscience. I don't have to believe blindly. The Catholic Church doesn't embrace thinkers. Who's most likely to be saved? I'll *tell* you who!

A nerve inside Nola's eye will be pulsing like a light bulb about to blow as Agnes stares back at her in blank amazement:

Come on, Katherine. *You* know!

Words will fail Agnes. She has never had an exchange like this with anyone before. She will doubt she is hearing properly. Nola will take a step towards her:

You must have heard it a *million* times – the docile shepherd in the field tending his flock! And *why*, you might ask? I'll *tell* you why. Because he is easily indoctrinated and doesn't ask questions. Protestants are encouraged, not dissuaded from thinking. I don't want my baby to vegetate in a so-called 'good Catholic home'. She'll be taken care of by her own loving mother. I'll teach her to be strong enough – to stand alone with her conscience. Presuming I'm having a girl, of course!

Stunned, Agnes will manage a guarded response:

There's something in what you say – I suppose.

Nola will seize Agnes by the shoulders:

Why don't you keep your baby and come to Melbourne?! Or you can adopt it out and come on your own? I'll help you! You found work against all the odds before, so you can again. I'll lend you money to get started and you can pay me back when you can. Think about it. Send your mother a letter saying good riddance to bad rubbish. Or say nothing and walk away!

But Agnes and Nola are set to go in different directions. Agnes will be unable to change what she has set in motion. She is nineteen, homeless and without money and she cannot leave the city that defines her. To Agnes's ears, Nola's words are sacrilegious. She will walk away from her friend, declaring that she cannot listen to her any longer. Agnes's faith does not require her to think. She hadn't known about the Protestant Reformation and didn't need to. She will conclude that the devil has taken up residence in Nola's mind and, despite liking her immensely, will feel forced to avoid her. The Catholic Church will remain Agnes's anchor for years.

Gossip will reach Agnes's ears that Nola is becoming increasingly fearful that her baby might be taken away at the hospital against her will. Thus, her aunt will be flying into Sydney to collect her and as her niece's pregnancy is too advanced for her to fly back, they will drive to Melbourne by car together.

Standing outside the home with the other girls as they wave goodbye to Nola and her aunt, Agnes will feel a surge of warmth for her courageous friend. Interestingly, although she has pushed Nola's guidance to the very back of her mind, she will stop writing to her mother as further fiction seems meaningless.

* * *

A week after Nola's departure, Agnes wakes with a strange cramp in her stomach that seems to run into her back, and she tries to remember what she ate the night before. It is 6am and she has much to do. As well as laying out the priest's vestments she will have to change the water in the vases and rearrange the flowers on the altar in the chapel.

Her neighbour on the other side of the curtain is scratching off another day on the cardboard above her bed. Jenny's body might be marooned next door, but her heart is home in Cairns. Although they only speak in passing, Agnes knows the name of her parents, aunts, uncles and brothers, along with those of a Siamese cat and Dalmatian dog. Parcels stuffed with goodies have arrived for her each week from up north. She appears continually homesick. Agnes waits until she sees her slouching past her bed to the bathroom and hisses:

Jenny? Did we have rissoles last night?

What? Well, yes, think so, and – don't you remember – apple crumble with cream to follow?

Agnes observes Jenny struggling out of excessive modesty not to look at Agnes's bare body, for she has taken off her nightdress in order to examine her stomach. Agnes says:

I'm feeling sick. A pain like a vice is squeezing my insides.

Jenny frowns slightly:

You might be going into labour. Have a look and see if the bump has dropped. When's it due? If it's true you're in labour, you lucky thing, you'll be out of here in no time:

Agnes tells Jenny she thinks she has two weeks to go and begs her not to tell anyone. She wants to leave it as long as possible, she explains, so she doesn't have to hang around the hospital too long before the birth.

Jenny puts her finger to her lips and crosses her heart, before vanishing to the shower room.

However, Agnes now suspects that, by the end of the day, she will probably find herself packed off to hospital. She has deluded herself into thinking the home won't be able to cope without her, even though Nola had warned her that nobody was indispensable. Nola's salutary words return:

My dear Katherine, another girl will take over your job, arrange the vestments and fluff up the flowers. They come and go from here like products on an assembly line!

The truth is that, unlike Nola and Jenny, Agnes doesn't want to leave. She is attached to the home because it's the first time she has felt safe since leaving the house on the corner of Rose and Edmond Street at sixteen. Another spasm takes her breath away. It dawns on her that she is, assuredly, in labour. Her girl is on her way. Like Nola, she is convinced she is having a girl and that she will call her Rebecca – after Daphne du Maurier's novel.

The second contraction will arrive conveniently – exactly an hour after the first one – just as she finishes preparing the vestments. She will be doubled over in pain when she hears Father Dominic's motorbike pull up outside, but she will make it through Mass, seated in her usual spot, beseeching God to guide her through the hours ahead.

When she feels another contraction coming, it will be easier than she thought to walk out of the office and away from her duties. Soon, very soon, someone will take over her desk. She will go to the laundry to steam-iron her blue wool dressing gown and, when the contractions are five minutes apart, she will shower and walk back to the office to ask Sister Ambrosia to ring the ambulance. She considers it demeaning the way the St Anthony's girls have to arrive at the hospital dressed for bed, but this will be no time for rebellion.

The sun will be setting as she waits in the garden outside the tower for the ambulance. Shafts of golden rays will illuminate the textures and imperfections in the cement surface of the path, a halo will surround the reaching arms of the jacaranda tree, and a shimmering light will glance off the raised hair on the back of a glossy black cat which, frightened by a barking dog outside the gate, will speed to safety up a gum tree. Streamers of thick clouds will be increasingly tinted pink and violet. Elated by the beauty of the sunset, an imaginary Hallelujah will fill her ears as darkness descends. She will walk hand in hand with little Annie to the ambulance. She will hand the driver her brown suitcase and then ease herself onto the front seat.

After the months of near hibernation, she will be startled by the neon lights and billboards on the Parramatta Road and, in an attempt to break the silence, she will venture a question:

Where is the driver we normally have?

He will tell her that he is a replacement driver and that there has been an accident along the Parramatta Road and that all the ambulances from Croydon are busy. Because of this accident, nothing will go to plan. She will not be spirited into the back of the hospital as is the usual clandestine way for the unwed girls to enter. The unfamiliar driver will double-park and dump her on the side of the road outside the main entrance. Cars will be speeding dangerously close. She will want to run away but know that, with the contractions bearing down, she will need to hurry.

She will be directed to a noisy waiting room where, clad in her dressing gown and slippers, her telltale belly exposed to public view, she stands out like a neon sign. It will be what makes it easy for Sister Angela – a beanpole of a nun with a spidery scar on the side of her face – to recognise her:

You must be Katherine! Sister Wilfred phoned and asked me to look out for you. She was worried when she saw the unfamiliar ambulance driver that something might go wrong. I *do* apologise for the circumstances of your arrival.

Overjoyed to be claimed, Agnes will wobble along the polished linoleum with the giant nun's arm linking hers.

I am upturned onto a trolley and buffeted from one nurse to another in preparation for the birth. The blurred rush of faces and bright lights feels like being back on the Parramatta Road. Someone shaves my pubic hair, there is an enema, a stint on the toilet, a soapy all-over sponge and then they all disappear. I focus on the familiar smell of a bar of Palmolive soap a nurse gave me to hold and forgot to take back. It looks like amber. I am alone in a windowless white tiled room. The only light seeps in from the glass panel above the door. I panic in enclosed spaces. I can't see. The room swirls around me. I sink my nails into the soap and press it against my cheek. I hear myself praying aloud:

Lord – I feel forsaken – like you did in the Garden of Gethsemane. Please hear my prayer and comfort me.

An Italian woman is screaming 'Mama Mia!' at the top of her lungs as she struggles to give birth. The pain in my back is intense. I want to scream too, but when I open my mouth, nothing comes out. I feel like I'm drifting away, locked in a silent straitjacket. I feel myself sink into a restless daze. I'm back in Lennox Street, a day or two after the electrocution, shaken by the bloodcurdling cries of Paul's mother outside our house. Neighbours tell her my mother has left the country, but she pushes them aside: Madge Keen should be in jail! Her negligence killed my son! You're to blame, Madge Keen! I know you're in there – you bloody coward!

They drag her away from our door, but she keeps coming back.

The judge in the nightmare prepares to pass judgement.

I'm locked in a struggle for a voice that never comes.

The impertinent girl's silence is proof of guilt.

The next contraction shakes my whole body. My insides are on fire, yet outside I feel cold.

I see a nurse beside me through the haze. They keep coming and checking between my legs with a bright light. I hear someone speak: She's only nineteen. Never utters a sound. Lovely face and beautiful red hair. She's a saint. Wish we had a few more like that in here.

More blurred faces pop their heads in to catch a glimpse of the modern miracle – the silent angel smiling in her distress. I don't know if I should be proud or ashamed. I have never felt such despair. I long to cry out like the others, but my throat is clamped shut.

I'm blinded by a powerful light. I close my eyes and hear my father slurring in my ear. He smells of whisky. I feel his dribbles on my back, but I never wake up. I stay asleep. The face that hovers over me breaks into tiny pieces like an exploding jigsaw puzzle. Uncle Parry smirks as he holds up the stump of his missing finger, squeezing a sultana eye in a lurid wink. Posturing Charles has joined the parade. A voice inside me whispers – they're all the same man… they're all the same man. I'm lost in a labyrinth of stained bathrooms. My mother and aunt are throwing children into a furnace. I'm afraid I will be next.

A crowd of gowned bodies with surgical-masked faces burst into the room. The sour smell of whisky on my father's breath is drowned in an all-pervasive wave of antiseptic. A mask is put over my nose. My legs are yanked into straps. I am overtaken by a powerful contraction which tears through me. A female voice says: Not yet… resist pushing, dear.

Obediently, I clamp my muscles against the urge. There is a volcano erupting in my guts. I am being split down the middle. The voice is louder: Now push!

I tell her I can't do it – finding my voice at last. She is holding my hand and I can smell the Palmolive soap:

Let's do it together – one, two, three. Now, push.

I push with all my might.

And again, child, push again.

This time I feel the baby's body slide out. A little later I hear a distinctive cry. The soft voice tells me it is a little girl. I feel my eyes fill with tears. I ask if

I can see her but am told 'Not till tomorrow'. I object but am told to sleep by a hypnotic voice that hovers behind me.

I give up.

* * *

Agnes wakes with an incredible thirst. She finds herself in a bed parked in a corridor with people walking backwards and forwards – as if she has been left at the side of a footpath.

She is terrified she will be recognised by someone and all her efforts at concealment will be for nought. A middle-aged nun is looking at her from under thick eyebrows – like tiny hedges. The nun slides a metal extension out from a contraption at the side of the bed on to which she places a little tray with a glass and jug of water. She instructs curtly:

Take these tablets. They will dry up your milk.

I don't want to take them! I'll give the milk to my baby!

The nun instructs her that this is not allowed.

But she's my baby! I just gave birth to her! It's my sacred right to nourish her. And could you *please* bring her to me and get me out of this corridor and into a room?!

Agnes watches the muscles around the nun's small, mean mouth tighten. The nun says:

You have forgotten your position. These are the rules. Unless you take the medication, you will never see your baby.

Stunned, Agnes watches the woman's white habit swish like a breaking wave around her legs as she disappears at a brisk pace down the hall. The euphoria of giving birth instantly tips into dejection. There is no buzzer or bell. No ways or means to contact anyone. She sinks down in the bed, pulls the sheet over her head, and weeps soft tears.

When she emerges, the shrewd eyes lurking under the little hedge are back. The voice is as brusque as ever:

Well? What do you want to do? Do you want to see your baby or not?

Agnes meekly swallows the pills in one gulp and drinks the whole jug of water.

But, when she finally holds Rebecca Lea in her arms, all resentment disappears. She kisses her baby and calls her by her name. She loves the smell of her. She examines her arms, fingers, legs, feet and toes. She is perfect. She is relieved to see she doesn't have her mother's red hair and thus the inevitable freckles the sun will bring – a hopeless colouring for the harsh Australian climate. She sings to Rebecca as she feeds her with a bottle. Then a young, jolly nurse comes to spirit her baby away just before the visiting hour. Fearful of being recognised as the throng of visitors surge past her in the corridor, Agnes, once again, pulls the sheet over her head.

She wakes the following morning, her head still under the sheet, to find she has been wheeled into an airy room where she is overjoyed to see Dawn, who is smiling at her from the bed alongside. Dawn apparently went into labour a day ahead of her and has had a baby boy. Happy, too, to discover her suitcase in the wardrobe, Agnes unfolds the pretty nightdress with its bodice of embroidered flowers, especially prepared for the hospital, and heads into the bathroom with the Palmolive soap, which has resided under her pillow like a talisman. She lathers body and hair in it, digging deep into her scalp to banish the dark hours alone in the labour room. After the early morning bed-baths administered by a clumsy nurse in the passageway, she luxuriates in the feel of hot running water. She notices her nipples have turned darker and that she has stretch marks on her stomach. She towels herself down and sits in a chair on the balcony outside the room to dry her hair in the sun.

The advancing sound of the food trolley is heaven to her ears, and she gets up to intercept it. She is starving, for when she was parked in the corridor, it had passed her by several times without stopping because, fearful of being recognised by anyone who might know her family, she had kept the sheet over her head. Scrambled eggs on toast have never tasted so good and she sips a cup of strong, hot tea with delight.

Visiting hour arrives, and Agnes is touched by the love between Dawn's parents. As one speaks, the other looks on with affectionate interest. The father is tall, the mother short, and they joke about the difference in their height all the time. And they look so young. Jim, the father, has a mass of brown curly hair and a boyish grin. Dawn tells Agnes that her dad grew a moustache so that his clients would take him seriously. The mother has big blue eyes, full cheeks, and a dimple in her chin just like Dawn. Her upper lip is scarred from surgery to repair a hair lip, which slightly affects the way she speaks. Agnes learns that they recently left their jobs as chefs to run a dry cleaner's business not far from the hospital, and that they make a detour every morning to see their daughter, and baby Tom, on the way to work.

When the warm-hearted couple see Agnes all alone, they ask her what they can bring her; Agnes can't think of anything.

Today, when Agnes and Dawn are just finishing lunch, Dawn's parents arrive with a dress shrouded in a plastic cover for Dawn to wear back to St Anthony's tomorrow with her baby. Agnes is so engrossed in a *Woman's Weekly* that Dawn's mother has brought in for her, she doesn't even notice the couple's departure and reappearance:

And here is milady's dessert!

With this announcement, Jim is handing Agnes a double ice cream in a cone:

I hope you like chocolate and vanilla. It's Dawn's favourite. We didn't think to ask you before we left, so just got two the same.

Agnes looks down at the brown and white scoops sitting side by side on the top of the cone and feels a giant lump spring into her throat. She has to stare out of the window to stop herself from crying. Dawn's mother's eyes are glowing like sapphires, her wild hair caught at the sides of her head in bunches like a little girl. For some reason, she unexpectedly bends over and kisses Agnes's forehead.

Agnes buries her tongue in the chocolate side of the cone in an attempt to ward off the swelling emotion in her chest, but to no avail. She hears herself crying uncontrollably – deep, primordial sobs. Distress that harks all the way to the annual school prize-giving. Back to the two seats she would reserve in the hall for her parents that always remained empty. Her whole body is shaking, and she drops the cone on the floor:

I'm so sorry… I'm so sorry…

She tries to explain herself but can't seem to get beyond 'sorry'. Jim is putting his arm around her shoulder and Janet is wiping her face with a handkerchief:

You cry all you like, little darling. Having a baby releases hormones that makes a girl emotional. It's normal. Our Dawn's done her fair share of blubbering and I made a complete fool of myself when she was born. Jim's going to get you another ice cream. You can choose the flavour this time.

She speaks with a sweetness that only makes it worse. But Agnes manages to request a strawberry and passionfruit cone – her favourite.

Coming right up!

Jim shoots her a cheeky smile and goes out of the door, his palm open like a waiter.

* * *

The cloth bag containing *Black Beauty* on her bedside table heralds the arrival of Annie and Jenny when Agnes emerges from the shower. They have come to accompany her back to St Anthony's. She is overjoyed to see them as she has occupied a dark place since Dawn's departure the day before. The nun with the hedge eyebrows, as nice as pie while Dawn and her parents were around, has turned on Agnes since they left, ordering her to stay in bed. Agnes asks:

Sister – if I *have* to stay in bed, could you bring my baby to me?

The response floors her:

You brazen hussy! I give the orders around here, not *you*! Stew in your sin, you young floozy! Deprivation is the only way the likes of you will ever learn self-control!

In the labour ward, when the Italian woman was screaming, Agnes had been considered the height of saintly decorum. Now she is a brazen hussy. The ugly nun's vicious attack has triggered a bout of high-pitched ringing in her ears and her distress will only deepen when she discovers Jenny and Annie have forgotten to bring her clothes. The brown paper parcel they offer her contains only the yellow jumpsuit and shawl she had knitted in preparation for the baby. The smart black suit she had planned to wear back to the home has been left behind.

Jenny is mortified:

Oh, I'm so sorry, Katherine! What about your gorgeous blue dressing gown?

I'm *not* going back in a dressing gown! I need my suit and a pair of shoes. My slippers have completely disappeared, and I can't leave here barefooted. I have long imagined a dignified exit from this awful place and *that's* what I'll have. You *have* to go back and pick them up!

They will be there and back within the hour, and Agnes will just about manage to wriggle in to the skirt without doing up the zipper. She has not realised she has such a belly. The weight isn't just around her waist – her thighs are like tree trunks. She will squeeze oversized breasts into a black polo-neck jumper that makes her look like Jayne Mansfield.

Fortunately, the long, loose suit jacket will cover her bulges and she will slip stockinged feet into a pair of black high heels. Twisting her hair into a neat bun, she will feel sufficiently dignified to confront the world outside.

Bidding the nurses farewell, head held high, baby Rebecca settled snuggly in her arms, her two heavily pregnant companions at her side, Agnes will leave the building.

* * *

I haven't prepared myself for the strong attachment I feel for my daughter. With each passing day it becomes harder and harder to think of parting from her. My duties in the home over, I go to the nursery at my leisure to bathe her, feed her and carry her around. I love watching her little legs bounce when I put her on a rug in the sun. I take endless photos of her and get the girls in the nursery to take photos of us both, so I will always remember these moments spent together. I try to think of ways I might keep her. But I have hostile, unpredictable parents, no home, no job, no career like Nola. I have no money and my absence has been spliced to a fictional story. How can I be a fit mother when I don't even feel like a fit person? If I give her up, little Rebecca will be loved and cherished by a mother who can't have her own baby. I shall be complying with the prophesy in the sacristy at St Patrick's Church. It is a tale foretold.

But regardless of my reasoning, my attachment to Rebecca only strengthens. I find myself haunting her crib at night. I love the way she sinks her head into my neck and snuffles when I squeeze her tight. I put off leaving her. I spend as much time as I can with her. I can't think of anything but her. My life has changed. Yet I am gently being edged towards the signing away. I know I am not unique. I have seen Sister Wilfred steer many a conflicted girl towards the adoption papers. She never forces anyone. She invites me to her office. I hear myself agree with her that it is for the best. The prevaricating was becoming intolerable and so I comply. I sign the papers with a broken heart. I feel like death.

The day arrives. I can see my baby's new parents pull up in a white Ford. It is midday. I watch them from the same balcony from which I watched Charles arrive that fateful Sunday. From that distance, I can't distinguish their features. They are, perhaps, in their mid-twenties, the rest I don't remember. Perhaps the new mother is wearing a blue hat.

Earlier that morning, before dressing my baby for the last time, I had carried her in a pink blanket to the little church where I mounted the red carpeted steps to the altar. Her tiny eyelids were heavy with sleep as she lay in my arms. Pink and white carnations entwined in maidenhair fern quivered above us. I laid Rebecca down. Down in front of the tabernacle. Cradled between vases of sweet pea blooms. I begged the Sacred Presence to guide my darling girl through the years I would never know her.

I watch them carry Rebecca Lea out of my life forever. I half know that I'm walking away from the one thing that is meaningful and valuable. That I am passing back into a shallow world. But, as usual, the forces are assembled against me, and I am vanquished.

25

THE HOMECOMING

It is a lovely, bright spring morning without a cloud in the sky. Agnes's footsteps reverberate in her ears as she drags her sluggish feet to Croydon railway station – hardly noticing the weight of her suitcase. She purchases a one-way ticket to Central Station and boards the train in a dream.

As Agnes glances at her watch, she realises that when the Western City train pulls into Central Station, she will have to rush if she is to meet her mother on time. The platforms around her looks unfamiliar, and she takes the stairs two at a time – arriving at a crossroad of unfamiliar underground directions. She can't find her way. She runs past platform entrances and down a labyrinth of corridors, dashing blindly, having to backtrack, panicking that not giving herself enough time will expose the months of careful deception.

Nerves at the prospect of seeing her mother affect her ability to listen to directions from a station guard. She finds herself swept along a crowded enclosed walkway. She is waiting for an exit that never comes and then, at the very end, like Alice through the looking glass, she bursts into the vault-roofed concourse of the main station. A brass clock, encased in a pagoda-shaped adornment, stands at the pinnacle. Twisted spherical plaster heads on either side resemble faceless bulls, infusing strength into frivolity. Drenched in overhead light from the vast glass roof, the three-storey stone structure of Central Station never fails to impress with its grandeur.

She stands in front of the huge railway indicator board, where she has arranged to meet her mother. The wooden slats with their printed destinations and station stops are rotating, along with the departure time and platform numbers. Agnes counts the twenty-two vertical slats in the frame to try and stay calm. She knows why the arrivals and destination board is familiar: it is the backdrop to a photo on the front page of an old *Sydney Morning Herald*, hidden in her mother's knitting bag. The picture is of Patricia Murphy, her mother's long-time nemesis, with her Yankee officer. They are locked in a farewell embrace. Forever to be regurgitated with envious bile is Patricia's Dorothy Lamour crêpe evening dress – designed with a bare midriff and worn beneath a leopard skin fur coat. That, together with the Ferragamo wedge evening shoes in gold kid with red satin that complete the ravishing outfit, will probably remain tattooed in Agnes's brain forever. The couple have been captured in time, along with other Australian servicemen taking leave of loved ones. Embarking on the first stage of a train journey to join army operations in Borneo against the Japanese.

Even now, as Agnes tries to calm down, she hopes that with the conversion of the cottage at the farm into a comfortable home, her mother's bitterness about other women's outfits and possessions will have diminished. She remains, despite herself, plagued with such a crippling responsibility for her mother's well-being that, until she can find a way of making her happy, she knows she will never be free of her.

The Roman numerals on the great clock are showing five minutes to the proposed meeting time. The arrival of the Melbourne train is announced on the loudspeaker. Still no sign of her mother. It occurs to her that her cover will be blown if she finds her waiting under the arrivals board before the train gets in and so she rushes down the concourse in search of the correct platform. Luckily there is no ticket collector at the gate. She slips through a side exit and smiles at a uniformed man who is trying to pretend he isn't eyeing her full breasts in the tight jumper. She has forgotten that in the heat of the moment she had taken off the jacket that covers her bosomy curves. Mortified by the lecherous look, she quickly slips it back on.

Aware of her attempt at modesty, he nods with a smirk when she asks him if the train just pulling in is the Melbourne train. She still feels his eyes boring into her as she wobbles down the platform in her black high heels.

Nearing the last carriages, with passengers already flooding off the stationary train onto the platform, she turns and tries to walk sedately to the exit gate – as if she has just alighted. The timing is perfect and, for once, she is glad her mother is always late. Then she spots her. Madge is striding into the enormous space from the George Street entrance.

Crushed as she is in the tightly packed crowd, Agnes remains invisible to Madge. As her mother draws closer, Agnes is struck by how plastic and unnatural she looks – the horns of her bouffant echoing the plucked curve of her arched eyebrows. This odd effect makes her look slightly demented, and her briskly determined stride only diminishes the allure of the stylish pink linen dress she wears. To Agnes, her mother's face appears to be contracting and stretching into the ugly image of a painted witch as she walks. She stares in horrified amazement, longing for the apparition to disappear.

And then, like magic, her mother's beauty is suddenly resurrected. Agnes fleetingly wonders whether what she was just glimpsing was the hidden inner psyche that Nola had described? Hadn't her friend insisted that Agnes should try to analyse what she sees and hears? But then how could Nola know that analytical thought was as alien to Agnes as the whereabouts of Upper Mongolia:

Hey Mummy! I'm over here!

I see my mother swing her head in line with my voice. Her recognition evokes a look of annoyance in my direction that makes me shrink. I feel instantly diminished. We don't run into one another's arms, as many new arrivals from the Melbourne train are doing. My mother stops short to survey my appearance. All my superlatives, all my 'missing yous', the legions of kiss crosses running off the pages of my fabricated letters, are for nothing. I might not have expected a hero's welcome but, at the very least, I had hoped for an affectionate one. Although nothing I imagine ever happens, I still carry on like the ripe idiot I am – hoping for change. Her first utterance proves she is a long way from showing me an even basic level of civility: 'What have you done to your hair?' I reply: 'Nothing, I just haven't cut it. I'm going to grow it long. Not a crime, is it?' It is when her critical eyes start boring into my body that I lose composure. I hate the silly, childish petulance simply being in her presence provokes in me. Then she says: 'You've got very thick around the middle and very bosomy while you've been away.' I feel myself blanche. I hadn't anticipated the change in my body. Signing the adoption papers and losing Rebecca Lea have consumed me completely. My mother metamorphoses into the old familiar monster with the burning coal eyes. Why did I bother to protect this mean, slothful bitch from any gossip? What does it matter if they all know I got pregnant out of wedlock? My father is illegitimate, and no one died! How important is all this reputation stuff? Perhaps it's a Catholic Church tactic to swell their ranks? Perhaps Nola had a point. A turmoil of truth and fury rises in me, exactly like the day I expelled my uncensored feelings onto my father: 'Oh, God – you, stupid, ridiculous woman!' I have exploded. I have taken the lid off, and I no longer care.

She is staring at me, her face frozen. I am shouting at the top of my voice: 'There WAS no governess job! I've just come from St Anthony's! A home for unwed mothers! I had a baby!'

I am screaming and sobbing and am aware that everyone can hear me, but I don't care. I want to strangle the cold, heartless bitch right there on the concourse. Normally, there's no way I can shut her up, but this time I appear to have succeeded. For once, the surprise exhibited in the arched eyebrows has turned into eye-popping shock. I feel gratified. I want to shock her into her grave.

The truth spills out of me in torrents. I tell her I invented everything. Invented it all so she could impress her vapid friends. I tell her that Sister Wilfred's sister redirected the mail between us. I tell her my beautiful little girl was taken away from me that very morning. I scream it in her face.

I am aware that people are stopping to look at me, but I am so overcome with emotion I don't care. A man with a handlebar moustache asks the uncaring woman who is my mother if I am alright. She puts on her best tragic look and tells him that I have received some bad news and will feel better in a minute. Then she grabs my arm and pulls me away from the crowd. Her fierce expression warns those who remain concerned to keep their distance. Her fingers are pinching into my arm. She grabs my suitcase, dragging me to a bench under one of the sandstone arches on the opposite side of the concourse where we can be alone and safe from prying eyes.

She hisses into my face: Stop this nonsense immediately! You sound like a raving maniac! STOP making such a scene! Someone should cut that loose tongue out of your throat!

I can only stare at her. It's crazy to think how long I went on expecting from her what was beyond her nature. Assailed by inconsolable disappointment, I slump over the bench with my head in my hands and sob my heart out. I have protected her for nothing. All the attention to detail in the letters, the enthusiasm with which I imagined her telling her friends, my huge outpouring of love and energy towards her, would bear no fruit. I had battled to preserve what didn't exist. It was all pie in the sky. Stupid dreams and silly fantasies. All imagined. None of it real.

But a plan has obviously formed in her twisted brain, for, as we walk towards the car, she puts her hand on my shoulder – an infinitesimally small gesture of affection that makes me sick with remorse. I hear myself apologising to her: 'I'm sorry for the outburst, Mummy. You know I never do that sort of thing. Please don't be angry with me.'

'Well,' she replies, 'you've certainly made up for lost time. I never SAW such a performance!' I can't really read the expression in her eyes when she says: 'Let's have a pleasant drive home – without any more of this talk. You never fail to get me churned up. It's hurtful, Agnes. Especially after the preparations I've made for your homecoming. I've put nice fresh sheets on your bed, bought sirloin steak, beans and baby carrots for you. I've even made your favourite chocolate blancmange – and this is the way you treat me.'

She sounds like a temperamental girl who has just been stood up on a date. And then it comes. The inevitable threat: 'Just as well your father is away in Adelaide. It's better he doesn't know ANY of this. Don't push me into having to tell him how you've dishonoured us. Be warned Agnes – this is one matter that is to remain a secret forever.'

* * *

Agnes has no memory of the drive from Central Railway Station out through the western suburbs. She must have drawn into herself and played dead like a possum when it is confronted by a predator. She is jolted into the present when the car pulls up outside the local store and Madge sends her on an errand:

Darling, run in and buy me a carton of Capstans. The store is the only place that carries them and I'm nearly out.

She is cooing in the trying-to-be-nice baby tone she always adopts to get things she wants.

Agnes readily agrees and jumps out of the car, painfully eager to make amends. They have mainly travelled in silence, and she has become increasingly furious with herself for breaking down and ruining everything. Another order comes:

And ask Maria if there's any mail!

Madge has shouted through the open driver's window. It is the imperial command of an Empress and brooks no questioning. Agnes is now firmly back on the staff. As she walks into the shop, the non-existent celebration at Central Station showers down like bright confetti when Giuseppe and Maria recognise her:

It's Agnes! How lovely to *see* you!

Maria is squealing with delight as Agnes gulps down the lump in her throat, struggling not to cry when each of them kisses her on both cheeks. She moves away from the window so that her mother won't see the fuss the Italian proprietors are making of her:

Look, Giuseppe – how gorgeous she's grown! Agnes, you've turned into such a beauty!

Agnes's face feels hot. She knows she must be blushing:

I'm nineteen now.

She has blurted this out like a small child. Battling an urge to apologise for the events that carried her away from this place against her will, she can only stand before them. Her bewilderment must be showing, for Giuseppe says:

Leave the girl alone, Maria. Can't you see you're embarrassing her?

But Maria is curious:

We wondered what happened to you. It's not like you to just disappear without saying a word. One day you were here and the next day you'd vanished. Nobody knew anything about you. Your parents never mentioned you. You can't imagine how happy we were when your letters started arriving from Victoria. Your mother said you were working for a rich family in a fine house looking after children. We knew you were destined for great things. How was it?

Agnes pulls herself together with difficulty:

It was a real adventure. The people were kind, and it was interesting to see how they run the place – they have Santa Gertrudos cattle, and they grow fruit – and even grapes – on the irrigated land that borders the Murray River. That's why they call Mildura the Mediterranean of the outback.

She feels horribly insincere repeating the slogan, repeating the fabrication – deceiving a couple as sincere as Maria and Giuseppe. The sharp toot of an impatient car horn cuts into their exchange, and Maria glances at the street and says:

Maybe she wants something else?

Agnes shrugs and opens the wire door to look out. Her mother's impatient mask is framed in the driver's window. Madge yells:

Come on! What on earth are you doing? I'm dying to get home and have a cup of tea!

Agnes feels instantly ashamed of her mother's rude behaviour, and quickly hands over some of her social security money for the cigarettes. Previously, she had always put things on account, but senses that it would be better to pay up front, for she has noticed Maria look at her husband in that way people do around her mother. It is about the debts. Though she knows her mother is dishonest, she cannot bear to see it acknowledged in the eyes of others. She intuits they have probably cut off Madge's credit and wonders how much her mother owes. But she manages to resist the crazy temptation to use the rest of her own money to pay it all off. She takes the change from Maria quickly, without looking at it, and runs back to the car.

Madge tosses the cigarette carton nonchalantly onto the back seat. The great preacher of good manners has none herself. She says:

Now I've got my own transport, I don't bother shopping at the store. She's a nasty piece of work, that Maria. She had the audacity to tell the neighbours I hadn't paid my bill when she knew all along your father had paid her husband. I don't need to shop with ignorant Sicilian peasants like them. I shop in Camden and Liverpool now, where I'm spoilt for choice.

Her stream of bile is stemmed, however, when Maria suddenly knocks on Agnes's window and hands her the mail. Madge looks the other way. The tension between the women is palpable. Neither speaks nor acknowledges the other. In fact, Maria is lucky to have her hand out of the window when Madge speeds off like a racing driver leaving the pit, narrowly missing running over the shopkeeper's foot.

Agnes sees that her last letter to her mother is on the top of the pile – a perfunctory short note, written after the urge to impress her died with Nola's departure. Seeing her own handwriting makes her feel profoundly sad. She is missing St Anthony's home already.

At the farm, Agnes jumps out to open the gate, infected by Madge's anxious haste to rush home to do nothing. She notices the gate is still pivoted on the upturned champagne bottle Uncle Parry sank into the ground during the first flush of building work. It must have rained the day before, as murky puddles are dotted along the dirt road. A new metal-tubed bridge has been erected in the lowest dip of the road, where cars used to get bogged down in heavy rain. Although the sun is shining, the place feels to Agnes as if it is submerged under a cloud.

While the front of the old timber cottage remains the same, the back has been transformed into an American ranch-style house. Intrigued, Agnes opens a further gate in a sturdy fence that encloses Madge's new garden. A golden Labrador runs across the lawn, barking and wagging its tail frantically:

Don't let him jump up on you, Agnes! His paws are all dirty!

Madge is scrutinising her daughter's every movement like a policeman with a suspect under surveillance. The dog, having initially run back to his kennel, has now returned with a ball in his mouth and is snorting and pushing it into her skirt. Agnes pulls it out of his jaws and throws it. A playful tug of war between the two is underway when Madge calls out:

Don't do that! You'll pull one of his teeth out!

But this unexpected friendly, boisterous presence has cheered Agnes considerably:

When did you get him?! What's his name?!

Madge sighs: His name's Sunny. Don't you remember? He sat by your bed when you were sick. He used to come in every morning and look up at you and wag his tail.

Agnes is floored that she has no memory of this:

No – I don't remember anything. It's all a blur. I only remember Ben's children asking their father if I was going to die:

Well, you were delirious. The doctor blamed us for letting you get run down, but I told him you wouldn't let us help you. You could have come here any time, Agnes. No one was stopping you. But, instead, you preferred gallivanting around with that boyfriend:

But you told me Daddy didn't *want* to see me and I was warned by Parry not to ring you!

Madge's eyes narrow:

Listen to me and listen carefully. I don't need any more of your smart talk. You were always welcome here. I don't know where or why you dream up these silly stories.

As Agnes has started to doubt herself, she decides to steer conversation away from the past. To break the deteriorating mood, she mutters something about wanting to see all the changes to the house. Her mother elects to do escort duty. It is hard to associate the extensive upgrade with the original downbeat shack once occupied by the Aborigine who went walkabout. A row of steps leads up to a new back door, and her mother directs her to an entrance at the side, with a laundry, storage area and new bathroom.

Agnes takes off her shoes as ordered, moving forward in stocking feet along a line of different coloured towels, past an open-plan kitchen with a bar top, and into a spacious new living room with a wall of fixed glass. This frames a full panorama to the stables, where Agnes can see horses grazing in the paddocks, and then the polo field beyond. The change is so striking she cannot help but gasp in admiration:

You must be so happy! It's so full of light! And that view!

She surveys the enlarged space for details. The old mahogany dining table with the pineapple-shaped legs, and the new chairs Grandma replaced after the Mack debacle, is the only surviving furniture from the corner of Rose and Edmond Street. The storm-crazed horses, along with the accompanying teardrop vases below, don't appear to have survived the move.

She notices, next, that an en-suite bathroom and mirrored vanity unit off the new 'his and hers' bedroom can also be accessed from the living room:

Stop! *Don't* go any further!

Madge has dropped dramatically to her knees, her bouffant in imminent danger as she directs Agnes's stocking feet forward one step at a time along a line of protective towels – like an orthopaedic nurse. Together, mother and daughter slowly progress over the new beige living room carpet before the step up into the old part of the cottage. These actions are beyond absurd as Agnes has already obediently left her shoes at the back door. Her mother has always been domineering, but this latest incarnation as house-proud wife is ludicrous.

Yet another towel is spread on one of the single beds in the small front bedroom – the one by the window where Agnes lay fighting for her life after collapsing in Sydney. She gazes through the window and sees again the rose bushes either side of the front path – the path along which she walked when she took her injured self out of the gate to escape her utterly indifferent parents. She tries, unsuccessfully, to remember if the roses were in bloom that night or not. On this early spring afternoon, buds and flowers in every colour proliferate from every stem. It is October 1961, three weeks since Rebecca Lea was born on 29th September – and seven years before her father's early death in 1968.

Now she notices that every available surface in the house is adorned with arrangements of roses. Agnes picks up the small vase of blooms on her bedside table and closes her eyes to savour their delicate scent. When she turns around, she is astonished to see her mother has opened her suitcase. She can tell from Madge's demeanour that everything pales into insignificance beside the allure of the contents. Her mother's eyes are riveted to the evidence behind the Dunroven fiction. She is in the act of plunging her hands deep into the case's contents and has already pulled out the two maternity smocks, now ragged after intensive use. Impatient, she upturns the case and tips the entire contents onto the towel on the bed.

Agnes feels horribly self-conscious, seeing her humble possessions laid bare. Now her mother is holding up the stained blue dressing gown for a second or two, dismissing it to quickly direct her attention to the maternity bras. Having had three children herself, they can't have been a novelty, but they make the story of the birth of her only grandchild concrete. Agnes spots the folder of photographs on the bedspread, and quietly hands it over to her mother.

The photos of Rebecca Lea are flicked through without comment, and Agnes imagines that this is how a humble housemaid might feel as she shares something of a personal nature with her employer. This house, new as it is, remains devoid of any photos of family because – in the true sense of the word – they are *not* one. She feels compelled to speak:

I knitted that shawl in the photos. And the white cardigan. She wore them this morning. To meet her new parents.

Tears suddenly sting in Agnes's eyes. It's all so terribly recent, but here, watching this woman gleefully invade her privacy, it already seems so dreamlike and dreadful.

Madge is now busy flicking through Agnes's sketchbook. Then Agnes sees her eyes dart towards the diary she had been keeping and panics:

Don't read that, please. It's personal. Put it *down*!

Agnes has spun across the room to reclaim it. Like a spoilt, recalcitrant child, her mother pouts, and puts it behind her back.

Give it back to me at *once*!

Agnes wrenches it out of her mother's hand with an uncharacteristic fierceness:

Oh Agnes. How *nice* to be together again, isn't it? Just the *two* of us. I've *missed* you.

Curiosity apparently assuaged for the time being, Madge will show Agnes her new white Pyrex dishes decorated with blue cornflowers, the kind that can go from hotplate direct to table. She is cooing at her daughter now, her tone utterly altered. Despite herself – and despite all her better judgement – her mother's suddenly ameliorative manner has a hypnotic effect on Agnes. Soon she will be mesmerised back into her old state of bringing a cup of tea to her bedside just as before, her mother sleepy eyed and still wearing nothing but the cultured pearls. But now, both wary and weary, and after devouring a ham and salad sandwich and drinking several cups of coffee, Agnes will snap out of the old, transitory delusion of maternal love and be desperate to escape her presence.

Obeying her mother's suggestion, she will go for a walk while Madge takes her customary after-lunch nap. She will put on a pair of her father's overalls, a pair of clean socks she finds in the laundry and will slip her feet into an old pair of her father's elastic-side riding boots. She will stride down to the stables, past the old barbecue where the extended family once cooked sausages in the happy stable-building days, past the row of poplar trees which are now taller than the stable roof. On she will go, further down the track to the polo field. The scar will still be visible in the trunk of a tall gum tree next to the field – the tree that Agnes hit with Ben's car when he was teaching her to drive. She will recall how she and Ben chewed gum to plug up the holes of a perforated radiator, constantly stopping to refill it with water all the way back to be repaired at a garage in Sydney. She will notice that the giant metal hotplate – where polo club members and their families used to cook lunches before the Sunday afternoon practice matches – is still in place behind the polo field. Then she will open the gate into the only wild, untamed area of the hundred acres Grandma purchased and will see that it remains uncleared – a superfluous, leftover area that few probably still venture into. Full of undulations, deep potholes, tall grasses, scattered clumps of trees, it will not feel like it belongs here. She will see glimpses of the creek through the wall of gums – the creek that runs along the full width of the property, creating a natural boundary – and she will reflect that a bandit could hide out there and never be seen:

I bang the ground with a stick to alert inquisitive snakes to keep their distance. I'm on the old path to the creek. On the right, I pass the overgrown track to a glade of stringy bark gums. They are covered in parasites and tangled vines. As a child, I imagined the glade inhabited by strange creatures. No longer a child, I still run past, feeling fear. I am entering a tunnel of strangely shaped trees,

361

covered in lichen, and where the sun never penetrates. My heart is beating so fast, I think it might jump out of my chest. Abruptly, I arrive at the clearing in the furthest corner of the block, where the creek forms a natural boundary. I have always imagined fairies dancing here – dancing under the tall trees that encircle the clearing as if in A Midsummer Night's Dream.

This is the only place with easy access to the water.

As I sit on the enormous fallen tree trunk, long embedded in the earth, and which acts as a retaining wall, a memory returns... before the inquisition at Rosemont... before jumping out of the moving car... before the forced rehabilitation in Maroubra.

I am fishing alongside my father. I see his line in the water before my eyes. I see myself wearing a swimming costume, leaning back on the trunk of a tall gum. I have struck a funny pin-up, film-star pose. I have a flimsy notion of once being photographed like that. I can see my white sandal falling off the back of my heel. It is odd because I have no memory of either parent ever taking a photo of me. And my mother cut me out of the one of the three of us I treasured. Me. Mother. Father. I should ask her why she did it. But what good would come from that? I am clutching at the dreamlike image of fishing in this creek with my father. I am trying to hold on to it because it is proof that I was living at the farm that summer. Was it summer? After I left school? My poor head rebels when I try and put such patchy memories together. Something is edging closer to me. An unseen presence. Ever since then, when the hot air cools at dusk and the birds call to each other, I feel shadowed. Shadowed by a presence in a bushland just like this.

I jump up. I am panicking. I cannot catch my breath. I run. And I keep running till I reach the gate. The late sun is hiding behind a cloud as I stride up the dirt road beside the polo field. Now I am on the slope leading to the stables and I can see my mother in the distance. She is bending over the old barbecue. My stomach sinks as I get closer. My suitcase is lying open on the ground with a petrol can beside it. I recognise the maternity smocks I made. They are bunched up amongst the weeds in the old fireplace. I hear myself scream as I run towards her:

No! No! Don't do it!

She knows I am shouting but does not raise her head. She strikes a match and, before I can reach her, throws it. As petrol and flame unite, she staggers backwards and falls. I run to her and lift her up. Her hair and eyebrows are heavily singed:

What do you think you're doing, throwing petrol on a fire!? You might have killed yourself!

She does not look at me. Perhaps she cannot look at me. I turn away from her and rush towards the fire to see what else she has destroyed. I see my diary pages twist and curl. My sketchbook, too, is now glowing red. She has scattered the photos of my baby randomly and I watch helplessly as bits of my child burn – a foot, a hand, the shawl, my smile, our faces close together – all disintegrating into silvery flakes.

I think of the newsreels of the Gestapo in Germany. The burning of books. Like my mother, they destroyed what they could not understand. And there are Rebecca's little yellow woollen booties – consumed in a gulp. And there is the edge of the envelope that contained a snippet of her hair. A rainbow of flames rises into the air. I can't save anything. The whole contents of the suitcase burnt. It's all gone. The ugly smell of destruction comes from deep in the earth. Comes from deep within my mother. She has eradicated all evidence of my crime against her warped family pride.

I scream my rage into her blackened face:
You bitch! You bloody, bloody BITCH!

PART FIVE

A wrong that cannot be repaired must be transcended.

Willy Brandt (at the Warsaw Memorial)

.

26
AUNT MARNIE REVISITED

Words have come to Agnes's rescue. Words that once turned their nose up at her. Words whose absence once relegated her to the dunce's corner. Words, the lack of which, had her occupying the lowest rung of existence. They have come back to her like manna from heaven. She has been scribbling in the Sydney apartment for weeks, fearful that, should she stop, her rekindled literacy will evaporate.

She stabs the returning words onto the page. She writes them in big letters. She inscribes them in a huge notepad because she fears to use her laptop in case of a technical hitch. The least distraction, after years of resistance, could sabotage her. Her hand flies over the notebook pages. Scrambled events start to unravel and take form. The biro she uses has wings and can barely keep up with her thoughts. It writes of things. Puzzling things. Dreamlike things. Distressing things. Things she has run away from all her life. All spills onto the page. Barely punctuated. No indications of speech or of who is speaking what or to whom. The outpouring throws up questions, but answers are few. And so, as she pauses to take stock of all she has written, it becomes suddenly urgent to see those who are still alive – who once bore witness to the events she is attempting to describe.

The rhythm at the Grantham Apartments rotates around her small space on the sixth floor. She feels sandwiched between check-ins and checkouts. She knows there are two white uniformed cleaning women at work around her. They are built like Russian discus throwers, and regularly flush out departing presences with a high-speed vacuum cleaner that sounds like the room in question is about to disconnect from the building. Soiled linen is replaced by neat, heavenly smelling piles of fresh snowy sheets and fluffy white towels. It surprises Agnes how light the two women are on their feet, for when not vacuuming they float as if weightless through the corridors in their soft shoes.

She is enjoying her stay. She suspects there isn't a better vantage point in the whole of Sydney from which to gaze upon the city's famous iconography. She thrills to overhear the gasps of delight when any new arrival flings open the balcony doors to view the wonders stretched out before them.

Each day she returns after a mid-morning break to find the discus throwers have spirited away the pile-up of takeaway cartons and wine bottles – detritus that she dares not attend to herself lest it distracts her from writing. The room is transformed after the maids' ministrations, and she luxuriates in the comfort.

Before ascending to her retreat in the sky, she usually exchanges a few words with Susie, the receptionist. The other day, Susie treated her to a close-up of a red robin and blue tit, one each side of a single twig, tattooed onto the flesh of her snowy white shoulder. The birds look oddly out of place without a garden setting, and she considers this could well be the way Susie views her, hidden away as she is – alone in the apartment all day.

Susie has replaced the green-eyeshadowed receptionist who Agnes thought of as a blonde Cleopatra. This new young woman is much more friendly, but the busy writer is conscious of resisting getting too chummy with anyone. She knows now that the least hint of rejection, or sudden change of mood, could detrimentally influence the urgent project upstairs. Her inner world requires her complete concentration. She walks on eggshells around herself. Be as temperamental as you like, she tells herself. This moment is *yours* and you don't need to explain anything. And you don't need to apologise to anyone. Yet, intriguingly, her powers of observation of the outside world remain acute.

King's Cross never goes to sleep. It is open around the clock. There is always a restaurant or corner shop where Agnes can grab a snack. Early morning hours remind her of films like *Taxi Driver, Mean Streets* and *Midnight Cowboy*. She is glad of an atmosphere where anything goes: streets full of tourists in costumes from other lands, office workers on a night out, heavily made-up transvestites – all false boobs and eyelashes – strutting their stuff. And the discreet – and not so discreet – sex workers on street corners and down the side alleys.

In the evenings she is often gifted with a 'second wind' – a surge of energy that has her scribbling with an even greater urgency, sometimes well into the early hours of the morning. There are desperate moments, too, but the solid sight of the brazenly lit Harry's Bar down at street level below remains a reliable comfort.

Today, from the apartment balcony, she notices a naval ship which has docked while she slept. The large grey amphibious form is crawling with sailors in white uniforms, some of whom stand in formation. There is a ceremony underway. She can hear the brass band as the Australian flag is raised over the ship. She thrills to the regimentation, to the order and discipline that, just like the reassuring girl at reception, seem these days to make her feel safer in her skin. She is forging a new relationship with Sydney. Also, she is alone here because she *chooses* to be, and not because she isn't wanted.

Her brother will arrive in a week. She decides that she must brace herself to see Aunt Marnie before he comes. After forty years, she wants to look her in the eye. This time she will not be ignored. But, at the mere thought of Marnie, the pain of the past resurges in waves, and Agnes wanders around the apartment like a caged animal, procrastinating about making the call. Then, abruptly, as if some outside force has compelled her, she picks up the mobile and dials the number.

* * *

Agnes walks down a steep drive and past an impeccably well-cut lawn. As she proceeds, she disperses a flock of tiny birds who are splashing around in an ornate stucco bird bath. As if scoffing at their frivolity, a kookaburra on a nearby overhead wire laughs his head off as she arrives at the entrance to Marnie's nursing home.

There are no gasps of joy when their eyes meet. She watches Marnie, searching her aging face for the girl she once was and immediately senses the old tension. With half her face frozen, Marnie seems even more inscrutable than ever. In her mind's eye, Agnes again sees her aunt let the newspaper disdainfully drop onto the green carpet on the day she first arrived to stay in the Maroubra house. She struggles to gain control of her thoughts. The woman marooned in the wheelchair seems frail. Marnie may be a former enemy, but it's still regrettable to see her in this state. Her speech is laboured:

Would you like some tea?

Yes. Let's have tea.

Agnes has replied quickly, glad of a chance to diffuse the atmosphere. Her aunt does not move:

Well… you'll notice, I'm not about to leap up and fill the kettle.

She is reminded of her aunt's ironic manner. A trait she once admired. As the other O'Connor women were sorely lacking in humour, Marnie's cutting wit could often thrill her. Agnes offers:

Leave it to me.

She has noticed a tea tray set on a high wall table. One end of this table is covered with framed photos. When she comes back from filling the kettle in the bathroom, and plugs it in to boil, she finds Marnie reaching out to retrieve a silver-framed picture of a man:

Remember him?

Her aunt has pronounced the question sharply – in a tone that smacks of accusation.

Oh – yes. It's Uncle Parry…

She is instantly revolted by the sight of her uncle's beady raisin eyes and the familiar sly smile. Marnie nods slowly:

Remember that expression? So typically Parry. He struggled with a horrible illness. We went to America for a cure, but nothing prolonged the years. He ended up in a wheelchair. And a pitiless deterioration to the end.

I'm so sorry to hear that.

You'll never know how fond he was of *you*.

Marnie has made this statement with slurred intensity. It is like a scene in a film when an older woman grudgingly forgives a younger one for a clandestine affair with her husband. And it further reminds her of the way her mother used to say: 'Your father loves you,' as if she would like to alter it.

As she observes Marnie stretching out her right arm to put the picture back into its place on the table, she senses an assertion of ownership. To overcome the distaste provoked by the image of her uncle, she excuses herself to use the loo.

Seated on the modified toilet, she surveys the shower opposite and the special equipment to manage bodily hygiene required by those confined to a wheelchair. It makes her aunt's predicament all the more real, and she feels a pang of sympathy for her. But what is she thinking? This visit isn't about being a good Samaritan but to have Marnie enlighten her as to why she ended up a suicidal teenager in a boarding house for the elderly on the edge of the Pacific.

A jar of Vicks vapour rub on the bathroom shelf catches her eye. She unscrews the lid and sniffs the ointment inside. Parry arises from it like a genie out of a bottle. She recalls now how he used to smear it up his nose to clear his blocked sinuses. Nothing about him is as vivid as this eucalyptus menthol smell. The pungency would cling to his body like a second skin, only temporarily vanishing in the foaming surf at the beach. She can hear him now – in her head. Hear him confronting her outside the entrance door to the Rosemont flat. The way he said:

You haven't told anyone, have you?

Told anyone what?

Well… if you don't remember… no matter.

He had turned from her as Marnie advanced from the lift to claim him, pulling him through the open door, into the depths of Grandma's Rosemont flat. It was Christmas morning – when the whole family would unite for a drink there. Barred from going to the farm, she had gone to visit when a trainee nurse. She had been looking for some convivial family warmth but had left instantly when Aunt Sill blocked her path to the living room. Stunned by her aunt's rejection, her mind had dismissed the event, but now… but now… what had Parry *meant*?

When she returns to Aunt Marnie, she sees a pot of tea, two flower-patterned cups and saucers, a small milk jug and a pot of sugar neatly arranged on a fold-out table in front of the wheelchair. A chair has been placed on the other side for Agnes. A plate of biscuits sits on the table next to the tea:

I phoned and asked the kitchen to bring it up. This is not just any old care home, you know. As you see, it's a refined establishment with excellent service.

There – again – is the snobbish O'Connor superiority she remembers of old:

My God! Iced VoVos!

Agnes has not been able to contain her nostalgic excitement. It is the sweetness of a lost childhood on a plate. Agnes picks up one of the coconut-covered pink biscuits, remembering how she used to imagine the jam line in the middle was a road through a snow-covered fairyland. But there had been no more sweetness from the age of thirteen. For some reason she cannot fathom, she now pictures her aunt as a young mother, clad in a white dressing gown, pegging wet clothes onto the rotary clothes hoist in the barren yard at Maroubra.

They sip their tea thoughtfully. Marnie lifts the cup to the good side of her mouth in an unsteady hand, quickly dabbing at stray drops with a lace handkerchief. With the movement, the diamond on her wedding finger sparkles as it catches an overhead light. Marnie turns her head and stares at her:

I suppose you know... I haven't had anything to do with your mother for years.

Well, that makes two of us!

After your father died, we used to go to the races together, but you know her. Always looking for a better offer. After Joan Bellamy passed away, she wangled her way into being escorted to the track by the widowed husband. Snubbed me completely. She never cared about anyone but your father.

She stares back at her aunt. An overwhelming need to speak of her pain takes her over. She *must* find the words. Words are the tools she must summon to come to her aid; words, like the manna from heaven that has flown onto the pages of the notebooks back at the Grantham Apartments. She begins:

Yes. My father was sun, moon and stars to her. I arrived at Liverpool hospital a short time after he died. She stopped me going to see his body: You don't want to see him, she said. He's all blue. Remember him the way he was. Jim's call to notify me was so unconvincing. He kept repeating – dead on arrival, dead on arrival. She cornered me outside the entrance to the hospital, raving about Ben. We have got to get home *instantly*, she said. Ben will be snooping around the farm. He's probably already there going through your father's papers. I've *got* to get back *now*, she insisted, dragging me to her car! That can't be the reaction of a loving wife, Aunt Marnie, can it!? Her husband not an hour dead and all she can think of is outfoxing her brother!

Marnie fixes her with a shrewd look:

Well – they are both tarred with the same brush, Agnes.

Her aunt is paying attention. It is a good start. She continues:

I know you don't like Ben, but in his own clumsy way he cared about my father and mourned his loss. Insensitive to his backbone, true, but he would have been shocked to hear the things my father said about him behind his back.

Marnie replaces her teacup into the saucer with difficulty, then says:

Parry and I were overseas when all this happened. That's why we didn't go to the funeral. And your mother never spoke about it.

Agnes relates the circumstances. That Eric Keen had died of a Staphylococci infection. How, having ignored a sore throat, he had pushed himself to go to a factory party at the Automobile Club, staying the night there, before driving to the farm the next day. How, on the way to the Club he had stopped off to see a doctor who advised him to take his badly inflamed throat home to bed. How, later that afternoon, her mother had brought him a cup of tea and that the hot liquid caused an abscess in his throat to burst and block his windpipe. How he had apparently managed to stagger to the car but had collapsed in the back seat. How her brother Jim tried to give him mouth-to-mouth resuscitation as Marnie drove them to the hospital. How only a tracheotomy would have saved him.

Marnie listens with obvious concentration as Agnes reaches the climax of her story:

Not only was I bullied out of seeing his body, Aunt Marnie, but she made me sleep in his bed! *Knowing* he'd been suffering from a contagious bacterium! I need to have you here beside me, she commanded me. You're my daughter. I can't sleep alone, for Christ's sake – I've just lost my husband! I slipped between his contaminated sheets and had to listen to her babbling incoherently all night.

She pauses to look at her aunt, aware that she probably already knows all this, or some of it at least. Would she think Agnes was back in the old madness? She had never spoken at such length to this woman before. Had never been given the opportunity, after all. But Marnie was making no protest, and so, emboldened by her close attention, she continued:

Children aren't responsible for the blind love they have for their parents – no matter how diabolical those parents are. Did you know I paid for his funeral and catering for the wake? Being financially successful didn't liberate me from being Madge's slave. I did put my foot down, though, when she wanted to bring the polo ponies to the graveside. I suppose it would have been appropriate, though, as he loved those horses more than any human being. The church was packed with polo players, workmates, and his pub mates – all singing his praises. I knew so little about his life, I felt like a stranger. It was nauseating watching Madge waltz back and forth between mourners at the wake back at the farm, like a girl at a birthday party...

Is it her imagination, or is Marnie now leaning forward as if to better catch every word? Heartened, she continues:

A few days later, Madge knocks on the door of my Paddington terrace house, wild eyed with his fever. Imagine! But I took care of her willingly, even though I'd been desperately ill with it myself. And, *then* she wangled her way into working in my real estate office! She just appeared! After six phenomenally successful years, my mad mother shows up out of the blue and expects to be given a job! I put her on the reception desk. It felt like the business had been taken over by an alien invader. As it turned out, she took little interest. Her ridiculous behaviour – giving orders, showing off, name-dropping – lasted just over a week. On the day she started telling my clients that she owned the business, I received an ultimatum from my staff – either she goes, or *we* go! It wasn't hard to persuade her that an office job was beneath her and so she wafted back to the skittish spending spree she'd been on since Daddy died:

What did your mother do with the inheritance?

She notices that Marnie's eyes are glittering with curiosity, and tells her straight:

She squandered it, of course! When the solicitor neglected to file for probate within the stipulated time, the estate reverted to us three children. Bert and Jim came to my Paddington terrace to discuss the matter. I told them I was signing it back to her. That it was a technical hitch – not my father's intention. I said I made my own living and wanted to be free of any connection with my mother. Jim signed as he felt the same. Bert, of course, who knew how to manipulate her, was keen to keep the money. But it was two against one, so he lost. Oh – and I almost forgot! A life insurance policy from the factory left her phenomenally well off.

As the unflattering tales of her arch enemy unfurl, Marnie's cheeks turn bright pink with outrage:

My God! How unjust that someone who did nothing for anyone should have it all handed to her on a plate!

Agnes is on a roll. Words are flowing like a river in full flood:

Then she asked me to invest her money in property. I should have refused, but like Scheherazade warding off execution with another story, solving my mother's problems was how I survived childhood. So, her money went into a block of twelve flats in Hargrave Street, Paddington – with views of the harbour. It included a block of land she could build a house on. There was also a beautifully renovated terrace house in Union Street. Both rental investments were managed by an agent. Honourable. One to be trusted. You don't have to do anything I told her. Just put the cheque in the bank at the end of the month and you can live the life of Riley. I thought I'd sorted her out. And myself, for that matter. But I underestimated how much my father's death had affected me. After he died, I lost interest in my business. I could hardly drag myself out of bed to go to the office. All that hard work – day and night, seven days a week, was about winning *his* approval. *His* love. I may have bought myself a wonderful house and amassed considerable investments, but once I achieved it, *nothing* had any meaning. And do you know, Aunt Marnie, he didn't even thank me for the two horses I bought him and had sent to the farm! Yet, back then, how could I criticise someone I had spent my whole young life trying to save?!

The tirade is wonderfully liberating. She believes she can still detect her aunt weighing up whether her recalcitrant niece is right in the head, but she can't seem to stop talking. This woman – this uncaring, unkind woman – must be the person who hears it all. All the pent-up hurt and distress. All the unfairness and desperation. She must hear *everything* she has to say:

My life changed when a handsome architect walked into my office. Self-absorbed as he was, his lack of interest in me felt comfortably familiar. He had the education I never received. I sold his house, and my own business, and three months after Neil Armstrong walked on the moon, we left Australia to discover the world.

Marnie nods and says:

You underestimate yourself, Agnes. You were good-looking enough to have suitors snap you up in bare feet. So – what happened to your mother's glowing investments? As I remember it, she put the squeeze on Parry and me for money.

Ah. Again. For Marnie it was always about the money. Well, here was the rest of the sorry tale for her to chew over. She tells her aunt how, a week after she left Sydney, the managing agent rang her in Bali and told her that Madge was giving the tenants in Hargrave Street notice as she wanted to renovate the flats and sell them on. That she had told the agent she was *not* coming back and couldn't help him. That the flats belonged to her mother.

That, after a month in Bali, she and the architect had travelled worldwide, finally settling in London. She tells her of the miles and miles of freedom she had enjoyed. Freedom from anything and everything to do with her mother. She admits to her aunt that perhaps she *should* have done something, *should* have come back, because Madge had put her trust in some showy, unscrupulous decorators in Double Bay who took her to the cleaners. She confesses to her that bulletins on the downward spiral of overspending had greeted her at each hotel during her travels. That the Union Street house was the first to be sold, then had come a first and second mortgage on the flats, until finally the loan providers foreclosed and sold Madge's little empire up.

She has paused for breath. Marnie is looking fatigued. She has talked the woman's head off. And, as she didn't come all the way back to Sydney to endlessly rehash Madge's sins, she decides to ask the one burning question that has spurred her to visit Marnie in the first place:

What I don't understand, Aunt Marnie, is why I was sent to live with you against my will?

Her aunt sits back in the wheelchair, adjusting her weight. A few seconds pass. Is her silence indecision? Reluctance? Perhaps she cannot even remember? Then Marnie speaks:

Your parents sent you to us with no money. They gave you no money and didn't pay us a penny towards your keep. Can you imagine being put in a situation like that?

This is no answer. Agnes must try again:

Then why did you allow it? Why did two people who had taken *no* interest in my life, suddenly decide to interfere in it? It's my *parents* you should have punished, not an innocent girl in need of kindness! And, if you feel I still owe you money, *do* let me know and I'll pay you back right now!

I didn't mean to infer you owe me anything Agnes.

Her aunt has responded in a muted tone and seems taken aback. But this is no time to waver:

Tell me, Aunt Marnie – *please*. Why, in Christ's name, if you really didn't want me, *why* was I kidnapped by Parry and brought to your house?! Torn from everything I knew, only to be tortured by the two of you! *Tell* me!

Marnie seems startled now. Her hand is hovering near the internal phone. Agnes says:

I'm sorry. I didn't mean to frighten you.

But she isn't sorry. Not really. She doesn't care if she has alarmed this woman. She can tell she is on the edge of something. That having pushed Marnie in this way could be about to yield fruit. She waits. She is trying to project the impression she is going nowhere until she gets what she wants.

Marnie sighs deeply, then:

Your grandmother gave the orders, as you know. She had a subtle way of punishing the least insubordination. You're not the only victim where she's concerned. Once, when I wouldn't comply with her wishes, she waited till Parry was away and sent a worker to take away my company car. Leaving me stranded in Maroubra – with three small children. What do you think of that? She was a cruel woman, Agnes. We were all scared stiff of her. Nobody dared disobey her. *She* was behind it. *She* told Parry to bring you to stay with us and try to make you see some sense.

Agnes cannot help herself:

Because I was off my head, I suppose? Around the bend? Stark staring mad? Well, if I wasn't crazy when I arrived at your house, I certainly was when I left!

Another sigh from Marnie. But she must keep on at her. She *must* pile on the pressure, for there will never be another chance:

Then why didn't our *father* look after us while our mother was in New Zealand? He didn't even come and see us at that terrible place where we were farmed out! Well?! *Surely* you must know?!

A tiny smile hovers around Marnie's slanting mouth:

Oh that. When you were little kids, you mean. I suppose you might say he was busy.

What do you *mean*? Busy doing what?!

Parry and I hadn't been married long. As soon as your mother left the country, Eric took up with another woman. I was shocked when he brought her to dinner at our house. Brazenly cheating on your mother in front of us.

This revelation momentarily knocks the wind out of Agnes's sails. But why should she be surprised? Deep down, she knew her father. As much as she loved him, this would fit the bill. The answer made sense, but it was still not enough. She needed more from this woman. She tells her how she and Jim were traumatised. That the neighbours made their lives unbearable. That she was left to believe at eight years of age that the electrocution was *her* fault. How, she demands of Marnie, could mere children defend themselves against those who were supposed to care for them? She can hear her own voice rising in anger:

Did it cross your minds how we suffered when Parry drove us to that awful place and just *dumped* us there?

What can I tell you, Agnes? I can't answer for Parry.

And what about the fire in your kitchen? I didn't start it or have *anything* to do with it! Why was I blamed?!

There *was* no fire. You imagined it! Just as you have imagined so much else that is *supposed* to have happened to you! There *was no* fire – do you hear?

As Agnes absorbs this blow to her sanity, her thoughts are obliterated by the ringing of Marnie's mobile in the pocket of her dress. Marnie fumbles to retrieve it:

Yes... yes... I'm having tea with a friend... yes... just a moment... it's my *mother*!

Marnie is acting like a girl who has been caught not doing her homework. She is holding the phone away from her ear. Marnie's mother. Pushing ninety and still going strong, apparently.

Agnes pulls back the curtain and steps onto the balcony to give her aunt privacy. She turns and stares back at her. She seems happy talking to the handsome woman Agnes remembers playing the piano in the sumptuous back room of the ugly Newtown pub.

This unexpected memory of the White Horse Hotel makes her stomach turn over and she feels her heart racing with adrenaline.

Out on the balcony she will slowly regain control of her breathing. She will become aware her aunt has no intention of cutting the call short on her account. She will intuitively know this woman has absolutely no regrets about the despicable treatment meted out to her niece in the past and, if anything, remains tacitly hostile.

Knowing there is no more to be gained here, she will walk back into the room where she will catch her aunt's eye briefly, cross the floor, and pick up the silver-framed photo of Parry. Then she will walk rapidly out of the door, without looking back. A final delinquent act for Marnie to remember her by.

27

THE REUNION AT ROSEMONT

gnes wakes with a start, feeling as if she's been drugged. The confrontation with Marnie has utterly drained her. The discus throwers are thumping on the door so it must be cleaning time. Bang! Bang! Bang! Relentless. If she delays further, the door might fall in. No need to put on a dressing gown, for she has fallen asleep in her clothes:

Coming! Coming!

Groggy with sleep, she unhooks the chain and finds herself staring into the ruddy-cheeked face of 'Wilma One'. The Romanian cleaners are twins, and even though they have separate names, they are known as 'Wilma One' and 'Wilma Two':

Sorry I trouble you, Lady Agnes. Mrs Jean O'Connor. She call your mobile. Got nothing. Now she say on phone downstairs, don't forget lunch party today 1.30. That is message.

Wilma One takes a deep breath after laying each word down like a building block:

Okay – thank you Wilma.

Agnes is nonplussed, having completely forgotten this arrangement:

You sick, Lady Agnes?

Wilma One is peering at Agnes through button-shaped eyes:

No, no. Perfectly fine. Long sleep. Just woke up. Thank you kindly.

You no worry. Sister and me clean dirty room in afternoon.

The maid strides away down the corridor. Agnes looks at her watch. God, it was already ten. She had turned her mobile off at the nursing home and hadn't turned it on again. But there was still plenty of time to get ready. She would walk to Rosemont from the apartments, in the hope that it would gradually clear her head. Ravenous when she arrived back from visiting Aunt Marnie, she had bought a box of takeaway tapas and a bottle of vintage red wine from the Spanish deli. Sitting in a trance in the evening on the balcony, she had finally run out of internal chat. Marnie had exhausted all thought and left her empty. With each glass of wine, Harry's Bar had seemed to leap higher and higher into the air as the gyrating neon lights danced apart, then blended together. It was a glorious sight and had lifted her inebriated spirits to the point where she was able to marvel at being in the world.

Now, as she drinks down a glass of cool water before leaving for Rosemont, she remembers with a tangle of pleasure and shame the photo she stole from her aunt. She fishes it out of her bag and puts it centre stage on the dining table. She fishes out the jar of Vicks rub, filched from Marnie's bathroom, and places it, like an offering, beside the photo. She stares hard at the long-dead uncle who, as usual, isn't giving anything away. She hears herself intoning: Fire… fire… fire… But Marnie had been adamant that there *was* never any fire. So why does her brain keep telling her the opposite?

Today, the keeper of family secrets, aging Aunt Sill – whom Aunts Charlotte, Tina and Jean take turns to care for in Melbourne – will be looked after by a neighbour. Thus, the three younger sisters are getting together today to celebrate Jean's new home. Jean is now the doyenne of the old Rosemont flat. And, it seems, they are also taking this opportunity to meet Agnes. Unlike Madge, big sister Sill has been prudent with her money, amassing healthy investments – generous portions of which will eventually go to each of the three caring aunts on her passing.

As revelations of past events in Agnes's early life start to emerge, she has realised her longing to be part of the Aunt Club has diminished. They might as well be strangers. Bereaved of sweet childhood memories, she had clung for years to the brief happiness around the farm barbecue with Jean and her artist husband Richard. Richards's drawing of the guardian angel above her bed had been a soothing talisman. Now, as she saunters along familiar streets towards the celebration, she realises the futility of seeking retrospective gratitude from Jean, for Agnes, years ago, had fought hard to find her aunt a cheap house in Double Bay in which to rehouse her large family. It would have been unthinkable to charge a commission for this favour, as she had felt so honoured and privileged to help a family member.

She had also listened patiently and with concern to the sad tale of Jean's marriage break-up. Was this residual resentment she felt mean-spirited? She didn't think so. It strikes her now that what was truly unforgivable was the shock and betrayal of having to fight off Richard's advances. She had been dining with him and his new wife in London and he had offered her a lift home, only to turn into a dimly lit Regent's Park, pull up suddenly and jump on her. Outraged beyond words, she had walked the rest of the way home. So much for the guardian angel.

The sight of the mottled shadows on the pavement, and the familiar steps leading up to the Rosemont flats, fills Agnes with a deep unease. It reminds her of the day she returned to Lennox Street at the very start of her Sydney trip and encountered Beryl. She feels profoundly disturbed. She looks up at the line of Moreton Bay fig trees opposite the apartment block. They impede the sun, producing an eerie pattern that flickers under her feet. Their blunt shadows stripe the parked cars and imprint mysterious shapes on the green garage doors that flank either side of the entrance foyer.

The building itself feels both familiar and menacing, right down to the ghostly pale grout that cements the solid, stubborn bricks of the façade. Once equivalent in her imagination to the great fictional residences at the movies, Rosemont strikes her now as an undistinguished block in an identical row of red-brick apartments. The late midday glare is intense as she scans the front of the building and wonders from exactly which third-floor window, all those decades ago, Grandma attempted to fly like a bird. Was it even true, this tale of Grandma's transitory madness? She still finds it hard to believe that the Grand Matriarch, the ruling despot of Rosemont, could have ever been plunged into such a state of mental debility.

She enters and ascends in the lift. As she stands, rooted to the spot, outside the entrance to the Rosemont flat, Parry's words, uttered outside the same door on that long-ago Christmas Day, are creeping back into her head:

You haven't told anyone, have you?

Told anyone what?

Well, if you don't know what I'm talking about, then forget it.

Now, here, in this same space, decades later, she can feel the rough edge of the stump of his half finger running down her bare arm.

381

Agnes bangs hard on the knocker on what is now Jean's door as if landing a punch on Parry's broken nose.

Jean flings the door open and blinks at her in disbelief:

Oh, Agnes, it's you! Why did you knock so hard? I thought something terrible had happened!

So sorry, Jean. Sometimes I don't know my own strength.

This is the kind of flippant quip she is famous for. This is the trusty sense of humour that has propped her up and dulled the pain for years. She hears voices coming from the living room and is glad she isn't the first to arrive. She hands Jean the magnum of champagne she has bought on the way:

Oh. Thanks. Everyone else bought a plate.

Jean takes the bottle and puts it on the hall table with little enthusiasm. Agnes notes the tone of mild rebuke and responds:

Well, I would have done the same, if you'd told me.

Never mind. What a lovely coat, Agnes. Is it mink?

She slips out of the coat and hands it to Jean. She says:

I was glad it was cold today, so I could up my rating by wearing it.

She wonders if this second burst of sarcasm would be lost on Jean too. However, the mink evidently proving to be a good icebreaker, she continues:

I bought it in the Portobello Market in London. I saw it in the distance, hanging on the side of a corner stall. Found myself drawn to it like a magnet. The seller explained it was one of a batch released from ten years in Harrods cold storage, safely away from animal rights activists!

Really? Oh – do let me try it on! How scrumptious!

Her mood improved, Jean swoons as she slips into the coat, burrowing her hands deep in the pockets and doing a twirl. Agnes ventures a compliment:

It looks lovely on you, Jean. Goes perfectly with your blonde hair and honey eyes. Her aunt smiles:

Go into the living room, Agnes. I'll put your coat on my bed and join you.

Agnes watches her mink disappear along the corridor. To avoid the intimidating prospect of walking into a room full of people, she slips through the dining room to have a look at the old kitchen.

With the exceptions of new mod cons, and a shelf full of vitamin pills, the kitchen is pretty much as she remembers it. She is delighted to see the disposal chute beside the back door that thrilled her as a child. How she loved putting stuff in it and then dashing down the stairs to the basement to see it arrive. Added to that, there was always the pleasure of running into Henry – the warm-hearted caretaker – and telling him what she had seen at the pictures. Unlike the pretentious gang upstairs, he had a penchant for the cinema, knew all the film stars of the day, and liked to listen to her enthusiastic childish chatter.

A tap on the shoulder makes her jump. She turns to see Beth, the only aunt, apart from the long-deceased Carmen the Kind, whom she remembers with any warmth. Aunt Beth and Uncle Ben have been divorced for years. He sent the cotton factory broke, married his secretary, and moved to a suburb out in the country that Agnes has never heard of. She's not sure in what order these events happened, but it was already ancient history:

Hello, darling girl! I heard your voice and came to find you!

Wow, you look wonderful, Beth! You've hardly changed a bit!

Agnes gazes into the attractive woman's smoky grey eyes, whilst savouring hearing again the sweet coquettish laugh she had once found so endearing.

And *you've* still got that *lovely* red hair! Jean tells me you've been studying at Oxford since your marriage break-up in London.

Agnes informs her that the studies in Oxford were undertaken in a small way. That she attended a few summer schools at one of the colleges. She reminds her that classrooms were never for her. She is strictly an autodidact, she tells Beth, and adds that she lives alone with a Persian cat and sleeps in a bedroom full of books. She hears herself laughing nervously at the admission. Despite the pleasure of seeing her aunt, she feels distinctly out of place. Beth takes a small step closer to her and, with a lowered voice, says:

If there is anything that I can tell you about the past, Agnes. Anything that might help your investigations, ring me. We can meet for coffee. I know from my own children how undiagnosed traumas can affect adult life. My son revealed that he was abused by a priest at school and it's only now, years later, he can talk about it.

Agnes is aghast. Such a revelation! And so unexpected! But she wonders if the promised private meeting would ever manifest. Family interference could put paid to it in a heartbeat and so she decides to push her luck:

Could we catch up a little now, Beth? Please.

Beth considers for a moment or two, then:

All right. I'm not sure how much you know, but after your parents moved to the farm, your mother became terribly possessive about the house. She was so hostile to Ben and me that instead of stopping off to see her, we would go straight to the stables. My youngest son, Daniel, played polo for Australia, did you hear about that? Before the factory went broke, Ben poured thousands into financing players, including your brothers. I was lucky to get a pretty cottage not far from here, and enough to live on, in the divorce settlement, before it all turned sour. My only problem is my children keep coming back to live with me! I just get rid of one and another one moves back in!

Agnes is looking quizzically at the pleasant, anxious woman standing awkwardly in front of her. Beth needed to toughen up before it was too late. She was always a pushover. Her aunt leans towards her and lowers her voice again:

Was it helpful to see Marnie?

What a question. Had they been in touch since her kleptomaniac visit to the care home? Agnes says:

To tell you the truth, I'm not sure. Please, Beth, listen. I have a memory of a fire. A fire for which I was blamed. Aunt Marnie denied to my face there ever was one:

Beth looks at her intently:

Oh. Yes. She rang me last night. She's very upset that, after all these years, you're still fixated on something that never happened. Do you think you might have muddled it up with some other event? Or accident? Memory plays funny tricks on us.

No! When I close my eyes, I see *flames* in the Maroubra house! It's the *one* thing I am *absolutely sure* of in the loveless mess that was my early life!

Agnes is aware she has raised her voice and sees Beth shrink away from her. She searches her face for truth and sincerity and sees the woman's expression remains sympathetic. Beth says:

My darling girl. You're preaching to the converted. Yes. I saw how badly they treated you.

Her aunt has reached out and is now squeezing her hand. Agnes is suffused with a sudden flood of tenderness for this kindly woman:

Oh, Beth – *thank you* for saying that!

A rush of secret, long unspoken words flood into her brain like a sudden gush of water into a pool. She can't keep them from spilling forth. She is compelled to speak:

I have no memory of the move to the farm, you know. The summer spent there. Nothing. Nothing until I entered this very building one day to hear I had failed my leaving certificate. Everything that lies behind that event is blank. Freud says nothing is ever lost and that it's all inside you. It's just a matter of getting access. But try as I might, I can't seem to do it!

She is aware of hot tears burning in her eyes and she swallows hard to keep them at bay. Beth leans forward earnestly:

You were a sweet, innocent girl, Agnes. Your mother made you out to be a delinquent. The family, well, they poured lies into your grandmother's ear too, I'm sorry to say. And Parry joined the chorus. I have never understood why they behaved like that towards you. Your grandmother succumbed to your mother's wishes and organised a place for you to board at Rose Bay Convent, didn't she?

Agnes nods her head fervently:

Yes! I told Grandma I couldn't concentrate! That it would be pointless! That something had broken inside me. Oh, this family... this so-called bloody *family*!

But she is stepping on dangerous ground now, for Beth is looking at her oddly. After all, her aunt is from a pious Catholic family and unused to such straight talk. Aware her outburst could be construed by Beth as tantamount to committing the sin of calumny and detraction, she backtracks:

What you told me is very helpful. Thank you so much, Beth.

Beth nods, flashes her a quick smile, but the candid atmosphere has evaporated. Agnes is relieved that Marnie appears not to have mentioned to Beth the stolen photo of Parry.

Beth cups her elbow, and Agnes finds herself guided firmly out of the kitchen away to greet the other guests. She is swept into a whirl of cousins she recognises but knows nothing about. As they greet her in turn, she momentarily loses sight of who she is and what she is doing there. She finds herself fighting a strong impulse to dash from the room.

The hurly-burly subsides when Jean rings a bell, inviting guests to help themselves to a smorgasbord lunch which has been laid out on a long trestle table, under the windows at the end of the dining room. Agnes has no appetite, but dutifully helps herself to a small serving of salad, plonking a chunk of garlic bread on the plate to fill it up. Seated at the same long dining table where, many years ago, Sill had taught her to eat a peach with a knife and fork, she turns to Jean as she settles into the seat beside her. Jean is now decidedly convivial on her second glass of champagne, and obligingly chatty:

You know, Agnes, when we were all children, for a quiet life we used to give Madge half the cake and share the other half between us. One Christmas, she stole my presents and wouldn't give them back. Everyone was scared of her. She controlled the family with her unpredictable violent rages. After a fight with her, Mother used to walk to St Joseph's and sit quietly in a pew to calm down. Pity her mighty decibel level couldn't be put to some constructive use in her life. I'll never get over the chaos she caused.

Well. Amen to that. Her mother's formative behaviour in the family comes as no surprise to Agnes. She can easily imagine the impact she must have had on them all. Jean, who is currently munching on a salmon and cream cheese roll, takes another gulp of champagne and, as if allotted the task of physical familial verification, Tina, the youngest aunt, who is seated opposite, suddenly announces:

Agnes has got my hands!

Agnes embraces the domestic comedy. It comes as a relief:

Yes, and I've got Grandma's legs, *and* my mother's bottom!

She hears herself laughing aloud as all eyes fall on her ink-stained fingers with their bitten nails. The sight of her hands alongside Tina's magnificent, long-red-nailed manicure makes her feel awkward, but the shape is, indeed, identical. In fact, it is impossible not to admire how attractive and well preserved these three women are in their middle age. All possess bright, dark eyes set in small, regular features, and have beautifully unlined skin. Alongside decades of applications of Elizabeth Arden night cream, their lustrous appearance has obviously benefited from religiously staying out of the sun. Hats in summer, gloves to drive in, and gloves also to be worn when hanging washing out on the line. Just like their mother before them. Tina speaks again:

Where were you when Mummy died, Agnes?

Travelling in Europe. 1970. Belgium. The date is set firm in my mind because I received news of Grandma's death shortly after I posted her a lace tablecloth.

The aunts exchange some covert glances, then Tina leans forward a little:

We thought it might be useful for you to know how your mother behaved – when Mummy was dying.

Out of the corner of her eye, Agnes sees Jean and Charlotte nod at Tina, signalling their approval from across the table. Agnes says:

I'm grateful for whatever you can tell me, Tina.

Tina relates that Agnes's grandmother had been in and out of hospital that winter with a bad chest. She wanted to die at home, so they all took turns nursing her at Rosemont. The doctor came every day and gave her oxygen. When he told her daughters she only had a few days to live, they split the task of notifying the rest of the family between them. Tina got the unfortunate job of notifying Madge who, apparently, made endless excuses, before finally agreeing to drive down from the farm. Two whole days passed, and when she didn't turn up, Tina rang her again to stress that time was running out. Madge finally arrived just after her mother passed away. Presumably for the benefit of the doctor, who was still in the room, Madge had loudly accused her sisters of failing to let her know that her mother was dying. She raved on and on. It was, said Tina, as if she was acting a part in a Shakespearean tragedy.

Tina does a passable imitation: 'How *could* you deprive me of saying goodbye! You *know* how close I was to my mother! If you'd only let me know in time, I'd have moved heaven and earth to be here at her side! This will be on your consciences *for the rest of your lives!*'

Agnes shakes her head as she listens. The doctor had been so convinced by Madge's outburst he had scolded the others for not letting her know. But it had not, says Tina, been a time for taking her on, for contradicting her, and so Madge's sisters had remained silent, hanging their heads in feigned contrition. Then Madge, cool as a cucumber, had thanked the doctor graciously and swept out without even glancing once at her own mother's corpse.

As Agnes computes this all-too-familiar litany of Madge's failings, Charlotte decides to cap Tina's anecdote from across the table:

It must have been very hard for you to manage such an unpredictable mother.

Agnes can only nod at this massive understatement. But the woman clearly means well. In fact, here, today, in this room, she believes all three sisters are trying hard to be supportive of her, even if it does not come naturally. They all appear to want to make some attempt at amends. To show, at the very least, some form of last-minute solidarity with her predicament.

She feels a strong urge to stand up. Her heart is racing, her breathing rapid. It is getting too much for her. Almost as one entity, the three aunts nod at her when she excuses herself to seek solace in the toilet.

She is amazed to discover that the beautifully preserved green bathtub and black-tiled shower have remained in the main bathroom after fifty years. Calming herself down, breathing slowly and steadily, she feels a need for further privacy and, hoping not to be spotted, she makes a detour through Grandma's old bedroom into the sunroom.

The setting of the long-ago inquisition is virtually the same, apart from one built-in cabinet in the corner. But there is no respite to be found here, for the cruel misrepresentation by her parents on that dreadful day now floods back in vivid detail. Amazing how she recalls all this, when so much else is lost! She raises a hand up to her face. Perhaps, if her father had consumed less whisky, he wouldn't have hit her so hard in the mouth? She wonders if she will ever stop making pathetic excuses for him.

Lost in her thoughts, staring blankly at the vast collection of ornaments arrayed on the shelves, she doesn't hear Charlotte's light step on the carpet until she is seated beside her on the sofa. The woman must have sought her out:

You know, don't you, Agnes, that 'famous' vase you broke wasn't an original but a copy?

Despite herself, Agnes laughs loudly, exclaiming:

Really?! The old con-artist! I gave her an exact replacement! Located from an antique dealer at *huge* expense! Aunt Sill milked my guilt for *years*. On my travels I constantly sent her all sorts of wonderful stuff as recompense!

The shared confidence of the phoney vase has made her feel strangely light-hearted as she surveys the nondescript room. Its every surface is still cluttered with the heavily ornate ornaments she had, long ago, admired, but now finds desperately gaudy and pretentious. She feels the urge to add a typical comic sting:

Sill was certainly a prototype material girl!

Charlotte is looking steadily at Agnes:

Agnes. I don't know if Jean told you, but Mother had a nervous breakdown. Poor Mother. Her life was completely dominated by the church. As a mother of five, I know what it feels like to have babies in quick succession. The pill has liberated young women, thank God. Mother was against any birth control, you know. She always obeyed what the church dictated.

Charlotte has paused, as if waiting for something. Agnes holds her breath. Will the next statement, or question, be what she thinks it will be?

Jean told us you had a baby. That it was adopted out.

Yes. I did.

Charlotte says nothing. Just squeezes her hand once more, then leaves the room.

This unexpected reminder of Rebecca Lea, and the cruel loss of her, galvanises Agnes to turn her back on this gathering. To leave all these people behind once and for all. In truth, when she braces herself to re-enter the room where chattering guests still linger, she feels no relief from the shared confidences, but the same desolation, the same loneliness as before.

The three aunts are now bunched together like an alien species of birds at the end of the table. They drink their coffee and do not notice her observing them. They are survivors – all widows or divorcees – just like her mother and Aunt Marnie. Perhaps, by pampering her sons, Grandma only weakened them for, with the sole exception of Ben, they have all joined her in heaven while her long-suffering daughters stoically remain.

Agnes is slipping into her fur coat and is about to exit when her brother Bert – with whom she has long ago severed relations – sweeps through the front door. He is too absorbed in whirling from aunt to aunt, titillating them with his caustic one-liners, to notice her. The girlish giggles that greet his glib asides only confirm her innate awareness that she is a duck in the wrong pond. But, before she can escape unseen, he turns and recognises her:

And what wondrous visiting angel have we here draped in mink? Don't ring us, we'll ring you! And let you know if you got the part!

He is gushing theatrically, obviously piqued by an antagonistic presence amidst his adoring fans. She knows he has quickly assumed his responsibility as the only creditable example of their parents' union and that he will happily rise to the challenge of putting her down on their behalf. He turns from her, instantly focusing his charm assault on Charlotte, keen to expunge any admiration for Agnes, who is now attracting some pleasant attention in her mink. It crosses her mind that he is the living image of their mother at the polo – chasing away any family member whom she construed as an intruder on her territory. She cannot, *will* not, let this man have the last word:

Your entrance is a signal for my departure!

She launches this remark at his retreating back as he walks away through the crowd. It is a version of the George Sanders' time-honoured line from *All About Eve* and really fits the occasion. He has heard her. Never a man to be gainsaid, she sees him turn on his heel:

If wit were shit we'd all be dead!

She might have guessed he would jibe back. And crudely too. She closes the apartment door behind her.

28

HER BROTHER BERT

Now snugly settled into a warm coffee shop at the Edgecliff Centre down the road from the Rosemont flat, Agnes's mind turns to when she had accidentally encountered her brother Bert when they were both young adults. They had all but collided in Queen Street one morning. Eighteen months younger than her, he had been away at boarding school since he was ten and, during the years she had been ostracised from the family, had grown into a man.

Initially she had not recognised him. In an unusually agitated state, he had led her by the hand to a run-down boarding house up the street. The entrance door was ajar, and they had waited as a couple of dishevelled old men shuffled out. She had followed him into a dark corridor that smelled of mildew and overcooked cabbage. Once up the stairs, he had kicked open the door of a small dark, untidy room, with damp-stained papered walls.

She didn't need any explanation of these squalid surroundings from him. She had instantly equated his situation with her own when residing at the boarding house at Coogee and felt she had to rescue him. Within minutes of smelling the overcooked cabbage she had found herself mothering him like a ten-year-old girl playing house. True to form, she had proposed a solution. They could share a flat. Her once spiteful and dismissive brother had looked sheepishly at the ground and nodded. With no further encouragement than this perfunctory tilt of his head, she had then spent the next couple of days scouring the rental possibilities, finally lining up a viewing for the following Saturday in Woollahra.

On the day of the viewing, she had woken to a sun-drenched Lavender Bay, situated across the harbour bridge. Here she shared a flat with two other girls and commuted to her job as a registration clerk in the city. She had showered, dressed, and walked at a brisk pace to Milson's Point to catch a train to the city – then on by bus to meet Bert at Double Bay. When she had spotted him in a coffee shop, he had looked at her vacantly as if he didn't know her. At the time she had read sadness into his seeming indifference but, doubtless, he was laughing up his sleeve at her blinkered impulse to care for him. His clothes were crumpled and dirty and his leather shoes scuffed at the toes.

Now, decades later, seated in the snug coffee shop, Agnes remembers saying:

Don't you have any clean clothes, Bert?

He had narrowed his cold, blue eyes into the hard stare that always unnerved her.

How can I buy what I can't afford? If you're ashamed of me, I won't bother coming.

Here. Buy yourself some. It's a beautiful morning! Come on! Let's go!

She had handed him some of the money she had withdrawn from the bank as a deposit on the new shared flat. He accepted it in silence. His face a sulky mask.

She had been excited at the prospect of reuniting more permanently with a sibling and had watched him stride up Manning Road, always slightly in front of her as if he couldn't bear her to take the lead. Everything appeared washed clean after the rain. They passed playing fields along the way with emerald-grassed lawns. A canopy of high branches from a central line of trees shaded both sides of the street they turned into.

They had stood together in a tiny patch of sunlight, in front of a single-storeyed pitch-roofed house. Potted pines stood to attention either side of the front door.

A pretty, auburn-haired young woman in a purple gingham dress had answered their knock and greeted them like long-lost relatives. She had grasped Agnes's hand and Agnes had watched her gaze moving from her brother's face to hers. She seemed to be picking up a resemblance many swore by, but Agnes could never see:

You must be brother and sister!

Yes, you're right.

The resemblance is uncanny. Don't you think so, John?

The woman had turned bright eyes on a husband who grunted, without looking up from his newspaper. 'John' was seated in an enormous wood-framed lounge chair that looked as if it was capable of floating across the harbour. His feet were crossed on the chair opposite as if directing the trajectory of travel.

After her recent years in the wilderness, Agnes had been thrilled that the woman had made a visual connection with herself and Bert. She could tell straightaway that Jean Vickers had taken them both to her heart and that her husband would go along with whatever she decided.

Smaller versions of the couple had looked up from the floor, where they were playing cards:

Let me introduce you to our two. This is Dom, as in Benedictine, and Tia, as in Tia Maria!

Jean had giggled at her own drinks-based joke, and Agnes, struggling to keep a straight face, could see that Bert was now staring disapprovingly at John's footwear, the man's sandals and socks singling him out as common. Plain socks might have tempered Bert's obvious disgust but running all over John's huge feet were intricate patterns of brightly coloured kangaroos.

They had followed Jean down the narrow passageway at the side of the house, Bert trailing sulkily behind, patently embarrassed by his sister's exuberance. To Agnes's delight, they had been greeted by an intimate garden surrounded by a semicircle of tall trees, like a secret clearing in a sylvan wood. A green ping-pong table stood in the centre of a spacious patio.

Her practiced eye had taken in the interior decor, which was uncluttered and adequate, although the two bedrooms at the back had no direct light. Her disappointment over the dark bedrooms had been swept away, however, by the enchantment of the garden.

Back out on the sleepy street, she had swooned with the possibility of it all. Russell Street was a dead end leading to a small rainforest park called Harbour View – a veritable miniature of the bush in Lennox Street! She had felt almost sick with nostalgia: the little park, the charming garden with the ping-pong table, the chorus of cicadas – all had augured the recreation of a lost childhood.

They had moved in one misty Saturday morning. She first, Bert sauntering along later with his small suitcase, intent on disguising his obvious pleasure in being delivered from the old shufflers on the downbeat corner. Having invested the sum of money she had given him in obtaining a haircut and some new clothes, he had barely been recognisable as the bedraggled young man she had bumped into less than a week ago.

Gazing at his altered appearance, she was aware in that moment that she hardly knew him.

He had never made connection with her, never confided in her, as Jim had done. When a child, he had shown contempt for the few possessions his younger brother and sister treasured, regularly breaking apart Agnes's painted shoeboxes to steal the sweets she saved for Lent, and gleefully messing up the meticulous arrangement of Jim's small cars on the bedroom floor. How he had relished their plaintive cries on discovering the destruction.

Watching him taking stock of his new bedroom, she realised she had no idea what he really felt or thought. Instinctively, she didn't trust him with knowledge of her dark past, for he used gossip to score points – like her mother – and she sensed he had internalised the same antipathy to his siblings as Madge had to hers. While she and Jim would laugh about the sacred cows at the polo their parents venerated, Bert would have none of it. So compelling had been his elevation of everything Eric and Madge admired, he might have been their only child.

Agnes had found enough money from her savings to pay the first month's rent. Fortunately, the large outgoing had coincided with the big pay packet she had received when she lost her job at the Greek solicitors. Not her finest hour. Her boss's secretary had found a weekday matinée ticket to the cinema amongst her papers and her kindly boss had no option but to let her go. The oversight had happened because she had developed a crush on a law student called Warwick. He had selected the cinema for their first date, so she had run around on the beat and finished her work early – in good time for the first screening of the day, and then had returned to the office. There had been barely anyone in the cinema, probably because of the bleak Ingmar Bergman films they tended to screen, and which Warwick found so deeply profound. It had been a short-lived romance, so hardly worth being sacked for squeezing in a date on her boss's time.

Nonetheless, she had landed in a perfect location to be self-employed. Bondi Junction was already a busy Sydney satellite and just a short walk up the hill from where she lived. With a glowing reference she knew she didn't deserve from sweet Mr Stephanopoulos, she had approached three recently established small legal practices, all of whom appointed her as their registration clerk – on an agency basis. Soon she was earning so much money that, having paid out for rent and food, she had still saved enough to put a deposit on a second-hand car.

Her social life now revolved around the lovely outdoor garden in Russell Street that, at weekends, transformed into a mini holiday camp, with visitors coming and going constantly. In an initial effort to dampen the amorous advances of a chap called Brien – a Pakistani architect ten years her senior and whom she had met at a party – she had proposed a game of chess. Beneath sprays of beer, high-pitched chatter, whirling dancers, and blaring music, she and Brien would sit either side of a garden corner table, absorbed in the pieces on the board.

Building on what she had learnt from Mr St Paul all those years ago in Castlecrag, she had soon developed a mastery of the game. Brien's obsession with beating her at chess turned him into a regular visitor at the new flat, and he would happily partner Agnes in weekend ping-pong tournaments against Bert and his girlfriend, Mary. Both Bert and Mary, at that point, were mutually commiserating after failing their first-year exams in architecture at Sydney University. The genius level Mary had attained in an IQ school test had fuelled such high parental expectations that her subsequent failure at university had made her *persona non grata* at home. Cocooned in the Russell Street flat, she had successfully evaded her disappointed parents and found comfort in spending the summer with Bert in a shared state of grief over their mutual loss.

Agnes's sense of being a ghost around her brother – the same feeling elicited by her parents – still prevailed, especially when he was with Mary. Bert had continued sharing nothing of his life with his only sister. All she had discovered about him in those days at the Russell Street house was what she overheard. Eavesdropping on his conversations with Mary was how Agnes learned that her taciturn brother, like her, had reading difficulties. She discovered, too, that Bert's boarding school once made the same fatal mistake of consulting their mother over the issue and had achieved the same disastrous result – for no child of Madge's could possibly be deemed word-blind and the accuser expect to get away with it.

In fact, Bert's dyslexia served to establish a deeper bond between him and Mary. Mary had sought professional advice and accompanied him to group sessions with others similarly afflicted. Future girlfriends would do the same, for Bert would master the art of evoking female sympathy and would manage to turn his dyslexia into an irresistible attraction. Comfortable in relationships he could control, he would settle into letting female partners read to him like a blind man. Informed that dyslexics are often highly intelligent, Bert, in his own eyes, would become a wounded and misunderstood genius. Eventually Bert will buckle down to show the world it is wrong to judge him and will land a job in a city finance company. The scrawny fugitive rescued by his sister will go off to work looking dapper and handsome in a smart business suit.

Agnes had remained silent when Bert's condition was first revealed, unsure if she was also a sufferer. There was a time in her young life when she had read voraciously, with no noticeable difficulty – that was, until the mysterious shattering of her concentration had taken its toll. Only two years between brother and sister, yet she had felt so much older.

Things between them had fallen apart when Bert got his driving licence. At first, seeing him behind the wheel of her car had made her feel like a proud parent, but shock had replaced pleasure when he consistently failed to replace the petrol he used. Her protests had fallen on deaf ears. When the car started to look as if it had been through the Normandy invasion, she had bitten her lip, tempted as she was to deny him further access. Change to this unsatisfactory status quo had arrived unexpectedly when she had discovered the car had sustained a broken axle:

What did you do to my car?! I had to order a tow truck to take it to be repaired!

Yeah? I'd *leave* it there if I was you. It's a rattle trap on its last legs. Bloody thing is falling apart. A danger to man and beast. You should get jack of it and buy a new one. Must rush. Got to get to work! Toodle-pip!

Then he had grinned at her as if to say: 'You'll never get the better of me.'

Today, seated in the Edgecliff café, Agnes can still see herself standing on that hot pavement, watching him depart. Handsome in his smart new suit. Confident in his stride. She had felt a glimmer of pride. The resentment always came later.

That poor old car of hers. She can still picture it in detail. Agnes takes another sip of her cooling coffee and remembers a short mechanic with a beer gut. The one who had helped the tow truck driver lower her car to a thudding stop on the cement floor of the garage. He had put his greasy hands in his pockets and said:

Looks like we've got some serious work here, Bluey!

But before he had a chance to depress her further, they were interrupted. A smartly dressed, middle-aged man, with a sharp nose and a thin scar on one cheek had appeared as if just parachuting in from the roof of the Catholic church next door. He had taken a long searching look at Agnes and declared:

You've got the look I've been searching for! You'd be perfect for what I want!

And what would *that* happen to be, Sunshine?

She recalls now how the squat mechanic had snarled as he grabbed the sleeve of the stranger's tailored white shirt, how secretly elated she had been to hear the mechanic gallantly intervene on her behalf. Stopped in his tracks, the Englishman's face had flushed pink beneath his greying fair hair, the white scar standing out like a brand. Angry, he pulled away from the mechanic's grip. She felt implicated, as if she had – somehow – provoked this altercation. The three look awkwardly at one another until the Englishman apologised, saying he meant no insult. That they were not to take what he said as a provocation. He introduced himself as Roger Johnson. Out from England to do a series of television commercials – for Senior Service cigarettes. He had, he told them, spent most of yesterday auditioning young women and was starting to despair he would ever find his Senior Service girl. Lo and behold, he stops for petrol and sees Agnes. 'The stunning redhead' he has been searching for.

The mechanic may have been smirking in disbelief, but any mutual suspicion evaporated when the owner of the garage walked over to greet the interloper deferentially by name:

Hello Roger! No further problems with the chariot, I hope!

No – she's purring like a contented tabby, thanks Ross. Couldn't be happier. Grateful for your help, old pal.

Agnes had followed the owner's gaze to a shiny red Jaguar sedan parked at the pumps, where a young man in overalls was meticulously cleaning the windscreen. She had noticed Roger's eyes travelling over her body and felt tangled in his gaze, like an insect on flypaper. Out of the blue, he had offered her a lift. The damsel in distress, devoid of transport till her car's broken axle is fixed, had said:

Thank you, yes. I'd be glad of a lift.

She had settled in the passenger seat with her briefcase on her lap. And, as the Jaguar cruised slowly through Double Bay, she had found herself hoping someone she knew might see her in this splendour. Roger has been so persuasive that, by the time he dropped her off, she had agreed to a screen test. And, by the end of the following week, she had become the 'Senior Service Girl'.

Professional photos printed, Agnes will register with the Gloria Patten Casting Agency in King Street and sign a contract for more money than she has ever earned in her life in one hit. But a natural pragmatism will still rule her actions. She will deem it advisable to keep her current employment going and get someone to cover for her. Better safe than sorry. You never knew.

She will wash and dry her hair the night before the first day's shooting and set her alarm for 8am, giving her plenty of time to arrive at the Cruising Yacht Club of Australia where filming is due to begin.

To gain heavenly protection, she will pledge 10% of her earnings to the starving black babies but, fearing she might have undercut the Almighty, will drag herself back into the prayer position and double her offer. Secure in the celestial deal, she will hit the pillow and sink into a deep sleep:

I consider it a miracle that I have managed to get through all three commercials – all shot on sea locations – without a major hitch: a yacht in Rushcutters Bay, a fishing trawler in Cairns and a catamaran at Pittwater. Smiling at men dressed in nautical gear as I puff on a cigarette has not exactly been challenging. Certainly not method acting. I have problems on the first day, as the filter-less cigarette keeps sticking to my lips when I pull it out of my mouth. I must have swallowed a whole packet of tobacco! This problem means extra shots. But, in the end, I get through.

I have rejected all Roger's overtures for off-set activities. I so wish I could just giggle and fluff off these inevitable male passes as I see other girls do. Instead, unable to speak, I can only turn to ice and stare at the ground. Even though I reject him, I still feel guilty when his wife arrives on set. As if I have somehow provoked his amorous advances behind her back.

With the proceeds from the commercials, I buy a new white VW Beetle that I categorically refuse to lend Bert. I am cast through Gloria Patten in other commercials, and this means I must travel to different locations around Sydney and interstate. The Russell Street ping-pong table goes silent. I am increasingly sick of paying for everything in the flat and am also disillusioned with my attempts to infuse retrospective sunshine into a relationship with my brother. A relationship that never existed.

Living under the same roof ends abruptly after I take Bert up on his offer to drive me in my new VW Beetle to the airport to catch a flight to Canberra for a Range Rover commercial. It becomes clear he is deliberately procrastinating in setting out to the airport. Tears stream down my cheeks as we crawl through heavy traffic, and I pray the flight might be delayed. But I arrive to find I have missed it and that the next flight isn't for another hour. But that flight is delayed because of fog. And so, landing very late, I miss out on the laid-on transport from Canberra to the snowfields set. There are no taxis, and I have to resort to hitchhiking, which fails to get me there till late afternoon – by which time the production company have flown up another girl by helicopter.

The agent drops me. My new career is over. Why did Bert deliberately sabotage me? Was it revenge for not lending him my new car? Or was it simply the pleasure of seeing me suffer? Confronting him is useless, as he will feign innocence. I am devastated. I give up the flat and move into a house with some girlfriends in Double Bay. I have no idea where Bert ends up.

* * *

Not long after the move, Agnes will bump into chess partner Brien in a street near her new house. In the process of establishing his own architectural practice, Brien is exploring ways of attracting work and she will accompany him to see a development site, set on a steep hill in Woollahra high above the old flat in Russell Street. He is thinking of taking out an option, designing a block of units, and selling the approved project to a developer:

What do you think, Agnes?

She will scent an opportunity and tell him:

You can't go wrong. Apartments looking over the harbour and the whole of the Eastern Suburbs. Can't fail to attract buyers.

And it will all come together. Brien will obtain the loan for the 10% deposit, take out the option and start work on the plans. For Agnes, entering Brien's world of design and colour will be like entering a hitherto unknown magical world. She will fall in love with everything she sees – from his brilliant office decor to the glorious paintings by Australian artists hanging on the walls. Particularly captivating is a series of primary block-coloured primitive pictures in the manner of Gauguin. They are by Ray Crooke. She will dream of learning more about the local art scene and imagines herself – one day – buying similar pictures.

Plans for the building on the steep hill finished and approved by the local council, she will accompany Brien, dressed in her best, to dine in fancy restaurants with developers who profess interest in investing in his project.

It is on one of these evenings that a short, red-faced man with a nose like Pinocchio will stride over to her table and offer her a job in his real estate office. His chest puffed out like a turkey, he has been circling the restaurant like a celebrity, calling the waiters by name, and greeting the property fraternity who are dining there. When Agnes recoils from the proposal, Brien will nudge her and, under his breath, tell her it is a great chance.

She will discover that Mr Bill only employs women – most of whom look as if they have stepped out of a fashion magazine. Agnes's desk, in a glass-partitioned cubicle in the front office, is where she meets buyers. The real money-making goes on in the back office, headed by Mr Bill's glamorous secretary, Cindy, who sends letters with cash offers to owners via addresses provided by the local council. Most owners seem delighted to sell their run-down terrace house for which they only receive a pittance in rental income from, often, difficult tenants.

Mr Bill – alone, and with partners – will buy rows of tenanted Paddington terrace houses, pay out the tenant and, after a quick coat of paint, sell them on individually via the front office. His business partners will include suave pinstriped solicitors and high-rolling bankers who choose to ignore the uncouth behaviour of their loud-mouthed partner as he fills their pockets with cash. The horror of being powerless, penniless and hungry when a teenager still haunting her, Agnes will vow to take full advantage of the present opportunity. Dedicating herself to the job, she will build up a good sales record and Mr Bill will let her keep the office open all weekend so she can continue to work.

One day she will pluck up the courage to ask:

Will you put up the money and go half shares with me if I find a good property deal?

You'd better get to the bank, Agnes! I just went past and saw the window open!

Apart from managing this kind of constant teasing, she will be sharply aware she has to be careful of Mr Bill, as she has seen him literally throw people out of his office. She was with him one day when he threatened an obstinate tenant like a gangster out of *The Untouchables*. Yet, for all his loud-mouthed posturing, she will have him to thank for the £1000 profit she earns from the deal she successfully pulls off with his capital.

In the following years, she will build on that £1000, buying and selling property herself. She will lie in bed counting her money and calculating the next return. Financial security will buffet her through the emotional rollercoaster ride that lies ahead.

She will fall in love with Paddington and come to know the area so intimately that, wherever she is in the world, she can lie in bed and walk the streets in her head. Friendships with local artists will lead to her involvement in converting several old corner shops into galleries and restaurants displaying art. Although she will have amassed a portfolio of rental property, will have helped friends onto the property ladder, will constantly have come up with solutions to difficult transactional problems, deep inside, she will feel as disconnected from the world as ever.

Her success will bring brother Bert back into her life. When he saunters into her office, he will ignore her as usual, instead focusing his charm on her female employees. But her impulse to help him will continue to override caution, as the sacred, inviolable nature of the family, infused in her from Grandma, will remain strong. She will applaud the way her staff and friends take him to their hearts but, to her, he will remain as inscrutable as ever. If, according to the Beatles, money really could not buy love, she had never grasped the full meaning of that sentiment till now.

The same chasm of misunderstanding will apply to Bert who – by denying his older sister any gratitude for lifting him up, for making him part of her world, for establishing a foundation for his future by buying him his first house at auction – will succeed not only in harming her, but also in ultimately denying himself all that is worthwhile in life. Given their seriously dysfunctional childhood, Agnes will arrive at the conclusion that, perhaps, Bert is only able to feel anything by pulling the scabs from the wounds of others and watching them bleed. She will accept that, when she is well, Bert's hatred could be dangerous but, when feeling at her weakest, it could prove fatal.

Many years later, following her discharge from a London hospital after a serious illness, he will visit her, accompanied by his wife, and she will realise she has made a mistake in permitting the visit. Their dismissive, insulting behaviour towards her does no more than reinforce her second husband's abuse. It will remain a final, unforgettable, and unforgivable audacity.

29
HER BROTHER JIM

The announcement that Jim's flight has landed blares over the loudspeaker and Agnes dashes through the airport to the arrival lounge, where passengers from the flight are already trickling through. She is intent on searching each face. After ten years or more, she no longer has a clear picture of the man she is looking for.

She feels a tap on the shoulder and spins around to see a barrel-shaped man with a bull neck and swollen red face. He is staring at her. The shock of the sight of him is enhanced by the scent of alcohol-impregnated sweat which swirls around him like an invisible halo:

Agnes, it's me – Jim. Good to see you after all these years.

His lack of verbal intonation throws her every time. A colourless monotone. Exactly the voice in which he had once told her by phone that her father had been brought to the hospital dead on arrival:

Well – here we are! It's good to see you. I can smell you've had a relaxing flight.

She feels bad being so direct. The snipe burst out of her because she is fearful of being driven miles into the countryside by a drunk. He shoots her a look, and says:

Yes, I sank a few on the flight to help me relax. The beers were included in the ticket you so generously paid for.

He gives her a tight-lipped smirk. Unlike Agnes and Bert, Jim has never taken much interest in his appearance and doesn't realise what an impact it has on others. Wearing a stained grey T-shirt, worn jeans and a faded brown jacket that even a charity shop would reject, he looks like a tramp:

Okay, well, I'll be relying on you to abstain while you're at the wheel, as I'm no longer able to drive with confidence on what, for me, is the wrong side of the road.

No worries, mate. You can rely on me. Like Qantas – never had an accident!

Agnes is searching for something to say:

It must feel strange to be on a flight again after so long.

Damn right! I can't remember the last time. When I lived in Mittagong I used to drive to an office in Sydney and fly interstate regularly. That was when Marline stayed home and looked after the horses:

Yes. I visited you there. Midway through the eighties, remember? I never understood why you moved from that lovely house – after all the effort you put into building it.

She is gazing at him now – painfully aware she knows very little about him:

Well, in a word – Mother. I lived too close to her. Her constant demands drove me insane. You know how lazy she is. Always better to get someone else to do it. She spent so much time in bed, it's amazing she didn't get fly blown.

He is grinning now, exposing a mouth full of broken teeth that look like the aftermath of a bomb explosion. Yet, through the ravaged features, she sees he is still the only one of the three siblings who looks like Madge. What distresses Agnes more than the broken teeth, puffed face and worn clothes, however, is how the colour has faded from his dark eyes. She doesn't want this worn-out man to be her brother. For months she has listened on the phone, in silent disbelief, to accounts of various disasters on a farm she will never see. All she can think of at this moment is that no financial institution will take him seriously:

Jim, you can't possibly see a bank manager looking this way. You should look like you don't need money.

Again, she feels bad, being so blunt. In line, waiting for a taxi, a voice inside her is telling her to hug him, and she finally does so clumsily – feeling even more awkward when her arms won't fit around his waist. He drops the old canvas bag on his shoulder and hugs her back. The awkward embrace seems to break the ice, and they relax together in the back of the taxi on the way to the Grantham Apartments.

Earlier that day, while at a loose end awaiting Jim's arrival, she had wandered around King's Cross looking for a gift for him and was pleased to find a book called *The Horse Whisperers*, which she had hoped would please her horse-breeder brother.

When they enter the apartment, the first thing he sees is the billowing red bow on the gift-wrapped parcel on the pillow of his sofa bed which had been prepared that morning for him by 'Wilma Two'. Agnes says:

Open it. It's for you.

She hands the gift to him and watches him rip off the paper with shocking ferocity. He holds the book in his rough hands, staring at the title. She smiles at him reassuringly:

It's to celebrate your new start.

Thanks. I've heard of it. Marline will like it.

It is as if he is merely an agent through which things pass to his wife, and Agnes feels instant anger at the way Marline has dissipated his retirement money. Compensation for years of work had been lost in months on her hare-brained schemes. She shudders to think of the last time she saw Marline – it was at the farm she and Jim developed in Queensland after selling up in New South Wales. Jim had landed another job and was commuting to a Brisbane office. He had still looked good back then, but everything had fallen apart when he left the well-paid Personnel Manager position and joined Marline as a full-time horse breeder.

Agnes knows all this because she lent them a bridging loan to buy a cheaper house while they waited for a buyer for the lovely place that they were forced to sell to cover their debts. She had feared the worst when she realised that Marline not only had more tickets on herself than the National Lottery but had Jim firmly under her thumb. Presumably feeling threatened by Agnes, she had used the presence of a ferocious white Italian sheepdog to make sure she never returned. Agnes can still see the enormous creature throwing itself against the glass door of the courtyard in a frenzy. She had made no effort to say goodbye to her hostile sister-in-law.

After settling in at their table, Agnes suggests to Jim that, perhaps, they have ordered enough, as she watches him add more and more dishes to their order at a Thai restaurant in Macleay Street. Henceforth, she will watch her brother with a mixture of disgust and concern, as he devours copious quantities of food at her expense. As if reading her mind, he says:

I promise I'll only drink when the day's driving is behind me.

She crosses her fingers under the table:

Well, Jim, I don't know if you've made plans for tomorrow morning, but I've organised a massage for you at the Ginseng Bath House. With Svetlana. You can follow it with a dip in the warm perfumed water in the pool. Then we'll collect the hire car and head out of Sydney:

He is draining the last of the wine out of the bottle:

Sounds good. Christmas has come early. Thanks a million. I'm having my first holiday in years!

He is mumbling – his mouth full of the last slices of beef with chilli sauce.

* * *

Agnes waits with her brother at the bath house till Svetlana arrives so she can introduce him personally. In the last months she has regularly crawled up the familiar spiral staircase, letting the musical waves on the stairs lap over her, longing for Svetlana's healing hands.

When Jim arrives back at the apartment, he is looking as much like a new man as is possible. He has shaved and put on a clean shirt. The smell of talcum powder, mixed with the minty aroma of the aftershave from the bath house, has expunged the stale alcohol that so panicked her at the airport.

As they turn onto the M5 motorway out of Sydney, speeding below ground over a smooth-surfaced road and through a series of bright new tunnels, Agnes feels her confidence in Jim's driving grow. This culminates in a point of utter relief when the police dismiss him in minutes after subjecting him to a random breathalyser test at Liverpool.

Compared to their father's long pilgrimage from the cotton factory back to the farm with the sun setting in his eyes, the westbound drive of Eric Keen's children is a silken affair. In under an hour, they have reached the Camden Valley Way. They are going to visit their father's grave.

Arriving at Forest Lawn Memorial Park at Leppington, Jim parks the car and leads Agnes off a side path and down to an elevated mound under tall gum trees. And there it is:

Eric David Keen 1919 to 1968.
Beloved husband of Madge Keen
And cherished father to children Agnes Bert and Jim.

The metal plaque is cracked through, as if struck by lightning. Once again, Agnes is hit forcibly by the fact that her father was only forty-nine when he died. But what surprises her more is the sight of her name inscribed alongside those of her brothers:

Look Jim! My name's right there!

What did you expect?!

He is giving her an odd look. But no tangible evidence can alleviate the profound depth of the alienation she has felt most of her life. She says:

Remember how Madge wanted to have the horses at the funeral?

She has ventured this remark because she is keen to change the subject. Jim seems eager to chat:

Do I ever! She turned the whole thing into a three-ringed circus. Lucky he wasn't there to see it. Enough. Let's get out of here. Why don't we drive to Mittagong and take a look at my old house? We don't have to be at Madge's till six.

Agnes readily agrees. This graveyard is a creepy, phoney place that smacks of advance funeral plans and false sentimentality. As they drive, she questions Jim as much as she dares:

Have you any good memories of our father?

But she didn't need to worry about any reticence on his part. Jim says:

Well, let's put it this way. He didn't give a shit about his kids. He never came to see me play football. Never visited me at boarding school or, for that matter, bothered to come and see me during my months in hospital. Once he even forgot to pick me up for the school holidays. Another time he stopped at the Crossroads Hotel on the way for the inevitable quick one and then drove on to the farm without me. I'd got out of the scorching car to wait under a tree. I watched him dash out and drive off! He didn't even remember I'd been with him until Madge asked where I was. Too eaten up with himself to take an interest in anyone else. You're right about the horses though. They didn't answer back.

She looks at her brother, finding it strange that, after growing up together, this is the first time they have ever spoken frankly about their parents.

As they reach Jim's old house they pull up at the side of the road in silence. When he speaks, his voice is slow and measured and she can detect a hint of sadness:

What I can see of it looks the same – although the garden's turned into a jungle.

Further contemplation is cut short when a woman in a red dress suddenly swings in front of the entrance in a white BMW. She gets out of the car to open the gate. Jim seems to take her appearance as a sign he is no longer wanted. Looking uncomfortable, he sets his shoulders and points the car in the direction of the main street of Mittagong. He tells Agnes he is heading for the restaurant where he and Marline used to order Marline's favourite – chicken in the basket:

There's the place, Agnes! On that corner. But it's called something else.

He seems disappointed. The trendy decor, with vegetarian gluten-free alternatives exhibited on the window menu, certainly isn't what they are looking for, and so they drive on out of town, settling for a cosy roadside café. Over their coffee and sandwiches, hoping to lift Jim's spirits, Agnes says:

Madge and Bert must have been impressed when they saw your Mittagong house.

Jim tells her they only came once. A few days before one Christmas. He had rushed to finish the decorating and had done the best he could with the garden to impress them. Marline couldn't stand Bert, so she had stayed in town. It was a lovely day. The horses were grazing in the paddocks and a cool breeze had sprung up just before they arrived. They had stamped into the house. Both perched on the sofa, just glaring around them, barely saying a word. It would have been better if they'd never come at all, Jim says.

Agnes is appalled:

Christ, Jim, how awful! The green-eyed monster had them by the throat.

He looks at her, a long-buried anger smouldering in his eyes:

Yeah. And it wasn't enough to piss on the house. As they left, Bert hit me with the usual 'off to see someone more important' rubbish and – you guessed it, Agnes – who else did they have to rush off to meet?

She grins at him, instantly knowing the answer:

No contest, Jim! The sanctified Maple Floods from Goulburn!

It's no wonder I feel like a heap of shit.

He is bowing his head over his plate, like a tired plough horse. But Agnes feels the need to explain a particularly pertinent experience of her own. She tells Jim how she reckoned Bert had the same antipathy to his siblings as Madge has to hers. How he only ever appeared in her life when the pickings looked good. She relates the event a few years back when she flew from London to Paris having heard he was there on business. She had asked him to book her a room in his hotel – which of course he didn't bother doing. They had dined at the famous 'Deux Magots' where Bert did his usual 'I'll pay for the wine, and you pay for the food' routine and shrugged off her comments about his past behaviour with the usual flippancy. Then, out of the blue, she tells Jim, he had started ranting about hating single women. That he could never stand it when his wife engaged a woman in conversation who was obviously solo during their travels. He had sounded like some sort of deranged misogynist, his devotion to putting her down having not changed one bit.

It was in Paris, she tells her brother, she had realised she was no longer afraid of what Bert was. It was what he *wasn't* that fascinated her. That sad lack of curiosity about others. That total lack of empathy. The emptiness she felt when they had parted had left her with no desire to ever see him again. Then, at the Rodin Museum the following day, she had read how Rodin's lover – a talented sculptress herself – was committed to a mental hospital by her younger brother. She languished there for thirty years until her death. Shockwaves had passed through her as she considered this outcome. What if she hadn't earned her own living? What if Bert had been successful in controlling *her* life? Her fate might have been identical to that of Camille Claudel!

Although she has spoken at such length, Jim has listened intently. He has concentrated his attention entirely on her. He sighs deeply as if drawing up the next sentence from a deep well:

You know, Agnes, you're the only person I could ever turn to for help. You were always kind to me – and I want you to know I'm grateful.

His eyes are watering as he puts his rough hand on hers. She says:

Well, Jim. Now you're on your way again you won't need any more help from anyone.

She has responded like this in the hope he would finally see the predatory nature of his wife and make the necessary changes for the better. But honestly, what were the odds of that happening?

30

MADGE AT HOME

Jim has parked the car inches from the double garage doors. They are lingering – neither of them inclined to move. Agnes is the first to rouse herself, saying:

All right. Let's get it over with.

Jim collects the bags from the boot. Agnes follows him along a stone path beside a lawn covered in leaves, to a set of cement steps cantilevered off the front wall of the house.

The lady of the house is glaring down at them from the porch above. As soon as Jim sets eyes on her, Agnes sees his body contract in the middle as if he has just been punched in the stomach. He ascends the stairs like someone mounting the scaffold.

Predictably, there is no greeting at the door. Agnes hears her mother hiss over her shoulder:

Close the door behind you!

As she steps over the threshold, the old dread returns – utterly undiminished by the passage of time.

She isn't prepared for the toll the years have taken on the old warrior. Her mother literally has the face she deserves. Spite is etched into every sagging muscle. The beauty that thrilled her as a child has left without trace. Standing before her is an overweight woman diminished in height, looking anything but stylish in a pair of beige slacks and a soiled open-necked white blouse. The coiffure has not altered, except there is now an unnatural sheen on the dyed bouffant. The stiffly lacquered curled horns either side of her forehead make her resemble a deranged bull about to charge. The lustre-soaked pearls are still visible around the wrinkled neck. Madge says:

What took you so long? Tammy has already been and gone. I told you to be here for drinks at five sharp!

Agnes looks at Jim for support, as he was the one who made the arrangements. He splutters an apology:

I'm sorry. I thought you said not to come before 6pm. Madge bridles:

Well, I don't know *what* I said. I wanted Tammy to meet Agnes. It will have to be on your way back now, as she's going away for the weekend.

Agnes is genuinely disappointed:

What a pity. I would have liked to see her.

Tammy Watson had made her previous visits with her mother half bearable. She lived opposite and came over every evening for a gin and tonic. She worked as a doctor's receptionist in a local practice. It was a gift knowing her mother had a concerned neighbour, as Agnes's greatest fear was being embroiled into looking after Madge in old age. Now that dreaded time had arrived and, thankfully, Tammy was still there.

It is twelve years since she last visited her mother, bubbling with news of Daniel's romantic marriage proposal – a proposal typically declared at Heathrow airport, minutes before Agnes has boarded the flight. The proposal had the air of authentication of Agnes as a 'proper woman' and she couldn't wait to display this hard-won triumph in front of Madge. And now here she is – returning as a failure in her mother's eyes, having had any hope of being cherished and cared for in her own later life dashed. Having, once again, been driven to the brink of madness.

Agnes hands her mother a bunch of white carnations mixed with blue clematis – all that was available outside a supermarket on the way. Together with a bottle of red wine, and says:

I hope you like this one. It's Brown Brothers. I often drink it in London.

Madge puts the bottle on the desktop next to her and dumps the flowers beside it in her usual uncouth fashion. There are no thanks. She skewers Agnes with a look:

What have you done to your hair?

Agnes explains that she has had it cut short. That it's easier for travelling. That she just washes it under the shower and flicks it into place with her fingers. She can tell from the shadow of a question mark in the old eyes that Madge senses a change in her daughter. It is an animal thing. As a result, Agnes is no longer on the defensive, even in the face of the familiar petulance. And here it comes:

I don't know what it is, but you children always get me churned up. If you only came at the right time everything would be different.

Agnes exercises her new resilience:

Well, Jim admitted he made a mistake, and now we're here, so let's make the best of it.

Her comment brings a well-worn response:

None of your smart tongue, Agnes. You know where it got you. A first, now a second marriage on the rocks. The trouble with you is you don't know how to keep your man.

Agnes sees red. She is not going to be defeated by this woman. Not any longer:

What rubbish! Euphemistically that's the whole problem! I *did* keep my man. Why on God's earth would I want to hang on to avaricious predators who steal my money and treat me badly? If holding onto your man means manipulating the shit out of him, like you did to Daddy, then you're right about me!

Madge rises to the occasion as of old:

How *dare* you speak to me like that, you *wretched* girl. Now you've *ruined* everything! I was *so* looking forward to seeing you, and now it's made me sick. You've provoked a turn. Where are my pills? Hand me those!

Madge is swaying on her feet for effect and pointing at a side table:

Yes – yes, *that's* them. Unscrew the top… hurry, hurry!

Agnes obeys the tyrannical command. With an air of resignation hanging over him like a fog, Jim goes to fetch a glass of water. He places it down on a small table beside the lounge chair into which his mother has slumped. The sister and brother watch as their mother swallows two tiny pills, after which she lies back in the chair and closes her eyes. She really does look her age:

Are you all right, Mummy? Do you want us to call anyone?

A sudden pang of all-too-familiar guilt has Agnes kneeling on the floor, with her hand on her mother's arm. In the house barely two minutes and they are at one another's throats. The lifelong patterns are indelible. Printed on the walls of their lives like hieroglyphs.

But Madge refuses to answer. Agnes looks at Jim, who shrugs, and glances at the ceiling in tired exasperation. Their mother waves them both away with her hand, her eyes still shut:

Just leave me alone. I'll come around in a minute. I don't need outside help.

Jim walks back into the kitchen and puts on the kettle where Agnes joins him. They sip their tea thoughtfully, leaning on the kitchen counter. The colour starts to come back into Jim's face. With a low voice, he says:

Why does she behave like that? What does she get out of it?

Agnes sighs:

Don't ask me. She's a monster. Jean told me that when they were growing up, she'd scream till she got what she wanted and that it's been the same ever since. It's got her nowhere. Everyone loathes her. Except Tammy.

I'll have some tea…!

It is a plaintive cry from the sick woman on the lounge chair and it curtails further chat.

When Agnes looks in the cupboard to find a cup and saucer for her mother's tea – just as she had done so often as a child – she notices much of the crockery is still dirty. She discovers the cutlery is soiled too, as are the pots and pans. Her mother was usually so fastidious about washing up. She has also noticed the big numbers on the dial of the phone which indicate her mother is losing her sight. There and then, she decides to send Tammy the money to buy Madge a dishwasher and arrange for an eye specialist.

Madge has just announced to her children that the pills are for her 'poor old heart'. Agnes carefully hands her a cup of tea and says:

We thought we could take you out for dinner, Mummy. There's a place we passed in town that looks good.

But no. Apparently Madge has the dinner planned. They were to have rump steak, potatoes in their jackets with sour cream and chives, along with mushrooms and peas. The English girls had done the pre-requisite shopping yesterday.

This offer of hospitality surprises Agnes, as her mother tends to jump at an invitation to go to a restaurant, where she orders the most expensive thing on the menu – usually lobster.

Agnes persists with her invitation, as she would far prefer to dine around a table in a neutral setting. She decides to wave a proverbial carrot:

I enquired and they have lobster.

But the ploy fails:

I've already told you, Agnes. I've got it all planned. Come, darling and I'll show you – it's all in the fridge.

Teacup in hand, her mother is sounding suddenly carefree, as if she is sashaying along the red carpet on the sixth floor of 'David Jones'. This typical mercurial mood change is another reminder of times past, and Agnes starts to feel as if the walls are closing in. She controls this unwelcome upsurge of anxiety by concentrating on the decor of Madge's home. The interior mirrors the exterior's absurdity. A narrow double-sided fitted kitchen, with no natural light, sits in the centre as if a railway carriage has come crashing in from the side. The living room rotates around it, merry-go-round style. It is more like the layout of a community centre than a home. Further exploration reveals a desk below a set of shelves – containing the now tarnished polo trophies. Several clumsy floral loose-covered lounge chairs are scattered around, and a dining table and chairs inhabit a narrow nook at the far end of the room. While her mother sips her tea, and Jim decamps into the garden to relax, Agnes wanders around.

There must be four, perhaps five, bedrooms and most of the small rear garden is taken up with a fenced oval swimming pool that looks like an installation in an aquatic research centre. A machine that her mother affectionately calls a 'creepy crawly' is farting its way randomly, and with no perceptible logic, across the pool floor and up the sides. It strikes Agnes, having listened when a child to her mother's endless descriptions of the glorious interior of the fabulous house on the grand property in the Great Dividing Range, how incongruous it is that – when finally free to choose a house for herself – she opts for one that resembles extra accommodation in a caravan park.

Seated at the dining table after dinner, prepared by Agnes under the close direction of her mother, and the usual mindless chit-chat having been exhausted, Agnes decides that enquiries about the past can't wait a moment longer. Unable to stomach the underlying tension, Jim gets up to clear the table. Now is the time. There will never be another opportunity. Agnes stares at her mother's tight, wrinkled mouth and says:

Mummy. I'd like you to explain a few things I never understood.

Well, make it quick, Agnes, as I'm tired and don't want to stay up much longer.

How did I end up at seventeen in a godforsaken boarding house for old people all alone and with no money?

Her mother dabs at her mouth with a linen napkin and sighs deeply, as if someone has told her that the next train is going to be late. She doesn't look at Agnes, but says:

Why on *earth* are you bringing this up after all these years?

Because, to me, it remains a painful, unsolved mystery.

Now Madge chooses to shoot a shrewd glance at her daughter. It occurs to Agnes she is weighing up the impact of what may be coming next. Madge says:

Well, if you *must* know, you were sent there because you were cavorting with your uncle and your aunt was jealous.

Her mother has dropped this bombshell in such a matter-of-fact way that it is as if the rationale should have been obvious to all but the most stupid.

What do you *mean*?!

Madge's facial expression borders on the incredulous:

Flirting! You were always a *dreadful* flirt, Agnes. *Everyone* said so. Your father and I cared about you *deeply,* but we couldn't handle you. You were a classifiable delinquent. Everyone thought so – your school, your grandmother, *all* the family!

Here it was. The showdown. Let it rip:

Cared about me! Nobody tried harder to annihilate me than *you* did. Those other people – that so-called family – belonged to *you*, not me! They only heard the pack of lies *you* fabricated. Even Marnie said you sent me to them with no money. Gave me no money and paid them no money for my upkeep. How caring was *that*?!

Oh, don't listen to *her*. She's *always* got an axe to grind. She's a poor pathetic woman who doesn't know what she's talking about. It's the stroke.

You O'Connor women are such wilting violets! I was no Lolita! If Marnie was jealous, why didn't she hit him over the head and send him packing? As I recall, he was a lazy bastard who did fuck all! You demonised me to get *rid* of me!

We did nothing of the sort. You're exaggerating all this. Grandma was prepared to pay for you to go to an expensive boarding school, but you thumbed your nose at her.

I couldn't concentrate! Something went wrong inside me, and I *know* it had something to do with you and Daddy. Something triggered such extreme anxiety I lost the ability to read properly. I've been extremely handicapped ever since.

Well, how would I know any of *that* Agnes! I'm not a mind reader!

Right. Well. Perhaps you can tell me then, Mother, how old *you* were when your father first showed you *his* penis?!

There is a long pause. Her mother's Adam's apple bobs in her fleshy throat against the pearls:

How *dare* you even *suggest* such a thing! My father would *never* do that!

Well, *mine* did and you *know* it! You didn't even seem shocked! Instead of sending the pervert packing, you laughed!

Oh, *that* day. With Rita Ryder, wasn't that her name? It was just a silly *joke*, Agnes!

Really? Well, you've got a poor sense of humour! Rita Ryder went straight home to tell her parents! *They* certainly didn't think it was a joke. It forced those I loved most in all the world to cut me out of their life! And, as we're on the subject of abusive behaviour, what about Lennox Street?

Madge sighs as if now profoundly bored by the proceedings. Agnes half expects her to retreat to her bedroom, but she doesn't move. Instead, she says:

None of that was my fault. The boy was a troublemaker.

Agnes holds back her rising temper with difficulty:

Paul was intelligent and curious and kind. And he'd still be with us *today* if *you* had acted differently. Why didn't you report the live cable spewed over the street to the authorities?

We didn't have a phone Agnes, so what was I supposed to do?

How about running down the road to the bloody phone box! Or asking a neighbour if you could use theirs? Or just screaming your fucking head off until someone alerted the police? How could you knowingly let little children play around a live cable with thousands of volts running through it? If I had kept holding his hand, Mother, I would have died *too*!

Madge purses her lips:

I made sure you were wearing gumboots.

What kind of twisted logic is *that*?!

In these seminal moments, these moments of pure, unadulterated truth-telling and its consequences, Agnes has it irrevocably confirmed that she has been protecting this idiotic woman most of her life, and what an utter waste of heartbeats it has been. Madge stirs in her chair, preparing to stand up:

Enough of this childish nonsense, Agnes. You've worn me out.

Agnes selects an armchair, sits back, and observes her mother make her preparations to retire to bed. Once Madge finally closes her bedroom door behind her Agnes and Jim, standing side by side, systematically wash and dry the pots and plates used for dinner. Then they scrub and rinse the old dry food off the stacked pots and pans in the cupboards. Agnes is the one who breaks the silence:

I had to confront her, Jim.

I know.

She tells him how she went to Lennox Street recently and how it all came back. *Years* of feeling responsible for Paul's death. Did he remember going to the orphanage? Did he know that Marnie said the reason their father didn't turn up to rescue them was because he was having an affair with another woman? That he even took this person to dinner at their house? She declares to Jim that she believes it is a miracle they survived. That it hit her tonight that she was always the mother and Madge always the child. That it was arse about from the beginning.

Jim hears her out. He is looking towards the door of Madge's bedroom when he says:

That woman in there, snoring her lazy head off, used to beat me so badly sometimes I couldn't go to school because of the bruises on my legs. She'd do it when there was no one around. She'd get this crazed look in her eye and attack me with a belt. That's why I ran away. I thought she'd kill me, so I took ten pounds out of her purse and caught a train to Hornsby. When I tried to change the big bill for cash the woman in the shop rang the police. The policeman saw the bruises on my legs, then someone else came in and asked about the bruises. Social workers probably. I said I had a fight at school. They kept fishing for information about my home life. I knew I'd be in for it if I ever complained about her, so I didn't answer.

Truth-telling. And its consequences. Agnes puts a hand on his arm:

My God, Jim. I never knew.

Jim leans in towards her, lowering his voice to a hoarse whisper:

I should warn you that you've been set up. Madge is out of money. She wants you to buy her house and give her a life tenancy. I should have told you earlier, but I couldn't face it.

Agnes smiles to herself:

Is that so? Well. I shall suggest she rings Grandma in heaven.

* * *

Agnes wakes the next morning from a nightmare, her heart pounding. She is in an unfamiliar bedroom in her mother's home. She tries to shrug off the dream but cannot.

Something… something… about scooping up filth. In a bathroom. Of removing an ugly brown mess of shit with a mop and bucket. Of wiping the wet floor dry with old towels until the white tiles sparkle. But, like an Alfred Hitchcock twist, the toilet lid had sprung open and belched out fresh turds like an oil gush over the floor. She had pumped at the flush handle on the toilet, but the level was rising. She was drowning. Slowly drowning.

She jumps out of bed and runs to the bathroom, throwing herself under the shower, letting the water cascade over her face. She scrubs at her body till her arms and legs ache. She washes her hair so many times that she finishes the shampoo in the Pears bottle – that same amber-coloured brand they used as children. The image on the bottle – of a sweet-faced mother holding out a towel to a wet-headed child – collides with Agnes's own memory of herself as a child proffering a towel in her small hands to her own babied mother.

She covers herself in talcum powder and eau de cologne, then touches her toes and runs on the spot to help contain the thunderstorm reverberating inside her. She knows she is firmly back in the terrorising hold of childhood and must face the woman who is her mother again today. Trying to control her breathing, she dresses herself in white jeans, white cotton jumper and white trainers – top-to-toe whiteness in defiance of the putrid nightmare. It is Good Friday. As a child she would spend all Easter on her knees with Grandma.

She opens the window. The world outside is drenched in sunlight and the sonorous drone of lawnmowers, and the hint of light laughter from the surrounding gardens fills the air.

She enters the lounge area where her mother and Jim are having breakfast, seated at the table at the end of the room. Jim has been to the bakery and bought fresh bread and croissants. The sun is bursting into the house through every dark crack to spotlight the dull walls.

As Agnes approaches the table, she spots three old books stacked on top of each other. The Art Book and the two ballet books she once cherished have mysteriously surfaced. She exclaims:

I can't believe it! Where have they been? I asked you for them hundreds of times and you said they'd been lost!

But it seems that, after the previous evening's exchanges, Madge is too busy eating and not willing to engage further. It is a predictably sulky post-argument state that is only too familiar. But it would be bound to change. If what Jim had told her last night was true, Madge would have to work the charm at some point.

Agnes opens the cover of the ballet books in turn, to find the dedications inscribed to Agnes have both been crossed out and replaced with her mother's name. There is a smudged ink spot on one flyleaf where her mother has probably shaken the fountain pen in her rush to claim it. She stares at the desecrated pages – transfixed. Books for her mother, had never been more than doorstops. Why did she claim what didn't remotely interest her?

Unaware of Agnes's discovery, her mother decides to communicate:

Listen, darling, I honestly had no idea what happened to them. I opened a drawer I hadn't opened in years the other day and there they were. I'm as surprised as you are. You can take them with you and send them to yourself from the Post Office if they're too heavy for your luggage.

The mood change, apparently. She is cooing at her daughter, now – adopting the once-longed-for baby tone that now turns Agnes's stomach. Still disturbed by the vandalism perpetrated upon her beloved books, she demands:

Why didn't you send *these* to me instead of the huge mass of heavy rubbish that kept arriving in Mallorca?

I have *told* you, Agnes, I only just found them.

Jim pauses from wolfing down a mound of scrambled eggs and bacon and looks up at his sister with a wry smile. She wonders if, by taking the books, she will be compromising herself. But the books are rightfully hers – even The Art Book that no one else ever appreciated. She feels she has paid for it a thousand times over.

She can't stomach bacon and eggs today, nor watch the ugly way her mother is collecting the drips of a boiled egg with her fat tongue. The woman is repulsive to her.

Agnes…

Her mother's tone is a little uncertain, tentative. Jim shifts uncomfortably in his chair.

Madge turns towards her daughter, widening her eyes as if petitioning a reluctant suitor:

I've got no money, Agnes. I thought you could buy my house cheaply and let me stay here. Stay here for life I mean. I'm already eighty-five and have a bad heart, so you won't have to wait long to get possession and then you can sell the place on at a profit.

Agnes leans forward in her chair. She must face her. She wants to make her suffer. She demands:

Why don't you ask Bert?

Is it her imagination, or is her mother looking nervous? Madge adopts a wheedling tone:

I did, but he's got no spare cash because he's expanding his business and Jim can't help me because he's struggling, aren't you, Jim?

Poor Jim lowers his head over his plate and Agnes can feel his shame. But Madge has no mercy on her youngest son:

Jim already owes me $5,000 and is hoping, aren't you Jim, that you could take over the debt.

This latest machination is news to Agnes but doesn't surprise her. Nothing about this family does:

What on earth makes you think I should help you?

But she feels guilty just saying it. Her brother is looking out of the window, avoiding her eyes. Scenting what is at stake, what could disappear over the horizon, Madge hits her stride:

Because Jim said you sold the big house you owned with your husband in London and because you're my daughter and I'm your mother and all children look after their parents in old age.

Agnes takes stock. Why did Jim tell their mother about the London house? Are they *both* colluding against her?

A fresh rage against her mother surges inside her – this selfish, self-regarding woman who has had more money handed to her on a plate than the whole family put together. But what would be the point of further interrogation? She might feel like strangling this excuse for a parent but, at the same time, is struck with a perverse sense of honour in being asked by such an abject failure of a woman for help. The conflict is unbearable. She feels hatred yet is still affected by the old guilt. Why? Will anyone ever be able to explain to her *why* this should be the case?

The sight of the floral carpet under her white shoes is making her dizzy. She feels suddenly claustrophobic. She can't breathe. Afraid of making a detrimental snap decision, she can do nothing but escape. Attempt to flee from the massive turmoil within.

She jumps up, opens the front door, and runs down the steps. She strides down the street past neighbours in their gardens larking about in the sunshine. Friendly in their domestic security, they wave and smile at her. She thinks of the cool-headed way she took control of the London house once she got Daniel out. How swiftly she put it on the market when the tenant returned to the USA after 9/11. How cleverly she avoided an earful of insults by not consulting Daniel personally but informing him via a solicitor. How competently she had managed what had been one of the most challenging crises of her life. She tells herself firmly now, as she walks along this unfamiliar street – you *did* it! And you did it single-handedly. Give yourself some credit, Agnes! By resisting reverting to histrionics with Daniel, by keeping a cool and calm business head on your shoulders, you managed to sell the house yourself and you *escaped*! SO DO THE SAME WITH THIS WOMAN!

Staring into a full-blown white rose that the least breeze would reduce to a stem, she sees her own fragility in its petals. The truth of her situation hits her. No amount of recrimination can change the past. Her mother could *never* love her because she is incapable of loving anyone. But she, Agnes, could learn to love herself.

She takes several deep breaths, lifts her head to feel the warmth of the morning sun on her face, and turns back.

Jim and her mother raise their heads as she enters and announces:

Thanks for the offer of the books. I'll have to think about your proposal and get back to you.

The last time her mother has looked this surprised was when Agnes told her about the adopted baby. But it hasn't robbed her of speech:

You can have it for $300,000. That's cheap, Agnes. The agent said it's worth $350,000.

Madge's eyes are darting gleefully around the room. She clearly believes she has won a victory over this vexatious daughter:

I'd need new carpets. And as for *you*, Jim – you can't leave without paying me back the $5000 straight away!

Seeing yet another look of shame pass over Jim's face will be too much for Agnes to bear. She cannot put off the decision and make him suffer, so she will agree to take over his debt. She will scribble out an agreement that is good for one year. Should her mother die and go to hell within that time, the $5000 will be paid back to Agnes out of her estate. She will write out a cheque for her mother. Jim will sign the agreement. Seated at the desk, she will watch her mother laboriously scrawl the name and details of her solicitor on a piece of paper torn from an address book. Because it is painfully obvious that Madge is struggling to see, Agnes will check these written details before she leaves and will be struck by how alike her handwriting is to that of her parent.

The only similarity between mother and daughter, thank God.

31

UNCLE BEN AND THE OPEN ROAD

Jim is turning north back towards Sydney on the old Hume highway which is now the magnificent M31 motorway. Huge pylons cut into vistas of rolling hills with pockets of new construction dotted on what had once been open countryside. They are rolling smoothly over the surface of the dual carriageway like a ball down the lane of a bowling green.

Off the motorway, on the way to Uncle Ben's house, they see the sign: St Thomas Moore Catholic Church. This must be Uncle Ben's parish church. Jean had told Agnes he had become religious in his old age, dedicating himself exclusively to church work.

Agnes sees houses built back from neatly cut grassy verges that edge curbs of wide streets. The whole area is impeccably neat and tidy. Saint Thomas would surely approve of its Utopian nature. Jim slows his speed, and swings the Toyota into a drive, pulling up in front of a garage with white painted doors. The single-storey house sits in the middle of a large symmetrical block surrounded by virgin bushland.

In contrast to their mother's hostile greeting, Ben flies out of the door towards them – grinning like a playful puppy:

Welcome! Lucky I just got back from buying a few extras for lunch!

His enthusiasm had always been his most endearing quality. But nothing, it seems, has changed in the cardigan-ogling department. He looks Agnes up and down through thick glasses, like a horse he's thinking of buying.

They follow him into a large bare-walled living room that feels uninhabited, as if new owners are still in the process of moving in. A coffee table is set up with glasses and bowls of snacks. Agnes smiles at her uncle:

Thanks very much, Uncle Ben, for agreeing to see us.

She settles herself down on a blue sofa. Jim sits opposite her, his gnarled hands folded over an extended belly. Agnes is relieved when he refuses a beer. Aware he is eating his way through a daily alcohol craving she offers him the plate of potato chips and he gratefully grabs a handful. Agnes accepts water, and Ben pours himself and Jim a Fanta orange. Agnes breaks the slightly awkward silence:

Uncle Ben, I brought you this…

She pulls a small parcel out of her bag.

Oh, my goodness! Let's see what we've got here!

He is tearing at the white tissue paper to reveal a small metal box with an image of St Peter's in Rome on the ceramic top. Then he pulls out a string of white rosary beads with a gold cross. He holds them up to the light:

Are they blessed?

He is lifting them higher as if searching for evidence of sanctity:

Yes, they were blessed by the Pope.

She is aware her affirmation doubles the enhancement, whilst not caring if it's true or not.

Thank you, Agnes. I'll keep them close.

She watches him slip the rosary beads into the pocket of his slacks, and notices that his face now exudes the smarmy goodness expressed on the faces of some priests. With his greying short haircut, dark trousers, and white polo neck, he could fit the role to a 'T'. Straight-backed, slim, with clear eyes and skin, at age eighty he appears in remarkable good health. He turns to her and says:

Tell me – how's dear old Maggie? I hear she's been having trouble with her sight.

Maggie. Her mother's pet name amongst her brothers. He has spoken in a cloying tone that matches the benevolent expression. Agnes decides she will give him the bare details. There is still a family grapevine, that's evident, and she doesn't want to feed it. She replies:

She seems to manage. Carers from the local council do her washing, take her shopping, and to the doctors and hairdresser. Meals on wheels bring food during the week. She doesn't want for anything – except money.

She knows her sarcasm is lost on him when he says:

Glad she's managing. Good old Maggie.

He repeats her mother's pet name like an aging Romeo extolling the virtues of Juliet. Puzzled by this, she asks:

Uncle Ben. Don't you feel any resentment about the way she treated you?

Oh, our Maggie can be a bit tetchy at times, but can't we all!

Jim is so amused by this understatement that he splutters in the process of taking a gulp of Fanta. He looks at his sister, eyes running, coughing, before standing up and shaking himself like a dog after a bath. He tries to conceal his mirth – and fails.

Ben glances at them both in turn, then excuses himself to go into the kitchen. When Agnes offers to help, he says:

No trouble. I've developed a liking for domestic duties.

But she follows him anyway, to find him pulling a loaf of bread out of the oven with a floral oven glove. He puts the bread down on a bench in silence, then beckons her to a corner near the fridge – out of earshot of Jim in the dining room:

I hope you haven't come here to make trouble, Agnes.

Here it is again. She is the perpetual troublemaker. The shaker of foundations. She says:

Of course not! What trouble could I – or would I – want to make? I was fond of you when I was young. You taught me things and made me feel special. I'm just trying to get to the bottom of the loss of memory I experienced as a child. It's gone on affecting me all my adult life.

He shrugs and says:

Oh. That's all right then. I just don't want my wife to be upset.

He takes the tinfoil off the hot loaf. She knows this man has every reason to love his second wife. The woman might be the prototype for the song 'Stand by Your Man'. Devoted secretary, clandestine lover, she has remained at his side ever since the cotton factory business collapsed. Estimated as over fifteen years his junior, she travels each day to Sydney by train to work as a secretary to support them both. A little later, when Agnes pops to the bathroom, she will spot the two towelling bathrobes hanging side by side, together with a heart-shaped card with the legend LOVE YOU leaning against the mirror.

Having helpfully shipped the used plates back to the kitchen and stacking them by the sink, she returns to the living room to hear:

Boy-oh-boy, Jim, when you lost your temper, you *really* lost it! After a run-in with her, you were so fired up, there was no one to match you. A real bull in a china shop. No – wait – that's not right. What the heck am I talking about – there was *masses* of room on the field! Nothing to break but your bloody neck and you came close a few times – especially when Maggie got your goat!

The two men seem to be reminiscing about polo matches they had played together but she sees that Jim is squirming as Ben cruelly underlines the power his mother had over him. The power to urge her youngest son on one minute and cut the ground from under him the next. Very much Madge's style. Agnes decides to rescue Jim by changing the subject. And, despite the earlier veiled threat in the kitchen, proceeds with:

And what about my father? Any abiding memories there?

Ben grins at her:

Only the good die young, Agnes, and he was a good man. Fantastic player. Made every post a golden mile. He was so proud, you know – when you bought him those two horses. He'd go on about your success. Running your own business.

Hearing this allusion to her father's praise – compliments that had never come her way – pulls her up short. She hears herself speak her thoughts aloud:

He might have been proud, but he never told me.

That right? Well, I can't tell you anything about *that* now, can I?

Ben's voice has increased a few decibels to the authoritarian boom that used to frighten his children and Agnes wonders if a life devoid of sensitivity has kept him looking so young. Nothing stuck. Nothing penetrated. All bounced off him without effect. But she will not let this show of bluster deter her. She says:

Aunt Marnie told me that when Grandma took my mother to New Zealand, when Jim and I were dumped in an orphanage, my father had an affair with another woman:

Her uncle narrows his eyes at her:

Did he, by Jove? He was a great one with the ladies. In America, they were all over him. But you know, Agnes, you shouldn't talk badly about the dead. I won't let you say anything against your father in this house, do you understand? You always had a sharp tongue on you. Your father is assuredly in heaven with Parry and Mother.

She couldn't help herself. The rejoinder just slips from her mouth:

Well, that's one place I won't be going, because I don't wish to meet *either* of them again.

The silence in the room will be palpable. She will watch Ben as he leans down to pick up a prayer missal from the coffee table and hold it against his chest like a kind of talisman to ward off incipient fury. She will notice the snowy five o'clock shadow on his cheeks that makes him look like a holy fraud. It seems she has shattered his saintly disposition.

Jim will break the impasse:

Well. We've got a long drive ahead of us, Agnes. We'd better be on our way.

Her brother will be standing tall in the room as if he means business, and she will see he has had more than enough. She will wonder if this fraught encounter might cause him to want a proper drink. She will get up obediently and follow him to the door.

Ben will shuffle after them like a dissolute shepherd, still clutching the missal to his chest. The last-minute apology Agnes is planning to offer him will be spirited away, however, when a wind blows up and forces her uncle to rush back into the house and close the shaking windows. She and Jim will wait for a few minutes in the car, but he will not re-emerge.

Instead, she will give him a final feeble wave when she spots him, looking out wistfully from what must be his bedroom window.

As Jim backs the car out of the drive, a storm of dry leaves and dust will cover the windscreen and obliterate Uncle Ben from her view forever.

* * *

The wind is so powerful, it is buffeting the Toyota from side to side. Jim uses the spray and wipers to clear the glass. She feels a surge of strange hilarity:

Reckon Ben summoned Poseidon to destroy the heretics maligning the dead!

See no evil, speak no evil!

Jim has added his tuppence worth as he peers through the fan-shaped clearing cut by the wipers. Cars move at a snail's pace with their headlights on. Then the appearance of a hearse explains this sluggish progress. A solemn, black-suited man is seated in the front. The hearse contains a honey-coloured coffin with brass handles which is covered in a line of wreaths formed of pink and white gladioli. Jim intones:

Nothing like a funeral to sober you up.

Perhaps he is making an inward vow to take better care of himself. She hopes so. As they pick up pace, she feels the grime of recent ugly events fall away. We only live in moments – she contemplates – we can't buy them, organise them, or steal them. She closes her eyes, hoping it will help her to hold onto this transitory perception of joy.

She wakes to the sound of water, realising she must have dozed off. Jim is cleaning the car on a garage forecourt. He catches her eye and nods – common parlance for 'the bill awaits you'. After settling the account and using the restroom, they move onto the motorway, heading south. After an hour or so, Jim exits at the sign to Goulburn and parks the car in a backstreet.

As they join the crowds strolling along the main street, Agnes suddenly recalls the nightmarish visit to the polo tournament in her early teens. A deadly chill pervades her bones, mirroring the despair of that terrible night of abandonment by her parents. Anxious not to cast a shadow over their day, she tries hard to shake the memory off so that Jim does not pick up on it.

Stepping aside to let a group of people pass, Jim accidently knocks over a display of riding boots in front of a shoe shop. She takes the opportunity to invest herself with fresh optimism:

Let me buy you a pair of boots, Jim, before you break your neck tripping on that flapping sole!

Necessity overcomes his initial reluctance, and within fifteen minutes of her suggestion, he is walking out of the store in a new pair of tan elastic-sided riding boots, having left the battered pair they replaced in the shop. The spending spree has begun. At a clothes supermarket across the road, wool socks are thrown into a self-service basket to replace the threadbare excuses he exposed when he removed his old boots. Socks are joined by underwear, belts, jeans, shirts, jumpers, and a tan fleece-lined jacket. Next stop the chemist for a new washbag, a toothbrush, toothpaste, and shaving gear, all of which her brother accepts in a kind of a haze.

Afterwards, over coffee, her brother surveys the carrier bags that surround him in stunned silence. She suspects the beatings that almost killed him as a child have robbed him of the ability to enjoy such simple pleasures. Just like her, he probably anticipates the worst constantly, and is dumbly relieved when it doesn't happen. She is kicking herself for not thinking of buying him new clothes before this. Facing Madge's critical eyes in his shabby rags must have been a torture to him.

Crookwell, where they plan to spend the night, is not only an historical rural town, but a popular tourist destination. There are 'No Vacancy' signs on the front of every motel, but they do eventually find rooms in the bizarre Spud Murphy's Inn. The incongruous exterior of this hostelry is echoed in the interior. Different sets of stairs lead through a labyrinth of corridors with sloping floors. All rooms appear to be painted in sickly pastel colours and boast ornate bedheads and rose-printed bedspreads. Paintings of flowers, of horses, of pre-Raphaelite women, of historic scenes of the town, hang incongruously alongside each other in reception, in corridors, and on bedroom walls – without harmony or order. None of the furniture is grand or old enough to be antique. The sheer mass of discord baffles the eye, as do the carved dolphins that leap from the wooden bedhead in the room Agnes has been assigned.

The scattering of bathrooms has proved hard to find and, once located, the trajectory back to the room sets a puzzling challenge. Having showered and changed, and got lost several times in the process, Agnes finds her way back downstairs. She settles in an armchair in the expansive open lounge, unnoticed, before an enormous raging log fire. The warmth makes her drowsy. Bleary-eyed, she hardly recognises Jim in his new clothes as he approaches her. He pulls up a chair beside her, and says:

Agnes. How did you turn into such a hotshot entrepreneur?

He has never asked her this before, and she gives him a shorthand version of the twisting and turning events that transpired after Sister Wilfred's fearless defence of her at St Anthony's home. He seems genuinely impressed:

God. You're a bloody marvel to have survived all that. I've never been able to sort myself out!

She tells him he can start the sorting-out process at the dentist and offers to send him the money to have his teeth done. He can pay her back when he starts earning again. Open a separate account in your own name, she tells him, and that way it can't go anywhere else. When he thanks her, she can only hope he has spotted the inference – to guard against his wife and her avarice.

She is feeling an ever-deepening commitment to Jim's well-being. It is a pleasant sensation, to have him under her wing again after all these years, but is she deluding herself? Is she foolish in believing he is joining in with this journey so that they may both understand and eradicate the effects of the past? Is she simply trying to convince herself that he, too, might finally want to comprehend their mutual attraction to being dominated by the will of others?

* * *

The next morning, she watches her brother as he tucks into a hearty cooked breakfast. She is drinking copious cups of coffee after a bad night's sleep. The return of the Goulburn nightmare still haunts the new day. Is it caused by buried memories, or is it simply stress manifesting in symbols?

Yet again, the recurring dream in which she is running away from her father had manifested. She was trapped in a suffocating fog. His piercing blue eyes had shone like searchlights as he gained distance behind her. When he had caught her and she had frozen before his wordless stare, she had woken up with a start.

Still trembling, she had turned on the light and felt comfort upon discovering The Art Book. She had clutched it to her breast the way Ben had clutched at his missal. The book had fallen open on the bed at the painting of Bruegel's 'Fall of Icarus'. She had examined the picture closely: Icarus drowns unnoticed. A peasant ploughs the soil. A shepherd leans on a staff – a dog by his side. A ship, with the crew on deck, sails past Icarus's sinking body. Terrible things happen and even those close at hand don't notice.

They finish breakfast and hit the road. At an altitude of 887 meters, Agnes has read in the room information, the temperatures can vary by ten to fifteen degrees in a day. Desperate for warmth in the cold morning air, she clutches her coat around her. Behind the wheel, dressed in his new coat, Jim looks like a country squire. But as he perks up, she finds herself sinking lower. She has just informed him that she would prefer to cancel their planned trip to the cemetery to look for ancestors. He has accepted this without question, unaware that the current renewal of turmoil over her relationship with her father has obliterated any interest in her forbears.

The deserted road out of town is lined with clumps of willow trees. Bowed down with seasons of bending to the elements, they seem to be fighting to exist. Now, in this moment, she finds the appearance of the Australian countryside deeply depressing. It has stolen her memory. Every tree, road, fence, house, animal – implicated in the crime. And the further inland they travel, the more she feels trapped.

Jim is slowing the car down. They are nearing the little town in which her father was born. It seems she cannot avoid Eric Keen. There is no escape from him, whether in her dreams or her conscious thoughts. A shaft of sunlight breaks through the clouds and lights up the spreading arms of a line of low-growing golden pines. The weather has turned hot and muggy, so Jim stops the car and they shed their coats. They have reached an elevated plateau from which can be viewed rolling hills dotted with clumps of green scrub, splayed out to the distant horizon.

They lose the panorama in a rapid descent to the small town below. She hears Jim insisting she has been there before, but her mind has gone blank. She tries to take in her surroundings. Most of the handful of structures in the main street of the tiny town are crudely built, with one exception – a two-storey Federation-style corner pub. This building is wrapped in an elaborate wrought-iron balcony, neatly cantilevered off the top floor. So here they are. Where the hotbed of intrigue – purported to have been played out during her father's youth – took place.

They take a short walk, then Jim announces for her benefit:

This is it. Where he came into the world and spent his childhood.

They are standing in front of a sagging green timber house that occupies a corner close to the road. Several panes of glass are broken in the crudely fitted louvre windows that enclose the front veranda. Twisted guttering, and a front door carelessly repaired with timbers that don't match, make it look decidedly unloved. Green paint for St Patrick is the only hint of the old inhabitants of Irish descent. She finds it hard to string words together:

So – this is it? It looks like a dump.

Jim nods:

I think it always was. There were a lot of them crammed in here. All up early and out to work on sheep stations in the area, then back home to eat and crash into bed. Next day the same. And the next.

Agnes shudders a little:

Perhaps that's why he lived like a bachelor with us? He had no blueprint for a leisurely family life. A pint at the pub after work and home to eat and crash into bed. Old habits die hard.

The anti-climax of the dishevelled green house in the empty town is underscored by the sudden descent of a swarm of flies. They are both covered in minutes. She begins to panic as she feels them in her eyes and up her nose. Her white cotton knit jumper has turned black.

The sleeves are hardly visible for pulsating black dots. Jim's shirt is swarming. The sun is fierce. The glare is blinding. It is unbearable here. In every sense. She bolts for the car and Jim is not far behind. Still waving their arms frantically, they jump in and Jim speeds off, dispersing the winged horror through the open windows. The long-planned pilgrimage is over in minutes.

Jim drives so fast, Agnes suspects he is escaping more than flies. She wishes she knew what he was thinking. The visit to the sad wreck of a house only confirms her growing awareness that this part of the trip is pointless. Her relationship with her father has nothing to do with his life before she was born. But why did she still carry his pain as if it was her own? The superlatives from her mother about his shame when he discovered his illegitimacy are as fresh as if she heard them yesterday. Was it because Madge had prevented her from seeing his dead body that he never died for her? Remember him the way he *was* – her mother's exact words. But *what* was the way he was?

Before she and Jim had commenced their road trip, Agnes had discovered on the internet that 'Pink Dale', the grand property where her father and Madge originally met, was still owned by the same family and that they rented out accommodation for short stays. Thus, she has pre-booked one of the little stone cottages for their last night. Such unexpectedly easy access to a place she has been dazzled by since childhood had arrived as a gift, but she now fears Jim might find the visit intimidating, and so has put off telling him her plans. Until now:

I should have told you, Jim, that I booked a cottage for tonight on the 'Pink Dale' property. Where our parents first met.

How's that possible? Will any of the family be there? I wouldn't want to meet them.

Jim has raised his voice. Anxiety is evident in his sudden heavy breathing.

No, there won't be anyone there who knows us.

But Jim is scowling. Underneath the silence, Agnes senses a volcano smouldering. She remembers his predisposition for tantrums as a child. He never relished sudden changes or surprises. Now she is tempted to cancel the booking rather than incur his wrath. Perhaps he is growing bored with their travels? Or is bored with her? She hears him sigh, then, as if reining himself in, he says:

Okay. If you're sure that's what you want.

The car kicks up a stream of dust on the dirt road into the property. The surrounding paddocks look as if they are dying of thirst – past grandness having offered no protection against the current drought. Once well inside the property, Jim stops the car and Agnes gets out to open the gate in front. In the distance, she will be able to see the goalposts of the polo field where, presumably, their maternal Guinevere met her dashing Lancelot. A thought then strikes her. How history is crowded with princes, tyrants, kings, and generals, all elevated above their worth on horseback.

She sees him. Her father. The great undead. Standing at the gate. Wearing his gleaming polo helmet, he is staring at her with the same blank gaze he wore on the day he ignored her in public. The day she had assembled with her school friends at the polo. The old pain will return and will return with such a vengeance that she will close her eyes and clutch the door handle of the car to stop from slumping over in her seat. Jim will notice this and say:

I'm not driving any further. Look at the state of you!

But she forces herself to rally back to her senses:

The people who live here are just people, Jim. They shit like everyone else.

Jim capitulates reluctantly. On the other side of the gate, when they pull up in a clearing and turn off the engine, they find themselves surrounded on three sides by gentle rolling hills – acres and acres of land – as old as time. The poem her mother liked to recite comes flooding back:

I love a sunburnt country,
A land of sweeping plains
Of ragged mountain ranges
Of droughts and flooding rains.

She recites it out loud because she can tell Jim, too, is moved by the beauty of the place. He murmurs, as if to himself:

This is some of the best grazing land in the country. Six thousand acres of perfect land for sheep and cattle. The Merinos they breed here yield the finest wool in the land.

And Agnes knows he is claiming his credentials as a country man.

Having always imagined the homestead that now presents itself as the equivalent of the gothic Mandalay in *Rebecca*, it will soon be obvious to Agnes this is not the case. The sweeping white timber structure that stands before them, shimmering in the late afternoon sun, has serene and beautifully proportioned sloping lines and is elevated above a perfect emerald lawn. It makes Agnes think of a fairy-tale house made of sugar.

Feeling steadier, she gets out of the car to drink in the sight. She says:

Look, Jim. It's like she said. There's the pergola with the wisteria. And there's the lake. The Chinese bridge and the weeping willow trailing in the water. And look beyond – the climbing roses!

Agnes turns in circles, intoxicated by it all like a small child:

Look over here, Jim! The famous wooden horse in a cage – to practise your polo swing.

Can I help you?

They both jump out of their skins, then turn to see a good-looking, open-faced young man. He is dressed in stained white moleskine pants and jodhpur boots. He smooths a fringe of streaky blond hair from a perspiring forehead:

You must be the people for the cottage. I've been keeping an eye out for you, but you must have slipped past without me noticing. I'm Jake.

Agnes extends her hand to him:

Agnes Keen. This is my brother, Jim.

Good to meet you. Follow me. You can turn in the paddock behind, then it's up the road and first right. I'll meet you in front of the first stone cottage.

The sister and brother find a white bowl overflowing with fresh fruit sitting on the kitchen table and a vase of freshly picked full-blown roses on a shelf above the fireplace in the living room. The grate below is set with wood ready for a fire and there is a box of matches on the hearth. Not only is the place delightfully pretty in an English cottage way, but it smells fresh, as if it has been recently painted.

Jake pauses at the door before leaving and says:

There's milk in the fridge, tea and coffee on the kitchen counter and biscuits. Oh yes. Nearly forgot. Your hosts were delighted to hear of your past association with the place and would like you to join them for dinner. They'll be arriving back from Sydney any minute. Hopefully roast beef and veg is to your liking?

Agnes looks at Jim, who is showing no trace of enthusiasm whatsoever. She raises an eyebrow at her brother who reluctantly takes the hint:

Yes. Thanks.

Okey-dokey. Settle in and I'll come by and take you to the big house around seven.

As the pleasant young man departs, Agnes gazes at her stony-faced brother and feels guilty about dragging him here, so obviously against his will. Worrying she has worn him out with it all, there and then she decides to invite him to visit her in Mallorca. She can easily picture Jim sitting under the lemon trees in her garden. Can see herself guiding him along ancient stone donkey tracks into the mountains where they will stop for a picnic in an olive grove that has a view of the Mediterranean. She would help him lose his beer belly and get back in shape. If he came in early spring, he would be there in time for the almond blossoms.

She voices her thoughts:

Why don't you come and visit me in Mallorca, Jim?

I suppose it's possible.

He is taking a deep slurp from the mug of tea he has made for them both. She tries to inspire him with the prospect, offering to buy him an open airline ticket so he could put the dates in when it was most convenient for him. After Mallorca, they could travel together: London, Paris, Rome, Venice. It's all waiting for you, she tells him. She will be fully aware she is gushing. She will want him to be as happy as she is in these moments. Because he is patently not. What was it about this place that he resented so deeply? Was it the thought of his parents being young, happy and with a brilliant future to look forward to in this sylvan environment? Was the bitter reality of their union, their failures, their casual cruelty, their utter indifference to their children simply too much of a contrast to take?

Jim looks at her glumly and her heart clenches when he says:

How did they know our father used to work here?

Because I answered the question on the website, Jim. 'Reason for visit'. *Please* try to pull yourself together. It's just one night, and I'm sure the food will be delicious. Where's the harm in meeting these people? You like a good baked dinner, don't you?

But Jim will not get the chance to reply to this attempt to appeal to his gastric juices for her mobile phone will ring. Puzzled, she will look at the screen and see it is the Grantham Apartments. She will listen to the receptionist with the bird tattoo asking if she'll be returning tomorrow. Should she take this as a timely omen? A sign she should go back? She will try and catch her brother's eye, but he will not engage with her. Regardless of wine and spirits flowing in the big house, with Jim in this dark mood, the evening would be a disaster. Her high mood would plummet, like a hunting hawk, to ground. Like so much she has looked forward to in her life, everything strange and magical about this day would be ruined in an instant. And, because she cannot bear this thought, she will tell the receptionist:

Yes. Yes. Expect me tomorrow.

Poor Jake will look bewildered as he waves them off a mere two hours after their arrival. Agnes will have made profuse apologies to both him and her hosts, citing an unexpected family crisis. Well, there was more than a germ of truth in that, after all.

Back on the main road, the brother and sister will speed towards Sydney in silence. On the outskirts of Crookwell she will suggest they spend a further night at Spud's and, over a quiet and reflective dinner at a Greek restaurant, Jim's curiosity will finally overtake him:

What really made you change your mind suddenly like that? It wasn't just me, was it?

She will have prepared her response, hoping it convinces him:

It's hard to explain. I panicked. I thought it might backfire in some way. Anyway, I know all the polo stories well enough to work at 'Pink Dale' as a guide! We'd have learned nothing new.

Later, alone in her hotel room, she will hope this explanation was sufficient, but she has certainly not convinced herself. When she sinks her head into the pillow, below the same leaping dolphins, she will remain wide awake and filled with a new disgust. But this will not be directed at herself. It will be focused on her father's eternal demands for sympathy and his inability to forgive. His raised voice in the car after the trip to Rosemont, followed by a fierce blow to her mouth. His hesitation in the car, before deciding to reverse to see if she was still alive. His complete indifference to her perilous state and the punishing exile that followed. It had been easy to unmask her mother. But why was it so hard to criticise the shadowy figure who fathered her? Instead of defending his only daughter, he had colluded in defaming her to Grandma. What had happened in those dark, shrouded months that she could barely remember? After the move from Rose and Edmond Street?

The question will reverberate like a drum roll in her head until she takes a sleeping pill and descends into oblivion.

* * *

Over breakfast, it is easy to dismiss the original plan to stop at their mother's house on the way back to Sydney. No extra visit, nor farewells necessary. They agree, instead, to make a final visit to the farm before Jim catches his flight back to Brisbane.

After crossing the Razorback Mountain, they circle around Camden on a bypass, arriving at the western end of the Bringelly Road. The trees which Agnes remembers standing sentry along the fence of the farm – now a five-acre subdivision – have been cut down, allowing a clear view of the land from the main road. The grand homestead Grandma planned for herself on the highest point has finally been realised. It stands, like the Lord of the Manor's residence, towering over the lower houses built on new roads across the block. The stables, and the groom's cottage which their parents converted into a home, remains hidden, as before, by the hill in front.

Initially, none of what Agnes sees has any impact upon her. Not even spotting the site of the fire in the distance where her mother had caused so much terrible destruction. But when Jim, at her request, turns the car to drive back in the direction they came in, she suddenly glimpses a flash of water through the thick foliage. It is the creek. She orders:

Stop the car.

Jim obediently pulls onto a grassy verge at the side of the road.

* * *

I'll be right back! I have shouted over my shoulder to Jim and am moving ahead with a compulsion beyond my control. I slip through a break in the fence and wrestle through a tangle of bushes to emerge in the corner of the lowest paddock. I stand still for a few seconds to check if there is anyone around. The fields and houses appear deserted. It remains the overgrown and pitted no-man's land I remember as a child, and when I visited my mother here years ago. It must have rained hard overnight, as the ground is saturated with water. My right foot makes a mournful sucking sound as I wrench it out of a muddy hole. I hurriedly wipe the mud off the sides of my shoe on some tufts of grass. I leap carefully from one raised clod of earth to the next. I am relieved to arrive, safely out of sight, behind the greenery along the side of the creek. I look back and see the place beside the distant fence where Ben blew the head off the injured pony.

I dash along the narrow path that flanks the water's edge of the creek. I feel secure screened off by the thick gums, tall grass and scrub that hug the water's edge. Just as when I visited my mother, I find the surroundings both familiar and frightening. Dead trees, branches and roots have fallen and jack-knifed into the water and are making strange shapes beneath the surface. They are like monsters that might leap out at any moment.

I have arrived at the far side of the old block where the creek flows into the next property, still shielded off by the neighbour's old fence. I am in the clearing beside the water. Once again, I spot the huge fallen log where I sat and fished with my father. The sight of his fishing line submerged in the creek flashes into my mind. Someone has hung a rope from a branch of an overhanging tree to swing out over the water.

I recall my visit to my mother at the farm when I was nineteen – after Rebecca Lea was born. It was over forty years ago when my baby was taken from me, yet this place has never been out of my memory. I can hear the whoosh of flame and petrol unite and can see my mother thrown back by the explosion of her own making. The contents of my suitcase still burn in front of my eyes. The carefully written diary of daily life, of the history of the little child I brought into the world, and with whom I fell in love, consigned forever to ashes. Fire has haunted me all my life. Fire and flames and the destruction of things I hold dear.

The memory of my father, quietly fishing, glances through my mind now, as I stare at the creek for what will be the very last time. I have a recollection of a photo of me. Posing against a tree. Wearing a swimming costume. But my parents didn't take photos of me. Ever.

I follow the path back towards the house, my feet sinking in a soft carpet of leaves, but hit an impasse. The path is completely blocked by a jungle of dense growth. I turn and wander back to the clearing to find another way out. As a child, I always loved this place. The way vivid lichens and ferns grew on the trunks of dead trees, shaded by gigantic overhead gums. The way reflections would constantly change in the water with the light. It was the one magical corner of the farm where I imagined fairies dancing in the moonlight.

I pass through the trees to the left, and here is the glade. I remember it. But, as I approach it, I start to tremble and am consumed by a strange and powerful sexual arousal. My stomach wrenches as I finally see the horror of what I have never been able to bear – have never been able to recall.

I am naked from the waist down, bent over, my hands balancing on the trunk of one of the trees – as my father thrusts his member into my behind. He sodomized his own daughter.

I throw up a disgusting mess of last night's meal down the trunk of that same tree. Legs shaking, I sit on the very same fallen log where he and I once rested. I dissolve into convulsive sobs. How could he violate me like that? Why didn't she, my mother, protect me? This is the reason why I have always felt him inside me. Invading me.

The photo of my parents. I retrieve it from my bag where I always carry it. She cut me out of it because she was jealous. Jealous because she knew what he was doing to me. This is what she meant when she said – 'Your father loves you.' As if she'd like to change it. I can still see his bloated face. Can still smell his alcohol-drenched body. Feel it pressed up against me. The same act I dreaded in my small bed at fourteen, that had me leave my body and levitate to the Guardian Angel in the drawing above the bed, haunts me now. It is his violation of me that obliterated my ability to read. To think straight. He mortified me to the point that I could not remember. A momentary brute compulsion, so summarily dismissed by him, led me to a life of self-hatred and further abuse at the hands of others.

I put the photo on the ground and in a feeble ritual of banishment, ignite it with the lighter I keep in my bag for the odd cigarette. I watch the flame eat into their faces and, once they become unrecognisable ash, I stamp on them and kick the tiny particles of grey dust into the air. The trees alone will bear witness to what has happened here today.

* * *

Jim is furious. She has been gone for almost an hour and he is in a real temper with her. He keeps looking at his watch as they speed towards the airport. She had no idea of how long she had kept him waiting. Torrential rain is falling, as if washing away the travesties of her life. She recalls how the early female Catholic Martyrs chose death over physical violation, but with no heavenly aid of any kind, how was she supposed to have protected herself against the father who was supposed to protect her? She struggles to bring herself back into the moment and says:

Ring me Jim and let me know you got home safely.

The good wishes toward her brother seem redundant. Jim has dropped her off outside the Grantham Apartments. Although he has occasionally shown her some vague form of filial affection on their road trip, she knows in her heart that her intense feelings for him are not reciprocated. His limp and lifeless demeanour on parting has left her feeling that, for him, the experience has been not much more than a free holiday he might have won in a raffle. One needs a full stomach to philosophise, she thinks, fully aware that his financial struggles must have made her present quest seem trivial to him. Apart from the voiced criticism levelled at their violent mother, she has gained no real insight into his true feelings about their parents. He seems, now, to be retreating into the mechanical persona she had met at the airport. She waves him off in the hire car, unsure if she will ever lay eyes on him again.

Alone in the apartment, she strips off and stands for a long time under the shower with the water as hot as she can stand. She soaps both feet and watches the mud from the paddock at the farm disappear down the drain. She shampoos her hair several times, scrubbing her scalp – once again trying to purge a guilt that is no longer hers. She knows she can never wash the stain away, but she *can* learn to forgive herself. The event at the creek was not her fault. Nor was the violation in her childhood bed from the age of fourteen. Not her guilt. She covers the scratches from the brambles on her hands and face with an antiseptic cream, dries her hair, and gets dressed.

Unscrewing the top of a bottle of red wine, she pours the contents into a fine-stemmed glass, swirling the liquid around the bowl. The streaks that cling to the glass confirm the wine has legs. Good. It needed to be special. Sipping her drink on the balcony, she looks out to the view which has been such a comfort these last months. But she cannot fully relax. After three days cramped in a car, plagued with conflicting emotions, she *has* to take a walk.

She clings onto the rail as she lowers herself down the high treads of the stone staircase to Woolloomooloo below. It's the same climb she navigated, in terror, the day after she arrived in Sydney. The air is still warm in the aftermath of the sunset, although a cool breeze is blowing in off the harbour. As the light fades, Harry's Bar is lighting up for the evening ahead.

She criss-crosses the road just as she did on that first visit, positioning herself opposite the Bell Hotel where groups of young people are standing with glasses of beer in hand, merrily chatting on the pavement. She crosses the road to gain some perspective and, leaning against the wall for support, is pitched straight back to the scorching summer of 1958.

She sees a picture in her mind's eye. A teenage girl is lying on the mattress of an iron bed in a dark room, surrounded by beer barrels. Shafts of light spill across the bed from the barred window in the wall behind.

Naked but for a loose shirt, the girl is half lying, half propped up, her long thin legs open, her blue eyes clouded as if she is blind. But this is not a new image. It has always been with her and, until this evening, she has wondered if she might have seen it in an art gallery, for it reminds her of a painting of a pubescent girl by a Swiss painter – Balthus. It is a painting she has always found offensive. But today, as the convivial buzz from the young drinkers fades from her ears, she closes her eyes and dares to look closer. There is blood between the girl's legs. And the girl? The girl is her.

She braces her hands against the wall behind her back. It was Uncle Parry. Uncle Parry had wrenched her legs apart in the basement of the White Horse Hotel and raped her. *This* is what had happened within the walls of the Newtown pub. *This* is what happened in that basement.

Blood. Fire. She knows now, beyond doubt, that she had always, until now, equated blood with fire. Crimson, consuming, painful fire. The fire that Uncle Parry and Aunt Marnie had denied ever happened. The fire that had gone on burning inside her for decades. It answered the baffling question of why she was not a virgin when Charles first raped her. Her first sexual experience had been with Parry. He had broken the seal and spilled the blood. 'You haven't told anyone?' It was abundantly clear to her now exactly what he was afraid she might tell.

The mystery shrouding his rejection of her is no more. Parry had joined her parents in demonising her. It was the obvious course for him. And the hideous woman, the woman who has just convinced her successful daughter to buy her house, had done the same. This woman had failed to protect her. Had never *intended* to protect her. Just wanted her gone.

In the days that follow this resurgence, Agnes will walk all over Sydney. She will decide to phone Jean and will meet her in the same Thai restaurant in Macleay Street where she had first dined with Jim. Jean will listen attentively to Agnes's revelations, curious for details, but strangely devoid of emotion. This juicy morsel of tittle-tattle about her father, and about Parry would, without doubt, do the rounds. But the truth is that she no longer cared who knew. The truth had to be told to *someone* in this excuse for a family.

What will make her waver somewhat in this commitment to honesty will be Uncle Ben's voice, chuckling down the phone several days later:

Jean tells me you told her Eric and Parry had a go at you. You were a cracking good-looking bird you know, Agnes. If I'd known, I would have had a go myself!

Shocked into silence by this cruel crudity, she will put the phone down on him. Where were the hypocritical rosary beads now? Undisguised malice in his voice, and obviously still stinging from her visit, he had thoroughly enjoyed the jibe. Well. Good old Uncle Ben would merely succeed in immortalising his gross nature for eternity.

Perhaps equally perplexing will be a call from his sweet ex-wife, Aunt Beth:

It's me – Beth! Jean just told me! How *terrible*! Do you think your father died young, and Parry got that terrible illness, because of what they did to you? God's punishment?

Her simpering voice and absurd notions of crime and retribution will simply die away in Agnes's ear. They will not matter. She will know she has no need to defend herself. Not to any of them. It is enough that she knows what happened to her beyond doubt.

To fulfil her commitment to her mother, she will go to see Madge's bank manager. It is all amazingly straightforward. Yes, her mother can borrow on her house. Yes, the inheritors will get what, if anything, is left over after payment of the bank debt. Yes, they will attend to all the paperwork on her behalf. Should they inform Mrs Keen, or will she be visiting her mother again before she departs Australia?

When Agnes alights from the taxi, she will see her mother standing like a bird of prey with a broken wing at the top of the stairs. She will stride into the lopsided house in business-like fashion to briskly inform her of the arrangement with the bank. Her mother will seem subdued, strangely contrite, and will accept the efficient arrangement without quibble – even the news that she will have to go on living with the purple floral carpet.

Madge will know it is over. That Agnes is no longer anyone's slave because, naturally, she will also have been a beneficiary of the family gossip grapevine:

I'm sorry that he did that to you, Agnes.

You should have protected me. Kicked him in the balls. Thrown him out of the house and changed the locks.

Madge looks genuinely incredulous:

But I would have had to divorce him. I couldn't *possibly* have done that!

She will gaze at her mother's lined, blotched face. Madge's hair will be in disarray, and for some bizarre reason Agnes will be reminded of the dishevelled appearance of Muammar Gaddafi and Saddam Hussein after they were captured. She will say:

You're right. You could never have done that. Because it takes courage to leave a bad relationship. Parry too! *He* did it to me too! You knowingly supported the actions of two criminals who should have been put in *jail*!

Parry?!!

It will be obvious from the startled tone and the shock on her mother's face that she has not been privy to this particular revelation. But it will make no difference. None at all.

Then Madge will turn away from her:

Don't say any more, Agnes, *please*! You're getting me all churned up!

Agnes will realise in this moment that she no longer needs to feel remorse. No longer needs to care. A voice inside will whisper softly, 'Walk away'. She will bid her mother goodbye. And leave.

32

DEATH, FILIAL EXTORTION AND NEW DISCOVERIES

ix months after her return to Mallorca, her mother will die peacefully in her sleep a few days before her eighty-sixth birthday. Upon receiving the news Agnes will reflect on the irony of how someone, whose chief concern in life was breaking a fingernail, was allotted such a smooth and painless end.

Her brother Bert will take control of Madge's journey to the grave. The day after their mother is found dead, he will ring Agnes to make sure she has no intention of returning for the funeral to cramp his style. Even if she wished to come, which she will not, the quick dispatch he has already organised will not give her enough time to get there.

Agnes will receive no sympathy cards or calls of condolence. Her only contact with the funeral proceedings will be to lend Jim the money to buy an air ticket to fly from Brisbane to Sydney to attend. Over the six months since parting in Sydney, she had consistently wired money into his account to pay for his dental work, and to fund urgent items on the farm. She will still live in hope that he will, one day, feel strong enough to face a bank manager looking as if he didn't desperately need a loan. She will enjoy giving him the love and support she has never been given.

Madge will elect to leave what remains of her possessions in equal shares to her three children whom she has also appointed as co-executors. After her mother's funeral, Agnes will fly to London to legally transfer her executorship to Jim at the Australian Embassy. She will hope the additional responsibility will build his self-esteem, along with the air ticket she has put in place for him to visit her in Mallorca.

Her two brothers will split their mother's possessions between them. And that will be alright because, initially, Agnes will want none of it. But the good-faith transfer of her executorship to Jim will prove to be a mistake. She will unwittingly play into his hands when, as an afterthought, she opts to take her mother's jewellery. By the time she discovers Jim's betrayal, the estate will be settled, and it will be too late to do anything about it. He will claim that the bank transfers she sent – which amounted to over $20,000 – were gifts, not loans requiring repayment.

As for the air ticket, it will remain a blur in the ether – probably to be used by him and Marline to go elsewhere in Europe. Yet another blow will be Jim's collaboration in falsifying a valuation of $15,000, deducted from her already small share of the estate, for a sapphire ring she will never receive. She will further discover that half the small package of jewellery intended for her as a legacy will have been stolen from her by her own mother over the years.

But the worst betrayal will come from Bert, who will inform Agnes by phone of a letter he has found in Madge's papers – from Agnes's adopted daughter. A request received, through Sydney lawyers, for contact with her birth mother and left to fester, unacknowledged, for years. Compounding his mother's cruelty, he will fail to forward it on. But love is not hard to lose if you have never really felt it. And where there is no love, there are only possessions.

With nothing to salvage from the ashes, Agnes will sever all further contact with her family.

* * *

From the moment I landed in Sydney, I had been gripped with a dread that I was going the wrong way. Perhaps what the Chinese say is true – we fight dragons because of the treasure they hide. My treasure has been apprehending the memory behind hidden wounds. After all, one day of liberation is worth a lifetime of struggle. At last I understand the cause of my vulnerability and why I went on unconsciously sabotaging myself on my parents' behalf. I will never be completely free of the anxiety that has plagued my life, but will learn to avoid the people, places and spaces that provoke it. I have no need for symbolic trappings. I gave my mother's pearls to Tammy – her one true and constant friend.

I feel now as I imagine Sleeping Beauty might feel, waking into the world. My prince's kiss is a fortified self to guide and protect me. Change is impossible to hold or touch. It happens unawares.

But what is a touchable and holdable truth is that I am: Mejor sola que mal acompañada!